BUT THE NATIVES AREN'T SUPPOSED TO *HAVE* GUNS

Lieutenant Jetter heard the hypersonic crack of a bullet. Without thinking, Jetter went prone and pulled his ruck strap disconnects. So did his Marines. Okubo managed to get her slender form in a depression mere centimeters deep. He wished he could do that.

Then he remembered that in theory no one had rifles here. Some idiot had given the natives access to modern materials and weapons.

"This is definitely going in my report," Jetter said to himself.

At least two of the interlopers were running away, back the way they'd come. He saw two others fighting with Corporal Garry. That wasn't well thought out. Garry was a huge, muscular Forward for the team. Not the first choice one should pick to fight. Two other Marines waded in to seize the attackers, while the rest kept the remaining captives at spearpoint.

Everyone flinched at a second shot.

"Okubo, Tahere, find that rifleman."

The two slithered off without a word.

"Marines, try *not* to kill whichever native has the rifle. We must be hands off. We also must get that weapon, at all costs." Dammit, he hated giving conflicting orders, but what else could he do?

This was just a giant ball of suck.

Baen Books by
Michael Z. Williamson

Freehold
The Weapon
Better to Beg Forgiveness . . .
Contact with Chaos
Do Unto Others . . . (forthcoming)

The Hero (with John Ringo)

Contact with
CHAOS

MICHAEL Z.
WILLIAMSON

CONTACT WITH CHAOS

A Baen Books Original

Baen Publishing Enterprises
P.O. Box 1403
Riverdale, NY 10471
www.baen.com

ISBN: 978-1-4391-3373-6

Cover art by Kurt Miller

First Baen paperback printing, July 2010

Distributed by Simon & Schuster
1230 Avenue of the Americas
New York, NY 10020

Library of Congress Cataloging-in-Publication Data:
2009005283

Printed in the United States of America

10 9 8 7 6 5 4 3 2 1

*To Dave Drake, Alexi Murphy,
Nicki Fellenzer, James Caldwell, Chuck
and Lynn Budreau, and Morgen Kirby
for keeping me sane that year.*

FREEHOLD UNITS OF TIME

1 Freehold second = 1.0153 Earth seconds

1 seg = 100 seconds

1 div = 100 segs

1 Freehold day = 10 divs

PROLOGUE

The survey ship phased back into space five billion kilometers from 107 Piscis. As ships went, it wasn't much to look at. It was a small pod the size of a typical tug, with its large engines matched by a large hull-canker of star drive equipment. Its name was *Hound Dog*, in reference to its mission.

It was a civilian vessel, but armed. Any ship registered in the Freehold of Grainne that was capable of mounting weapons would do so whenever local customs or rules didn't forbid it. As this was an exploration mission, it made sense to prepare for possible hostile intent.

The distance from the primary was a routine precaution against detection. Of course, this system, like all others so far, was uninhabited so no threats existed, but it made sense to plan for the eventuality. Sooner or later

1

a system would be inhabited. Besides, it was safer in terms of navigation to phase in away from a star's gravity well.

Within the ship were ten contractors and employees of Halo Materials Group, LLC. HMG was a multisystem supplier of high grade ores and crude materials, mostly metals. The phase drive's expense was offset by the ease with which it allowed planetoid and belt resources to be transshipped, in lieu of the expense of transmuting materials locally.

In a very short time, the materials survey came to a hurried end. The third planet of this star was known to have an oxygen-nitrogen atmosphere and indications of plant life. However, a closer scan of the atmosphere indicated there might be technological development.

Jackpot.

"This is a potential disaster," pilot Mike Helfstein said, sitting loosely in his couch. *Hound Dog* coasted in free trajectory, power at minimum, as stealthy as a civilian research vessel could get. The control room walls were all screens, showing photos and data. He could smell the company rep. That wasn't bad; it was an indication of how well the new aircycler worked. The ship had no smell.

"This is a potential gold mine. More than a gold mine," said Damon Egan, the other occupant. He was the survey's official head. He knew materials science. It was clear he didn't know social sciences.

"That's what makes it a potential disaster," Helfstein replied. He'd called Egan up to inform him of the event; he didn't want a pissing match.

"First, we have to get a probe out." Egan was antsy. Very antsy. He twitched visibly in excitement.

"First, we have to not get noticed by whatever is on that planet." Helfstein was damned sure going to stay calm for this.

"Assuming there's anything down there. No one has ever found sentient life before. Check for radio or other EM emissions?"

Helfstein sighed. "A lack of EM does not indicate a lack of civilization. They could use laser or maser tight-beam, for example, have cabled the entire planet for optical or electrical, or have some sub or hyperspace method of communication. If that latter is true, worry, because that's technology we don't have."

Egan seemed to parse that. He held whatever he was going to say, and concentrated in thought for a few moments.

"What do you advise?" he asked, turning and actually looking at the pilot at last. He drifted in position as he did so, experienced but not a master in microgravity.

Not bad, Helfstein thought. Only five segs to do what he should have done in the first place. Who said executives couldn't learn?

"First we check for EM," he said.

"But didn't you—"

"Then we can deploy a passive only drone through the outer halo, and slowly move in. This could take a month or more."

"That's a lot of ship and crew time," Egan said. He shifted in the small command globe.

Helfstein reflected that he'd wanted this job for the experience, the challenge and the money. In exchange, he had to put up with short-sighted, bean-counting middle execs who would either learn how to think long-term enough to be managers and Citizens, or would dead end into third rate jobs for life.

"Otherwise, we risk being found by something as powerful as us or more, with bigger numbers, that may be hostile. They could take us out, backtrack, and attack the Freehold. That would make HMG liable in court, should we survive the event."

"Point," Egan admitted. "I'm more familiar with spectral readouts and cost analysis." Right. The kind of geek who was a narrow-focus engineer, then turned out to be not quite good enough, because he spent all his time schmoozing. So he turned the first class schmooze and the second class education into a job. Sometimes it worked. So far, he was aggravating, but not dangerous.

The survey for intelligent life went smoothly, and took seventeen days. The initial passive scan of the outer system showed no EM, no gravitational waves, nothing any human outfit used for communication. Telescopic surveys showed no large IR emissions off the planet that would indicate large power plants or industrial cities. There were no indications of ships in trajectory or powered flight, no spacewhips or mass drivers tossing cargo.

The probes of the second round were slightly larger, with better resolution. There were no large visible surface facilities on the planet's satellite. The landscape hadn't been filled, cut or shaped in any large fashion. There were large areas of forest, desert and grassland along two continents and a substantial archipelago arcing between them. Areas of the grassland were geometrically precise and differentiated.

"Cropland," Helfstein said. "That's how I'm calling it until we have better intel."

"Cropland, but no modern industry?"

"Yes, Iron Age, even Bronze Age had substantial agricultural zones."

"So we're looking at primitive life," Egan said, alert and interested, tapping notes instead of speaking them, to maintain secrecy. As if everyone aboard couldn't see the throbbing commercial erection behind the currency symbols in his eyes.

"Probably less technologically advanced, though there's no guarantee they don't have some odd philosophy of living in huts with bioengineered crops, light and waste disposal. We've done experiments with that. A working society is possible. And even if they're Iron Age, I wouldn't call them 'primitives.' They could have a civilization in the billions. Unless we plan to exterminate them, we'll have to negotiate with them."

"Of course we'll negotiate," Egan said. "It's a massive market we can exploit, and they'll do well in return in high tech goods and services."

"I advise taking it slow," Helfstein continued his mantra. "I expect they're going to react far differently than humans."

"All we need to do is find their motivations and needs, and work from there. You stick to piloting," Egan advised. "Economic development is my area."

It's one of the mysteries of the universe that no matter how fast things can move under laboratory conditions, no matter what test equipment shows to be a "maximum" speed, rumors will always travel faster. They may not be accurate, however.

Within the day of *Hound Dog* phasing back into Freehold space, people knew of something odd. Some had heard "alien attack." Others had heard another company/nation had beat them to the site. Someone using "common sense" insisted it was merely a complete failure to find anything of value, which explained the empty-handed return and refusal to release data.

Within a day, it was bad tabloid news and largely forgotten, except by those with a professional interest. There were a *lot* of parties, however, with varied professions, who had such an interest.

CHAPTER 1

C itizen Mark Ballenger wondered how he'd been so
lucky. Of all the hundreds of Citizens available in
the Halo and near out-system, why had the Council
picked him to be the first envoy to a possible alien civilization?

It wasn't strictly luck, he reflected. The situation
required something be done fast. Halo Materials Group
was already planning a response, according to an informant, and there was some buzz at high levels. Deep
Space Resources, HMG's main competitor, was trying
to get in on the act. Since the system was inhabited, it
couldn't just be staked by HMG. So whoever contracted
a deal with the natives first, no matter how flaky and
questionable, could start shipping ore and continue until
resolution at least, and then, even if ordered out, could

sell any charts or surveys. Nothing like a credit symbol with a "1" and a few groups of zeroes following to motivate people. He wondered who else would horn in on this.

There was nothing the Freehold government could officially do. At the same time, it was obvious some kind of moderating influence, or at least an observer, was necessary to this pending orgy of good old-fashioned land grabbing. Mark had a degree in international relations from Western and had made his fortune as a contract sales rep, brokering deals between manufacturers, and later, megacorps. That, and he happened to be at Faeroe Station when the word came down. He had the background, knew most of the players, in fact, and was closest. So it was his task by default.

He foresaw a small chance of success, and a large chance of a giant goat rodeo. He really did feel honored. He also wondered just when it would all fall apart.

Faeroe Station was a 16km chunk of rock, situated near Jump Point Four. It was as far from anything as one could get and still be within the Freehold of Grainne. Mark's business here was resolving yet another dispute between mining and spacing employees and their bosses. It had been an ongoing problem for decades. The locus had been reasonably high in KBOs and ore-bearing rocks, though it was now largely worked out. JP4 handled traffic to systems that were populated only by researchers and mining engineers, and had a small Star Guard garrison to support that. Fortuitously, that meant lots of scientists were handy. It did minimize immediate spectators, which was why the news of the event was almost entirely rumor and speculation. It also meant a military ship had to be brought from elsewhere, which was going to add to those rumors.

The station was sparse and spartan, but modern enough. Mark wasn't uncomfortable. Despite the station's raw size, the actual amount of cubic and passageway was fairly low. He could find his way around without too much trouble. He half-walked and half-swam the hewn corridors in the marginal gravity, following illuminated tags triggered by the mapping function in his comm.

Dr. Landrieu McDonald had been appointed as the lead scientist for the project. On file, he had years of experience running expeditions and dealing with other scientists, and had produced results. In person, he was as "normal" as a scientist could ever be. Mark was thankful he wasn't an unrepentant geek. He'd met McDonald previously, and found him to be steady, thoughtful and remarkably unprejudiced. A good scientist.

McDonald was in his office, with the hatch open. Mark tapped on the frame and drew himself through with both hands.

"Good morning, Doctor. Amazing opportunity, isn't it?"

"Absolutely, Citizen," McDonald said, bounding off his stool. Faeroe had centripetal gravity, but it was only thirty percent at the perimeter. At this level, it was barely fifteen percent. He caught himself on the rock wall, deliberately. That fall was a learned maneuver in this environment. He extended a hand and Mark shook it. He was a good twenty centimeters taller than Mark, with lankier limbs. He was about as broad, but that muscle stretched over a long frame raised in space, not Mark's more compact high-G build.

Mark said, "I hope we managed to get a good cross section, since we had to go with who was available and did it by committee, across several light years."

"I think we'll do okay, sir. I approved of most of the choices, and I don't see a real problem with any of them." He bounced by, then led Mark out into the passageway and down it. "Do you want introductions, sir?"

Mark followed along and said, "Please give me a quick face to face and then thumb bios and pics I can look at later. I won't remember everyone at the moment. And call me Mark, please, Land."

"Yes, Mark. Congrats on your status." McDonald grinned and gestured the way. Ahead was a closed pressure lock, marking the change to another compartmented section. A rack of safety gear, emergency lights and warning signs reinforced that fact. The lock was big enough for several people, and they cycled through together. The equal pressure meant the chore took moments only.

The lock opened into a large workroom. It was filled with what looked like a class of college kids and profs, all gathered around screens, pointing, talking, making notes on screens and in mics. Three were in uniform. There was moderate light from glowtubes, and more from the screens and commsheets.

"Thank you," Mark said to the earlier comment. Then, "Good to see they're already at work," more softly. Indeed. That made several things easier.

In a few moments everyone was paying attention to him, so he figured he should say something.

"I'm Citizen Ballenger, the official Envoy," he said. "Don't let me interrupt you. We can get introduced later. We'll be boarding on short notice, so please be ready. The military in general does not yet know the nature of this expedition. Once we are in system you are free to talk as duty permits and on anything cleared by your department heads. There is still a risk of intel compromise even aboard ship. Until then, refer any inquiries to me, even if it's from the captain. No discussions at all. Understood?"

Assent ranged from nod or mumble to "Yes, sir." That was fine for this type of group, and he knew they'd all signed nondisclosures. Already, perfection gave way to expedience. These were the best people available in the Halo or within short travel time, with training in the proper fields and who were known to be discreet. Better scientists could follow along later.

McDonald said, "We have forty segs to arrival, and we expect to board as soon as it's docked and clear. It's going to be a mess aboard, but we'll straighten it out."

Mark drifted back and let them work. He overheard some poli-sci discussions he understood, and physics and technical ones he didn't. Halfway in between were history and anthropology that he could mostly follow. There was no telling what kind of sciences would be needed, so a broad spectrum of all was being taken—materials science, biology, chemistry, astronomy, logic, mathematics, zoology, botany, politics, anthropology, linguistics, cryptology, philosophy, cognitive science combining several of those together. Other, less known disciplines and a platoon of assorted engineers were along, journalists and documenters in official capacity, not as news shills. As soon as this bundle of brains came aboard, the military would pretty well figure out exactly what was going on. He wasn't sure what to do about that. He left them to work and went to check on other matters.

Mark realized he didn't even know what ship had been arranged by the ad hoc committee. The messages took segs to reach the capital, then more to return. The Citizens chosen were scattered across the system. In two days, he'd sent several hundred messages, and got several hundred back, some of which were long outdated by the time he saw them, regarding threads long since closed. Documentary skill was something he used often. However, not all Citizens had his background. It was a jumbled mess. He called to Faeroe Control and asked.

"The *Healy*, sir," one of the controllers on duty said. "Arriving exactly on time, they just called in for anchoring. They won't be docking, correct?"

"Correct. We're taking boats out. Thank you." He closed and realized he'd have to move. He wanted to depart fast, and there was just time to board boat.

Two station hands assigned to watch the bumbling mudsucker met him at the boat bay with his gear. He had far more than he should, because formal clothes could prove as important as environmental gear or body armor. The scientists were already gathered, most with a single duffel. They'd been told mass was at a premium. Some looked curiously at Mark, some nodded, and a few looked annoyed.

He pushed his way to the front, his temporary aides following, and pulled himself into the first boat. The occupants were three crew and a bunch of what looked like grad students, in ten styles. They nodded politely and stopped talking. He hated that, but he couldn't do much about it.

The launch was far gentler than he expected, but then, they were traveling only a couple of kilometers. Velocity paid for now would have to be paid for in return. It took very little time as it was; the boat shuddered, clanked and chuffed as pressure equalized.

Two eager academics dove for the lock. Beyond it, Mark heard, "Party, tenSHUN!" The two slipped back flushing crimson. They'd just received a salute intended for the Citizen. He wasn't angry, only amused, and sorry for them making a faux pas. The protocol probably hadn't been covered in school.

Mark moved quickly through, waved acknowledgement to the reception party and said, "As you were." He reached out for a quick slap of palms with the captain, in lieu of shaking. It was about all one could manage in a boat bay with no gravity.

"Citizen," the captain greeted with a nod. "Captain Commander Rulon Betang. I've been placed at your disposal. Can you tell me what this urgency is about?" They swam away from the lock to allow others to debark and to gain some measure of privacy.

"Only that it involves the security of the Freehold, and that a small amount of military presence might be needed," he admitted.

"Can you define 'small amount'?"

"Perhaps a gunboat. Sending a cruiser is overkill," Mark said.

"Good. I always like to know I have more than enough resources for the job at hand."

"That was the Council's thinking on the matter." *And my own. And you were the only ship available, so hope it doesn't blow up big.*

"No other details?"

"Not until we are underway. Then I can give you a briefing."

"Understood. We have several personnel meeting us here from leave. I assume we can wait for them?"

"No, we need to move fast."

Betang raised his eyebrows. "Our SOP also includes fuel surveys and maintenance reports."

"Leave without them. I'll authorize the situation so the crew are not in violation of missing a movement. If these reports are not urgent safety issues, skip them, please."

His expression said Betang realized this was serious. "Yes, sir. I hope whoever we are meeting is reasonable." Yes, it wasn't hard to figure out why a ship would move that fast, with civilian experts aboard.

"As do I. Enough said for now."

"Understood."

The captain was good to his word. Segs later, *Daniel Healy* was topped with conversion mass and ready. With no fanfare and no notice other than data in a log, the first human expedition to an alien intelligence got under way.

Mark woke up groggy. He liked micro-G for resting, but it took a couple of days to adapt. They were also in phase drive, which didn't quite feel like emgee, more like tottering on the edge of a cliff as shifts took place. He didn't know the technical details, but did know it was complex, and keeping the ship in one piece was part of the task. If energy levels got out of whack, boom! He wasn't overly worried about that, since he could do nothing about it, but the combination itself, as well as it being a constant reminder of the seriousness of this mission, did not make for good rest.

Shipboard food was still shipboard food. The menu was a bit more elaborate than he recalled, the quality adequate but not inspiring. He was left alone to eat. While he wasn't a celebrity, everyone aboard had to know who he was by now, and his civilian coverall, while spaceworthy, was not a uniform. He'd known that his status would create a huge social barrier, but knowing

so was not the same as the feeling of aloneness he actually felt now.

Once done eating, he checked for updates. Little from
the Council or committee, a few more details. HMG had
done the right thing so far: identified the situation and
left. However, they planned to return on their own. This
was where the laissez-faire minimalist government of the
Freehold was a drawback. A conglomerate with a profit
motive and few sociologists should not be allowed to act
like the East India Company, the early American settlers
and the Conquistadores rolled into one. Those lessons
had been learned the hard way. There was nothing in the
Freehold constitution to stop that, however. Officially,
Mark's mission was separate and unrelated. Unofficially,
they needed to get there first, set up shop, possibly get
introduced, and preempt any one-sided trade deals.

There was also the unknown of just where the natives
were technologically, or how they'd react. No data.

That left Mark in a holding pattern until he could
learn more.

The official party was scheduled to meet in one of the
cargo bays. He sought directions and followed a blinking
light through white metal passageways. The white color
was intended to make searches easy. It got sterile and
depressing fast.

The captain had done his job. The cargo bay was
empty, stripped, with intel gear set up to stop eavesdropping, security posted, and active countermeasures
to kill bugs. It was a large open compartment with cable
and pipe bundles on overhead and walls, deckplates
below and a few chairs.

He nodded to Betang and his staff, who walked in
and looked around at the occupants—the same scientists,

plus a few more and a very few crew who'd be providing satellite and boat support.

"Please let me know as soon as the cabin is secured," he said behind him.

"It's tight, sir," a commo tech said with a nod.

"Thank you," he said, and raised his voice. "As some of you know, Captain, Dr. McDonald," he nodded, "I'm Citizen Ballenger. I've basically hijacked your ship and crew for a technical and diplomatic mission."

"What mission?" the XO asked, unprompted but timely.

"HMG found a resource-laden system that is in contention, and that presents some unique diplomatic issues," he said, testing the waters.

A female officer near the front, intelligence from her insignia, said, "Let me guess, it's inhabited by sentients?"

"It is inhabited by sentients," Mark agreed. Damn, that was faster and smoother than he expected.

"Really?" She chuckled nervously. "I was joking."

"I wish I was," Mark said. Ah, well. He hadn't expected great secrecy. Nor was it hard to deduce.

"Why one cruiser?" the captain asked. "Why not an entire fleet, armed?"

"Their technical level appears to be preindustrial, possibly Iron Age."

"That's interesting," the captain said. Lots of people were jerking upright now. This was for real. First contact.

"The Council's primary concern is our presentation. Both HMG and DSR are already responding. HMG's ship departed before we left. There are bound to be other commercial interests, plus possibly missionaries and kooks. Also, the UN will obviously send someone when they find out, and the Galactic Alliance." That name still made him chuckle with its pretentiousness. The seventeen systems of the old Colonial Alliance, plus the three secondary colonies, hardly constituted a "Galactic" anything.

"So you expect any shooting to be at other humans, not aliens," the intel officer said.

"Secure that, Phelan," the XO warned.

"Sorry, sir," she replied, eyes still grinning.

"Let me keep this brief," Mark continued. "What we're doing is not only unique, it's something that calls for a substantial mission, in the political and diplomatic sense. We don't have that, so I'm going to be dependent upon all of you to cover the necessary roles, to keep me apprised of our actions, and to act on behalf of the Council as well as your respective organizations. This mission is technical, diplomatic, political and possibly social. We cannot, should not and will not stop legitimate industrial and commercial operations from dealing with our new neighbors. I'm hoping to persuade them to join us and present a unified face for a favorable impression. But if someone goes off half-cocked, we could have a diplomatic mess at best, and we still aren't positive their technology is only Iron Age. Nor would that stop them from allying with some other group and bringing modern power to bear. If we can offer deals, so can they.

"So, while the government has no official interest in trade, it does have a de facto and legitimate interest in national defense—in not creating a situation that will adversely affect the Freehold. Once the initial mission is over, and an embassy established, at that point everyone can have at it with the aliens and whatever representatives they so choose. With all human systems, that mechanism existed from the beginning. Here it does not."

There were mutters and whispers. None of these people, scientists or officers, were fools. This could turn ugly quickly, especially for the people on the ground. Nor did anyone want their name attached to a screwup in the history books.

"I'll be consulting as follows: Dr. McDonald's scientific group, shipboard intel and recon, shipboard support and transport, and landing party support. We will also need a security element that is discreet and can effect recovery, or retreat under fire. If anything else occurs to anyone, please bring it up to me, the captain or Dr. McDonald. I should be talking to each of you individually to get more background and information, but until I have the basics set up, that's going to be impossible. I will be consulting with everyone after we enter the system and start working. In the meantime, my distance is not meant to be rude or condescending."

The only response was a few nods.

"With that said, everyone please get to doing your jobs, and give us as much head start as possible. Thanks and good day." He turned, lowered his voice and said, "Captain, I'm going to get some exercise and start work from my stateroom. Anyone can reach me as needed. I hope you or one of your officers can stop by for lunch and give me a briefing on what the military needs from me."

"Will do, Citizen. So it *is* first contact?" Betang quivered.

"Yes."

"Thank you deeply for letting me be part of it, even if it was largely chance." The expression on his face was easy to read. It was one of wonder, awe and excitement. This could give his career a tremendous boost, but that wasn't the point. The point was to be there, doing something that had never been done before.

"You're welcome." Mark grinned for the first time in days. "We're all going to make history."

As he left, he thought to himself, *let's make sure it's as heroes, not villains.*

He entered his stateroom to find a crewwoman straightening and cleaning.

"Thank you, Spacer Two," he said, "but it's not necessary. I'll call if I need anything."

"It's not necessary, Citizen, but it's discreet." She stood up from making the bunk and smiled. "My actual rank is Blazer Captain, and I'll be in charge of ground security, and your personal security element. Chelsea Jelling, pleased to meet you, sir." She offered a hand.

He shook and said, "I imagine 'Blazer' is not quite correct." She was probably a Black Ops officer, he surmised, but one of the Blazer Recon or Pioneer units was possible, too.

"You know I will not comment on that, sir," she said. Her hair was slicked and tied back, and was a lustrous red. Her eyes were sea blue, with a skewering gaze that peeled him down, determined his competencies and threat level, categorized him and watched for his response. Now that she was upright, he could see she was nothing but rippling muscle, slim but solid. She was beautiful the same way a shark, ripper or leopard was, in perfect development for her purpose, which was to kill people.

"You need to pick a new cover name. I recognize that one from a war history thesis I read."

He gave her points for not twitching. "I'm not sure what you're referring to, but I will use a different name for discretion, when opportunity presents. Thanks for the information, sir."

"Drop the act. What are you planning for security?"

"Yes, sir," she said, and relaxed visibly. "As soon as we know what their tech level is, I will consult with you and arrange the appropriate weaponry. Some will be ceremonial, some brutally practical and some completely hidden. We'll arrange commo and gear so we can recover anyone missing or abducted, or, if that is not possible, make it impossible for them to be a source of intelligence against us. We will arrange to destroy or recover any equipment that could compromise us, and we'll act as bodyguards, both formal and practical."

"There's a good chance the weapons will be bows and spears."

She nodded and grinned. "We've trained with those, and refresh periodically. That will be fascinating if it happens."

"In the meantime you'll stop by here for briefs?"

"And to check your cabin for any intel gear, yes, sir. It's clean today, as best I can tell. I would not assume HMG doesn't have a shill in the crew who'll try to get in here. They can offer a tremendous bribe or blackmail, under the circumstances."

"Understood, and thank you." That had occurred to him, but he hadn't taken steps to prevent it yet, other than silence and sequestering of the ship. Signals came in nonstop, though, and people who worked with signals could also manage to eavesdrop.

Two days later, *Healy* phased back into normal space, in the outer halo of the system. It didn't take long to find HMG's ship. It was in the outer system, doing surveys of KBOs, outer planets, planetoids and chunks of rock. That actually was eminently practical, and Mark gave them points for it. The information would be of scientific and commercial interest to anyone who did open things up here, and was salable. They'd likely recouped their costs so far and then some. He had no illusions that would be enough to satisfy them, though.

There was nothing for Mark to do the first several days, except receive updates on remote sensor data and integrate the little that came through. The warship had better tactical sensors than the mining survey ship. It did not have the capability of a dedicated research vessel, even with upgrades and supplemental software. However, a few things became obvious.

107 Piscis was a K1 dwarf, its approximate age and spectra were on record, and it was easy enough to deduce mass. There were five planets. One was a burning rock in close, one was the inhabited one, and the three outer ones were gas giants, too small for brown dwarfs. The metal content was about 63 percent that of Sol, which for stellar purposes meant "anything other than hydrogen."

Astronomer James Zihn hardly slept or ate during that time. He didn't have the best instruments available, but he fine-tuned and took multiple scans. Then he and McDonald sat down with Mark to go over the findings. The briefing table was in one corner of the bay, and other activity was going on around them, with a respectful few meters of distance for privacy.

"There are a few obvious facts," Zihn started. He was a dapper, bearded man with a thick shock of black hair and an expressive face that was smiling in professional satisfaction. "I've got probably half the information HMG does already. The halo is marginal but exploitable. The gas giants are high G, so a little harder to exploit, but loaded with helium, neon, argon, methane. They're exploitable by scoopship, and will provide a lot of material for any kind of ongoing operation, as well as marketable resources."

Mark twitched. He didn't want a market survey. HMG would have that. He realized, though, this was necessary background and waited.

Zihn continued, "One notable lack is an inner planetoid belt. There's very little debris, most of it swept away. None of the denser ores most life systems have." He flashed some charts onscreen, which meant little to Mark, but apparently matched the briefing. "The inner planets have nominally typical cores and structure. What metal there is is all in planetary cores. 'Metal' in the chemical sense, not the astronomical sense."

Mark knew this was significant but wasn't quite following yet. "In other words, the system's marginal as a source of high grade ore, decently conducive to space habitation, and has locals on a normal-type planet we can't use."

McDonald said, "You'll have to spell it out, Jim."

Zihn nodded, now serious. "Sir, that's a correct summary of the system. You're more interested in the planet. Most exploitable metal ores on Earth, Grainne, any of our planets, are near the surface due to either volcanic action or meteoric impact. There are near zero metal impactors in this system, and while volcanism isn't my field, the inhabited one seems stable enough to have minimal heavy metal output."

That made sense. It sounded impossible, though. "So the definite signs of technology we see are Stone Age only, because they have no metal? Is life possible without metal?"

McDonald said, "There is metal. All the lighter metals used in biological processes are present. What is not present are large masses of copper, iron, cobalt, nickel, anything that could readily be smelted and used for tools. Aluminum, titanium and other light metals require sophisticated chemical or electrolytic means to reduce. No iron or copper means no electricity. I've handed this over to the anthropologists to kick around, and we'll need to make a closer survey."

"I understand," Mark said. Indeed he did. Whatever species was down there was trapped by its environment and would never be able to leave. Agriculture was certainly a Stone Age invention, Late Neolithic. Those photos of rectilinear land indicated they had it on a fairly broad scale. For how long? Recent? Some time? Their social development could be anything from savagery to say, Mesopotamian. He'd have to read up on those aspects to see where it went. That, and HMG would want to move in, strike a deal for anything exportable in exchange for tools that would make whichever group got them the planetary warlords, and massively disrupt whatever societies there were.

He noticed Lieutenant Shraybman waiting behind the two scientists. He raised an eyebrow, she nodded. He waved her over. Shraybman was assigned to control communications for the expedition. She had final say on anything going out or in, unless he overrode her. It annoyed the scientists greatly, but the security was necessary.

"We have incoming, Citizen," she said. "I just got word from Command."

"Incoming what?"

"Two ships, sir. A cruiser with a UN delegation, and a survey ship from Deep Space Resources, HMG's main competitor in this direction. They both tightbeamed, both polite requests we not do anything until they arrive."

"How polite?" he asked.

She grinned. "The UN was in diplospeak, sir. Requesting indulgence, in the spirit of joint human endeavor, et cetera, signed by an Ambassador Nurin Russ. He checks out. Do you know him?"

"Never heard of him. Who is he?"

"Some undersecretary of Indigenous Persons Affairs. I think that's for Earth indigenes, but it makes sense to send him here. DSR was less flowery, but requested HMG not be allowed to proceed without their presence, to help moderate the event and provide the locals with more options, and so they can have a chance at a deal themselves."

"I'll grant the UN because they're not being demanding assholes, and DSR because they were honest enough to admit to a profit motive," he replied. "Tell both they can dock and meet here. Three person max per delegation. Call HMG and tell them they're outnumbered, outgunned and will do everyone a favor if they come to the council fire. Land, do you have anything to add?" he asked McDonald.

The scientist seemed amused. "That seems to be it for now. We can share whatever you want to share when they arrive."

"Got it, sir." Shraybman nodded and swam back to her station.

McDonald cautiously asked, "Are we going to be sharing?"

"Certainly," Mark agreed. "The more brains working on this, the better, and the less likely someone will sneak off to find their own data and screw things up. Sorry for that. Dr. Zihn, do you have anything to add?"

"No, fortunately I had concluded." Zihn smiled with twinkling eyes. "I'll go back and look at more graphs."

"Good. Captain Jelling," he spoke into his commlink as they left.

"Right behind you, sir," she said. He jerked. Dammit, he hated that.

"Very perceptive," he looked at her. She wasn't grinning in triumph or amusement. He decided it hadn't been any kind of point mechanism, she was just eager and efficient. "I'll want you to stop anyone bringing in any recording device we don't know about, and be sure we can scramble or suppress those we do. Sidearms only, no heavy weapons, and I may limit that completely when we land. I hate doing it but it's going to be tense and I don't want anyone trying to argue the point on who gets data."

"I'll talk to Shraybman and my Special Projects people, and have it ready, sir," she said. "Call if you need anything."

CHAPTER 2

The mass briefing started the next day, with everyone aboard. Per Mark's request, Ambassador Russ had been shown standard diplomatic courtesy on arrival. While he'd prefer to have the company shills met by latrine cleaners, he settled on the executive officer. They hadn't done anything too extreme yet, except for HMG deciding to not inform the Council. They were not legally bound to, but there was the moral issue. The social contract of the Freehold discouraged mistaking profit for rapine. Out here, though, were few witnesses and no one to call them publicly to account. Mark wished he had press along to that end, but that would also open a lot of things he needed to do to public exposure.

Dammit, the basis of their society was to be open and honest. He'd have to ask for some moral guidance on this. Whom could he trust? McKay? Ngota? Waltz? Someone who would listen honestly to the conflict and offer advice on what he must do? Who wouldn't scream to the Council that he was too inexperienced and had to be removed? All three, he decided. He pulled up an encryption program that almost no one knew existed, strictly for communication between Citizens.

Then he remembered there was no Jump Point here. Unless a ship was heading back under phase drive, no message could be sent. It was all up to him.

Lieutenant Shraybman caught his attention. She had three people with her. He grabbed a corner of desk and swam over.

"Citizen Mark Ballenger, may I present Ambassador Nurin Russ of the United Nations and his assistants."

"A pleasure to meet you," he said sincerely, bowing his head a fraction in the emgee.

Russ seemed surprised. "And you," he replied. His assistants bowed slightly and said nothing.

"I'm sorry I didn't meet you personally at the lock. However, let me welcome you to our operations center for this study."

"Thank you. Though I wonder why you didn't inform us you had discovered sentients?" Well, that was direct. Mark pretty much had to reply to that.

"We weren't sure what was here, and we're still figuring out what it is. Also, information like this needs to be kept close. Even tightbeams can be intercepted, and any encryption we share, others can crack."

"Fair enough," Russ nodded. "Can we combine missions?"

"From your point of view, yes. Our exploration and research is intended to be open, once we decide what we have. However, that's not the only issue here. I have to deal with two corporations so far, and they're not really answerable to me, under our system."

Russ grinned. "They are under ours."

Mark paused a moment. That seemed to be an offer of aid in choking HMG down. However, it came with a hugely loaded assumption attached. He raised his eyebrows and waited just a moment to reply.

"Please don't go there, Ambassador. It was ugly last time."

Russ's sudden change in tone indicated that had been part of the offer. "Yes, you like to hold that threat out."

"Since I was five when the war ended, that's hardly fair." He took a surreptitious look at the assistants. One male, one female, mixed race, young and obviously understudies or factota. Their expressions were neutral.

"Forgive me," Russ said. "Obviously I'm anxious. This does affect the entire human race. The UN is the only body with the moral authority to treat, not some lone state."

"Do you really believe that?" Mark asked, trying for incredulity.

Russ said nothing, just smiled.

"Nice opening bid. Want to try for something a little more reasonable?"

"Citizen, listen—"

That wasn't what he wanted to hear, and Mark cut him off. "No, you listen. This is a system staked by a Freehold corporation, perfectly legit within international law and with plenty of precedent. The natives have an obvious overriding claim, if sentient. That should lead to discussions of how best to approach them to preserve their society or ours, and how to mutually benefit from it. I missed the part where 'invite in some third party that attacked us with nukes and bioweapons twenty years ago, ask their opinions, and assume they have the right to take over' came into it."

"It's the first inhabited planet the Freehold has found," Russ said. "Irrelevant."

"Ah, so since UN ships found the previous ones, that's a perpetual lease on the universe? Oh, wait! Tancorp founded Grainne, without UN sanction. Kuwait founded Ramadan. Mtali, Salin were private missions. We're at four systems the UN didn't discover or found so far." Mark was enjoying this part. It was like an asset fight between conglomerates. Actually, that's exactly what it was. He'd made millions in this game, all on contingency.

Russ replied, "The UN was involved in development after founding, on all except Grainne."

"That still gives us a precedent, first claim and stake, political, scientific and military missions on site. What are you bringing to the table?"

Russ was silent. Mark kept his face still, but grinned inside. Silence from a UN diplomat was a score and a compliment. They never shut up.

Finally, Russ tried a different tack. "You don't plan to let HMG move in and start operations at once, then?" he asked.

"There's no reason for me to be here if that was the case. It's very probable this system is inhabited by sentients. That changes the rules for everyone, since it hasn't happened before."

"What do you plan to do then?" Russ asked, then added, "If I may inquire?" Better.

"Investigate until we know enough to make a decision. That's not an attempt to be evasive. I honestly don't know what to do yet. How deep is a hole? How long is a rope?"

"I would like to offer our assistance, technical and scientific to learn more, then. In addition, I'd appreciate being able to offer amicus curiae for the obvious questions that will arise."

"Agreed," Mark said. He'd give that one as a freebie. It would give him position to disagree later for balance.

Once again, Russ was at a loss. "That's not a problem?"

"I value more scientific input. I'd like to keep any communication with HMG or other nongovernment interests through me, and cautious."

"Obviously."

"By all means bring your people in. Please coordinate with Lieutenant Shraybman."

She arrived as soon as her name was invoked. "Yes, sir?"

"The UN delegation will be joining our research efforts. Can you please contact the appropriate personnel to make arrangements?"

"Will do. Also, Deep Space Resources' representative has arrived."

"And now the money fight starts." Mark sighed. "Please tell him I'd like to talk to him."

"It's a she. Yes, sir. The usual compliments and courtesies?"

She. He was almost certain he knew who that was.

"No."

He kept his face blank as he enjoyed the shocked and amused expressions of all those nearby.

Shortly, Shraybman brought over the DSR representative.

"Citizen Ballenger, Tayalin Margov, Deep Space Resources Associate of Exploitation Ethics."

"Taya," he greeted with a grin. "It's been several years."

"Mark. Good day." She smiled back, thinly.

A few things were apparent to Mark. First, that she was still distractingly gorgeous even in a shipsuit, and the scheming glint in her eyes made her more so. Second, she'd obviously been picked based on their previous negotiations. Score one for DSR for researching that. Third, she was no more trustworthy now than back then, when he'd been the purchase rep for Gealeach Metallics. He'd listen and read very carefully before agreeing to anything she offered. She wasn't a backstabber. She was a throat slitter.

"Is that a new position?"

"Of course," she said, brightly and with mock innocence. "Since it appears there may be sentients here, a different type of negotiation will be needed. We need to balance our needs with those of the natives to ensure a long-term, strain-free relationship."

"Cut the bullshit, Taya. What's your position?"

Her grin could melt steel. "HMG is claiming stake based on entering the system. That's standard policy for an unoccupied system. Were it habitable and without sentients, it would be put out for conglomerate or consortium bid and development. If this system has sentients, DSR's position is that there are no rights until feet down and contract inked."

"That's close to the initial position the Committee is taking," Mark said. "Of course, I am not conceding or agreeing to anything until all parties have discussed this."

"Obviously not. I am here to conclude the best deal possible for DSR vis-à-vis the Freehold Citizens' Committee, the indigenes, our own margin and that of our public image. And, of course, to shut those HMG bastards out and have their balls for breakfast." She grinned again.

"Nice of you to admit the obvious without a fight."

"You're welcome," she said.

"Taya, may I present Nurin Russ, Ambassador for the UN."

Russ had been silent, trying to be invisible, and had clearly followed the exchange with interest. He greeted her cordially with a bow, which she returned. It was not an accident that a modest but enticing amount of cleavage showed when she did so. Mark felt better now. He had two corporate sharks to deal with. That was the venue he was familiar with, so that's the fight he'd pick. Russ could keep up or be shut out himself.

"I must talk to the captain and Dr. McDonald," Mark said. "I encourage everyone to contribute their collective knowledge and wisdom to the research effort. Once we have a better idea what we are dealing with, we can negotiate the fine points. Good day."

As he left, he saw Taya sizing up Russ like a lab project. That would keep both of them busy. Now to see about getting HMG into the melee.

That same day, Egan arrived. Mark knew him by reputation, but they'd never met. He lacked the control and viciousness of Taya or the formal obsequious assumptive pressure of Russ but was still very acquisitive in his own way. It took a while to deduce that his method was to start with the assumption that he owned the entire system personally, and whine about every injustice that would take the smallest rock away from him. He was far less subtle, but at least as stubborn.

"So, Mr. Egan, your position starts with a claim to the system."

"Not quite, Citizen. All we claim is first rights. If the system is inhabited by sentients, we should have first offer and right of first refusal. If not sentient, we should be able to form our own consortium or dispose of it as controlling party. We would have claimed the system, as is standard, had it been uninhabited."

"Under those circumstances, you're agreeable to waiting for the scientists to resolve such questions, then?"

"We're agreeable to a reasonable period. By all means determine the actual status of the native life. To that end, I'd like to share some of our findings."

"Certainly. As you can see," Mark said with a wave, "this bay is a temporary science center. It makes up for what it lacks in dedicated equipment with training and expertise."

"Our equipment is better, and I am authorized to extend the courtesy of our resources."

That was a good offer. Of course, it also led to a situation where everyone was beholden to HMG, who would be sure to play the card. That, and having personnel there increased the risk of a leak, blackmail, extortion, all the usual bargaining chips. An entire star system's wealth and life was at stake.

"I will discuss that offer with the UN and Freehold scientific contingents, of course," Mark said. He kept his negotiation smile in place. "Define 'reasonable period.' "

Egan feigned casualness and ran fingers over his jaw. "Well, I'm sure this could take additional days. We've determined they're tool users and have agriculture. They're almost certainly not spacefaring. Once we narrow the range we're dealing with so we know what approach to take, I expect to move into orbit and plan a landing mission."

Legally, there was nothing Mark nor the Freehold government, such as it was, could do about that. Practically and morally there were huge issues around it. HMG was obviously aware of those, and either didn't care or didn't regard them as important. Stick enough zeroes behind a credit sign and anyone's morals were flexible.

Still, "We'd like to approach that slowly, so as to minimize any impact, while of course retaining any and all rights your company has."

Egan said, "Good. So have the scientists pool with mine and we'll take it from there."

He said it very casually.

Mark didn't miss it. He was quite eager to have the scientific partnership, Mark noticed. Could it be his scientists weren't quite as capable? Or that he hoped to gain more than he gave? Either was likely. He wouldn't be offering to share intel he could profit from unless he would gain as much or more in return.

"You realize DSR has arrived with its own survey gear and would like to be part of this, too."

"Of course. Obviously we have no say in what deal you may come to with them. I can't allow them aboard our ship for obvious reasons of corporate privacy."

Mark considered that. Did he not think noncompany scientists would notice any useful info? Or did he not have any? It certainly seemed as if his main worry was his competition. If either group found something useful, it would get shared soon enough. So, he had nothing, or little enough he thought he could benefit from the partnership, and sure as hell didn't want his competitors finding out directly how little nothing he had. Or else he knew the natives' status and didn't want it spoiling his claims.

Mark replied, "I'll discuss that in turn. Shortly we'll have to have everyone get together for a round table and share openly."

"Within reason, yes." Egan's nod was an attempt to hide a poker face.

That wasn't necessarily evasive, but he wanted help without compensation.

"Let me talk it over and see what we have. Updates are coming in pretty constantly, and you're welcome to observe. I also see that Lieutenant Shraybman has information for me," Mark said to end the conversation.

"Very well, Citizen. Please let me know." Egan shook hands again and moved away. He obviously was recording with his comm. Mark wondered if he should have a scrambler put into play about that, or just ignore it.

He discreetly signaled McDonald. The tall scientist nodded and swam over leisurely, checking systems and talking with people as he did so. Good man.

"Land, what do you have?" he asked, when the doctor finally arrived.

"Nothing substantive and new. I spoke to the military intel people and we have tactical drones on a decreasing sweep at high boost. If anything untoward happens, they'll shut down and go ballistic, after ejecting the power cell. We're five nines certain they have no space capability or advanced sensors. Once we get in close, I'd like permission to send active tacticals in, if it seems safe."

"Let me know. We need to find information fast before someone succumbs to greed. Not that I blame them."

"I understand. Though I'm not clear on how adding more zeroes to the credit sign makes the task more worthwhile. My motivation is a little different." Again the amused smile.

"People like them and people like us will never meet on that issue," Mark agreed. He'd had millions not so long ago. In order to be a Citizen he'd had to divest himself of most of it and donate it to the government he now worked for. There reached a point where more money was merely point counting, and there were other, more interesting ways to make points. He was certainly earning those points here.

After three days of back and forth on the technical data, Mark agreed to the roundtable he'd mentioned. The longer the scientists had, the better. But he had to offer something or the two mining firms were likely to race down and settle matters with survey charges and power beams.

Captain Betang graciously offered a conference room on the command deck. Mark checked it over the evening before to get a good feel for it. He'd never seen a warship wardroom before. The table was dogged down, and the seats had belts for emgee, as well as additional harnesses in case of battle or maneuver. The bulkheads were plain polymer panels with a few schematics of ships and a framed starscape to break up the blank faces, with assorted screens and displays at each seat, recessed into the table, on bulkheads and overhead.

When he arrived he made a point of being on time. Exactly on time.

"Good morning," he said. He sat and stared down the table. Betang was present at his request, along with

Shraybman, McDonald and two of his experts, Russ, his female assistant whose name he still didn't know, two UN scientists, and Egan and Margov. Without preamble he said, "I'd like to let Dr. McDonald summarize our current findings."

"Ladies, men," McDonald began. "I'm feeding a variety of displays and documents to your screens. Summary is behind me to my left, and a photo slideshow will appear to the right. The technical specs for the images are available through your systems.

"Basically, the natives are definitely tool users and city builders with agriculture. Obviously, sentient. They do not have anything close to space capability, even low orbit, to the best of our ability to detect. Air travel is exceptionally unlikely. The specific probabilities are listed, but they're several standard deviations from the baseline. We don't know what ground-based sensors they have, but there's less than a point zero five percent chance of electrical power. We're not sure what visual frequencies they may use, but low infrared is possible, given the spectrum of the star. Ultraviolet is conceivable.

"We make a sixty percent probability of their technology ranging from Bronze Age to early Industrial Age, mechanical tools without modern power."

Russ asked, "What do you recommend as the next step?" His own scientists had obviously advised him, but he was helping Mark present all facts. They hadn't discussed doing this, but Mark appreciated it. By the time they were done, the assumption should be that the system be left in isolation. The speculators would have to argue for every concession.

McDonald said, "Move in closer and determine their technical level with greater accuracy. Assuming we prove they don't have modern sensors, we can use more active equipment ourselves and place them better."

Mark asked, for the record, since he knew, "What do you think of a contact scenario?"

McDonald answered, "Obviously, we have to ascertain their technical level, attempt to deduce their sociological level and mythology, then make assessments as to how they will react. After that, we must try careful meetings without exceeding their technological level in a fashion that will arouse or upset them."

Egan asked what was obvious for him. "How long do you estimate this to take?"

"It could be anywhere from weeks to years," McDonald said. "It's impossible to guess without actually seeing the indigenous society or societies."

"Citizen? What do we do about that?" By "we" he obviously meant Mark, whom he expected to produce an answer to his liking.

Mark replied, "We continue the examination. We don't want to be incautious and alarm the locals. That will obviously complicate any interactions or trade. That concerns you more than us."

"I don't see how it would be harder than the regressed tribalists on Salin or the outer areas of Mtali."

Taya Margov saved Mark by saying, "They at least grasp the concept of technological society. These people may not. Imagine . . . no, I don't think there is a comparison. Even if we saw something impossible, we'd attribute it to a new technology. They may not have actual technology beyond the simple Archimedean tools."

Russ said, "I must agree on restraint."

"Am I being asked or ordered?" Egan asked, looking around and bristling a little.

"Asked," Mark insisted at once. "Your interest is economic, but the other interests are still valid and subject to discussion, in court if need be."

"Frankly, I move to step up the exploration fast and see what the surface looks like. I don't see how doing that would violate any lesser interests, as long as it's done cautiously."

Now was the time, Mark thought.

"That information is already available," he said.

Once everyone was looking at him, he continued. "I authorized an unarmed tactical reconnaissance by some of our intelligence boats."

"When?" Egan demanded. "We've been monitoring the entire system with sensors and didn't see any launches or atmospheric entries."

Mark smiled and stared for a moment. When it was clear Egan was slow on the uptake, he said, "So you can assume our military stealthing exceeds the capabilities of your surplus military sensors." The troops had loved it, too. Sneaking and scooting past an active "enemy" had been a challenge they'd enthusiastically embraced.

Russ looked perturbed. Clearly, he didn't like those implications, either.

"Here's the edited and annotated footage and images," Mark said, pulling up four screens and a 3D tank. "The surface is very poor in metals. What's there are light metals in hard to process ores. Iron is not available in any quantity that's exploitable without industrial machinery they haven't been able to build. The same for copper. I limited the pass to remote sites and long range images, but you can see that the villages are communal and simple."

"So, they're Stone Age?" Egan asked.

"They're not a metal using society," McDonald said. Everyone faced him. "Since we're admitting this, Citizen, may I?" After Mark's nod, he said, "However, they seem to have advanced somewhat above that of Neolithic societies on Earth. There are other technologies that developed concordantly with metal. Agriculture, animal husbandry, early chemistry, mechanics. There's no reason such would not happen here, and in fact, appear to have done so."

The scans were stills taken at high speed, during a supra-atmospheric pass. They seemed slightly better resolution than a microball drone would shoot, but they were not great. However, the military photo people had cleaned and sanitized them, to give more clarity and to hide capabilities. One of those people was in the cabin watching right now, to determine if any capability might be revealed.

"Fascinating." The speaker was Marguerite Stephens, one of the UN scientists, whose title was Historical Developmental Anthropologist. She craned across the table. "They look like medieval communities with an open field system. Far more advanced than you'd expect of a Stone Age culture. Can I get the raw data?"

"I will make the raw data available to everyone," Mark agreed.

"Did I see boats and tracks?"

"We aren't sure," McDonald said. "Obviously, they don't have engines, but they might have pedal power or levered wheels."

"You are positive on the engines?"

"Yes. No bronze, no iron, and aluminum takes either electrical power, almost impossible without the former, or advanced chemical reduction. Also, there's no reason to develop aluminum if you don't know about the more basic metals, and nothing to suggest looking."

Stephens said, "DaVinci described a number of mechanisms, and the old English narrowboats were horse drawn, as were the early rails. I can accept that. But I certainly want to get feet down and see. Both culturally and technically it's a gold mine. I suppose we could say that's the real mission here."

Mark snickered. This grandmotherly intellectual was a great help. Egan was being treated as side issue. It would be good for him. A glance showed him to be twitching again.

Russ asked, "Do you believe we should move in closer at this point, or continue doing remote scans with our best equipment?"

"Dr. McDonald?" Mark prompted.

McDonald tilted his head slightly and said, "I believe it safe to send recon craft in closer, and take better resolution images. I must recommend against atmospheric probes or impactors."

"Why against probes?" Margov asked. She looked quite alert.

"There is very little meteoric activity in this system. A flare or fireball could be seen by the natives as significant."

"I understand," Margov said. "So, I propose we wait for more information, and land together. The natives will eventually deal with whoever they feel is the better company for their needs. Unless HMG is afraid that's not them?" She stared at Egan. Her smile was casual, but vicious.

"Not afraid, and don't feel a need to prove it," Egan said, in a manner that belied his words. "We'll land when we feel like it." It was a clear challenge.

"Inadvisable," McDonald said. He had a faint edge of annoyance. Very faint. For Land, that was the equivalent of calling someone an idiot.

Egan missed it, or didn't care. "Right now, perhaps. Since the data will be available to all, I'll ask my staff to review it, and decide from there what our best option is."

Mark still had no response to that. He wasn't sure if there could be a response to that. He had to come up with something.

The meeting adjourned with handshaking and fake smiles. At this point, there was the HMG versus DSR fight, the UN versus the commercial agendas, UN bluster versus the Freehold's claim, and the officially neutral position of the Freehold, and the unofficial one in favor of keeping the interference as low as possible. In theory, that was the UN's concern, too. In reality, its concern was in grabbing power, as it had been for five hundred years.

He had to concede one point to DSR. It was necessary to land soon and resolve this. The problem wasn't going to get smaller with waiting.

As everyone departed, most with phones already in use and encrypted messages flying, Mark caught Captain Betang's attention, and indicated privacy. Betang nodded and opened a side compartment, about twenty percent as large as the wardroom and sealed.

The hatch closed, and he said, "Tell me about the UN ship."

Betang shrugged and said, "Comparable class and capabilities as ours, really. Retrofitted with phase drive and not purpose built. It's Sloan's mechanism, not Brandt's, but that doesn't make much difference. Would you like deck plans or a capabilities sheet?"

"No, similar to ours is good enough. I don't want to be massively outclassed, or have brought too much. Status quo helps."

"I see where you're going. Yes, sir. Let me know what we are to do."

"Thank you, Captain."

As Mark left the wardroom, he found Russ waiting in the main passageway, alone.

"I'd like a word with you, Citizen Ballenger."

"Certainly."

"Your reconnaissance, without consulting with us, is somewhat disturbing. Moreover, the implied threat such flights pose to our ships and interests is a point for discussion. You could, in theory, attack one of our craft."

Blunt and honest. Mark replied in kind. "If you're not hostile, you have nothing to worry about. If our concern was hostile, it would already have happened. We did help rebuild after the War. There's no long-term animosity toward the people of Earth, and as we're cooperating here and elsewhere, not between governments, either."

"The War is not a subject most people find tasteful."

"Nor do we, when it comes down to it."

After a moment of swapped stares, they parted ways.

Mark sighed. He was the new guy, on a mission unlike any before. He felt like he was juggling sharp knives, just waiting for one to come down the wrong way.

CHAPTER 3

Mark quickly tired of breakfast on the run. Intel was coming in at too fast a rate to keep track of. He didn't need to know finer points of evolutionary development, geography or species distribution, except as they related to political ramifications. Even with that, he rarely left the research bay, and when he did he returned as soon as he was rested, sometimes before.

To add to the stress, today they would enter orbit around the planet, at geostationary distance. Everyone was certain there was no threat, but, as he had to keep reminding them, political and social threats did not need to reach orbit. Just being seen could create any number of disasters humans would ultimately be responsible for. It was ironic that to determine the potential threat, they had to get close enough to be such a threat.

Egan—and Margov, though she didn't say so—wanted to land now. McDonald and the scientists would be happy to take years, creeping slowly closer and writing entire libraries of information before actually contacting natives. The military and diplomats were somewhere in between.

He kept track of the approach on a separate window on his desk, while dealing with the multitude of nitnoy crap and real issues constantly being generated. Would he approve an active scan of the near space? Had he seen these improved biome charts? Here was a tentative tectonic history for the last million years and an environmental history of growth and climate. No additional news on alien technology, except that it was clustered around river estuaries and mountains.

Three fact-filled but otherwise uneventful mornings later, he entered the bay chewing a bland nutrient bar and saw McDonald waiting anxiously.

"What do you have, Land?" he muffled around a mouthful of food, if it could be called that.

"Well, there's good news and bad news," McDonald said with his trademark slight smile.

"There always is," Mark agreed.

"The air is breathable. We knew that. We can drink the water, as long as it's filtered. I wouldn't even touch anything else unprotected."

"Oh?"

"Toxic chemistry. All the plants will burn like acid ferns or blister like Earth poison ivy. Any wounds are going to burn like firethorns. Ingesting anything is going to cause massive damage to the GI tract, and likely be toxic as well, possibly at the enzymic level."

"Will we need respirators against pollen?"

"Uh . . . " McDonald obviously hadn't thought that far yet. "I don't think so. It wouldn't be a bad idea to take some, though. Long sleeves, bloused pants, tight fabric, gloves wise for those who like to touch or lean on things. We may be able to devise a salve to protect skin."

"Please do all of that. We can lighten precautions afterwards if it seems prudent."

"Yes, sir."

Mark sighed. The good news, from his point of view, was that it would limit interaction and make it more controllable. The bad was that the more gear needed increased the likelihood of technology transfer and would make it harder to create a comfortable environment. He decided that was a worthwhile payoff, for now.

"Can you use a worst case scenario for that when presenting the data to HMG?"

"I already did."

"Excellent."

Mark heard a sudden voice in his earphone. Lieutenant Phelan, intelligence officer, said, "Citizen, I need you now!"

"At my desk, talk and show," he said, facing the 3D cube set in it. An image of the surface rippled and expanded. It was a flat image from high altitude.

"What am I looking at?" Mark asked.

"Watch as I zoom in," Zihn said, hooked into the same circuit.

"Watching."

The continent grew and spread in the screen, terrain features growing and rising, with a vague brownish area defining an area of habitation. As the resolution passed 2000 meters, lines became visible, irregular in width and brightness, but dead straight, surveyed and precise.

It took Mark a moment to recognize it, because it was so unlikely in the context he had so far.

"That's a Pythagorean model," he said.

"Yes, a right triangle and square areas, laid out across fifteen point three kilometers of grassland. Unless it's an annual celebration of mathematical knowledge—"

"They know we're here," Mark finished.

"So they have telescopes," Zihn said.

"Or an informant." Mark wasn't sure why that was the first thing he thought of, but a healthy dose of paranoia was called for.

"That . . . is a disturbing possibility, Citizen," Phelan offered.

"It's not likely," Mark said on reflection. "They wouldn't announce a presence in that case. But I am assuming our real estate moguls have seen the same signal." He pondered for a moment. "Tell me about telescopes."

McDonald was on net now, and said, "Telescopes require a glass technology. That's a reasonably clean quartzite sand, and a clean, hot fire, then abrasives in increasingly finer grits."

"I assume the tube for the lenses doesn't have to be complicated?"

Zihn said, "No, a tube isn't even necessary. A frame will do. Especially since light pollution isn't a problem for them. They may be using aerial telescopes—on tall towers—as a means of combating chromatic aberration, but compound lenses are not that great of a step, though chemical treatments would be. I doubt they'd be able to manage a motor drive for timed exposures but any photographic telescopy would require metal anyway, so—"

Mark could follow that, but didn't need it. "That's fine," he said. "So they may have telescopes and can see us. Can we confirm that?"

"Given time. I can start scanning high peaks for construction appropriate to an observatory and proceed from there."

"Please. I'm not assuming any knowledge on their part."

"Let me know too, please," Stephens' voice said. "That boosts their tech level to seventeenth or eighteenth century." Everyone was joining the party. Mark cringed. This was exactly why he'd have preferred not to have any interference.

A bit later, Phelan said, "Sir, we found another one. A perfect circle with radians marked."

That was impressive. Whatever tech base this society had was well above Earth's Stone Age, closer to at least the higher levels of ancient Greece or Rome. If telescopes were confirmed . . .

"How are these set up? Open fields? Wilderness?"

Phelan said, "With Dr. McDonald's approval, I authorized a sweep by a Pebble. We'll find out shortly."

"It's staying out of the atmosphere?" Mark asked, nervous. They couldn't have anything that might be perceived as hostile.

"Yes. No chance of tracking it with their technology."

"Yes, Lieutenant, but I'm remembering that this morning, they were just Stone Age savages, Neolithic agriculturalists. Now they have telescopes."

Zihn said, "It's not too tremendously unlikely. It actually speaks well of their scientific nature and social base. You'd know more about that than me, though."

"A bit," Mark replied. He wasn't an historian. His degree was international relations, as it applied to interstellar trade and marketing, he'd covered the basics of societal development twelve Grainne years before. "Let me discuss it with Marguerite Stephens."

A div later, they had more intel. He ordered it presented in the conference room. The frames were projected along one wall, with a steady loop running at slow speed below them. Phelan met everyone with a nod. She was tall, lean, and obviously military in bearing. She used a finger light to indicate points of interest.

"Keep in mind the resolution on a drone the size of a plum is low, and that it was moving at a fairly high rate of relative speed," Phelan said. "But we have a decent view of the first area. You can see the pattern is built of brush, likely cleared in that forest. Regular parties with draft-drawn wagons are bringing it, and there are substantial stockpiles. The burn is very controlled, and I wonder if they aren't doing some forest management at the same time."

"That might be coincidental," Stephens said. "That would be a substantial advance even over what we've seen so far." Mark could place her accent now. Caledonian. She'd been raised not far from the capital, with that formal, almost archaic British English delivery. Her enunciation and delivery were perfect and well schooled.

Captain Jelling spoke up. "I see clear signs here, and here, of security checkpoints bottlenecking the arrivals. This looks like a crowd of spectators who were denied entrance and set up camp."

"Very much like a camp," Stephens said, squinting to try to see through the photo's graininess. "You'll note the improvised corral, a cluster of tents that were probably initial arrivals, and the rest in organized rows. That could be sanitation facilities, and that could be a midden heap, though they appear to be landfilling as they use it. Quite sophisticated. That's a level of discipline that was endorsed in the Middle Ages, but rarely accomplished in reality. They're smart."

"Anyone else?" Mark asked.

"Intelligence Sergeant Louise Thomas, sir," a blonde soldier said. He hadn't even noticed her. "I'm a photo intelligence specialist. Looking at the roads here and over there, it looks as if they were very crude dirt tracks. But I believe those lighter areas have been selectively filled with debris, either dried vegetation or gravel, to maintain integrity for load use."

"I concur," Jelling said.

"Enough for now," Mark said. It would be too easy to get sucked into a days-long analysis of each frame. "So, they're mathematical symbols, not visible except from high altitude, in more than one location, restricted to participants only with no spectators allowed, and built on apparently short notice with the expectation of an extended operation," he ticked off points. "Certainly deliberate, then, is my call. We'll assume so for now. Everyone back to work."

No sooner had he reached the lab than Egan came storming in, and said, "I understand the natives have contacted us. When are we landing?"

"We aren't," he said. "They've drawn mathematical symbols. That does not equate to contact."

He exploded. "You said that if contact was made, we could land. Now you're trying to squirm out of it! If you had any idea of the business potential involved—"

Mark cut him off. "If you recall my background, you'd understand I do have some idea of the business potential involved. I also understand the sacrifices and ethics involved. As a veteran I understand the personal risk involved. It will cost you little to wait a few more days, and may keep you out of Citizens' Court claims and bankruptcy proceedings, and it just might keep you out of the dueling arena. Now, unless you have further business aboard this military vessel, I suggest you return to yours." His voice didn't rise, but the tension was palpable. Egan's troop escort gestured to him, and he twisted his face in impotent rage.

"Very well, Citizen," he snarled. "We'll do it your way. For now. But the Council will hear from me about a constitutional violation." He turned and left.

Stephens was nearby, and acted as if Egan hadn't been present. "One more item. There appear to be covered or enclosed vehicles, quite large, which may be powered by some mechanism. Although, daVinci also described such enclosures for draft animals. Those were military vehicles."

"Yes, I've seen those sketches," Mark said.

Margov called a few segs later. The industrial ghouls were not about to let up for a moment, if they thought they could make a buck. "Citizen, I've been talking with my opposite number. Obviously, we're both eager to land, but I understand your caution. However, as an interim to allow better study, I propose moving into low orbit. They know we're here. You can't argue that."

"I can argue that," Mark said. "It is not yet proven, and may not be until and if we land. Also, multiple craft increase the possible perception of threat. Your presence is antagonistic to several factions. My orders remain. You can argue it with the Council back home. I want as much intel as we can acquire up here before we land."

"No, I'm comfortable with your guidance. Please proceed." He didn't believe for a second she actually cared what he thought, except as it affected her ability to land. Still, she was the easier one to deal with for now. Was it deliberate good thug/bad thug with Egan? Was she exploiting his attitude? Were the two of them even in contact at this point? Mark waved Shraybman over and asked her.

"I'll see what I can find out, sir," she agreed.

Another military officer came over. "Zig Hensley, sir," he said. He was a captain, lieutenant for spacer ranks.

"How can I help you, Lieutenant?"

"Sir, if there is a landing, I'm in charge of flight operations. I need to get an idea of where you're considering."

That was a damned good question. "I would have said somewhere quiet, like an island near a coast, to give us some privacy. We could deploy from there by boat for discretion. At this point, though, we've got a probable deliberate attempt at contact several kilometers inshore, off a major waterway. We're more likely to land there since they seem to be inviting it."

"I can prepare both projects. Inland would have to be a direct ground to orbit craft. I can make the same plans for the coast, and also plan to drop an assault craft, with a masked approach from open sea."

"Man, I haven't done either in twelve years," Mark said with a wistful grin. "It'll be different."

An entourage of scientists came over. There were McDonald, Stephens, and one he recognized only from his badge, Navin, a UN optical scientist.

Navin said, "We've found what looks like an observatory. It's an open building on a mountainside, with a road leading up to it, and is situated behind the peak from the city, which would cut light pollution."

"I'm confused," Mark admitted. "We're still discussing a Stone Age culture here?"

"Yes," he agreed. "They have gas lighting. It's doubtful that it's centrally piped. They still seem to have pressure vessels, though, and tubing."

"Obviously," Mark pondered, "if they don't have metals, their technology will develop without them."

McDonald prompted, "Show the Citizen the shots of the city."

A moment later, a city map flashed on screen at 5000 meters resolution. It flashed quickly down to 1000 meters, and features became clearer.

It looked like a city. A large one.

"This is native?" he asked rhetorically. Of course it was native. He was surprised, though.

"Yes. I'll zoom in on some interesting parts." McDonald grabbed a remote and ran his finger over it. Pan, zoom, and a section of river grew huge.

"Wow," Mark said, "that is some serious engineering."

The river was dammed in stages, and viaducts and sluices ran from it, to large buildings and installations. It was clear that water pressure and volume were used for industry. A scan in various colored overlays showed temperature, chemical content, flow velocity. Mark saw what looked like settling beds, canals, quite sophisticated engineering. Boats. Barges. Ships at anchor . . .

McDonald said, "We're estimating population around five hundred thousand. There are nine cities so far that we believe are over one hundred thousand, more than a hundred over fifty thousand and thousands over ten thousand, on this continent. This is definitely the base of the largest population and greatest technical development. Continental population is on the close order of one hundred million."

"Not bad for Stone Age."

Stephens sounded bothered. "I don't like it. There is no reason they could or should have developed the technology for this. It's sixteenth century at least, some of it is nineteenth, and might generously be twentieth. Technically, it's staggering." Her expression was intense, studious.

Mark said, "You're not thinking about social development. Religion, philosophy and social networking all affect development. I'd speculate they skipped large numbers of cultural wars that Earth had."

"Those wars resulted in development and transfer of knowledge, though. And I certainly do think about such things. Sir." She sounded annoyed. Under her curly blonde hair she wore a disapproving expression.

"Generally from vanquished to victor, and a great many sources were wiped out. The library of Alexandria, for instance, and the Mayan codices. If they *shared* cultural knowledge, even limited technical information would be synthesized and incorporated."

"We've looked at that, Citizen. We estimated they'd reach classical Greece or Rome at best." She was insistent. This was her field, so he assumed she knew what she was talking about, and asked for more.

"You don't think it's possible you were wrong by a couple of millennia? Since we have this concrete example in front of us."

"Obviously we were," she admitted. "We can't figure out where, why or how, though. That's a chance to learn and develop, but it's also disturbing in this context."

Mark nodded thoughtfully. It was a significant level of error. On the other hand, it was completely new territory, and the locals clearly *did* have that level of technology.

"First of all, do they have electrical power, modern weapons or anything that could be a significant threat?"

McDonald said, "Well, obviously there are environmental factors. We don't anticipate diseases or other cross contamination, but chemical incompatibility, enzymes, toxins are all possible, as we've discussed. They have no substantial metal. They might have jewelry or some artifacts, but the precious metals are almost nonexistent, too. If HMG offers them gold and teaches them how to work it, it would be a tremendous trade medium, assuming the locals appreciate it, of course.

"It's barely possible to make firearms without metal, but the results cannot be too sophisticated. Polyceramic barrels are certainly beyond them. No electrical generation capability that we know of, though they might have some crude chemical batteries in labs. That's 'crude' in a relative sense. They could be highly refined for research, but they'd not be portable or of concern to us as weapons."

"Still, archery was devastatingly effective for the English and Turks, among others." Mark raised his comm and said, "Add body armor to landing gear."

"I was going to suggest that," Stephens said. "We don't want a misunderstanding to turn into war."

"No, we're juggling culture shock as it is, and our aspiring Freehold East India Company is not helping."

"Is that a hot air balloon?" someone asked.

Everyone stared intently as McDonald grabbed a remote and zoomed in.

"I'll be damned. Eighteenth-century tech," Stephens said.

"Nothing past twentieth, though, right?" Mark asked.

"Nothing so far. It seems unlikely," McDonald said. "Of course, this is one grid square of one continent, but it seems reasonable that technology will be on a general par, even with surface travel only. Balloons increase the reliability of that assessment."

Shraybman came over as Mark said, "So, an initial contact would seem to be what they are asking for, then."

"That's what they're getting," she said, looking frustrated and angry. "*Margin* has launched a shuttle."

"Dammit!" he swore. "Can you intercept?"

She nodded. "We have a gunboat in pursuit. However, the captain has no authority to stop him. It's your call."

"Stop him, tell him to wait, and we'll go down together," Mark said. "Is Egan still aboard?" He knew it was a mistake to have Egan along, but he didn't have much choice. Egan could go down now. Undoubtedly, his crew had come to the same conclusions as the government had. The only possible compromise was to make sure he was escorted, hope that whoever they met wanted to discuss politics before business, and play it by ear.

Mark realized how ridiculous that seemed. The representative of a laissez-faire capitalist system praying for political intrigue to slow the rush of business. *Well, you know what they say about strange bedfellows,* he thought.

"Egan left as soon as you dressed him down," Sergeant Thomas said. "He seemed to be planning something, but I wasn't sure what. Sorry, sir."

"Not your fault. Thanks. Continue with your research." He left to follow this latest disaster.

Russ called through just then. "Citizen, I observe and protest your corporation's initiation of contact. We consider this an aggressive, preemptive act of occupation."

It was a formal statement, but he sounded angry.

"Give me a few segs and I'll have them back, and you can hold your protests."

"Very well, sir." Russ probably wanted to say more, but bit down on it.

It was gratifying to see the military hadn't lost its edge. They'd almost lost a war against a massively more powerful UN military from Earth, winning through a combination of brutality and stubbornness that had become legendary. Mark had served after that, while the Forces tried to rebuild their numbers and equipment with little budget and insufficient recruits, because the Marshal refused to lower standards to gain bodies.

The gunboat commander literally drove his craft out at full G, on a direct collision course, all active sensors blazing. As soon as he hit range, he locked on a full complement of missiles. Mark wasn't sure what Egan thought about it, but his pilot understood that if he didn't stand to, he'd be shot or rammed, and the military commander was unlikely to choose ramming. Either way, debate was pointless and the flight was over. A div later, the shuttle was back and docked to *Healy*.

Emgee could be fun, or relaxing. It could also be a hindrance, such as when swimming and climbing aft to a conference. Mark hoped the initial experiments in generated gravity panned out. It would simplify a great many things in space. He couldn't keep track of how many times they'd transitioned from free orbit to centrifugal rotation and back.

He arrived last, just late enough to reinforce the suggestion that he was running the show without being rude. The officers were present, McDonald representing the technical mission, Egan, Margov, and Russ.

"My plan," he said as he dragged himself through the hatch, without the dignity striding would have offered, "is to land as a group. I will speak. The scientists will advise me. The military will be along against any threats. Assuming we can communicate, I will then present each of you, and you may begin your own negotiations on trade or diplomacy under the guidelines I create with the advice of the scientific contingents of both the UN and the Freehold."

Before anyone could start objecting, he pointed and said, "Egan, you're first."

"I'm not clear on how the government has the authority to interfere with my free actions and trade, especially as we're not in the Freehold. In fact, my company has the initial claim here."

"I have the authority because I have a warship. Your claim fails of its merits because the system is already the property of its inhabitants."

"That depends on how those inhabitants view it." He didn't mention the threat of military force. Cool operator, when he wanted to be.

"No. It depends on how they view it, *after* we have determined how their society works and if they understand the ramifications of your deal."

"That could take years."

"It likely will."

"Not acceptable."

"Talk to the Council."

"Oh, my people already are," Egan said with vitriol, "and I will own you when this is over."

"Good luck with that." He deliberately turned away from Egan. He did so with enough disdain that the man said nothing, just sputtered for a moment and then locked up with a tight expression. He faced his U.N. counterpart. "Mr. Russ, over to you."

Russ was far more reasonable. He leaned back in his chair and said, "We'll be present and allowed input in this meeting? You're just funneling through one party to keep things clean and controllable?"

"That's my plan, yes. I need all the input I can get from scientists, diplomats like yourself, even economic interests. We don't want to overwhelm or confuse them, or we could screw it all up."

"And we'll have free access to your findings?" Russ's stretch and shift was probably feigned casualness, but he didn't seem antagonistic, just alert.

"I see no reason why not. You're bound to notice things we don't." Good so far.

"What of other parties?"

"Galactic Alliance, Earth development groups and such?" At Russ's nod, he said, "As long as they check in with me, or through you to me, they're welcome. But anyone going past me without discussing it is getting tossed out with prejudice."

"As long as we do get actual input, I have no objections at this time. I will expect to create our own, independent mission as soon as, and assuming, the aliens consent. At that point, we can continue to share information." The statement was matter of fact, but clearly made it a deal breaker if declined.

"Agreed."

Egan didn't snarl, but looked disgusted. "Basically, you're cutting us out of our investment."

"I'm sure your ROI on existing systems is profitable. I know you find a substantial percentage of unusable systems. Worst case, this is one such. It doesn't affect your margin. Best case, you're here and do have a claim for initial negotiations once the relationship is ironed out.

I know you've spent years developing Shade, building surface and orbital habitats, and have yet to bring out enough material to get in the black. Don't try to play me for a fool. I was doing this while you were in primary school."

Margov said, "My company finds the deal acceptable. We're ready to proceed on your schedule." She smiled in a way that was charmingly agreeable to the diplomats while being a triumphant sneer to her competitor at the same time. Mark made a note to get an image and study the technique. It was good.

"I'm going to see about setting this up. We will land tomorrow, barring any unforeseen changes. I will consult with everyone either way." He left before he had to argue the point.

Later he wished he'd stayed. Apparently, in an ensuing debate, Egan had said something callous about native development, and Stephens ripped a chair loose from the deck and threw it at him.

Back in the bay, Lieutenant Hensley showed Mark potential landing sites, Shraybman worked on a disclaimer and nondisclosure agreement for all concerned, which a legal officer would neaten up and formalize, and Jelling came over with more bad news.

"It's not quite my department, Citizen, but we have a security issue. We found surveillance bugs in here from two different sources. Two fixed ones that are probably HMG, three floaters that are definitely UN technology, though that does not mean they initiated them. In fact, I'd suspect not, because it would be too obvious. Of course, that could also be a cover." She dropped the electronic carcasses in front of him. Two were small round nubs that could pass as rivets or repair plugs; three looked like small insects.

"They've been disabled?"

"Yes, and we do regular sweeps."

"Should I keep quiet about this, or can I pin someone to the wall?"

"I'd recommend against it, sir. They've found at least one of ours." Her grin suggested they hadn't found any of the others, however many that might be.

"I see." This was going to be that kind of game. "Even though we invited them in, they're skulking around. Or is it just in retaliation?"

"I'm not sure, sir."

"Citizen," he heard behind him. It was Captain Betang on intercom.

"Yes, Captain?" he said as he turned.

"The UN is building a Jump Point. We're seeing indications of a breakout. That's one of the drawbacks of phase drive. It costs as much as a government full of crooked politicians, but once you have one, you can use it for transit, then build Jump Points in days, not years."

"Understood. What can we do and should we?"

"I've taken the liberty of deploying drones that will jam the operation when triggered. They're in sleep mode now. We can't stop people coming in, but we can stop them leaving. Except, of course, in phase drive. But communications will be under our control."

Standard interstellar communication was via pods that were dragged through the Jump Point by passing ships, to dump their signals for relay or tightbeam. Once that was up, Mark could theoretically get advice from other Citizens within sixty hours, twenty-two divs.

As fast as the situation was changing, he doubted that would make any difference. He could report his progress, though.

"I guess you should continue with that, and try not to give our hand away. I assume they know they're visible?"

"The construction? Certainly. It's impossible to hide. They likely suspect we have some kind of surveillance or jamming, and they likely have some countermeasures. None of that need be discussed, though. It's all part of the game."

"Indeed it is. Keep me informed and try not to take action without consulting. If you feel it's necessary, do what you have to and inform me soonest."

"Understood, sir. Betang out."

CHAPTER 4

He woke the next morning to his phone buzzing for attention.

"Ballenger," he answered, well-rested as he always was in emgee, and set about wiggling out of his bag.

"Lieutenant Shraybman, sir. Just so you know, the media are here."

"When did that happen?" He slipped his phone into the room's console and brought up video. Shraybman popped into view at almost life size.

"Russ reluctantly brought UN shills along, who are limited by their rules of 'fair' speech of course. DSR had a few pet shills along. The Jump Point is now intermittent while it's focused and brought online, and apparently some came through on a co-op, from Caledonia and the Freehold."

"Are we still able to jam outgoing transmissions?"

"We can when we want to, but they'll whine at once. We can probably get away with it three or four times as 'technical faults,' after which we will have to let them have at it. I recommend saving those opportunities."

"Yes."

"There are two requests for interview. Do you want to take them?"

He grimaced. "I don't want to, but I really have to."

"I can take them, sir. It's not a problem."

"Except for the perception that it's a military mission, especially to non-Freeholders."

"Not at all. I'm Capital District Reserve. I just happened to be aboard for training at the time. I'll have the XO write me permissive personal duty orders for a couple of days, put on civvies, and you can have your office compensate me later. All legal."

That was sweet. "You're a diabolical bitch, Lieutenant."

"Thank you, sir. It'll be fine. I'll be using these to my advantage," she said with a heft of her generous chest. She grinned. "Seriously, though, in civvies, they have no idea of my rank or status. With your permission I'll have the same done for Sergeant Thomas. In civvies, she's 'ma'am' and harder to argue with."

"Do it." Mark felt better. If they wanted to play games with the rules, so could he.

The time from then until lunch was crammed with paperwork. The initial landing would have close to a hundred people. He'd started with around ten, but that hadn't lasted seconds.

DSR, HMG, himself, the UN, crew and security made it twenty. Jelling had insisted more security was essential, between the craft, the persons and any risk of technological compromise. Then of course, the Citizen had to have a large enough entourage for his position, as did Ambassador Russ. More security to keep the UN in line was essential. A linguist would be needed, a couple of culturalists, McDonald should fairly come along after all his work, plus engineering scientists to judge the native technology before any discussions. Medical personnel, especially with the potentially dangerous atmosphere. Once it was that size, the press wanted to come along. Shraybman and Thomas insisted the military would send documentation specialists for their own purposes, and as neutral observers. The UN was invited to do likewise. Add more security, and of course, engineers to secure a landing field and either erect sunscreens or build fighting positions. Cooks.

The fifth time Jelling said, "We need more security," he replied in a restrained snap.

"I appreciate your professional paranoia, Captain. If this were a combat mission, or hostage negotiations, you'd be the first person I would call. This is a diplomatic and peaceful mission. Even if there's some risk involved, we have to appear to be naïve, fluffy and gentle. That increases the risk of casualties slightly, but the chance of actually coming across as peaceful a lot."

"You're correct, sir. Noted."

Shraybman had appointed herself PAO, and was in civvies. Her definition of landing wear was stretch slacks, ruffled sleeves and cleavage almost to her waist. It was within contemporary news standards. It also showed a lot of luscious looking flesh that she obviously did plan to use to her advantage. A deep breath or a tug at the lacing would have every male within sight looking at her, not Mark, combat troops or the aliens.

"Remember there's a risk of injury from local life and possibly the atmosphere," he said quietly in passing.

"You remember that, sir. If I go down, I can't do anything about it." She grinned but it was a bit sickly.

"I've got your back," Jelling said with a nod.

"As do I," said Thomas. She was also in civvies, though far less flamboyant. Jelling was in service uniform, modified with plastic buttons that looked like horn, field boots and gloves, spear and bow and a quiver full of ceramic-tipped arrows that looked knapped. Her normal poise made her unmistakable for anything other than a killer, and there was no way she was going to be relaxed, given her demeanor so far.

Hopefully, human body language wouldn't be discernible to the natives. In case it was, he'd keep the military back and discreet. The bona fide offense would be uniformed for honesty, the rest in civvies for discretion.

Nurin Russ arrived with his assistants. They wore neat contemporary suits, dressy but not excessive. Margov smiled politely and without guile, which really made Mark wonder. She wore a very tasteful, basic tunic over tights. Egan said nothing, settling for a nod. He was the dressiest, but it wasn't too much, just pushing the envelope. The scientists were a mixed bag. McDonald and some of the older ones, like Zihn and Stephens, clearly knew how to dress for formal events. A lot of the younger ones and scholar-students obviously had to borrow, share or fake it to look the role. It likely didn't matter. The aliens would have no idea what human clothing meant, even if they wore clothes themselves. Still, other humans would follow, and it was important to have the first impression be held in regard.

Mark was curious about the press, but decided it was best if he remained aloof and used the argument of being too busy to interact personally, while allowing the military to control their access. He could play good guy and give them a few drabs of info to sweeten things. The pair from the UN had one of Russ's assistants attached like a leech, and he clearly had ultimate say over their reports. Wistfully, Mark wished for that much control. He simultaneously loved the freedom the Freehold gave to the media, and loathed the liberties they took with it. It might be better than the alternative, but they were still ghouls. Egan seemed to love their presence. That said it all. "Ms" Thomas and "Ms" Shraybman wandered in orbits around the three Freehold reporters between other duties, and Jelling's assistant/exec/second, a Warrant Connor, stood next to them with an angry scowl. They looked nervous around him, which Mark enjoyed.

Everyone seemed used to waiting. It took until lunch to load the craft. Part of the delay was due to Mark's insistence that everyone be scanned for metal at an intrusive level. Even jeweled tooth inserts triggered the gear. To his relief, everyone had taken his order seriously. The palletized gear was checked separately. Circuitry was either fiberoptic, molecular or encased electronics with minimal metal connections, those well covered in polymer. The good news as far as the press was that they were dependent upon stealth military gear to transmit, all of which had to come through the encrypted channels on *Healy* before it would go anywhere else. Still, their job was to get information out, and they undoubtedly would.

He entered the umbilical tube to the front hatch, unable to see any of the outside even through the maintenance hatch ports. It was completely ensconced in a launch cradle.

The passenger section was fairly rudimentary. The seats were better than troop benches with straps, but not individual. Each entire row had to recline as a unit.

The loadmaster addressed them from the front as they got seated. "Citizen, Ambassador, Doctor, ladies, men, welcome aboard. It's not as comfortable as we'd like, but we wanted to save mass for maneuvering, and fit everyone in one craft. Two more will remain in orbit, per the Citizen's instructions, while we make the initial landing. Citizen, Jelling, McDonald, you have headsets to keep in touch with the command deck. All, if you have any problems, address me. Any soldier with experience in this type of craft raise your hand. If you need basic help, check with one of those people first. The pilot informs me we depart in about four segs, that's four hundred seconds or six point seven minutes for those not familiar with our clock. Lunch will be field chow, I'm afraid, and you may as well eat now. Once we enter atmosphere we'll be down almost at once. Let me run through the standard safety briefing, as modified for this mission . . ."

Mark gave that half attention. He was familiar with it. He did memorize the locations of all doors and hatches. He caught the part about, " . . . only cardboard aerial flares and no modern weapons in the kits, so in event of a crash, ignore that entire section of the manual."

He felt the pressure change as the hatches sealed, and the air took on a different odor, that of a smaller military craft. This landing took both of *Healy*'s direct ground to orbit craft and one from the UN's *Aracaju* as backup in case rescue was needed. The *Healy* had a larger lander, but it was intended for at least an expedient field or a one-way combat mission. If need be, one DGO could take them all, but Mark and the captain agreed that a staggered landing allowed better odds of recovery, simplified security with the additional personnel, and would reduce the appearance of a massive invasion.

Thumping sounds indicated the docking clamps opening, and a slight shove of a pneumatic ram shoved the lander out. Thrust built, detectable by acceleration and sound. There was no significant feeling of it, as far as vibration went.

His headset came live. "Sir, this is Pilot Lieutenant Hensley. Welcome aboard."

"Thank you, Lieutenant. I'm here."

"Good. If I can skip the usual formalities, sir?"

"Please do."

"Thanks. We're dropping a set of beacons ahead of us by one orbit, thirty segs, to mark a landing field. As agreed, it's in the large meadow just to the southeast of the Pythagorean. My landing engineer shifted it slightly for best terrain. We'll also pass over twice in lower altitudes, then hover before landing to ensure the natives have it clear. If they don't, we'll break off to orbit, refuel from the other doggo, and try again. After that, I'll call you for advice."

"Sounds as good as we can plan. Obviously I will defer to your expertise."

"Thank you, sir. Always good to have a superior who recognizes the obvious."

Mark grinned.

Hensley kept him informed in periodic detail. Launching beacons. Deorbiting. He felt gravity return and the buffeting of stratospheric winds. First pass over the LZ at ten thousand meters, with smoke. Pass at two thousand meters.

"They appear to understand we intend to land there and are well outside the beacons, sir."

"Excellent so far." Goddamn, this was exciting. Sentient aliens!

"I'm going to slow to a hover at three hundred meters and descend. We will have enough fuel to reach orbit, or to return to *Healy*. Another attempt will require refueling."

"Understood."

The basic facts were relayed to everyone, and their expressions reflected nervousness, excitement, a gallery of emotions. Mark knew this because everyone in his row craned forward to look at each other, wanting to see how their fellow humans reacted to a once in a species experience. He chuckled. Everyone here was about to share something no human had experienced before. He felt a bond, an excitement, a thrill.

"I am turning stern to the alien crowd," Hensley said. Thrust and gravity fought in a trembling dance.

"Understood. Trouble?"

"No, sir. That's where the cargo ramp is."

"Ah, yes." He flushed momentarily. That should have been obvious.

"We're down," Hensley said as thrust faded to nothing. It was barely noticeable. They'd been under the somewhat light local gravity for the entire vertical descent.

"Please wait for me before opening up."

"Of course, sir."

The loadmaster indicated they should unharness. Mark stood, grabbed an overhead strap and moved swiftly to the stern. The loadmaster, flight engineer and some other crewmember moved purposefully around, grabbing tools, checking monitors and lines. It appeared to be routine, likely standard for any noncombat landing.

Three landing field engineers looked at some kind of readouts on the surface and terrain.

"Attention, everyone," he said, and got it. "We will debark carefully, form up, and then proceed if it seems safe. We will not allow the aliens to get close enough to potentially threaten the ship. The military understands to use minimum force required for this. Also, do not take any gear at this time, unless you've been given specific instructions by myself or Dr. McDonald. This is a greeting session. Science, exploration and trade come later. Am I clear to all parties?" He fixed Margov and Egan and ensured they met his gaze and nodded.

"We will wear hats, gloves and filters until we are sure the atmosphere is safe. Evacuations will be difficult for now." A couple of people fumbled for masks. Most had them ready. He slid his on, and a broad hat that would look ridiculous as a fashion statement.

Jelling stood at the hatch next to the loadmaster, equipped with a slim, conformal backpack he knew was all water and weapons, wearing body armor under her uniform and with her weapons slung. She had a visor on, connected by wire to the ship's instrumentation.

"They're not approaching, sir. Awaiting us outside the perimeter. They seem eager and nervous but not afraid."

"What do they look like? Hell with it. Open the ramp and let's do it."

He hoped they weren't revoltingly hideous. Jelling was the type who'd give no indication of that while making a report.

The ramp seal popped and native air mixed in. It was a bit richer than Grainne's, fresh, clean and oddly scented through the mask. The plants here were not Earth plants. An atmospheric specialist took readings on a sample.

When colonizing Grainne, the landing, debarkation and first camp had taken an Earth week. Here they had segs at most.

The soldier-scientist nodded at Mark, held up a hand in the battle sign for pause, and pointed at one of the junior personnel. He recalled the procedure per the manual. Lowest ranking, least trained individual. The private stared wide-eyed, but pulled her mask free for a moment, then replaced it. After five seconds, she took it off completely and sat still. Then she squinted her eyes shut, breathed deeply and shoved the mask back on. A breath later, she opened her eyes, slipped the mask off and smiled over a shiver. He made a note to be sure to get her name. She deserved a mention.

"Take them off, keep them at hand," Mark ordered. If the growth was toxic, dust, pollen or otherwise could still build up as an irritant in short order. The medics had plenty of oxygen bottles, just in case.

The loadmaster slapped a switch and the ramp resumed its descent. The outside air was warmish.

Mark and others strained and peeked over the ramp as it came down. He could hear the security detail behind him, warning others to stay back and seated. It was impossible to tell much about the locals at this distance by eye, but they seemed to be erect and probably bipedal. That was logical and predictable. Fewer limbs meant more brain available for cognitive functions, and being upright enabled manipulation. So far, the theories were correct.

"I'll lead," he said.

Jelling's exec, Warrant Connor, said, "Is that wise, sir?" What he meant was, *That's not wise, let me go first to stop spears.*

"It may not be wise," Mark said, "but it's necessary. I'll go first. Scientists behind me, Mr. Russ and our economic parties behind them, military last. We want it clear that you're defensive in nature."

"Lying to them already?" Connor asked with a smile. Mark chuckled, too. Operatives were as deadly as you got. "Defense" was not a word they often bothered with. Even with knapped flint spears and arrows, he expected they'd be at least on par with the locals. They trained in that much detail.

With that to break the strain, Mark nodded.

A breeze eddied in. It was fresh, with the scent of strange plants and a whiff of animal. The landing site was pleasantly warm, sunny, and breezy, with mild humidity. The light seemed a little yellower than he was used to, but not uncomfortably so.

With a deep breath, he stepped forward and down off the ramp into waist-high grassy plants. He carried nothing, as a status issue to differentiate him. Those who needed to carried cases. They'd open the gear in the presence of the locals if possible, to show they weren't a threat. Odd-looking devices can reasonably be assumed to be weapons. But if they are boxed, and one has to bend over to open them, they're less threatening and more obviously scientific. Of course, the boxes were rigged with incendiaries to slag all contents should they be taken. No risk of technological contamination if it could be avoided.

A small part of him wished for his sidearm, but the advanced composites and metal were a no-no, and a peaceful diplomat shouldn't. He was still getting used to that, after twenty years of being armed.

The locals were silent. He wondered if it was respect, awe, fear or if they didn't use vocal communication, though what they'd use in lieu of the latter to develop technology, he had to wonder. They were well outside the beacon perimeter, which showed sense and concern. Still good. The ground was uneven prairie, grown with grass and shrub. They'd have to clear that for safety. He waded along. He estimated their height against the grasslike growth at a little taller than humans.

Basically, he was keeping track of every detail he could, to try to distract himself from the massive, historical moment rushing up to crush him.

As he walked, a small group of locals detached from the mass and came forward. They carried spears and bundles, and were dressed in clothing of some kind. The boat would be recording all this. Mark had not even brought binoculars. Less to worry about. The distance was less than five hundred meters now.

Egan stayed true to his word. It was obvious he had something up his sleeve, but as long as he didn't spring it now, Mark wasn't concerned. He had plenty of other issues.

As the two groups neared, he turned to his entourage and said in an even voice, "Military, please stop now, and advance after we make contact. Scientists, move slowly so we don't alarm them." The party split up. Adrenaline rippled through him. This was it.

The locals came on as a mass, and those spears looked huge. He swallowed. They shouldn't be aggressive, given that they'd invited a landing from a presumably higher technology. Perhaps they were fearful of their safety? Or used weapons for status?

Then they suddenly resolved, and he realized they were wooden tent poles, and the bundles were fabric. Good. That indicated a desire to talk. There were spears, but the guards were behind the group, as the humans' were.

"I want to go ahead. Slow down, please. Ambassador Russ, I will introduce you after myself."

"Yes, sir," Shraybman and McDonald both said and drew back. The others reluctantly did, too.

"Very good," Russ agreed. He sounded a bit over-whelmed. Understandable.

He dropped back one pace to give Mark a slight lead.

Mark held out bare arms at an angle, palms forward, and advanced steadily. One of the locals did, too. He . . . she . . . no way to tell. The creature was bipedal, over two meters tall, broad and shaped like a caricature—not much waist, broad thorax, knobby joints, with reverse articulated legs. The semi-snouted face had no nose but a probable blowhole above the eyes. The mouth was almost under the chin. The skin was pale pink with brown points, like those of a cat. They had some kind of hair, but it resembled fluffed feathers, and grew in a tonsure. The hands had a thumb and three fingers. He, as Mark designated the alien for now, was probably very strong, even in this light gravity. His outfit was plain woven fabric in green, with orange and yellow trim. It was a tunic and skirt, with a wide belt of some kind of leather. He wore leather shoes, sturdy but with simple stamped decorations. On a further examination, the "skirt" was more like an old Japanese hakama. The plain clothes indicated that they were beyond the trinkets and geegaws stage. This might go well. Mark had hopes, at least.

They both slowed as they approached and stopped about a meter from each other. The local spoke, and Mark knew he'd never be able to repeat it. He felt another tingle of excitement. Mark bowed slightly, and extended a hand slowly. The alien barely hesitated, and reached out his own. Mark gripped it firmly, shook his wrist with his other hand, looked up and said, "I am Citizen Ambassador Mark Ballenger of the Freehold of Grainne, representing my nation and the nations of humanity. I greet you." It was humanity's first actual contact and interaction with a sentient alien species. One for the history books. Mark felt a ripple and a thrill up his spine that turned icy and prickly as it hit his head.

With a gesture he said, "This is Ambassador Nurin Russ of the United Nations of Earth and Space, speaking also for the Galactic Alliance." He stepped aside and let Russ move up.

This time, the local offered the bow and handshake, in a very good mimicry of Mark's.

They dropped hands, and in a few gestures, the alien—"local" would probably be a better term to start thinking—indicated that he wished to have the tent erected. Mark nodded and gestured and the alien crew got to work.

He turned and said, "Dr. Cochrane," and the linguist came forward from the quivering but motionless crowd. Slowly, she opened her case and took out her translation gear. It was hoped that it worked with aliens. If they had at least the concept of fixed nouns, it should work, but it had never been tested.

"Suggestions?" he asked.

"Stick with nouns," she said. "Avoid proper names and titles until we can translate the definitions."

That confirmed what he understood the process to be, and seemed easy enough. He pointed at the rising canopy and said, "Tent." Their host said another word, and

Cochrane programmed it as a match. He said, "Tent," again, and the computer replied with the throaty local word, something like, "wlargh." His counterpart was delighted, and they went on a tour. Grass, shadow, pole, person, leader, tree, wood, sky, cloud, and on. They worked on basic verbs. It would be clunky translation for some time, but would contain the essentials.

His opposite number was male, claimed the title, "Tribal District Leader," and welcomed them. The discrete term "ambassador" seemed to be a stumbling point. Mark got the impression that all their leaders acted on their own behalf, and that was confirmed when they agreed on "messenger."

"Query: Messenger not leader you?" The box was only fractionally behind the inflected native language, adding a strange stereo effect.

"Leader. Messenger to other leaders," he replied.

"Comprehend. Great leader." Well, that wasn't quite right, but it would work for now.

"Query: Star come?" was not too hard to decipher. It sent adrenaline ripples through Mark again.

"Called Iota Persei, show at night," he replied. So, they did have astronomy, and understood the concept of stars. Impressive.

"Query: Show now?" he said, and gestured. Another local—they called themselves "Ishkul," as near as Mark could grasp—brought forth what were clearly star charts. "Dr. McDonald," he called, and McDonald came forward to identify their point of origin.

Behind him, Warrant Connor said, "Is that wise, sir?" The man had snuck up and seemed more relaxed with the close proximity. He'd left his visible weapons behind.

"Certainly. If they can determine for themselves, it doesn't hurt to tell them. If they can't, they aren't a threat," Mark said.

"True, I hope," he agreed.

Their host, "Vlashn," gave out information, too. He defined the boundaries of his territory and of the other district leaders, the local towns, and the tribes. McDonald scribbled hasty notes despite the ongoing recording from the DGO, and looked fascinated.

Other Ishkul approached, and other humans. Mark met Shraybman's eyes, and she gave a hand sign of comprehension and moved to corral and direct people to keep order. A few specific scientists came forward.

The native government was by committee. Most matters were considered private or local; those needing resolution were harangued at length until a consensus was reached. Patriarchs and matriarchs acted as figureheads, but had advisors and didn't speak without a debate first. Vlashn asked about human systems.

"Each star different," Mark said. "Our star, leaders special. Strong. Caring. Wise." How to define it?

"As ours. Query: Choose how?" Of course your leaders are good people. How do you choose them?

There was no way to explain constitutional requirements with the terms they had. "Committee," he said. How many nuances were they each missing so far? Historically, how many cultures had been destroyed over assumptions and faulty terminology?

"Ambassador Nurin Russ is also a messenger to leaders the same rank as I."

"Greetings," the translator spoke. "You are the same creature."

Russ replied, "Yes, we are the same species, but of different tribes."

"Query: Come here why?" was next. The thing Mark had been hoping to avoid, but he supposed it was obvious.

"See. Learn," he said, indicating the scientists. "Trade," he said. Reluctantly, he pointed at the corporate reps, and Egan and Margov nodded and bowed. Now they were officially involved, and officially pains in the ass.

"Trade good," Vlashn said. "Many things interest. Large number planets mean different goods."

"Yes, we have found that to be true and worthwhile."

"Query: See (untranslated)?" He was pointing at the ship.

That would take some thinking. There was metal all through the ship. The question had been and still was, would they know it for what it was? Would they somehow get a hint of the technology and be contaminated by it? Could he refuse without insulting them? They weren't mere rock chippers who would think humans gods; they were a developed, intellectual species. Amazingly so, in fact. The presence of aliens didn't seem to bother them much. Had they met others? That wasn't the issue at present, though. They wanted to know about the boat, and he had to answer now.

"Explain first," he said.

Vlashn agreed, "Explain."

How to phrase it? He was waiting, staring. "Our leaders and soldiers keep secrets, hidden things, even from our own people. I can show you as leader, as a favor and gift, but no soldiers or scientists can come yet." Actually, now that he'd said that, no one else could come. Ever. Relatively "ever" from the viewpoint of his mission.

The Ishkul warriors didn't like that, came forward and argued furiously, trying to keep it from the translator. It picked out a few words. Then the few words stopped although they kept talking. Cochrane said, "They've changed dialects! Good!" and started making notes.

Clearing his throat and gesturing for attention, Mark said, "Perhaps it would be easier if you choose someone to show you and I will remain here in your place."

This made the decision much easier, and Mark missed the expressions on Vlashn's face as he was shown a direct ground to orbit shuttle. DGOs awed him, and he'd grown up with them. He wondered, though, at their acceptance that he as spokesman was valuable. If they were really suspicious, they'd assume he was just a shill. Was that a matter of actual trust, or was Vlashn playing the diplomat at his end, too?

While the ship lifted, with Hensley promising a short, suborbital flight and return, he met Vlashn's assistant Somle, as near as a human could pronounce the name, who was a charming female. That helped keep his mind off the fact that he and a handful of humans were alone on an alien planet with nothing more sophisticated than chipped spears and novlar body armor against potential mobs. It felt safe, though. They discussed the tent, which had been woven on a loom, shrunk and treated to be waterproof, and was even nonflammable. Mark was impressed. These Stone Age "savages" had technology at least equivalent to sixteenth-century Europe. The humans might not learn much technologically, but they would learn a lot about cultural development and problem solving.

If he had to define them in human terms, they were part bird, part saurian. The tendrilly hairs were definitely reminiscent of feathers, the skin faintly nubbed like bird skin, with vestigial scaling on the head. Their movements were quick and darting, and they held motionless in between.

Their warriors wore a cured hide armor with supplemental scales of some satin black substance. He suspected it was a polished wood, horn or another leather of some kind. It looked quite sturdy. Like human armor, it covered torso, shoulders and head, though it was shaped differently. A lamellar hip skirt protected the lower regions, and they wore wraps around the backwards knee joint. That made sense. They were harder to reach than human knees, but the reverse joint made a hard cup impractical, and any hard armor inside the joint would be in the way.

Their spears weren't knapped stone. They were either laboriously polished stone or some kind of ceramic. Their bows were sophisticated laminated models, with reflex, deflex and blocks that would cause the string to give an additional slap to the arrow as it reached full return. He recalled seeing something similar, as Stephens said, "Turkish composite bows." He wasn't sure of the nomenclature or physics, but it was appeared as efficient as a bow could get without a compound pulley mechanism. The arrows looked turned and the fletchings were a graceful ogive.

He suspected Captain Jelling would talk to her technical staff about upgrading their cruder gear within a day or so.

The native engineers put that large tent up in a hurry, using guy ropes and wooden mallets, the kind the military called "Bam-bam hammers," with plenty of stakes. Several of the stakes split during insertion. One of the techs with a ceramic axe made more by lopping bits off a spare limb and notching and pointing them. It seemed routine.

"Somle, how big are your machines for weaving cloth, your looms?" he asked, to keep the conversation going, the language in use and to learn some technical details.

"Looms about as wide as you are tall. Big looms about three times that. Fabric made from crushed plant fiber, animal pelting, and (untranslated)."

"It's interesting how similar a lot of our equipment is. It seems there are standard ways to accomplish given ends."

"Logical," she replied. "Your fabric also appears (untranslated)."

Russ said, "That word isn't working. May I show you the fabric?" while extending a sleeve.

She examined it briefly. "Tight weave. Consistent. Practical. Not elaborate."

"We have different modes of dress. Plain and elaborate both see use in different environments."

"Yes," she agreed. "Too complex for simple translation. Query: Ship power?"

"I'm not sure that translated," Mark said as a stall.

"Query: What fuel ship?" she asked.

Fuel. Not hard to guess they understood the mechanism. They seemed to have hot air balloons, after all.

"Do you understand heating plants to derive flammable liquid? We call it distillation."

"Obviously distillation. Query: Arrangement of small parts?"

"I think you're asking for the chemical formula," he said. "I am not a scientist and don't know. Our scientists are here and interested in talking to yours."

Her body language closed up for the first part. He deduced that as a mistrust. The latter caused her to reverse a little.

"Query: Why you don't know chemical formulas but are leader?"

Russ said, "I think she expects you to know." He seemed a bit bothered, and watched Mark for his response.

"So it seems. Somle, I know basic chemistry of food energy and basic distilled fractions, carbon, water and air. The fuels for our spaceships are very complicated. We have scientists who specialize only in that field." Besides which, the craft was powered by a combination of ionizing, superheating and reacting the fuel to achieve tremendous pressure and efficiency. Even if they could grasp it, he wasn't sure the information would do them any good, and if it did, he certainly wouldn't discuss it. Still, it was interesting that leaders or spokespeople were expected to know such things. Their system was merit-ocratic in some fashion.

The DGO returned in a loud white roar of dust and crud, and Vlashn debarked, escorted by Lieutenant Shraybman. The two bowed and shook hands as they parted. Mark and others grabbed for chemical wipes to clear the acidic burning debris from their skin. He blinked several times but decided he didn't need eye-wash yet.

"Small ship, large party," Vlashn said. "Assumption depart from larger ship above."

"That is correct," Mark agreed, still squinting. "This is a landing craft. It can't travel far."

"Query: Distance measurement?"

"Our basic unit is a meter." He waved his hand and one of the techs ran up with a meter stick.

"Noted," Vlashn said, holding it to his arm for comparison. "Estimate ship above at general approximation two hundred times one thousand times one meter."

That was pretty close. Their astronomers were good.

"That's within close order," he said. "Distance varies with orbit."

"Distance far for us."

"I understand. Do you know distances to stars?"

"Translation will fail. Distance to nearest star is one meter times six times ten times thousand-thousand times thousand-thousand times thousand."

"That's quite close. I would give the same approximation." Impressive, and very advanced. Shit, if they'd had access to metals, they'd have already visited humanity. That was scary. Definitely eighteenth-century science. And they didn't seem scared of aliens.

"Our tent is built. Welcome inside, all party."

As big as the circus tent was, that would still be a tight squeeze. However, it was an excellent step. Mark nodded to Russ, who said, "We are honored by your hospitality and thank you. We appreciate the shade and shelter and we'll move at once."

They both turned, signaled the mass, and waved. The scientists grabbed their gear and surged forward as the troops tried to maintain some semblance of order.

If the humans were disorganized, the Ishkul were a friendly mob. Thousands of spectators from the camp were held at bay by the warriors. Tens were allowed in, and an impromptu receiving line formed with the two races greeting each other, examining garb, looking at each others' features.

Shaking hands with aliens was an odd experience. So far, they all seemed to have been vetted, and were courteous and brief. "Greeting," they said, one after another. He returned it, and moved along. One group were probably press, writing on tablets and speaking to creatures that he surmised were akin to parrots. It was all very exciting, if anarchic.

"Jelling," Mark spoke into the air. Sure enough, she appeared in seconds.

"Yes, sir."

"Stick to Margov and Egan. Do not let them talk technology, pass over samples, radios, codes, anything. Shout them down, interrupt, plead appointment and drag them off if you have to."

"Yes, sir," she said, and disappeared again.

This was going to be a nightmare, sooner or later. Mark wasn't sure if sooner or later would be worse. Humans and Ishkul milled about, chatting, pointing, friendly and excited. That was good, which was bad. It would be easier to keep control if they were scared.

He caught Shraybman's attention. She came over quickly, after directing someone else to watch the cameras. Connor had attached himself to her and came along.

"I don't think I should go back to the ship. Any further action is going to take place here. Add in all the infighting, and I should remain. I'll need a shelter and guards. I don't mind how crude it is, as long as it's safe. Correction, dammit . . . " He sighed and thought for a moment. "I'm a high plenipotentiary and the uberpanjandrum of humanity. Get the engineers to make me something fitting my status. Not flashy, but definitely first class."

"Will do, sir. I assume you'll need a full commo station?"

"Yes. I need to see everything the ship sees, as close to real time as can be managed, and I need to be able to slag it on a word. Figure Russ will stay, too."

Warrant Connor said, "That means a small camp. We can do some of the engineering to keep the numbers down, but you're looking at twenty or so people. Ideally, I'd insist our people handle it all."

"That's not going to be an option." Sigh. He knew they were stubborn for a reason. It still got in the way.

"I expected that, sir. Use as many of us as you can, though."

"Understood."

"Should we use native materials? We don't have wood or canvas aboard ship, though we could fabricate artificial fabric easily enough."

"I think plastic would be safe. It can be made from trees, right?"

"I'd consult with the scientists."

When called, McDonald said, "Oh, yes, sir. I'll go into detail later, but plastic should be completely safe. Any common polymer."

Back on the matter at hand, Mark said, "I need to rein everyone in. They've had their gawking; they need to be where I can control the interaction." He raised his phone and said, "Ambassador Russ."

Russ came over at a brisk but dignified walk. "Citizen?"

"I want to get the bloodsucking ghouls out of here, and the industrialists they're watching with those cameras. You and I can pass people through in escorted small groups."

"I agree. I can order such for UN persons, now that the landing has proven out. Can you?"

"I can't give orders as such. I do retain space control, landing privileges on this site, and other such resources."

"Let's do it."

The two ambassadors strode back through the crowd with their military escort.

Vlashn and Somle stood side by side, patiently dealing with questions from the human media. The concept seemed strange to them, but they were doing so gamely. The Ishkul press merely watched and wrote and chattered to their birds. They didn't speak to anyone.

"Vlashn, Somle, we must interrupt, for which we apologize," Russ said.

Shraybman addressed the press. "Folks, we've got limited time on surface on this trip, due to the size of the contingent. It's time to wrap up. A few of us will remain, and a schedule for regular visits and development will begin at once."

There were mutters of disappointment, but no overt complaints. Egan visibly steamed, but he went along with the crowd.

Shraybman said, "I've coordinated the other lander to bring an engineer platoon and the best materials we have. It may be very clunky. The tools are an issue."

"I understand. Clunky is better than social contamination."

"They'll be down within the div. Do you want to remain, all depart, or have our lander wait for the second one?"

That was a tough, exciting question, as simple as it was. "I believe it will be safe and diplomatic to remain here, with my security detail of course," he said. Jelling had twitched as soon as he mentioned staying. "We can survive a day if the craft runs into trouble. Get them up."

"Understood."

Russ had six guards with him, who seemed to be ceremonial and to protect him from human threats. His two assistants seemed trained as such, which was atypical of Earth thinking, but made sense. It also made sense to rely on the Freeholders to be the outer perimeter, and have his detail worry only about him. It was useful to know he was that rationally cautious. It was also prime information for building a profile on the man for negotiations and calculating his threat.

As far as Mark was concerned, everyone except Shraybman and the Operatives was a potential threat, and even they were questionable. There had been rogue Operatives on rare occasions. The sheer credit value here alone made it possible.

The Operatives and UN security chivvied everyone back to the lander. After a few pro forma protests, the civilians complied. The military technicians brought up the rear, and the noise level in the tent dropped, as did the humidity, with fewer sweaty, exhaling bodies. The weather was quite pleasant, and pollen didn't seem to be an issue. It might be seasonal, or the plants might have other means of spreading. Still, Mark recalled an Arabian sandstorm, and a heavy windstorm in the agricultural spread of Capital District. Wind could stir up dust that was probably toxic here. Masks would be a necessary accessory until they knew more.

Shortly the craft powered up. The engines rose to a roar, necessitating hands over ears. The Ishkul looked bothered, but not surprised after the previous takeoff and landings. The ship wobbled, rose and roared away.

Mark suddenly felt quite alone.

"Tell of your worlds," Vlashn said. It wasn't an order, but there was a definite hint of imperative case even through the translator.

"My system has one habitable world, similar to this one. We can breathe each other's air, but probably not share food. We have a brighter sun with more energetic radiation above the frequency of visible light, which we call 'ultraviolet,' and a variety of plants and animals. We settled it about two hundred and forty years ago. Our year is five hundred and four days long, our day about fifteen parts per hundred longer than yours. We came from Earth, where Ambassador Russ is from. We have habitats in space in our planetoid belt, our outer halo, our moon and around several large planets, as well as at four 'Jump Points' that connect us quickly to other systems including Earth."

"Query: You travel faster than radiation?"

"Yes, in two ways. Jump points require a construction and only work at specific locations. Phase drive is more expensive and energy intensive but works anywhere."

"Expression of appreciation. I query more later. Ambassador Russ, tell of Earth."

Mark was relieved to be off the spot. These were not savages by any means, and he wondered how much intel he'd let slip by what he said, or what he hadn't said. Vlashn was pretty blatantly looking for a pecking order so he could fit in and demand as much as possible. It might actually be a good idea to match him up with the company reps in that regard, if they could be trusted.

So first, sort out precedence. Then, cut a deal with Margov and Egan somehow. Match that deal up with Russ. Offer it to Vlashn, and let him worry about dealing with other cultures here, except that latter was impossible. Twenty different deals would have to be cut at once, in a shifting maze of alliances. This was going to be as tribal as a negotiation in Central Asia, Eastern Africa or on Mtali.

All those had failed and led to war.

However, if it did work out, it would gel a bit at a time, until suddenly firming up and locking into a very fragile place.

Once again, Mark wanted a drink.

Russ was delivering a similar treatise on Earth. "—while we're the origin of our species and several others, humans now occupy more than twenty planets and a variety of habitats. Earth is still the most populous and directly influential, though we welcome the distant and different insight of our explorers and settlers, who are at the forefront of our exploration of space."

Vlashn said, "I strongly expect our discussions to be highly complicated and quite rich, with many ramifications. I am moderately convinced of your good intentions and strongly convinced of your peaceful approach. A sizeable minority here are sufficiently conservative that they will require moderate time to accept the situation and explore it in more depth."

"As with us," Mark said. "We should move slowly but in good faith."

"That is why we are here as a team," Russ said. "Other planets and cultures will send their own envoys shortly, so that you can see a section of our race, and others when they arrive."

Nice hedge, Mark thought. Leopards, dolphins, dogs and octopoids were not sentient in the same sense as humans and Ishkul, but that didn't need to be released yet, and they were other species and races that humans got along well with . . . finally.

"Statement. Query: You present as equals. Is this so?"

"Our goal is to be equal," Russ said, short for words.

"We each have our strengths and weaknesses, but operate better together than individually, and find extreme difference to lead to a number of problems that are costly, so we try hard to get along," Mark said, a bit more honestly, if stretching it.

"Strong appreciation of your statement," Vlashn said. "The area is secured against animals and the local population. We will leave you to your rest," Vlashn said. "I with others will return after your shuttle lands." He shook hands with them each again, and Mark grinned inside as he realized the handshake was a two-hand Freehold style, not the bow and touch of Earth.

The tent included an internal partition for privacy, inside its outer wall. The weather was wonderfully pleasant so far, even if the air did smell very odd, almost astringent. That was likely due to the acidic chemistry. The handful of humans had a few cots and chairs, a couple of folding tables and some comms. They'd have to nap, or at least rest, in shifts.

"Three hours between now and the scheduled return time," Mark said. "Let's get our gear into the inner room."

"We'll have to move it out again later," Shraybman said.

"Yes, but we need it secure for now."

"Of course."

"You will rest the entire time, as will Mr. Russ," Jelling said. The Earth security nodded assent. "We need you lucid as long as possible. I've sent for metabolic drugs."

He chuckled. "I feel like royalty, allowed so little say. I agree though."

He might rest, but he wouldn't sleep. He took a cot in the corner, lay back, and let his mind wander. It was the same style cot he'd used in the military, unchanged in two decades, and no more comfortable. He kicked over the idea that Russ was likely right—other nations, groups would arrive shortly. There was a need for patience, and be quick about it! Vlashn had hinted at similar issues at his end. Hopefully, he had more control, since most native travel was surface-bound, the balloons scarce and not fast. He'd have to look at their government, their industry, see their entire cross-section. This wasn't like meeting a spacefaring culture, where presumably once intentions were established, trade would commence at once, with oversight against insults that could lead to violence. Nor was it like meeting complete primitives who'd have to be quarantined, then possibly offered guidance if consensus was reached. This was the nasty in between; a technical society, sophisticated and modern, just not quite modern enough.

CHAPTER 5

J elling tapped his shoulder gently and said, "They're landing." He started awake. A div, not quite three Earth hours had passed.

"Good," he replied. "Have you told Vlashn?"

"No, sir. It all goes through you."

"Thank you," he replied. He'd forgotten that, at least while napping, but was glad to see the orders had stuck.

Shortly, he heard a sonic boom. So apparently did the distant camp of Ishkul, who cheered. Then the DGO landed amid a roar of hot wind and a cloud of blown debris.

Vlashn returned. "Greeting, Citizen Mark Ballenger." Wow, that face was a heck of a thing to wake up to.

"Greeting, Chief Vlashn. It's not necessary to be so formal. Citizen Ballenger is sufficient for official needs, and I would be honored if you addressed me by my given name of Mark. Ballenger is my family name."

"I will do so, Mark."

"Thank you. If you will excuse me briefly, I need to talk to my staff. Mr. Russ can assist you with any current questions."

Vlashn made a gesture that was probably a nod, and turned.

With McDonald's cryptic advice about polymers to work from, the engineers got to work with panels and struts. Mark had a hut to sleep in before dark. He used an induction set to rest deeply, and by morning, a miniature field embassy was erected, complete with showers, toilets, meeting rooms and lodging. The meeting rooms opened through curtains out under awnings that ringed three sides of a courtyard. It wasn't particularly elaborate, about like a hunting pavilion in the Grainne tropics, only larger, being polymer half-cylinders sprayed inside with structural foam and painted outside in clean white with green and black trim. It compared favorably with the Ishkul tent, however, and seemed to place them about par. That was good, very good for now.

Russ was also awake. He looked like hell, though. The man probably wasn't used to sleeping outdoors. Either that, or . . .

"I think the atmosphere is getting to me," Russ said.

"Do you think it's the dust?"

"Maybe, but I've never been on any planet except Earth, unless it was a fully conditioned space. Brief trips from starport to meeting center probably don't count."

Jelling had a medscanner out, and oozed through his guards before they could object. "Look this way," she said, holding it up. "Now breathe." She glanced over the screen and said, "Try a hit or two of oxygen periodically. It should help." She gestured to one of her people and they brought over a small compressor and filter.

"That makes sense, thanks," he said. He seemed to be tracking, if groggy. Two deep drafts of oxy did refresh him quite a bit.

"What did you discuss?" Mark asked.

"More of the same. This is a very rich culture. I have to recommend we move slowly." Russ coughed again.

"So do I," he agreed, "even if certain elements won't like it."

An engineer officer led the way to the embassy, stood aside and let them pass.

"I'll follow, sirs. Please ask if you have any questions." He handed over a pair of floor plans.

Mark sought the designated private areas. The quarters were comfortable enough. The bed was a cot for now, but with a cushion mattress one could sink into. The floor was solid, as were the walls. Russ's personal space was identical. There were permeable membranes that could be set to allow light and sound, or opaqued and damped. They had plenty of commo, both local net and an encrypted military tightbeam to the ship. They had toilets and showers, with water and waste treatment in a discreet hut. They had a kitchen and a cook. That covered the basics for now.

"I appreciate the courtesy," Russ said, genuinely impressed by his own apartment.

"Of course," Mark agreed. "It is my intent to make this a joint mission. You may have to remind me now and then."

"Yes, you do seem to get intensely focused."

"And become a self-centered ass?" He shrugged slightly. "You can say it."

"As a diplomat I would never say it that way." Russ grinned. "I will remind you when your focus becomes too intent."

Well, good. It was important that they get along, in order to help keep the rest of the interests reined in. He made a note to ask more of Russ.

"So why don't we hold separate meetings this morning?" he suggested. "I'll meet with Vlashn, then you can. I know you're not a security risk. I'll ask, and offer, that we not conclude any deals without consulting."

"That's fair," Russ nodded.

Good to know, Mark thought. Yes, give the man what he was likely to ask for, and use it as a chip later.

He led his counterpart through the rest of the shell and checked it against the floorplan. The living quarters and service areas were in the rear. In front was a laminated platform with an awning, big enough for a reception for twenty or so. Behind that was a patio that could be left open or closed off. To the right about halfway back was an airtight and filtered barn similar to the section of cargo bay aboard *Healy*, with a duplicate of the equipment. The engineer warrant leader handed Mark a transmitter.

"That will slag everything on your command. UV, thermal, X-ray pulse and incendiary. Keep pressing it and they'll actually detonate. They might recover some micrometer shreds of conductor if they look hard enough, but there's as little, er, . . . element as we can arrange in there."

"Thanks," he agreed. It was good to see his order never to use the word "metal" was sticking. He was concerned about the scientists, though. Science was all about information.

The rest of the compound was still largely tape and marks at present, but would have a military barracks, several bunkers, and a few service buildings for storage and maintenance. It was a miniature forward base, standard and familiar. There were already signs of where a berm would be dug for privacy and defense. Mark felt much more comfortable in a familiar environment.

Vlashn's party was larger that morning, with a gaggle of obvious scientists carrying measuring equipment, a library of scrolls in tubes on a cart, and a bare handful of warriors. The warriors were dressed up to look pretty rather than vicious. They were not quite uniform, but all wore a bright blue not obvious in the natural environment. Apart from that, some wore snug clothes, others loose, with various splashes of color that could be awards or decorations. They carried spears and wore bandoleers of large throwing darts. Armor peeked from under the garments.

Mark had only McDonald for now, and Connor. He wanted to keep things pared down for security, and to boost his status by not needing a large entourage. He wasn't sure if the latter would work on the Ishkul, but they seemed to respect efficiency and it was a good evasion for his real rationale.

Vlashn came forward with one of the researchers and a cage of animals. They were brown and green and plumed in light, tendrilly scales that were probably close to feathers. Their forelegs were far back, like necked dinosaurs, and their tails split in two. They had beaks, not jaws, and the same top blowhole.

"This is a (untranslatable: animal species). We as a culture have bred them for six hundred and seventeen years to record events. They as units will be replaced periodically, and we will of course transcribe to paper their recitations."

"We have something similar," Mark agreed, taking a chair and offering one to Vlashn. He remembered the creature from the day before. "We call it a parrot." He pointed and the commo tech on duty flipped through a bound book for an image.

After a glance that scanned the page almost like a camera, Vlashn said, "I deduce that is one species of aerial creature." His reverse knees didn't allow a standard seat. Mark pointed and someone dragged over a lounger. Its length allowed Vlashn to sprawl in a reasonable fashion.

"Yes," Mark agreed. "We use its name to refer to the act of repeating what is said, verbatim. The class of animal is called 'bird.' "

"Good. I am amused at the irony of this meeting. Both our collective groups approach in predatory mistrust while intending an agreement to their benefit, with the implied threat of force responsive to force administered. It is near zero probability we can both acquire advantage of the same goal, so we both collectively hope for sufficient differences to enable us collectively to agree, while maintaining sufficient similarities for that same agreement." He made a gurgling sound that was probably a laugh.

Geek humor, Mark thought. "That is a good summary and I agree with the irony," he said. "About that: Ambassador Russ and I have decided to meet separately, if it suits you. This allows more candid discussion. While we are allies, our cultures are different and have different aims. We can consort as a group as needed. The same will be true for our other partners. Besides which, I'm not a physical scientist and wouldn't understand a lot of the discussions."

"I regard that as practical and excellent," Vlashn said. "It is important that all groups offer as much clarity as possible. I will pose a query as to your organization." He stopped and paused.

Ah. *May I ask a question?* Such a question was redundant and illogical, so Vlashn had expressed it as an intent, allowing for permission.

"Go ahead," Mark prompted.

"You have probable scientists, warriors and politicians. Query: Is that typically how your society is constructed?"

"No, those are the classes we use for meeting other races." He tried to make it smooth and obvious.

"Interesting. Query: How many races have you met?"

"Some of our own planets, few of others," he said. He wasn't about to admit to being first at this point, but he couldn't lie, either. Dolphins, leopards and chimps were at least semi-sentient, laws existed for their treatment, so they could be considered "races."

"Do warriors prove needful often? I am only curious. We have our own, as you are obviously aware." He gestured toward them with a wave.

From the corner of an eye, Mark noted the Operatives and the local troops staring and gauging each other. It was professional, not threatening, but both wanted to know the others' measure.

"We have met some very aggressive races, but we were able to come to agreements that benefited both without violence." If you wanted to consider domesticating leopards and engineering them to do their violence on behalf of people an "agreement."

"That is encouraging. Inquiry: Your culture is a mono-structure?"

"I didn't quite get that."

"Query: You will be the setter of policy and communication for your entire race?"

"I will be speaking for one planet and its outer habitats in space. There are groups for other planets. I will advise and hope to create an initial trust and communication. Policy will be more complicated. We have over twenty inhabited planets and a variety of interactions."

"Query: When will other groups talk? I intend no offense, but a variety of inputs almost certainly allows for a more accurate conclusion."

Fast. The man was fast. His conclusions were easily on par with a twentieth-century philosopher or politician. Technically, they weren't yet Iron Age, but they'd skipped straight to ceramics, it seemed. That had to be considered comparable, given the sociological responses so far. No panicking at the landing aliens, no genuflecting, an assumption of self-possession and a desire to come to terms peacefully off the bat, with the best deal possible.

"You have met Ambassador Russ. Some others accompanied us. I can introduce them shortly. Others are several days away even with our star drives. Your planet is a delightful find for us. The group that found you was seeking knowledge and did not expect sentients. They are from my planet, and we are closest, so we responded first. Our intent was to establish contact and meeting, which we have, and then introduce our partners. They agreed with us in this plan." Eventually.

"Query: Which of your cultures is most powerful, in your estimation?"

That was one hell of a probing question, and set alarms off in Mark's head. They wanted to find out the playing field and cut deals with the biggest, or possibly, with the others against the biggest.

"One is larger," he said. "One is more widespread in space. Ours I think is better at exploiting opportunities fairly, but that depends on the philosophy one uses for a system of government."

Vlashn's gesture was strange, but had to be a nod. "I propose that our scientists talk and study here, especially yourself, myself and the linguists, so that we can more readily understand each other. As soon as a quorum of your groups are represented, we should have a formal meeting to promote friendship."

"That is an excellent idea," Mark agreed. "You should know that we can breathe your air, but we cannot eat your food. It is possible you might be able to eat some of ours, but that should be left to your and our scientists to determine."

"Excellent," Vlashn agreed. "Your translation device is quite notable, but it seems to need further information or refinement. Your words come across imprecise and with several choices of meaning."

"I think your language is more structured than ours," Mark said. "I am speaking the language 'English' which is one of our dominant ones and the most common. It has absorbed words from hundreds of different smaller languages and grammar from at least two predecessors, if I recall."

"This tends to indicate your ancestors were often successfully aggressive in occupying the territory of others, and or in generally subverting aggressors to your benefit."

Shit. It was flat out dangerous to talk to this man, but he had to.

"I will make arrangements for our other representatives to arrive," Mark said to avoid the subject. "Their ships may be larger, and their cultures are different from ours."

"I look forward to meeting them. Query: Do they also speak English?"

"Most of them will, and we can continue to do so if you would like a single development of translation for now."

"That would seem to be the most logical answer for now, given the need to develop the translation, if it is agreeable."

Mark made a note to ask about that. Translations should become more colloquial and straightforward as the AI learned. Vlashn's speech was becoming formal and exceptionally precise.

"I will leave our scientists to talk. I have limited the range of topics, but exceptions can be made by Dr. McDonald," he indicated with a point, "or myself." McDonald looked ready to burst. If he vibrated any more in excitement he was liable to undergo fission. "I will consult with Mr. Russ and make arrangements for other cultures. Their arrival will take time, though. Expect Mr. Russ in a few segs."

"I understand. The distances involved are great."

"Yes. Good day to you, and I am at your service for any questions or help beyond what you see here." He bowed and reentered the building.

Once out of sight, he took a deep breath. He had an end destination—a peaceful exchange between the species—and no idea how to navigate there. Had they been truly primitive, it would be easy enough to have a review board approve ranges of offers. With them being sophisticates . . . he didn't know.

He turned to his UN counterpart, who seemed far too comfortable, the bastard.

Russ was sprawled on a comfy chair.

"How is the air?"

"I'm breathing better, thank you." He did have more color.

"Mr. Russ, we need to discuss how we're going to allow others in."

"As slowly as possible. Next question?" The man grinned.

"The circling sharks want to be fed."

"Citizen, our offer still stands, with no attack on your sovereignty. This system is not territory under your constitution and can't be. It's not private property. It's not even human. I can designate it a foreign nation under our laws, and you can agree to abide by the rules and go through us. I can make all parties operate by our rules."

"That wouldn't be unwise, but besides the moral issue of conceding, there are the nationalistic concerns. The corps will fight it heavily, it could set a bad precedent, and I'd be conceding a lot of future authority. So I can't accept."

"Of course not. The offer stands, and you can use it for leverage." Russ didn't seem offended.

"Thank you. How are your scientists fitting in?"

"Some of them are not happy being second to others whom they feel are less capable," Russ admitted, "but they're exchanging information fairly. I appreciate it."

"We know scientists are pursuing Truth in order to classify it. They'll swap information anyway, and it's true that your own specialists, like Marguerite Stephens, have insights we don't. I welcome it. I'm not your enemy either culturally or personally."

Russ grinned. "You didn't mention professionally."

"No, I didn't." Mark grinned back. He was starting to like this bureaucrat. He played hard but fair. That was the best one could hope for. "You're up next."

CHAPTER 6

Mark woke and flicked his eyes at the clock. It was just shy of the alarm. Twilight peeked tentatively through the polarized skylight. He sat up and stretched, not really ready to tackle the day but knowing he had to.

He sighed. He'd spent the entire day, when not talking to human interests, examining multiple references, looking through history to see how to do this first contact thing correctly. He was forced to the conclusion that it pretty much hadn't been, and he could be the key figure in wiping out a culture. No pressure.

The first steps were done. System entered, landing, greeting locals, taking of explorers to leaders, made much easier when some type of leader showed up personally. Next was to talk, fast, in detail, while giving nothing away without gaining more in return, so as to gauge their response. After that, discuss information exchange, then who would do so, and let them haggle over a rate that would not cause undue resentment or war. Through all this, don't mention or wear any metal.

Russ seemed happy to leave the load on him, no doubt waiting to exploit any failure. Good old Ambassador Russ, you can trust him. See how Ballenger offended or hurt you? Russ won't do that. Agree to a cultural exchange and get everything you want, in exchange for piecemeal surrender of independence and cultural distinction. Mark couldn't prove it would take that direction, but it had before, often enough under the UN, and was their standing offer to the Freehold and other systems. Let us rule you and you'll get a lot of free services in exchange.

Perhaps he was being too cynical. He did have the ball, and as long as he was handling it, why change?

He rubbed his eyes and stretched again, and rose from the bed. All he could do for now was keep collating information, and waiting to see what it might yield. Eventually it should coalesce into something more concrete.

Suddenly, he was coughing, gagging, choking. He felt something in his throat and couldn't dislodge it. He leaned to his knees, then to the rough floor, and bent forward. It seemed to help, but he couldn't get his throat clear. He coughed, coughed and gasped, before shaking loose a large mass of phlegm. He spit and grimaced, then spent seconds drawing slow, deep breaths to recover.

An Operative medic slammed through the door and knelt next to him.

"Sir?" the troop asked, grave severity in his voice. He was moving, glancing around, looking for threats.

"Breathing trouble," Mark rasped. "Woke up. I'm congested now." He paused for a breath. "Sinuses hurt, throat constricted."

"We've had other cases. Allergy induced asthma due to the local chemistry." After some rummaging he shoved an inhaler in Mark's face. "Take two puffs thirty seconds apart as needed. I'll bring you a tailored nano later."

"Right. Eyes itching a bit, too," he said, and sucked a breath through the inhaler. It tasted astringent, but did immediately ease his breathing.

He recovered in a few segs, and sat carefully, making sure of his breathing. Aggravating, but he'd have to deal with it. Ultimately, they might all be in masks. At least that would increase the cultural distance between the species, as he'd hoped.

He showered quickly in the field expedient washroom, and dressed. One good thing about this event was that he and Russ had both agreed to resume casual clothing. Khakis and canvas were much more practical, and more comfortable than formal wear. He added a kerchief he could snug around his neck for show or around his face for dust.

So, back to the negotiations. Focus on cultural stuff? Sports, gardening and such? That would help with language and sociology, too. He grabbed a cereal stick, being disinterested in actual food and with his brain already alert. That finished his morning preparations, and he stepped next door to his office.

Landrieu came in, and said, "Mark, I know you're busy, but there's a small issue."

"Not at all, Land, go ahead. What is it?" The research and negotiations, at least between human interests, didn't sleep. Every morning was the same so far. Wake up, walk through, piss on some fires. Hopefully this was something simple. Land looked eager but not too bothered.

"The Ishkul are very specific about whom they deal with. I believe you noticed their greetings resolve to 'who is in charge?' in a search for status."

"Yes. I can imagine several evolutionary reasons for that."

"They seek credentials and status. So far, the UN is getting the short end. They find our scientists have done more field work, and are therefore more interesting. The natives have a practical hands-on culture rather than an Aristotelian philosophical type."

"Has this caused problems other than noses out of joint? They're picking people they can deal with, who know the subject at hand, it sounds like." He approved of that, actually.

"They are. I'm offering the information so you can deal with Russ before his people do."

"Good to know. Thanks muchly." It was also good that the scientific mission would come first. Mark grinned a bit at that. Egan could be petulant, Margov could be politely insistent, and if the natives didn't raise the issue, they could sit and wait. Mark could shrug. He was an intermediary and referee, not their paid representative. That was very convenient.

Shraybman and Thomas arrived together. "Busy, sir? And are you okay?" Shraybman asked. She looked concerned. Apparently, word of his earlier bronchial attack was out.

"I'm available," he said.

"We're working on a tour schedule. The Ishkul want to show us local activity, and we need to arrange to show them something in return."

"What, though?" he asked. "We can't show still or video that would reveal anything technical. I'm not even sure we can show still or video yet."

"I have graphic artists working on that," Thomas said. She was average height, average range of build, though on the curvy side, average looking. She was likely close to the perfect intel type. She'd disappear in a crowd of two. When she spoke, though, she was very noticeable, for those few seconds. Was that talent or training? Either way, it was impressive.

"That will keep them busy," Mark said, with a raise of eyebrows.

Thomas shook her head marginally. "They haven't been used much at all. They're fine with it. Do you want to approve their work, sir?"

"I'll leave that to the Lieutenant and Doctors McDonald and Stephens. I'll make periodic checks to keep informed. If I don't delegate, I'll go insane."

Shraybman said, "Good idea, sir. If you need help from me, let me know."

"I shall. What are you working on now?"

"Right now, Ms Thomas, Press Liaison for the Citizen, is telling them 'no' and giving them sanitized briefs from the science team. Ms Shraybman," she thumbed at herself, "is apologizing for the busy diplomatic schedule, but is sure there will be time for more appointments over the next few days. If all parties can please summarize their needs with certain info, she will see that the Citizen, and of course the ambassador, look at it as soon as possible; however, with both nations involved it might take some negotiation to make things acceptable to all parties."

"Excellent," he grinned. "Please continue. I've sent for a couple of vertol couriers, to allow some medium-range travel. We're acquiring a proper little base here."

"I heard, sir," Thomas said. "The engineers are muttering about defensive berms, razor wire, towers and sensor nets."

"Yes, the craft come with support elements, more security, ongoing supply flights . . . each of them another risk of contamination." He sighed.

Shraybman said, "Hang in there, sir. We've only just started."

"I'd hoped for something to raise my spirits, Lieutenant. That wasn't it." Just past breakfast, and he was already fatigued.

No one was sure how the fight started.

At some point, the UN sent down a squad of Marines to cover its personnel. They wound up in close quarters with Freehold Operatives and Mobile Assault troops. Both groups had members whose families were military dynasties, and had lost relatives during the war. Something was said somewhere to someone, and then several troops were in a free-for-all brawl, fortunately with bare hands. The rest separated them, but some minor damage had been done, tables and comms tumbled, equipment spilled. It wound up on Mark's desk shortly thereafter.

"I'm not sure why I'm seeing this," he said to Captain Jelling, as she placed it in front of him and stood to attention. "As the ranking officer for our ground forces, shouldn't you talk to the UN OIC and resolve it?"

"Sir . . . " she started, then said in a rush, "the UN OIC and myself were participants."

"I see. That makes it awkward and sets a very bad example, of course." Damn. Old tensions, but very real. UN and Freehold both had hard feelings, even eighteen years later.

She flushed almost as red as her hair. "Indeed, sir, which is why I am presenting it to you myself, with apologies."

"What exactly set it off?"

"Comments were made, sir." She looked very embarrassed and uncomfortable, and almost fidgeted.

"Comments?" he prompted. There was only one thing he could think of, but it seemed unlikely.

"A comment in particular, sir."

"Out with it, Captain, we both have things to do."

She inhaled, stared straight ahead, and said, "Sir, one of their NCOs asked if we were the same unit as the cocksucking little babykillers who attacked Chicago."

"That was Team Seven, unauthorized, now disbanded. You're Team Four, I presume from your location and assignment."

"Yes, sir. But for . . . other reasons . . . I couldn't deny it and couldn't find an appropriate response. And I lost my temper. So I hit him."

"You apparently also threw him through a bench, tossed one of his buddies on top of him, and one of our own Mob troops who tried to restrain you." Her report was quite specific.

"Yes, sir. Then their commander hit me and it gets vague."

"So I see. It apparently didn't end for some time."

She said nothing, just stared straight ahead.

He understood, though. Her father had commanded the Earth mission. Still, in Special Warfare, she was going to get hit with that frequently around the UN. She'd have to deal with it.

"What was the tally?"

"I took out three, sir. One of my NCOs took out two more. Then we got dogpiled. Of course there's the blue on blue I made with one of ours as well. My ribs will need bandaging after the Marine lieutenant hit me."

"Would you do it again?"

"I . . . " She paused for a moment. "In a fucking second, sir. But not on this planet, and not in a diplomatic forum."

"Very well. Can your exec handle management of your unit?"

If she were normal, she'd have had tears in her eyes as she replied, "Yes, sir." Her voice was firm and confident, though.

"You will transfer authority to him and stand regular duties with your unit until such time as I need your skills. If anyone offers a similar inducement, I suggest you say, 'You forgot to call us "puppy rapers," ' and let it drop."

"Understood, sir. What rank should I wear?" She was still as a statue.

"Captain, of course. I just want you to reflect and unwind for a while. I am going to need your skills, and I will need discretion."

"Thank you, sir." She seemed to shed several kilograms off her shoulders. "To keep it discreet, may I simply say the schedule is changing due to operational needs?"

He nodded. "Now you're thinking. But it must not happen again here, as you are aware."

"Oh, yes, sir. Absolutely."

"Of course if it happens in a social venue, say a spaceport or military bar, I expect you to hospitalize the son of a bitch." Yes, she'd overreacted. But the comment did call for a response.

He had to hand it to her. She still didn't crack as she replied, "Noted for record, sir." Absolutely icy. The insult must have really hit home to break that professional reserve.

He did notice she favored her left side after he dismissed her to the medics.

No sooner had she left than Egan pushed his way in. The man had no grace. Of course, he also had several billion credits to threaten with and was used to getting his way.

"Good day, Citizen," Egan said, politely enough.

Mark was having none of it. "Mister Egan." He didn't offer a seat.

"Sir, I've kept back and out of the diplomacy, and intend to continue. While I obviously have my company's interests at hand, nothing good will come of shaking things up at this point."

"Excellent. Is that all?"

It obviously was only an opening, and Mark had blindsided him.

"I was going to ask if I might receive updates on the government's activities as they progress, so I can develop a strategy that will not interfere." He clearly meant it as a reminder.

"I'm aware of your right to information," Mark replied, and Egan smiled, "however, all our negotiations involve the UN, and most involve the military. So they are not as transparent as we'd like them to be." Actually, they suited Mark just fine. He knew Egan would disagree.

"Obviously, that's a problem for me, sir. However, I will work around it, and continue to defer to you and the ambassador."

And I'm Simon Bolivar, Mark said to himself. "That's appreciated. I'll let you know what happens. Since I am about to meet with Vlashn and don't want to keep him waiting, may I ask you to leave us?" Goddess, this plenipotentiary thing was the greatest debate technique ever. Matters of state. Piss off. It would have been awesome in his professional venue as a corporate negotiator. Of course, that was why the Freehold required as broad a separation as possible between business and politics.

"Yes, of course," Egan said, departing with an expression that said he didn't know if he'd gotten an answer he liked, or even an answer at all.

Mark spoke into his collar mic, "Irina, I need it cleared out so Vlashn isn't kept waiting. I want him to feel special."

"Of course, sir," Shraybman replied. "His entourage is crossing the field now."

"Excellent." He rose and headed for the pseudo-atrium. One of the Operatives fell in behind him. He reminded himself to get names and be social. For now he simply nodded and said, "Thank you, Blazer Murah."

"Of course, sir," he said, preceding Mark through the door in case of threats.

Vlashn's party consisted of himself, one with a recording animal, one with weapons and one other. Good. Mark preferred streamlined and direct operations to waltzing around. So far, he liked the Ishkul. They seemed to prove the adage that rich democracies never fought. Though were they actually a democracy? He had no idea about their political system. Something else to ask.

"Greetings, Vlashn. Is it appropriate to also greet your assistants?"

"It is, but they are as I for this discussion. I greet you, Mark."

"Thanks. Can you explain how they are as you?" He indicated a couch.

"Apologies," Vlashn said, sitting. "Imprecision not intentional. The term predates our language and is metaphorical. They are accompanying me but not participants outside of their duties of protection, documentation and consideration."

"Got it. I will have more couches brought." He'd had momentary flashes of dealing with some kind of hive entity. That would have been a pain.

The warrior replied, "With thanks and permission, I officially prefer to stand."

"Absolutely. My own warrior will doubtless stand across from you."

"An excellent position to study the other."

Yes, Mark liked them. He was even getting used to the half bird, half lizard, half monster face.

"Customarily, I should offer refreshments, but we have nothing that fits your metabolism, Vlashn. Please accept the offer in concept."

"Likewise, I should have brought a gift of status, but I am unaware of your needs or customs."

"I hope I don't keep you from your people, visiting at this remote location," Mark said.

"No. My Equal Somle has authority in my absence, and I in hers. I note you are a single entity. If you had a partner with you, what status would you share?"

"We don't share status generally. The individual bears the status, but may appoint someone to handle affairs on a limited basis." That was interesting. Also, were they a couple, or an elected duo?

"This suggests a high level of stress associated with your position."

"At times, yes. I confer with others on most matters. I'm entrusted with a lot of authority at the present."

"Conversely, I have great many represented Ishkul strongly interested in my actions. Your distance would tend to negate that, presuming a lack of communication at a distance."

Was that a deliberately probing question? Or just curiosity? Either way, Mark did have an out.

"My messages must be sent by ship," he replied. It was literally correct, until a Jump Point was stabilized. Even then, without a comm tunnel through it, a ship would have to be the means of transfer. He wasn't going to mention radio even in passing.

"Mark, we should have a party."

"A party?" he asked, momentarily surprised.

"Yes. We should collectively plan and implement a gathering of our peoples in order to socialize and interact, while sharing cultural expressions between us."

"Yes, I know what you meant. I was just surprised that you have the same concept."

"I'm quite sure your and my sensual cognitive symbols for the concept differ. It will be interesting to a moderate degree to see how they differ."

"Certainly. We traditionally do such things in the evening. May I suggest five days from now, starting about the time of sunset?"

"That is earlier than we usually choose, but is acceptable. What involvements do you recommend?"

"Food, beverages, entertainment and talk are what we normally use."

"You speak of them as separate concepts, not combined."

"They can be combined. Some of our chefs are entertainers at the same time."

"I agree for those I speak for on the time and concept."

"Excellent. May I ask that you provide a large enough tent, with private needs facilities?"

"Yes. Since our foods are not compatible, we shall arrange a common area, and sit around those who prepare the animal."

That was an interesting phrase, Mark thought. Obviously carnivore or omnivore. He'd keep letting them lead and offer him tidbits he could use to build on, though so far they were as practical as he could have hoped.

"Excellent. I will arrange for the human side of things."

Actually, he'd delegate that, which was a shame. He'd much rather plan a diplomatic banquet than the stuff he was doing.

"Query: Have the technical discussions been informative?"

"Very. While we have spaceflight and you don't, your development is very impressive, and better than ours in some areas."

"Query: Which areas?"

Shit, he would ask that. "I'll have Dr. Stephens put together a summary. She's our expert on cultural technology."

"Thank you."

"While I welcome your presence, if these discussions can be handled on your behalf, I will not be offended. You have many tasks, I'm sure."

"That you describe is my standard method. However, as we have not met an outside race before, I greatly enjoy the opportunity."

"As do I. Please visit whenever you like."

"Your generosity is highly appreciated."

As the Ishkul left, Mark reflected on the odd mix of similarities and differences. It was indeed a lucky privilege to be in this position.

Mark raised the issue of information exchange to Stephens.

Stephens said, "The problem is, for everything we see, they want to know how we do it differently. We're seeing highly developed tools, with the materials involved, and meeting master craftspeople, whom we then insult by telling them we can't show or tell them how we manage a task." Her expression was dour.

Another complication. "Do we need to stick to more basic production? Raw material? I'm sure we can set up something. We also have the argument of only having a ship along, not any serious factory."

"That's possible, yes. Though I'm not sure where we'll find people skilled in the basic materials involved." She squinted in thought.

He offered, "Aren't there some reenactors aboard? Primitive materials people? And I'm sure some of your staff have done anthropological living."

"This might work. I really need someone who can create diplomatically phrased talking points for us, though. We want to present as equals, but we know our technology is superior."

"Shraybman seems to have good ideas on that. I'll try to get her to add it to her schedule. Also Cochrane can tweak the language." He pinged the linguist.

"The other problem is recording what goes on."

"Can't you fake sketching and written notes to cover the scans and video?"

"Yes, but the Ishkul like to review the notes and make additional comments. They're too bloody sophisticated and helpful."

Mark made a note. "I'll have a search done for more graphic artists and anyone who knows a shorthand." He was glad of the support of a military vessel. A lot of those troops and spacers were going to find themselves interacting with aliens, in order to present humans as more primitive than they were. "Should I gather there aren't a lot of resources in that area aboard *Aracaju*?"

"There are some," she admitted cautiously. "There would be more if it was a dedicated scientific mission. This was put together rather hastily."

"I understand," he said. The Freehold mission was also hasty, but they seemed to have a better cross section of personnel out the gate. "Of course we'll help. My concern is how the Ishkul will react when they eventually find out the deception."

"That's going to be soon, no matter what happens," Cochrane spoke up on radio. "Their anomalies extend to language, too." She came through the entrance as she finished speaking. She was in workout uniform here in private.

"Tell me," Mark said.

"It's an artificial language," she said. "Constructed and maintained for communication. It's analog and precise."

"So they created a uniform language? That's not too surprising with a need to communicate on a large scale and a society this large."

"That's the point. They shouldn't have a society this large. They don't have a means to disseminate information fast enough to prevent dialectic differences. Yet they have."

"It's that unusual?"

"The construction is what makes it unusual."

"Can you give me an example?"

"Certainly. Look at the sky and tell me what you see." She nodded toward the window.

Mark glanced out and replied, "It's blue with scattered cumulus."

"In Ishkul, which is their language as well as their societal name, I might say, 'The sky is a blue two-thirds of the way to its maximum clarity of low humidity and dust, with scattered cumulus of a third the density of that which would indicate bad weather to follow in a short number of segs.' "

"That's why I never hear an absolute from them."

"That's why you almost never, so far in our engagement, hear an absolute answer on anything subjective or variable from them, taking into account we are speaking to scientists and intellectuals with a highly refined grasp of their surroundings and events."

She'd nailed it.

"Damn. No wonder they're such wordy bastards. They're being precise."

"Very. English is clunky and wasteful to their ears, and translation back to them is a bitch. We come across as the stereotypical lowbrow savages whose vocabulary ends with 'Ugg strongest, Ugg kill deer.' "

"So they look down on us?"

"No, but they are confused at our grasp of technology but not language. The confusion works both ways."

"Do you think we have anything to learn from them?"

"Another imprecision," she said. "Facts or technical knowledge, they have little to teach us. Culturally and philosophically, we can learn a lot from the study, which we will add to our cultural anthropological science."

"You think they'll figure out we're hiding tech soon, though."

"I'm almost positive of it," she said with a frown. "Vlashn asked why our warriors changed spears."

"Did they?" Mark asked. He hadn't been aware of that.

"On landing, we carried knapped flint and obsidian, or at least ceramics that looked like it. After we saw their weapons, which are stone or ceramic but ground and polished, the Special Projects team came up with a polymer cored, ceramic edged matrix that looked much the same as theirs, while having tremendously better toughness. The latter wasn't obvious, but the change in appearance was."

"Did someone authorize that?"

"I don't know." She looked uncomfortable, and it really wasn't her department.

"Right. I'm assuming Jelling did. What did you say in response?"

"That we had a variety of weapons available and wanted to remain equivalent. I hope that wasn't wrong, but I figured evasion would be bad."

"No, that's likely the best answer you could give. It does hint we can outdo them, though. Sorry you were put on the spot."

"We all are on the spot, all the time," she said. "I'll manage." She did look a bit relieved, though.

Mark was annoyed. Presumably, Jelling had decided that matching the locals' tech wouldn't hurt anything, and had proceeded. No one had told her not to, though.

Nor did it really matter at this point. The Ishkul knew the humans not only had better technology, but had been hiding it, and could jump dramatically in level in a matter of segs. That was neither diplomatic nor reassuring as to friendly intent. Or it wouldn't be for him. He presumed the locals would feel likewise.

Shortly, Russ came in, looking steamed.

"I assume you have a complaint. Please go ahead," Mark said, canting his tone to be accepting, not abrasive. "Is this about the fight?"

"Fight?" Russ looked confused. "No, that's not something for me to deal with. The military has it. That bitch Margov seduced my assistant."

"Really," Mark replied. He'd had reason before to wonder if she swung that way. Or was it the male she'd seduced? "I'm not sure how that's my problem. She's not part of my mission, nor does it affect my dealings with her."

"I was hoping you could exercise some control over your Residents."

Russ should know better, and there was no point in arguing. Instead, Mark replied, "What about you over your assistant? I assume this was more than just social?"

"I believe some encryption was compromised, whether willingly or by deceit I don't know. I've sent him to the ship with a reprimand and will follow up later."

"Heh. Doesn't surprise me about her. Watch yourself. She's a snake."

"Clearly."

"I'm afraid I can't do much. I'll try to have a better watch kept on her. If you furnish a list to us, I can keep her away from people and areas as an official favor, but I'll need to be paid later."

"Paid how?" Russ was suspicious.

"Not sure. I won't hold it over you, but it is something that will take effort here."

"Understood, then. Please do."

CHAPTER 7

The large tent, circus tent as everyone was calling it, was dressed up for the occasion. The thing was huge, bigger than the one erected on landing. All day, laborers had brought additional poles, stakes, ropes that were apparently similar to nylon, fabric panels both outer and inner, and tables, benches, and other accoutrements. The Ishkul chairs were bizarre, almost a kneeling surface, but with shin and hip rests as well, to handle their complicated legs.

It was fascinating to watch. Some technologies were parallel, and the Ishkul went for large round tents as some human societies had, with low-angled walls like desert dwellers. Logical.

The younger scientists arrived early, whispering amongst themselves in a gaggle under the embassy awning. No doubt they'd pulled loose from duties to keep an eye on this, and what did it hurt? They'd learn things here, too. Some of the military technicians wandered in, then; security, of course. Mark didn't see any journalists, but he did see Louise Thomas, so that was under control. The diplomats and senior staff would probably be fashionably late.

True to Mark's internal prediction, Doctors Stephens and McDonald arrived in fine suits, she with a flounce, he with a ruffled collar. Russ and his one assistant arrived in Earth dinner jackets. Connor and Jelling wore Class A uniforms with ceramic-bladed sidearms and batons, looking attractive and deadly. Most of their team was already in place.

Egan proved he knew how to dress, and Mark admitted the man looked handsome in kilt, pattens and coat.

Then Margov arrived, and he cringed at her outfit.

It wasn't that it would bother the Ishkul. They had no idea what human fashion or mores were. It was obvious, though, that she wanted attention and was determined to get it. She wore a sleek deep blue bodysuit, tight as paint and coutured. Her long hair was raven blue-black, flowing under a static field, accented with some sparse clear stones. He suspected natural diamonds or natural Grainne moissanite. The effect was striking, and it showed and accentuated every curve of her lithe body. Every curve.

He knew that if she was seeking that much attention, she either planned to make a play, or have someone else do something while she provided the distraction.

Russ came alongside and said, "I hope you have a plan to handle this." His tone wasn't offensive. He'd just seen the same thing and was as concerned.

Mark was about to speak when Shraybman arrived and said, "Of course he does. How do I look, sir?" She popped open the hooked clasp on her cape and twirled it off, over and around her head. It wound up in a neat coil around her left forearm. It was a great effect.

That effect was lost in the shimmering green gown she wore. It draped around her neck and firm shoulders, framed her bare breasts and wrapped around her hips, hiding but concealing nothing. She wore emeralds in her short but elaborately woven hair and from her ears, and on her nipples.

"I take it you play chess," he replied. He eyed her over discreetly and politely.

She smiled modestly, in amazing contrast to the rest of her. "It was the obvious time for them to make a play. You'll also see Egan is trying very hard to get close to our host." She indicated with a nod of her head. "Captain Jelling has that under control. Dr. Stephens is corralling his assistants. Ambassador Russ's aide is watching the Earth press, and Thomas is covering ours. If anyone has any questions, they should come find me. You haven't commented on my outfit yet. Are they not spectacular?"

It was obvious she either spent a lot of time on pec workouts, or took nanos, or had surgical splints. He suspected the former, and that any suggestion of the latter would be insulting.

"They are spectacular, and even more as part of the ensemble," he said.

"You're not worshiping them," she joked.

"Certainly not in public." He grinned. "What would the aliens think?"

"Since they have no idea what our dress standards are, and since I'm perfectly within evening standards for

Freehold civilian attire, and not in uniform, I decided to make sure I was the star."

Russ said, "I don't think anyone from Earth would have thought of doing that, but I'm certainly glad you did."

"And you worship them, yes?" she said as she turned to him. She was certainly joking, though proud of her physique, and Russ was certainly nervous and not going to say a word, with his position and the societal standards of Earth.

"I think you'll get all the attention."

"So I had better hunt down the media and start making statements, shouldn't I? Privilege to be here, so much to learn, opportunity of the millennium, gracious hosts, boon to humankind, am I missing anything?"

"I trust you implicitly," Mark said. "I want to see the vid afterwards. How many thousand words can you use to say nothing at all?"

"The outfit comes with an invisible bullshit shovel," she said. "Good evening, Ambassador, Citizen." She bowed slightly and swept away. As she did, Mark noticed her shoes were slight heels, but with broad bases and terrain cleats. There was certainly a weapon or three in that bone-fastened clutchpurse, too.

The ushers/maitre d's were paired human and Ishkul, all trying hard not to be bouncy with glee at the event. A pair came to the two diplomats.

"We can seat you now, if you like, sirs," the human said. He wore a petty officer's mess dress, minus metal buttons and with a stone knife instead of the dirk he'd likely have worn otherwise.

When an usher offers to seat one, it's generally taken to be an order. Mark had nothing critical that required him to stand, and he gave Russ a quick look.

"Shall we?"

"Of course, Citizen."

The Ishkul made a slightly dramatic variation of the waved arm, and indicated a pair of seats at the end of the arc. They were Ishkul construction, but human style.

That was quick, Mark thought. *I wonder how comfortable they are.* He followed. He could always take pain killers later, and the gravity was light.

"Please stand until Vlashn and Somle arrive," the petty officer whispered.

"Yes," he agreed. He stood behind the chair and studied it.

It may have been made on short notice, but it had a lovely satin oil finish, a rich grain and a few tasteful but spare carvings along the arms. Well done. McDonald and Stephens filled in to his left, and Russ was at his right. He'd deferred and let his counterpart have the head position, out of a desire to push the theory they were equal.

In moments, the two Ishkul leaders were at their stools across the aisle, and various scientists and officers were filling in. Ishkul warriors and researchers settled on their side. The media, with microscopic cameras hidden in bouquets and buttons, writing with pencils on paper, were still interviewing Shraybman. Margov tried to loiter, but was politely and firmly ushered to her seat. She looked annoyed. Next to her, Egan tried to mask a grin, mostly successfully. Putting the two competitors side by side was a stroke of genius. They were honored guests, very uncomfortable, unable to talk strategy with obvious sensors around, and unable to ignore each other.

Turning his attention back to the table, Mark said, "Nice glassware." His goblet had obviously been made for human hands. It was a little on the heavy side, but looked sturdy enough and clean.

"Very," Landrieu McDonald said next to him. "If it was blown, it was done perfectly, without inclusions or bubbles. If it was spun, I'd love to see the equipment."

"Land, you're staring," Mark murmured.

"Sorry," McDonald agreed and sat back, placing his own goblet back and discreetly capturing some images.

A host walked down the aisle, stood near the middle. Behind him came staff who set up a roped area. Dancing? Wrestling?

The host spoke, translated into English. "Greetings, guests of other worlds, and Primary Leader Vlashn-Somle. On behalf of Conceded Great Preparer Rithalg, and Chef Finley, I thank you for your attendance and trust. Let us begin."

They brought in the cow.

It wasn't a cow, obviously, but was quadrupedal, tusked and hirsute. The tusks were cut and capped, indicating domestication. It was led into the roped pen and hobbled to four stakes that were driven into the ground.

"That's an odd presentation," Shraybman said from down table. "Are they going to kill it here?"

"I'm not sure that's . . . " Mark said and then stopped. *. . . all they plan to do*, he thought.

The cook walked up holding a long haft with an obsidian blade, and a carved stone bowl.

"You've got to be kidding," Russ muttered.

They really were. Damn.

The cook held up the bowl, chose his stance, and stuck the blade a good five centimeters deep in the beast's haunch. Blood gouted neatly but in substantial volume. He caught the stream in the bowl, then poured it into a nice piece of ceramic dinnerware his assistant held.

It trumpeted, clearly in pain, and the Ishkul applauded, whether the cook's style, or over the volume of the animal's howl or lack of it, Mark wasn't sure.

The first assistant kept passing bowls. The second took the filled ones to the table to serve.

Five humans rose and moved urgently but with dignity toward the private area.

The butcher, since that seemed a better term, chose another flank as his assistants kept the bowls of blood moving.

A human waiter hurried up, placing a plate of decorative sushi in front of Mark. He grinned at the irony.

The beast's howls subsided with blood loss, and it staggered its way to the ground as it lost consciousness. All in all, it didn't appear to have suffered much more than an Earth animal hunted by predators.

Some of the Ishkul used ceramic ladlelike paddles to heat the blood over the braziers, thickening it into gray juice, seasoned with sprinkled herbs, then spooned it out. Others enjoyed it raw. It seemed to be a cook your own glop affair.

Human conversation picked up slowly. McDonald said quietly, "Please do talk, people. We want to at least appear to appreciate their culture, even if it is strange to many of us." The words repeated through earbuds and comms, and others relayed the message until it was distributed.

That was about as diplomatic as he could manage, Mark figured. Certainly, this wasn't what he'd been expecting. "Killing a fresh cow for dinner," had a certain expectation for humans that it would be held at least in the kitchen or off site. This was macabre, and fascinating. He couldn't take his eyes off the scene.

One of the biologists, Jim Gregory said, "I'm impressed at the butcher's skill. He's taking a whole animal apart in slivers, rather than sectioning it first. Definitely a high grasp of anatomy."

"God, please stop," someone farther down muttered, clenching lips tightly.

"Thank God for incompatible chemistry," Russ said. "That's a little more than I'd care to get into."

Some of the humans, notably the Freehold military, the anthropologists and biologists, started eating their own food. The others followed the lead to the extent of at least picking at it and moving it around their plates.

The butcher now took to waving his blade around, making slices and slits and pulling at the still twitching carcass with tongs. The meat came off in sections, with hide attached, somewhat like pieces of coconut in the husk. He moved almost in a dance, balanced, poised and with motions that were fluid and elegant but not wasteful.

The Ishkul enjoyed their meat the same way as the appetizer: *Sur le brasier de sang*. They'd slice a chunk from their serving, to personal preference, sprinkle or dip in seasoning and blood, then wave over the fire to taste.

Once the animal was merely a carcass with protruding bones, most of the humans found it possible to intake at least a little food. Some were a bit glassy-eyed; others wore the artificially relaxed look of tranquilizers. The life scientists and the Operatives didn't seem bothered at all, and were eating politely but with gusto.

"I can definitely smell the acidic chemistry in the smoke," McDonald said. "Be glad they're using charcoaled fuel and not raw wood. It would be worse."

Mark agreed. "I'm getting some small whiffs. A bit like a mild tear gas at present." He figured the nanos most of them were taking against the airborne contaminants were helping.

The humidity, though, was not.

It got worse when the vegetables came out.

For centuries, most humans had eaten grain turned into some kind of bread or cake. However, a few tribes had gone the same route as the Ishkul.

The grain was brought out as a gruel or porridge. It smelled of faint decay. As near as Mark could tell, the grains had been allowed to sprout, malt and ferment before being seasoned and served. It wasn't a bad odor as such. About like what one would get at a brewery fermenter. However, added to the abattoirlike smell of the beast, the cooking and the acidity of the fumes, it was definitely another kick to the guts. A few more people took their leave.

The entertainment helped take everyone's mind off the food. Ishkul music used a different scale, which wasn't surprising. They also didn't have brass, obviously. The ensemble, a group of ten Ishkul, played a soft, melodic beat on hollow wooden blocks, the material and shape chosen for its resonance. Several of the science team stared and snuck photos. Mark smiled. It was likely they'd be able to get hands on the instruments by just asking.

A straight, trumpetlike horn in a dense wood gave an almost oboe sound. A singer used a wooden megaphone with various mutes to shape his vocals. There was one stringed instrument in the bass frequencies, played by slapping and plucking. It had shell inlays, but whether for decoration or tone was impossible to tell yet.

Once he got past the odd tonal qualities, Mark enjoyed it. The music was heavy with rhythm and dripping with harmonic resonance. One of the percussionists played a solo, and the singer was able to hit a strange high note, with the atmosphere, his voice box and his wooden amplifier all working together.

The Ishkul gurgled a cheer that was similar to their laugh but distinguishable. Their applause came from table slaps and castanetlike clappers. The musicians marched around the entire party, waving, pointing and swapping polite greetings.

Mark was eager to see how human music was received, especially in the modified form allowed. No metal on any of the instruments and no electronics. They were pushing it already with cameras and comms.

Petty Officer Marre Beattie, a missile tech aboard *Healy*, was a violinist. She also played it the traditional way, in wood with nylon strings. She was accompanied by a classical guitarist and a drummer playing some kind of Celtic drum, plus a harp. The sound was mellow yet striking. Her outfit was the same way; bodice, blouse, skirt that was stylistically ancient but still contemporary.

The Ishkul seemed fascinated by bowed strings. They were rapt as she started a lilting piece. Mark recognized it, but couldn't name it. Some sort of jig.

She really was good. Fluid, graceful, with feel for the instrument and the song. She started moving, stepping around the venue, a high-booted foot on a chair, then springing over to Vlashn's table, the pace of the tune accelerating, galloping. She swept through the chorus and began a solo over the guitar and harp, while the percussionist tried gamely to keep up.

The Ishkul watched in fascination, talking and pointing, while one of their musicians edged over to the table.

Russ said, "The Ishkul drummer asked if it was acceptable to ask if he might join in. I told him he could proceed."

"Excellent," Mark said.

Indeed. To have something both cultures could share was an important and exciting step.

Beattie was at full tilt now, stepping one foot on the table, bow arm flying while her fingers danced on the strings, her thick, red hair broken loose from its band and waving as she played, her bright smile morphing into a rictus that was part grin, part focus.

With a flourish, she reached a crescendo. She, the harpist, drummer and the Ishkul percussionist all hit the same beat and jarred to a perfectly timed stop.

This time, both races cheered and applauded.

The combined ushers/maitre d's wrapped things up with gracious comments after a div, three hours. It was clear some of both races would linger and socialize informally, but many had duties awaiting. Mark wound up leaving with Stephens and McDonald, with Zihn not far behind.

"That was certainly an interesting cultural item," Zihn commented as he caught up. He looked mildly nonplussed.

"Clearly a predatory origin," Mark said. "We knew that, of course."

"Still, very graphic in practice," Stephens said. "I don't approve at all. Kill the beast quickly and be done with it. Though I wonder if the blood feast is akin to the Masai practice. It allows high protein without killing the animal. What we were seeing could be a combination of evolutionary behaviors. The biologists will be all over this." Her expression was neutral, but with a sour hint.

"Agreed," Zihn said. "I'll stick to stellar devolution and planetary development."

McDonald said, "Still, our food was tasty, and I gained a new appreciation of it. I also now grasp what 'fresh' means." His expression was part smile, part distaste.

"Indeed," Mark said. "I expect to be busy tomorrow, with more findings. Keep me in the loop. Good evening, folks." He waved and wandered into his bungalow, as he'd taken to calling it. Not a palace, merely a bungalow.

He woke early, to shouts and chants. They were familiar, and not hostile. It took him a moment to identify them.

Baseball? he wondered.

Yes. A glance out the window showed two mixed teams of humans and Ishkul playing baseball. A resounding crack indicated a clean hit. The natives apparently learned quickly.

The Ishkul running gait was bizarre. It looked sort of like a cat running upright, sort of like a wobbling bird, and very ungainly. However, it was quite fast. The runner reached first base easily. The lower gravity meant balls flew a long way.

The second one shattered the bat.

In moments, players of both species huddled around, conferring. Mark pulled on pants and ambled out and over, and caught the end of the conversation. The Ishkul were surprised at the breakage, good stout hickory, but offered to replace it with a stronger wood of similar density. The game resumed with another bat, this one polymer.

Mark kept a glance out the window all morning. After baseball, they switched to an Ishkul game which he learned translated as "catch the rock." It was reminiscent of rugby and dodgeball, and had no boundaries. Scoring was based on distance traveled, not any set goals. Teams changed as the game played. It also seemed to have evolving rules as it went on. It looked like a lot of fun if one didn't mind an occasional bruise.

He needed more intel before offering anything. There wasn't a good way to do so, though. He was developing an appreciation for the difficulties earlier explorers faced. They at least had a commonality of species. The Ishkul were different. How different, he didn't yet know.

On his desk, an update from Captain Betang flashed for attention. He opened it, read, and nodded. The military were giving an assist. Incoming vessels would be queued, required to clear a UN inspection to ensure they had no military weapons, assigned parking slots far back, to "avoid alarming our native hosts," then cleared one at a time, without hindrance, other than delay, by Freehold traffic control.

From there they would be passed back to the UN, for its extensive adminwork, referencing, acknowledgment of policies and rules for dealing with the UN and the natives. Any complaints went back through the UN, back to Captain Betang, then through Shraybman, finally to Mark. By then, most of the inquiries would be approved anyway. Shraybman had designated "Ms" Thomas to field the post complaints, apologize with a form statement, remind the complainant that they were allowed in so there was no real issue, and politely tell them to kiss off.

The end result was that no one would even be able to ask for a landing slot for fifteen days or so, at which point Landing Control would stall them another day. Before being allowed aboard the Freehold military lander they'd be inspected for metals, technology and purpose. Mark would have to do nothing. If he had no objections they were proceeding with this plan.

He was tempted to ask for a detailed explanation, which he would approve in five or six days, but decided he should look like the good guy. Instead, he sent a message that while he found the delays unfortunate, the safety of the locals and the diplomatic mission was his highest priority, do please continue as you have planned, then added commendations for the quick thinking and implementation.

The press were going to scream.

CHAPTER 8

That afternoon, Mark sat listening to the scientists. He didn't follow more than a quarter of the discussion, but he was building a picture from it. The new information, after the banquet, caused a revision in the social concept of the Ishkul.

While he pondered that himself, Shraybman came over and whispered quietly. "Update on screen. You need to see it."

"Understood," he muttered back. With a nod to the staff, he made his way to the secured and screened terminal.

The officer on screen said, "Citizen Ballenger, I'm Senior Sergeant Ahern, communications intelligence. We've got a radio squeal from mid-continent, about three hundred kilometers from you."

"One of ours, right?" he asked.

"Yes."

"That's good and bad. At least I know it's not the locals."

"It's a Dash Fifteen, last generation. Surplus sale, most likely."

"How did it get there?"

"I'm working on that now. It's barely possible someone hiked from your location, though they'd have to be balls out Olympians to do it."

"I account for everyone here every evening." For exactly that reason.

"Right. So they landed. I'm working with orbital recon to find any evidence. The problem is, we're neither an intel boat nor an orbital station. There are two techs here with the training, and we'll have to make do with the sensors we have."

"Meantime, I need to arrange a response. I don't have a lot of troops, though."

"We have some Mobile Assault troops, of course. You'd have to discuss that with the captain."

"Right. Let me check with people down here. Please funnel additional intel to this terminal."

"Understood, sir. Ahern out."

With that gem of intel in mind, he went to meet with Ambassador Russ.

As he passed back into the lab, he heard an exchange that made him chuckle.

One of the social scientists said, "I would say that when a technology transfer takes place, it should be limited to raw materials. Allow them to develop the production and distribution. It will slow things down. We don't want to create a competitive, exploitative system among a gentle race."

" 'Gentle'? We just watched them sushify a whole cow!"

"I'm told by paleobio and paleopsych that that's indic-ative of a fossil pack hunting mentality. Normally, the meat is killed well ahead of time. That technique is reserved for banquets and formal events, as fresh sushi—from live fish—was for the Japanese."

"Which ended around four centuries ago."

"Hardly a noticeable amount of time. So far, we're estimating the age of this technological growth at ten thousand years. They developed practical lithic tools about the same time we did, they're just progressing slower without the jumps that bronze and iron brought."

"All that aside," Mark cut in, "we're conceding that technology transfer will take place?" The two looked at him, obviously surprised and nervous about being moni-tored by the Citizen, and fumbled for responses.

"We can't stop it," Russ said with a grimace as he came over. "I don't like it, but at least one UN development company is now in the mix. It's going to happen. We can only hope to retain control of the process. So the 'information wants to be free' twits are right in this case."

"Not really," Mark said. "It's going to be paid for, one way or another. We'll need to make it cost effective enough that the Ishkul prefer to deal with our official source, and expensive enough at the other end that out-side operations are reluctant to risk the capital." He saw McDonald coming over and gestured to him.

"That's all yours," Russ said. "I'd have no idea how to negotiate that."

"Whereas I have a background in it. Still, it's going to take time."

"We're running out of that," someone said.

"I can't get away from that."

"Culturally, I'm reassured," McDonald said. "Their leadership is cautious as well, for the same reason. Their diverse tech level among the various groups works in our favor. They already have a background in this."

"Yeah. Nurin, I need to talk to you for a moment." He waved his counterpart to a corner.

After he summarized the unauthorized landing, Russ looked very perturbed. "What next, then?"

"They're using our surplus radio gear. They're probably our people. However, to avoid arguments over whether or not they should be there, I'd like to send some of your troops to get them."

"Fair enough. I can ask for some Marines. We have a few extra on board."

"More than complement?"

"Yes. *Aracaju* was taking the Marine Rugby Team to a match, when we got the call."

Mark smiled. "Sounds like just the people we need." Then he added, "Which UN company is involved?"

"ExtraSolar Ores."

"I'm familiar with them. Rather conservative, and openly friendly to the government. I gather they're less so when not on the spot?"

"Four hundred years, Mark. They didn't last that long by being timid."

"Got it. Keep me up to date, please."

"I will."

He just turned around when McDonald called, "Citizen, how are you at handling shocks?"

"That depends on how much of a shock I'm in for, in light of all the recent ones." He waited for Land's revelation.

"They have steam power."

He said nothing, just pondered for long moments. "How?"

"Plastic or ceramic at a guess. They potentially could manage either. They have limited rail and limited steamships. They mostly use the steam upstream and uphill, relying on gravity and flow the other way. The efficiency can't be great. No better than that of 1840s Earth."

"Which is still four *thousand* years better than Earth stone workers."

"I think we need to look past the material to the technical development. Even in the Iron Age, most construction and tools were wood. Iron was only used for cutting edges. Stone is inadequate by comparison, but it did suffice for half a million years."

"Let me know if you find rockets."

"That's barely feasible. Jet engines are, too."

"You're kidding."

"I wish I was."

"I don't want to know. I'll stop joking."

Shraybman rushed in, "Ego wants another meeting. He says there are new considerations in the tech level."

Mark snapped, "Tell Egan I'm watching that develop right now and I'll let him know as soon as we've considered it, and hear his request."

When Connor called and said, "We have another unauthorized landing in the archipelago down south," he wanted to explode.

"Who?"

"Unknown."

"Dammit, find out. Get someone on them fast. I don't want to kill natives, I can't kill our people, but someone needs an ass kicking in the worst way." Damn, people were determined to piss him off. If they'd just sit down and wait . . .

"I'll let the captain know. She'll get on it."

"Fine."

It took him a moment to realize the captain in question was Captain Jelling, not Captain Betang on the *Healy*. Then he remembered her background, and her father. Her real name was "Chinran." The Earth contingent could never be allowed to know that.

"Tell her to use discretion. A lot of discretion. The kind of discretion I'd use."

Connor almost smiled. "I'll relay the information, sir."

"Lieutenant Shrayb—that was quick," he said as she arrived again.

"What do you need, sir?"

"Look, you're public affairs, but you're rapidly becoming liaison and advisor, too. Are you okay with that?"

"I'm a Freehold officer, sir. If I can't handle it, I'll find someone who can."

"Good. What's the likelihood that information is being funneled out of here? Bribes or interested parties?"

"I'd say it's statistically certain we have at least one. Not likely the senior scientists, they're too focused. Assistants possibly. The press might overhear things and leak. They tend to keep info close for bargaining power, but it's still possible. I hate to suspect some of the younger, or even older, troops, but money talks." Her expression was very matter-of-fact.

"How do we find this possible leak?"

"That's where I'll find someone who can. Just throw me the questions, sir. I'll get them where they go. That's part of what Public Affairs does. I have more information for you," she added.

He took a deep breath.

"Go ahead," he said.

"The first lander of press and third parties is down. That's the press we didn't bring or authorize. They're now asking for tours, appointments, et cetera."

"Tell them I'm dead. No, stress the urgency of the moment and I'll get with them as soon as possible, likely tomorrow, by which I mean to keep stalling."

"Yes, sir." She grinned, nodded and left.

Russ was waiting again, with Connor.

"I have contacted Lieutenant Senior Grade David Jetter, who's captain of the rugby team and platoon leader. He's more than happy to follow up this potential leak, and I've made introductions with Warrant Connor."

"Excellent. Warrant, I see no reason for excessive discretion as . . . wait, intel could leak both ways. Get them in silently, squash the transmitter, round up any humans, UN or Freehold or other, bring them in."

"All taken care of, sir. They're using one of their ships, so we can completely deny any knowledge."

"Good." He turned to Russ and said, "Ambassador, my nation must protest any apprehensions of any Freehold Residents, and ask that you deliver them to us immediately . . . eventually."

Russ replied, "Noted. I apologize for the misunderstanding, as I was not aware they were your Residents. Obviously, they will eventually be immediately returned to you, pursuant to an investigation to determine if their claims are true."

"After you have investigated, please furnish their IDs to me, and I will forward them for verification, which will unfortunately take time for communication back home. Unless, of course, some organization or entity will vouch for them."

"Would you care to place a bet?"

"Actually, Ambassador, I would. I bet that everyone will come clean within thirty days."

"No bet." Russ smiled.

"In the meantime, I'll have our people handle the archipelago, just to avoid any allegations of UN interference. I'll order them up now."

"I appreciate it, sir. Of course, I protest the apprehension of any UN citizens."

"If there are any, I'll let you know."

It seemed appropriate to reach over and shake hands.

"Not to interrupt the party," Shraybman put in, "but a contingent from the *American Times* and *World News* specifically want a press conference."

"Then I suppose we better hold one," Mark said. He sighed. And here he thought he'd been making progress.

"I can handle that," Russ said. "I'll speak for the combined team."

"That will also make you look more in charge," Mark said. "Do it."

"Well, we can at least have the perception."

His look wasn't exactly challenging, but was definitely intended to remind Mark that he wanted more input.

CHAPTER 9

Operative Captain Chelsea Chinran couldn't show fear, even in the approach to a suicide drop on a toxic alien planet. She had literally been born and raised in battle, as some few people knew, and even those who didn't picked up on the vibe. She was also the commander of this operation. The Old Lady couldn't show fear. End of discussion.

That made the ordeal even tougher. The insane orders around it were even worse.

Rule One, Absolutely Inviolable: No metal weapons or tools taken along. Plastic, at least, was okay, as were ceramics. That was a small improvement.

Rule One, Absolutely Inviolable: No loss of commo or other advanced gear. Personnel were expendable to secure equipment against loss. Equipment could be freely destroyed on her word if need be.

Rule One, Absolutely Inviolable: Any contact with the indigenes had to be at her instigation, only if necessary. No accidental discovery was permitted. Personnel or gear could be vaporized to maintain this security.

Rule One, Absolutely Inviolable: The only necessary reason to make contact with the indigenes was to prevent unauthorized interests—meaning the UN, any corporation, any freelancer, any missionary or anyone not bearing a coded holodoc from Citizen Ballenger—from doing so first.

There were several other Rules One, Absolutely Inviolable. Every department, operation, branch and faction had an unbreakable rule for aliens, the Ishkul specifically and this current situation. Then there were the Rules Two, Absolutely Inviolable If The Captain Wanted To Stay A Captain. Then the Rules Three, Absolutely Inviolable If The Captain Didn't Want To Be A Jackass In The History Books . . .

Her troops sweated from pre-drop fear. She sweated from fear of the bureaucracy. And while the power of a god over anything she encountered was heady, it was also sobering. She hadn't been given that much authority on a whim. Succeed in this and she'd achieve her dream of being a Special Warfare Team Commander, or even a Regimental Commander. Fail and she'd best fall on her sword.

No pressure.

It was while pondering this yet again, and seeing the red light blink to orange, presaging the drop, she realized how alive she felt.

A touch on her rear indicated everyone knew they were pending. She raised a thumb awkwardly, being swaddled in jump gear. Her abbreviated team was only ten including herself, and there were even odds of losing one of them on this insertion. She wondered who might not make it while her eyes stayed on the warning light. There wasn't much else to look at anyway. The rear of the stealth boat was cramped with the support gear needed for this jump, and the ten troops.

Gravity came back smoothly but fast as the boat maneuvered in stratosphere. *Hashashim* was rigged for atmospheric stealth, but any disruption of air could be tracked eventually. The pilot brought them in fast.

The orange light flashed twice then turned yellow, then started counting from "20" as the bay opened onto black space. It didn't count evenly, as maneuvering affected the drop point, as did improved assessments of wind. It lagged from 17 to 13, raced to 8, then slowed to a fairly steady count that seemed to take forever. The rarefied wind screamed past in a high keen.

And 3, and 2, and 1, and a thundering whuff of air blew them into nothingness.

Immediately, it was silent. She had room and darkness and the odd feeling that came with no gravity and no atmospheric pressure. Gravity gently cradled her and returned at a slow, steady rate. As it did so, the wind resumed the same way, from a whisper to a whine. There was a tiny leak in her helmet somewhere, so she closed her left eye to avoid it freezing in the incoming blast.

Could she be the one who wouldn't make it?

The air pressure increased and her fall slowed, though it was only a number in her visor. Below was dark, and the draft whipped past her, too fast to be warm even with the pressure increase and friction.

It wasn't her so far. Her visor indicated nine other lights. As long as the release didn't fail, they should all survive, though injuries up to broken spines were still possible.

They were definitely safely over the target area, though she'd chosen a larger part of the island for this, preferring a hike on the ground to a long swim at sea.

Her altimeter finally came live, estimating 9000 meters. The rushing sound deepened as they fell through high cirrus, and fell, and fell. A buffeting roar indicated high cumulus, and she checked pressure, altimeter, visual and risked a quick UV laser flash. Good. She steadied in a relaxed arch, and saw faint movement around her. At least some of the team were maintaining close proximity.

A beep in her ears indicated 2000 meters. They were falling slower here, despite the thinner atmosphere, because of the lower gravity. Thirty seconds per thousand meters should do it . . . twenty-eight seconds later, another beep indicated 1000 meters. Close. She drew her hands in slightly, not enough to affect her attitude, but a little closer to her shoulders. Then she was at 800 . . . 700 . . . 600 . . . 500 and beep . . . 400 and the dark ground rushing up in a dizzying blur, as if a giant anvil was about to swat her . . . 300, as every fiber clenched, intellect fighting the primal fear of falling . . . 200 and a muffled bang as two automatic openers popped two drogues, as she grabbed both handles at her shoulders and yanked. The unfurling, rustling, billowing fabric snatched at her, straps cutting in all over, and she glanced up to see two good round chutes. No need for the reserve, for which she'd have had about two seconds to pop.

Her altimeter showed less than 100 meters and falling. She reached down fast and cut her ruck loose, letting it slide five meters down on its rope. Then she braced for landing, still falling fast, until the ruck hit and the reduced weight slowed her just enough to slam in to a roll, as if jumping off a house.

Nine green lights. She'd survived her first suicide drop, and her team were all alive and relatively functional.

She limped up on a tingling ankle, and grinned at Sergeant Sandy Sanderson.

"I came in on reserve," he said. "Free drinks for the duration."

"And a statue to you with giant brass balls," she grinned. "Secure perimeter, cleanup and trash the evidence."

At some point, after they were both dead and deniable, she and her father would enter the history books: He for his brutally devastating attack on Earth, she for leading the first actual military mission on a non-human planet.

They needed to move fast toward their target, then get low, discreet and unseen. It took moments to peel back sod, scrape a depression, scatter dirt, toss in the canopies and an enzymic solvent to destroy them.

The good news was that backup was mere segs away, should they call. The bad news was that they couldn't call except to abort.

With that unspoken thought, her nine troops shouldered what were called "sustainment loads" and trudged into the night.

Lieutenant David Jetter, UN Marine Corps, had a marginally easier task than Chinran, even if he wasn't aware of the fact. In his case, he had a short platoon of fifteen, two squads, to effect a reconnaissance, apprehension and containment of an unknown number of humans, possibly armed, definitely with intelligence assets, in the continental middle of nowhere. He had a very extensive brief on Ishkul capabilities, and a warning that those in the area he was now flying over were probably not as technologically sophisticated, with a slim chance of them being equal or better.

Really, that didn't concern him. Numbers mattered. No matter how effective he was, the locals could slaughter his force if they decided to. Even if they couldn't, if it came to that, he'd failed.

His rules of engagement included not contacting the natives unless necessary, deferring to them while forcing any humans to leave—he had some ideas along those lines—using none or minimal force, if persuasion would suffice, and stopping any potential information transfer cold. Having space to do so, and being close enough that time wasn't as much of an issue, he elected to rappel from low level and march in. The transport they were aboard was rigged for such insertions, and quite quiet when necessary. He hoped it was enough. Ishkul society was very quiet, outside the city.

It was a hell of a war, when a former enemy asked you to attack its own civilians, and okayed the use of lethal force if necessary. The whole issue made him cringe, but the ambassador approved, and had signed off. With that on file, he was prepared to risk it.

The drop went smoothly enough, as they weren't under fire. The craft slowed, doors popped, and they hit the ropes, him last for once. Slow was quiet. Hovering took airflow. Airflow meant a very loud white roar. The result was his platoon stretched across a couple of kilometers of terrain, with him at one end. He was farthest, and would gather his men en route.

A strange engagement indeed, he thought, as the craft hissed away and he started hiking.

The first interview of the day stuck his head through the open door, with a polite knock.

"Citizen Ballenger?" the man asked. He was balding, in decent shape, with a serene and calming expression.

"I am."

"Father Dunn, of the Jesuits." He stepped in and extended his hands. Mark rose to meet him.

"Good to meet you, Father." So far, so good. The freaks were going to be far more interesting, and not in a pleasant way.

"And you, sir. You have no idea how exciting this is for us."

"I can imagine." The Jesuits had an excellent reputation for scholarship, pragmatism and faith. Though he suspected this would be a challenge even to their reputation.

"Indeed. I was told I must clear through you, and then through the Ishkul embassy?"

"Actually, this is the Freehold embassy, but Leader Vlashn has arranged for us to manage contacts through an agent."

"Very well. How may I go about that process?" Dunn seemed ready for a bureaucratic maze.

"Step next door and put your name on the list. I see no obstacle. There's a short list of issues not to discuss. They are technological, not spiritual, though you'll have to rephrase Jubal and Tubal and some other parts of Scripture to avoid metal. You must abide by that. But I must warn you, Father."

"Yes?"

"You can learn a lot from the Ishkul. But I don't think they'll be receptive to any proselytizing."

"Are you forbidding it?" Dunn didn't bristle, but did look more alert.

"Not at all. That's entirely your business. However, they seem to have very keen, very scientific, very orderly minds. They don't use any terminology that would indicate a faith or religion at all."

"That's a challenge I can only hope God makes me worthy of," Dunn said with a smile. "The Vatican is discussing the ramifications of an alien sentience. Do they have a soul? We must assume so, until it can be studied in depth. Have they heard of Christ and God? If so, it would lend great credence to both the existence of God and the immortal soul. Since they apparently have not, how will they receive the Gospel? It's a privilege to be at such a pivotal point in the history of the human race and of the Church."

Mark prickled in mild shock. Dunn spoke much the way Vlashn did, in precise but analog gradations.

"I'll be watching with interest, Father," he said. "I certainly appreciate your enthusiasm and how exciting it is in that perspective."

"And I thank you for your gracious cooperation," Dunn replied with slight bow. "May God bless and keep you." He turned to leave.

"Thank you, Father," Mark replied. Well, at least the Catholic Church wasn't posing the problem of some other outfits. Though he did wonder at the reaction there'd be.

He had a little time before the next bunch. He spent it reviewing McDonald's summary of new findings. A test on a graciously traded Ishkul torso armor had shown it would withstand most heavy bow and crossbow fire, stone pellets from slings, spear thrusts or throws and even light pistol fire. Twentieth-century technology. He made a note to ask what the natives thought of human body armor. It was far more resistant to impact.

So far the native technology ranged from an extreme of sixteenth-century to early twentieth, most of it in the range of 1820–1880. Very impressive, and still the study of much debate.

He had digested a page of summary when his next supplicant arrived.

She opened the door and leaned in, a grinning smile on her face. He vaguely knew the name of Bernadette Chavez. She was involved in a lot of low-scale, largely irrelevant causes. He'd never met her.

"Please come in," he said, and rose. She went for a slight bow, so he did, too. He was going to be giving her bad news, so he may as well be as polite as possible.

Her appearance indicated she didn't move much in high circles. She wore a snug pair of pants, stylishly heavy boots and had a sort of tunic over it. It wasn't business wear, but was obviously not casual, either. It seemed to be an attempt at individuality that said almost nothing.

"Thank you for seeing me," she smiled.

"It's my privilege to serve Freehold Residents in system, our interests, and those of our new friends," he said. "How can I help you?"

"If I can be brief and blunt, Citizen, we—my group, and others we represent legally and in moral position —are worried by HMG's obvious intent to exploit the Ishkuls for technology."

"That's a concern of everyone here. I'm in constant discussion with the UN ambassador and our joint scientific outfit, and have military force at my disposal if diplomacy fails."

"Yes," she said with obvious distaste. "Governments always feel the need to resort to military force. What we want to propose is far less harmful."

He had a general idea of her proposal, and figured it was either harmful or useless or both. However, the longer he could keep them talking, the longer it would be before they did anything. Such people loved to talk, "start dialogs," endlessly.

"Can you summarize? We can always use more ideas." He didn't let his own distaste show.

"Obviously, the solution is to give the Ishkuls the technology in question, free of charge. This avoids any need for dispute or violence, will put them on an economic par with humanity, and prevents any economic exploitation."

On the one hand, it would be a good thing if the Ishkul had foreknowledge of the depth of their bargaining position. They had an entire star system to negotiate with and for. At the same time, these whackjobs didn't care about any negative effects, as long as HMG and its ilk got screwed.

"I follow the idea," he said, "and we've discussed similar things here as backup to our primary idea of exploring the limits of Ishkul technology and then allowing them to determine which technological courses they want to pursue. At that point, we will certainly encourage them to seek out the best deal for transfer of knowledge, based on their own cultural needs."

He took a slow, deep breath after that response. He could do this as much as needed, but he did have other things to do.

"I expected that to be the official position, sir," she said. "However, I'm hoping we can persuade you that a new, nontraditional approach is needed. This is a new situation, and standard methods are not going to resolve it, believe me. These are a people who need, deserve to be our equals, not economic slaves. Someone has to make the decisions for them at this point."

"I understand your concerns, Ms Chavez," *you elitist bitch*, "but the Freehold government is limited in our ability to interfere. The Ishkul will have to make the decision themselves, though we will ensure they have as much information as possible first. That's why this matter is taking so long. Also, the UN is offering its own guidance. They have more experience in providing a level of external equality, as you know." Goddess, that sounded condescending as hell. *Bet she loves it.*

"I already spoke once to Ambassador Russ," she said with a frown. "I had hoped he'd be more helpful, but the government is, if I can say so, firmly in the pockets of the corporate estate."

The amusing thing was, she was correct about Earth. It was improving, but the war had struck it a cultural blow. For centuries, it had been an increasingly fascistic state. The more laws one passed to control corporations, the more loopholes they found, the more influence they bought and peddled, and the more they exploited it as yet another means of competition.

"I'm certainly following that, and it's of concern to us." Dammit, he was mimicking her collective we, "And we'll do all we can."

"Thank you, Citizen." She smiled that near-grin again. "When do you think I'll be able to present our position to the Ishkuls' delegation?"

"That should properly go through the UN first. I tend to approve most things they suggest. I'm titular head simply for conflict resolution."

"Ambassador Russ said I had to see you."

"I see," he said. He knew that, of course. "Then I will schedule you to present your ideas to our social science section. They're keenly aware of the risk of exploitation of various types. They'll be glad to help."

"That's not what I was hoping to hear," she hinted.

"Of course. Everyone wants this to move fast, and there are good reasons it should. However, there are other reasons it can't. I'll certainly follow the advice of the scientists, though," he said as he rose. "Along which, I'm meeting with them in a few segs. I'll make sure they're aware of your presence. If you'll excuse me?"

He ushered her out despite her squawks. Yeah, the social scientists. Some of them agreed with her. The only saving grace was that they were more circumspect, and of course that McDonald had final say over their actions. Hopefully, they could delay her a week with daily section meetings, then warn her heavily about restrictions and have her write proposals to be approved for a few more days. With luck, it would all be moot by then.

His next applicant was waiting. He was bearded, robed, wore earrings and carried a staff with a small animal skull attached. He rose and met Mark at the door as Chavez left fuming.

"Citizen. Pleased to meet you. I bring greetings and hallucinations on behalf of the Church of the Sub-Genius."

"The Church of the SubGenius?" Mark asked, trying not to sound incredulous. He'd never heard of them. He ushered the man in, moved to his desk and quickly brought up a summary file.

"I am Shaman Lo Thing, Exalted Speaker for J.R. 'Bob' Dobbs, Lord of Slack and Derider of Pinks. The

Church is the Spazz movement of Brilliance against the decay of normalcy and boredom." He struck a dramatic pose while sitting.

Mark could read fast and doubletrack his attention. He'd reached the end of a page-long summary of the Church as Lo Thing finished his piece.

"You'll pardon me if it sounds as if your sole purpose here is to mock everyone and every group, with no respect for faith, diplomacy or culture."

"Why, thank you, sir!" Lo Thing beamed and pulled back his hood. It looked as if he was wearing a basic casual tunic underneath. His staff was obviously home-made and rather crude.

"I don't have any way to stop you. I do intend to inform our host of your intent. However, I think an old-fashioned court jester might be just the thing to make certain parties take themselves less seriously." He grinned.

"Excellent, Citizen. I shall retire to my excremeditation chamber. Praise Bob."

At least that nutjob knew he was a nutjob and enjoyed it for itself.

After that, Mark was supposed to actually get to that meeting with the social scientists, but he took a moment to call Shraybman.

"Irina, I hate to pile more work on you, but is there any way to filter out a few more of these nutjobs?"

"I have been, sir."

"Really?"

"Oh, yes. There was one guy with a set of Tesla coils and a Van de Graaff generator, prepared to show the primitives lightning and declare himself their god. Apparently, no one has bothered to do enough research to find out what the Ishkul myths are."

"Including us," he said, suddenly disturbed. "I'll note that. Okay, that's a nutjob."

"At least he had bigger goals and a plan. One guy showed me his pocket lighter. The traditional sparking flint type used for cigars and pipes. He was going to declare himself Prometheus by showing them his magic firemaker."

Mark said nothing for several seconds. Finally, he uttered, "Wow." There was nothing more to say.

"Indeed. Spamway marketing reps wanted to talk to them. They even agreed to sell only nonelement goods. Insurance salesmen, even offering culture shock protection. Ten or so really weird cults offering all kinds of enlightenment. I ruled them out because they expect fees. If they can't underwrite their own expenses, they can't afford to sue."

"I apologize for doubting you. You have my sympathy."

"Can I have your booze?"

"If you run out, by all means." He nodded.

"Someone has already started Radio Free Ishkul on 'pirate satellite.' They don't seem to comprehend there are no radio receivers."

"They might not care. I've met that type." Now he shook his head.

"That's possible," she said, seeming to consider it. "We also have drug sellers, both medicinal and recreational, demanding to know the biochemistry so they can start tailoring pharmaceuticals. Sir, do you really want to hear all this?"

"I'd love to hear every detail to cheer me up, but I probably should not waste time on it. Save the good ones for when I'm depressed. How are we keeping them under control?"

"Three gunboats and regular communication with Captain Betang. He deserves a medal."

"You all do."

"How about half a percent of any final deal we—"

He cut her off with a grin. "Get out."

He found the firemaker most amusing. The Ishkul had fire pistons and chemical matches. Fire pistons had existed on Earth, and he was stunned at the sophistication that Indonesian primitives had displayed. Given that, a lighter would be a novelty only. Some of the others were as potentially bad as HMG.

HMG, though, had billions of credits and an endless supply of greed, cheap labor and negotiable morals.

At least all the visitors were at his sufferance, and billeted in crude shacks at the back of the compound, where the military could keep a close eye on them. If he had to deal with them, at least he had them corralled.

CHAPTER 10

Because of the need to get scientific information, and have expert eyes on site, Mark wasn't on the first trip to the nearby city. He spent days juggling social matters. It was close to a week before he got on a tour. He, an armed guard, and Russ and one of his escorts flew in together. The security detail screamed at the idea, but accepted his decision. They wanted tours of twenty or more, half of them military. That wasn't diplomatic. Nor was there any indication so far that the Ishkul would try anything dishonest, even if they didn't respect their new neighbors' technology. Not that Mark thought it would come to that, even on the off chance something went wrong. The situation was too valuable to waste for the death of one mere Citizen or ambassador.

He intellectually had no concerns, but still a lot of trepidation when he and his alert, polite but taciturn escort, an Operative whose name was irrelevant, being fake, and unnecessary, being the only one along, debarked to a waiting Somle and her small entourage. When the craft lifted and dopplered away, he felt a shiver.

Somle watched the vertol briefly, and the other Ishkul paid quite close attention. They seemed curious and impressed, but not awed. Of course, without more study of their body language, he might be imbuing a lot of human response to what he saw.

"Greeting, Mark," Somle said, hand extended. He shook it.

"Good morning, Somle."

"Greeting, Nurin." He noted she bowed in Earth fashion, as nearly as her skeleton allowed.

"These are my staff, I introduce as a courtesy. You are not expected to give significant attention to them, as our business is to present our citylode to you." Mark snickered quietly at the blatant but refreshing disclaimer, made a point to surreptitiously punch their names into the translator by task so they could be addressed, and shook hands.

After the round, Somle said, "It is our hoped expectation that you find our citylode most interesting and informative."

"I'm certain I will. It's bound to be different from anything in human space."

"I didn't parse that phrase through the translator. It sounded as if you said our citylode is restrained."

"Sorry, the translator mixed up a word. Your city will be different from any I've seen before. We're eager to start."

"Very eager," Nurin said. "It's a privilege."

"Please follow me, then. I have arranged intermediate transport." She gestured in a way that was almost human, almost bird and almost feline.

The vehicle was a well-constructed wooden carriage, with an awning. The wheel trucks pivoted, were sprung, and the whole thing was drawn by four draft beasts. He stared at them in fascination. They were vaguely bird-reptilian, lean, whiplike, clearly bred for speed and strength. He'd be surprised if they were good for anything other than hauling a carriage on finished roads. Definitely selectively bred, and definitely related to the slaughtered animal of the feast. He stepped up, settled onto a couch, which seemed to face the wrong way, but he recalled the stance the Ishkul used. He stood, straddled it and leaned back to get as comfortable as possible.

Once she reclined, Somle spoke to the driver, who yanked a bridle. The beasts moved from walk to trot to smooth run in seconds. The vehicle was comfortable, too. Nothing comparable had been developed on Earth. He made a note to have someone dig up plans of Earth animal-drawn carriages and let the Ishkul feel good about the accomplishment.

The industrial section of "Ishkuhama," as the humans had taken to calling it, was staggering.

Mark had seen it from orbit. Up close, it wasn't just impressive, it was amazing. He figured there could be huge money in tourism, partly for the sheer scale, and partly for the sophisticated low-tech approach.

The tour started upstream, where billions of liters of water were diverted through four large canals, two on each side. At least half the river flow roared through the concrete lined troughs, which also supported a large timbered bridge, sunk into concrete pilings. Some of the main beams were near sixty meters long, all one trunk.

From there, the water split into a variety of tanks, reservoirs and depressions, which fed smaller canals and aqueducts. Another series of pipes fed down and across, offering running water for the residents. It did bear a passing resemblance to ancient Rome, and to nineteenth-century London, with an odd mix of blocky industry and fairy architecture.

Mark wrote discreet notes as he went, avoiding talk that could be recorded by the engineered parrot creatures. His communication with Russ was limited to discreet nonverbal expressions and surreptitious signs on paper.

Massive vitreous pipes indicated an advanced ceramic industry. There was plumbing, with ceramic valves gasketed with rubber or fiber. Earth's Iron Age had been predominantly a wood age, with iron the means to shape it. This culture had refined ceramic, stone and water power to a high art. They used a lot of timber, but not as much as they did ceramic. Somewhere there was a factory, several factories, that produced ceramic pipe and brick.

Rafts and barges came down river, and logs, reminiscent of the era of the California sawmill. Ishkul loggers leapt nimbly over them, poking and pulling with pikes, steering the timber into holding ponds.

He realized he didn't dare ask questions, as he had only vague ideas about the Stone Age methods of splitting or sawing lumber. He simply said, "Very impressive. We have similar resources, but not many rivers mighty enough for this."

Somle led him inside. "This is the largest mill for hardwood processing on this continent," she said, gesturing through a doorway designed to take large wagons.

A manager was waiting for them. *The* manager, it turned out. He was introduced as "Factory Operation Leader Twul." He had apparently been coached. He extended a hand and let Mark control the shake, and bowed badly to Russ.

"Greeting, honored guests," he said. "It is my (unique?) pleasure to guide you in my well-regarded facility."

"We are very excited to see it," Russ said. "Do please show us anything you like."

Twul gave an odd expression for a moment, as he heard the translation. Once over that apparent novelty, he gestured and led the way to an elevator. It was an open cage, probably water driven, but smooth and reliable. That led them to a long mezzanine overlooking the labor below.

It wasn't dark in the huge building, but the light was limited. Huge windows across from them let it splash down onto the work floor. The "dark" areas of shadow were not that dark, just lit indirectly from the other side. There were some limited gas lights run from cylinders. Mark wanted to see one up close, assuming them to be some kind of ceramic or plastic.

Noisy hydraulic power ruled. Large rams carved from whole logs with ceramic wedges mounted on their ends were in use to split entire trunks. The sections landed in huge nets, rolled down and into troughs filled with cast ceramic bearings. They were split again, crossgrain, into fairly standard sizes. Shouts and work songs chuckled through the translator, half-heard and half-lost, and timed gongs added to the cacophony of cracking logs and shrieking splits, the hiss of steam and hydraulic pressure, with an overall din of feet, bearings, rumbling mass.

Crews of workers, both male and female, sweated and cursed, lifting split sections into place where more rams, gear driven by water power, could shove them through shavers lined with sharp stone, doing the reverse of broach cutting, turning out finished planks and beams.

From their observation gallery, he could see the whole process, with the river a tumble of white outside open windows. The workers glanced up occasionally, but kept their attention on their tasks. They likely couldn't see much from that angle, and failure to concentrate could easily get someone killed in that massive maelstrom of machinery.

"Climate control," Russ commented.

Air conditioning? Yes, it was cooler than he expected. Mark looked and saw ducts, but the air was treated, not just ventilated. The heat pumps must be water driven. He'd follow up on that.

As to the industry, it really did resemble nineteenth—and early twentieth-century factories. The scaffoldings and mezzanines were of solid timbers, pegged and mitered. The building was more timber with a dressed stone foundation.

"I see the shavings are being collected. Where do those go?" he asked Twul.

"Residue is processed to alcohol, cellulose fiber and also used as fuel for processes. Limb trimmings are pro-cessed into carbon for additional production and as fuel."

"Excellent. I am impressed."

"As am I," Russ agreed.

"I think we'd find it hard to make any improvements to this operation. It's very modern." That was literally true. It was far ahead of any comparable human factory.

"I strongly appreciate the compliment from your very distant and effectively unbiased viewpoint," Twul replied.

Very efficient indeed. It would be necessary to define terms. Neolithic wasn't correct, but they didn't refine metal. Ceramic age? Non-metal industrial age? Whatever it was to be called, it was sophisticated, technical and efficient. Technolithic. Subject to discussion he was coining the term.

Mark realized it was critical not to contaminate its development. The knowledge available, about the development of science and society, might be a "soft" science, but was essential and valuable. Also, such a highly developed culture would crash hard, once it realized it had taken a "wrong" detour of several thousand years.

There was also the slim possibility they might bypass metal completely. That was too fascinating and valuable to risk. HMG and DSR had to be kept out of here indefinitely. How, though?

Somle interrupted his musing with, "I will show you a sample of the mass transport systems that evolved and were developed for transport of massive and/or bulky goods, in order to considerably increase the efficiency of production delivery over that of carts drawn by draft animals."

"Please," he agreed.

She turned and said, "Host Twul, we are very grateful for the tour. Apologies for hurrying quickly away. This is due to other commitments."

"I understand and concur," he replied. "It has been a unique experience for my life and I also am very grateful."

Somle led them down a long stairway with landings at various catwalks, which allowed maintenance of the drive shafts. The factory was noisy, but in a far different way from any human operation. It had to sound like the larger mills of the 1800s, before steam power or electricity. Mark wondered how often the shafts needed to be replaced, but human mills had run that way for almost a thousand years. Even the economy of scale wouldn't be a problem. Entire forests came down that river.

He asked Somle, "Do you have any idea how long the timber will last in this area?"

"The relevant committees continually review production needs and direct an appropriate amount of seedlings to be planted."

"Excellent. Our cultures developed that eventually, but it took some time."

"I deduce that your technoculture developed at a faster rate, with less time to collate and consider ramifications of developmental philosophy. I remain curious as to the agents and instruments of that technical progress."

"We will certainly take guests to our planets and demonstrate our different technology. In exchange, I believe we can learn culturally from your generally very mature views on philosophy." Goddess, that sounded like a political speech. Ugh. He'd managed to avoid the question, though.

Still, he was eager to see their rail, which apparently had some kind of motive power.

He checked that his necklace-mounted camera had a clear view. Russ's camera was mounted to his collar. They'd have a lot of images to compare and share.

"We will wait here," she said, and pointed.

Mark looked at the indicated area and felt something punch him. He tried to cover a massive adrenaline dump, hot, cold, electric and neural shock.

Log rails, pegged on sleepers. That wasn't too strange. Railed wagons were an easy development across rough terrain, or from rutted roads. The approaching vehicle, though, had a mechanical sound. Intellectually, he knew they had this technology. Seeing it, though . . .

How in the hell did they develop steam?

"We have similar vehicles," Russ said. "A practical and efficient means of transport on the surface. Far more economical of fuel than air travel," he offered.

"I assume from your comments you are familiar with the physics of gas pressure of vapor phase water."

Mark said, "Steam power, yes. We use it extensively, but I am not a physicist. I can recognize it but not calculate it." That wasn't quite true, and he really wanted to see this contraption. He tried not to stare. He caught Russ's eyes and saw the same expression he must have.

It was vital not to let any tech slip to the Ishkul. Any thought past the short term made that obvious. They had millennia of refinement in philosophy and science and would jump on new technology, conceivably surpassing humans in a short time.

Even below that, Mark recalled how a Dutch trader had sold a few matchlocks to the Medieval Japanese for an exorbitant sum. A year later, most of Japan was equipped thusly, after reverse engineering. The Dutch did not have the last laugh.

As it approached, he could see the functional similarity to Earth steam engines was amazing: Eight spoked wheels cut to straddle the rails, two large two-stage pistons carved from whole trunks, bound with shrunken leather and cord for reinforcement and glazed in resin, a boiler and firebox of some mix of bakelite and ceramic. A Stone Age steam engine. The boiler was small and the cylinders probably couldn't hold the pressure of the later Earth engines, but it was sophisticated enough. His guess as to efficiency was confirmed when it didn't stop. A chute mounted over the track dropped several tons of wood chips into open-topped cars. Those cars had doors on the bottom, presumably to drop the load somewhere else. Obviously, they preferred not to stop if they didn't have to. That was likely due to a low torque level, the small boiler and a desire not to wear the tracks with changing friction.

Crew swarmed over the eleven cars, pausing to stare curiously at them. Obviously, they'd been told humans would be in the area, but they wanted to see. He stared back and raised an open hand of greeting. Some grinned and returned the gesture.

Next downstream was an operation producing ceramic blades—cast vitreouslike porcelain, and ground obsidian and quartzite.

Somle said, "There are issues specific to axe heads. First is the grain of the working material. Then the angle of bevel changes in a generally predictable way based on that grain and density. Of course, some are sold for the aesthetics of that grain. Those are marked thusly." She pointed at a bin full of gorgeously variegated colored stone blades. "Our failure rate is typically about three percent with current materials and methods, though the vein we are using is playing out and we will need to relocate the factory soon. That brings a variety of economic and social issues into play."

"I can see that," he said. They had started as agrarian migrants and still were, to an extent. Villages, factories, even entire cities moved across the landscape, leaving rich archeological troves. Archeotourism could be huge here, in fact.

"Your failure rate is very low and I am impressed. How long does an axe last? Your stone and wood differ from ours," he said, lying truthfully.

He was led out behind the facility to see some tests.

The ceramic was capable of far more abuse than he would have expected. Granted, even a primitive steel axe would cut an entire tree, with periodic sharpening, but one head lasted through an entire trunk. It seemed to take two or three ceramic heads for a thigh-sized trunk. The resultant chipping was sudden. First a nick, then failure. But it might be salvaged and sharpened, he thought. He assumed they burned most timber down to save wear and tear.

Stone axes were used to trim smaller branches, and of course, ceramic saws and hardwood wedges were used for a lot of splitting. Certainly the work looked to be on par with what he'd seen of native village recreations in human society. As good as anything up through the age of steam.

Still, geography dictated their civilization. Power required streams, transport required rivers. It was more efficient to work the material on site, and ship only finished goods, rather than transport raw product, fabricate it and ship it again.

The less power needed for the industry, the farther downstream it was, as the massive head pressure dropped from use. The next facility cast and formed vessels for chemical industries. The outside was bakelite, as he'd deduced, reinforced with shrunken hide and wooden braces. Any boilers tended to be fire tubes. Then there was the glass . . .

Lovely clear quartzite glass for various low-pressure processes. Here charcoal from the residual wood, and assorted tarry oils were fired in furnaces. The glass was extruded by gravity, blown by machine and hand, and cast in coated ceramic forms. Marguerite Stephens was going to be ecstatic. It was at least nineteenth-century Earth technology, possibly twentieth, and all without metal. The treatises to be written would keep a platoon of technohistorians busy for decades.

Last was the distillation plant, running alcohols, petroleum and coal and wood esters in three different lines. The stuff was decanted into ceramic or resin-lined wooden barrels, for loading on barges, trains or wagons. Like modern human facilities, it ran nonstop for efficiency.

Several meters from where he watched, shouts rose to a warning level, and there was a loud *crack*! One of the vessels burst; its contents sprayed and washed across the floor, then ignited in a low fire.

He watched in fascinated interest as crew ran up with cylinders, upended them and sprayed pressurized liquid. What had early extinguishers used? Soda acid? That fit. He assumed there was some bonding chemical to render the liquid less flammable. Soap?

"Good response," he said. "How often do you lose a vessel?"

"I recall from recent generalized reports it averages one per day and a third fraction."

Ouch. That would keep the economy moving. Still, he recalled that Industrial Age factories had similar problems with tracks, drive belts, gears, etc.

Mark was surprised at the time. More than three divs, ten hours had gone by. He'd forgotten to eat. In that time, he'd had a cursory view of one track of industry of one side of one canal. There were at least ten others running through this upper industrial area, and another low-power section downstream of the town.

Their wagon awaited, under one of the tall viaducts that brought water this far for plumbing.

As they took a road up past the factories, he saw another clever adaptation—a circuit of track with open containers for charcoal, drums and crates. It stopped at each factory downhill, where cargo was removed, and the mass coming down also drew the empties back uphill. It wasn't fast, but it was free as far as operating costs went.

Somle said, "You should give serious consideration to landing your craft inside the city, closer to your desired destination. While your care is appreciated, our people are not generally so excitable as to be fearful, now that information has been released regarding your presence."

That raised a question of where the Ishkul press were. He hadn't seen any specific reporters or documentarians since the first couple of days and the party. He had seen printed documents, though.

Instead, he replied, "We prefer to avoid any potential risks. Someone running nearby could get hurt, and the impression could be bad. Besides, it gives me more time to observe your culture in overview, and I can collate my notes before I have to submit them to be ridiculed by the scientists."

She glugged at the joke. "Nor do we mind. The offer was for your benefit. Your reasoning is rather sound, if rather cautious."

They parted at the marked perimeter, and Mark ensured the draft animals were well clear of the area before he authorized departure. He spent most of the short flight draining fluid, then rehydrating. An entire day, and he'd forgotten to do anything except watch. He didn't even have much in the way of notes.

The flight was only a few kilometers, but that distance created a safe zone since there were no roads in that direction. It was a hard concept for the Earth people, but familiar to anyone from elsewhere. The Ishkul population was within a close order of that of the Freehold, about three hundred million worldwide, with similar unsettled tracts.

Upon debarking, he headed directly for the embassy, as the primary dipped toward the western horizon. The guard detail awaited, and he drew out his ID as a formality.

The outer guard was largely for show; he was waved right in. Their main purpose was to ensure no Ishkul ever got inside to see even this detechnologized facility, even if it meant destroying several million credits worth of equipment. It was all mined, and the guard had controls to detonate if needed. The berm wasn't so much defensive as a visual block and containment. Mark and Russ had graciously invited Margov and Egan to set up their quarters in one corner, close together so they could spy on each other, far away from the research facilities and farther away from the embassy, with guards on constant watch. Those inner guards had orders to kill as necessary. The press quarters were tents in the other far corner. No one was to be comfortable, just sheltered. It encouraged them to stay in space.

Inside, he tossed his camera to a commo tech, who plugged it in and started pulling files. Three intel techs, three photo techs including Louise Thomas, and a variety of analysts, scientists and military sat around a table with a holotank in the middle and monitors at each station.

There weren't enough monitors, and people crowded them. Russ was already here, and Stephens came in right behind him. The mass of bodies raised the temperature and humidity to an uncomfortable level.

He came in in mid conversation.

"—Yes, they've chosen timber from all over the planet, selectively bred it to improve various traits and straighten it, as well as improve the growth rates. They've got species and strains for structural use, vehicle springs, wear resistant varieties for shafts, for barrels and other containers, water resistance. There's a fortune in research and knowledge here, and I suspect they could export a lot of it for both the exotic factor and for its utility. Certainly we won't need to bring any materials in system for normal construction."

"I saw the production factory," Mark commented. The researcher didn't seem to hear him, and continued enthusiastically.

"Spider silk analog, various plant fibers and bacterial grown polymer chains. They have protective clothing that could be ballistic armor. That body armor their warriors wear is layered ceramic and plastic with a silk type binding."

Another said, "Chemically, they produce detergents, nitrate fertilizers, alcohol for drinking, fuel and as solvents, some petrochemicals and plastics, lacquers, paints and adhesives and cements."

Marguerite Stephens said, "This place is a fucking gold mine for researchers," then added, "Sorry," to the resultant stares. Grandmotherly scientists weren't supposed to swear.

"So I'm looking at the photos of the steam engines," McDonald said.

"Yes?"

"Very sophisticated. Ceramic can't take the shifting heat and pressure of a large boiler. The pressure vessel appears to be glass fiber reinforced plastic. The heat source seems to be pressurized gas with air mix in ceramic burner tubes, insulated by glass and asbestos. The cylinders are bound trunks outside, but I'm guessing from the pressure curves they're plastic sleeved inside."

"How tough is plastic for the Ishkul?" Mark asked.

The scientist finally noticed him and answered, "They seem to be using surface tars and other petrochemicals. I imagine they can also bioengineer plants to do so. It would take some time. They're obviously just moving into this stage, though the sophistication says lab design, not trial and error."

Someone said, "Coal gasification, wood gasification, sugar plants for alcohol, bred for efficiency, tar and petroleum refinement, thermo depolymerization. Plenty of fuel for industrial use at their current tech level. They're slowly moving into ceramic-bearinged steam plants for industry. Propane lanterns are becoming common in houses. I expect they'll avoid most of the petroleum related problems Earth had, though of course, without it they'll never develop the massive urban sprawl."

"I hate the use of the word 'never' in relation to these people," Mark commented with a wince.

"Understood, sir, but there are energy limits on a culture. Without uranium, fusion or petroleum, certain levels are unobtainable."

"They had air conditioning," he mentioned.

"Oh, that makes sense. Ammonia or certain methyl or propane refrigerants are easy enough. They must be using ceramic castings for capillary tubes, but the efficiency has to suck without elements for thermal transfer. Even ceramic tube blocks wouldn't be very good."

Marguerite Stephens said, "Water power, lots of it. They seem to be diverting another stream. The natural stream here reminds me of the Zambezi River at Victoria Falls. Instead of a series of gorges, they have one large cataract before the sea. I'd speculate much of their development is geographically dependent, fitting the Diamond Theory, only more so. It's fascinating."

McDonald said, "It also seems they're increasing their exploitation rate. Their early civilization—literacy, mechanics, sewage—apparently predate ours by several thousand years. They've been working on this industrial age for close to a thousand. They're just now reaching the technical development rates we've developed with since the nuclear age."

Mark moved in close to McDonald and muttered, "Some days I can't help but think how much easier it would be if I could have certain people shot."

McDonald lowered his voice. "Egan? Yes, he needs to be kept away from here. Far away. By all means cut a deal with HMG, but insist on payment in something they can use that won't wreck things." McDonald looked bothered.

"Other than future funds in escrow, I can't think what to offer. What do you estimate their, the Ishkul's, future development is?"

"I'd say they're going to plateau and stagnate, but I'm not sure. Their development rate has been slower than ours, and it would take a long time, but I think they might eventually develop elastic ceramics. With their chemical base, they could get into space. Possibly within the millennium."

That was an awkward concept. If that was potentially possible, hands off was the only safe way to play it. There was no way, though, to guarantee a phase drive ship couldn't get through. Garrisoning the planet would have showstopping political ramifications and different risks.

"How did the tour go, Mr. Russ?" he asked as his counterpart entered.

"Quite well. I agree with the overall impression. It's good we didn't underestimate them, and I owe you an apology. You're managing against a very open system to maintain controls that are clearly needed."

"Reality and theory are often antagonistic," he said. "Thanks for understanding. What's that?" he said as he pointed to a native bottle Russ held.

"Local booze. I already turned it in for analysis."

One of the chemists spoke up. "We've managed to filter some of it. It contains a strong bite, the chemical contaminants and enzymes from the fruit. But in this form it's drinkable if rough. Just so you can say you did." He offered a sake cup half full of a clear liquor.

Mark shrugged, nodded and said, "Sure." He took the cup and sipped at the fumescent beverage.

"Holy CRAPerrrrrrg," he said after he tasted it. "Rough. Bitter, astringent, acidic, like scorched, spicy food."

"It's only seventy proof."

"It tastes like burning fuel. If they can drink that, they're tough."

"They seem to enjoy alkynes and ketones, too. Those are not fit for human consumption."

"It occurs to me," Russ said, "that we could start authorizing certain trades to keep HMG happy. We'd require the trades to go through here, and monitor them."

"That's because you're a reasonable man motivated by consideration for society," Mark said. "These people are ravening sharks and will push every limit at every chance. We'd have to dismantle every shipment down to the component. Too much work. I'm not inclined to cross that line until I have to."

"I'll defer to your judgment."

"Their printing technology is amazing," someone said.

"How so? And I'm sorry I don't know your name." Mark recognized him; he'd been here since the beginning.

"Leon Bamcis, sir. They're using fiber and rubber belts with ceramic and hardwood blocks to do limited offset printing. They also have something akin to a typewriter that prints on a large sheet." He fiddled and projected pictures. "The sheet is flash paper. They lay it on a wax tablet and hit it with a fireball. Black powder or the like. The ink is oil based and impervious. The paper burns off, then they sluice it with photochemical etchants. A couple of Earth hours later, negative plates ready for printing."

"These people have turned basic chemistry and agriculture into high art."

"I did see woodblocks in use, too, for less precise imagery and basic text."

"Woodblocks worked for a millennium, didn't they?"

"About that."

Someone else came in. Mark recognized the bioscientist and sighed.

"Dr. Adair, I appreciate the info, but biology is not my field and I do have other matters I must discuss. I do want to hear this, but I hope you won't feel offended if I ask you to hurry."

"I'll summarize, sir," Adair said. He was yet another dapper looking slim academic. "They don't have teeth, they have a hornlike ridge that grows at a fair rate, with a hard pseudokeratinous edge. Sort of an internal beak. They don't seem to suffer from any kind of oral decay. Slightly cartilaginous bones, hollow and ridged. It seems to be an element-saving measure, but they're light and very strong. Their blood is an aluminum and magnesium globin, and rather acidic. That's necessary for proper oxygen exchange. Should I explain why?"

"No, I'll take your word on it. Tell me more."

"Definitely some analogies to both theropods and birds. They're the dominant hunter and tool user of this planet, of course, though there are apparently some other species that are high tool users, like chimps on Earth."

"They are omnivorous, yes?"

"Yes," he agreed, "mostly grain sprouts and roots, but some fresh vegetables. Little that's grassy or leafy. Their shearing plates, what I'm calling their tooth analog, can't chew it. They rip and shred, then swallow.

"Stereo vision, of course, stereo hearing. Strong sense of smell. Good balance. They're closer to a base hunter package than we are. Yet they've become very sophisticated. I'd describe them as pack type clans. Dominance seems to be intellectual, physical and somewhat social. They debate, argue, form tribes and lead from there. If you don't like your leadership, you're welcome to move. I don't know much about the sociological end, though."

"I can parse that, but I'll have to think about it. That's a very odd dominance strategy. I wonder they don't have more fights about it." Mark realized he should grasp the sociological end. He had the training. What was this similar to?

"That could explain the quality of the warriors and armor, sir. Far better armor than we'd expect. They might be used to keep the underlings in line."

"Certainly something to inquire about."

Adair said, "It seems rather harsh. Take it or leave, so to speak."

"I expect they swap around a lot at the local level, and largely don't worry about the higher echelons generally. There was quite a bit of moving in the twentieth and twenty-first centuries in North America for that reason. Few left their nations, but lots moved between cities or provinces."

"True. It may be less severe than it sounds. I also got to look at their surgery." He paused to gauge Mark's interest.

"Go ahead." He wanted to hear this.

"Decent surgery. Obsidian blades, silklike sutures, needles looked to be fine fishbone or the like. They understand sterile procedure, have a variety of anesthetics, antibiotics. Early—to mid-twentieth century there, too."

"And technically Stone Age."

"I like your new term better, sir. Technolithic. It's amazing. I could make a living just documenting what I see here and writing theses on its development. I hope you don't mind, I shared some ideas on tumors and on precision grafting."

"It shouldn't be a problem. We need to do more of that, but very carefully. Clear it all through senior science staff first."

"Understood, sir."

"I want to show them Earth horse-drawn wagons and carts. The most sophisticated ones that existed. Make them in wood and let the Ishkul get a feeling for superiority. It doesn't need to be much, but if they don't exceed us in something, I foresee problems."

"Good idea, sir," Stephens said. "I endorse that heartily."

"Okay, that's where we'll begin, then. Biological techniques above the cellular level, and physical surgery, and discussions of vehicular transport."

"I took about the same tour you did, sir," Marguerite Stephens said. "A couple of things stood out."

"Yes?"

"First, the fact it's a canned tour could indicate they're concealing certain things from us. It might be just for convenience, but we have to assume they picked the tour they did for a reason. We saw technical production, all of a peaceful nature. We know they have warriors, though."

"Certainly, and I wouldn't endorse much information about that getting out myself. No foul there. They didn't seem to try to conceal the fact."

"No, they're just not offering info."

"I'll see if Warrant Connor can get anything from them. A training exchange or such."

"We'll be admitting a lack in combat tactics," she said with a warning look.

"Do you think there's that much difference?"

"Absolutely. I can show you texts, and parts of texts, from sixteenth to nineteenth century, that cover fencing with bayonets, pole weapons, spears. Most of those died out with the improvements in small arms and the influx of Asian unarmed forms. No one with a pistol bothers carrying a spear. Of course, Freehold troops would know more about those techniques than I would, but I suspect I'm better read on the older techniques."

"Could you teach them?"

"Not really." She shook her head. "I'm no soldier, and haven't tried to learn or analyze them; I only know about their existence and the social ramifications."

"On the one hand, it will be good to learn from them, assuming they have techniques we can adapt, and it will be a great study for you, I'm sure, to see them firsthand rather than in books."

"Absolutely," she agreed.

"On the other hand, I wonder if it will hint or reveal that we really don't use those weapons and have something far more effective."

"I can't say, sir."

She probably could, but clearly didn't want to.

"I know. I'll have to handle it. I guess there isn't much choice." It was his turn to frown. "We do it, and try to avoid any questions about our weapons. We'll give them the upper hand in this debate."

"Oh, two other items," she said. "They seem to have an excellent grasp of cellulose chemistry, judging from the production to waste ratio."

"I believe it. What's the significance?"

"It means they've been refining it for a long time, both the distillation techniques and the selective breeding of the plants they use."

"So you think their industrial processes are more sophisticated than equivalent Earth era?"

"I do. Their breeding programs are definitely well into twenty-first century, possibly twenty-second. Is that Dr. Adair still here?"

"I think so," Mark said.

"I'll get him," McDonald said. A few moments later, Adair came back in.

"Can you look at their breeding and compare it to ours? The difference being they don't have molecular manipulation, that we know of. Optical microscopes only, though they might have enzymic tools."

"Delighted, sir," he said, appearing as if he was a boy who'd been handed a bucketful of puppies.

After Adair left, Stephens said, "There's one more thing."

"Oh, sorry, go ahead," Mark replied, though he was pretty well wrung out already.

"I've been following the photos of various inhabited areas. I'm quite sure that city to the north, on the smaller river, is another nation."

"Oh? Significant differences?" he asked.

"Certainly cultural differences. The construction and layout are quite at odds with that of Ishkuhama. The images weren't detailed, but I got a definite sense from them."

"I'll arrange more photos, then," Mark said. "That's very much of interest and I'd like to see followup."

"Not a problem, sir."

That was very much of interest. It was also a potential complication.

CHAPTER 11

Mark was beginning to cringe inside when Vlashn came for their discussions. The Ishkul was so damned insightful. They exchanged greetings, and chose to sit under the awning, enjoying the ruddy sun and gusty breeze.

"I have another list of requests for visits," Mark said. "Most of them scientific. A few are publicity. Some are that odd category that is neither."

"I will have the visits arranged. I appreciate the quite good discretion your warriors show when escorting other than scientists. Query: Are they trained for this?"

"Not specifically, but those warriors are trained for diplomatic problems in general."

"Query: You find warriors necessary for diplomacy?"

"Not necessary generally, no. It's an old tradition. They also can enforce my decisions if there is need."

"It was necessary in the past."

"Yes, at times, and still occasionally today. In human societies we have fringe groups who cause trouble. Usually a show of force is sufficient. At times, diplomatic warriors will interact with local government enforcement —police—or local warriors to resolve disputes. It's very rare to actually have problems that involve fighting."

"I recognize the substantial problems of our communication barrier. At the same time, I am aware of reticence and secrecy on your part. A better knowledge of your problems would reassure many I represent, and myself, as to your nature. I am told of a human phrase."

"Which one?"

"Stop shoveling shit."

Mark choked and laughed.

"Vlashn, we will make real progress with that attitude. I will agree to swap political information in equal amounts, from the past, until recent times." It was risky, but nothing would be gained with the Ishkul playing the same game.

"We should have a small group discussion. Somle and myself, our best subject of encyclopedic study scientist, and another. Likewise from your groups."

"Agreed. Politics out in the open. Technology still restricted for now."

Russ appeared in the doorway.

"I heard and also agree," he said.

Vlashn stood and said, "Welcome, Ambassador. I thank you for joining us. On that subject, I will arrange it. I have more questions."

"Go ahead," both humans said together.

"Obviously, you weren't able to transport many of your machines. You travel in space, but you walk on our surface."

"Our animals would be poisoned by the growth. Restricting them, or bringing sufficient fodder, was deemed impractical," Russ said.

Mark took over with, "And without them, it made little sense to bring vehicles. We could bring our own powered engines, but they would add a lot of mass."

"That closely matches my deduction of the situation," Vlashn said. "This should not limit the ability of your technical staff to advise on differences and probable improvements in design and strength of materials of our vehicles. I want to establish such discussions immediately as it does not interfere with other operations, and as it does not offend your cultural position." His presentation wasn't offensive, but it was certainly more direct than previously. He wanted to start swapping info with these offworlders, or he was going to start questioning their motives. No one played tourist for the hell of it. One didn't have to be human to grasp the immensities of cost and scale involved. Transporting a large team to a distant planet and bringing diplomats, scientists and warriors meant one wanted something.

It was a reasonable request, and there was no way to stall under the circumstances. "I'll have Dr. McDonald assign a fluid dynamics engineer and a mechanical engineer to talk to your researchers," he said amiably. Aw, crap. He'd have to vet them, and then rely on them. How many more people would be coming into this, and when would one of them let slip?

Russ stalled again, with, "It doesn't offend us, and we are eager to share information in that fashion. However, Citizen Ballenger's nation is in charge of our operations, by mutual agreement, until the Galactic Alliance can create its own team, as we came a farther distance. I will be happy to put our staff at his disposal for this as soon as practical."

Yeah, he stalled, and dumped it all on me. I better get my name in the history books for this, he thought. It just was never going to get easier.

"I'll talk to the appropriate people and have them meet here tomorrow morning, if that's convenient for you," he said.

"Very pleasing. I'm highly excited at what will be discussed."

Mark could almost read Ishkul expressions, and that looked like a gleam of triumph.

Just how did their political system work and how much strain was Vlashn under?

And how would Egan react to technology being handed over freely as political bargaining chips? The longer this took, the worse his position. Mark understood why the man was so antsy.

McDonald came at once when called. He looked thrilled and nervous at the prospect.

"Ishkul want advice from humans on improving their tech. That's a good idea, great for the relationship. The problem is, humans don't have much experience with that tech, and not recently," he said. "I think the best approach is to have our people do a detailed analysis of theirs, under guise of examining the differences, which is true and legit. Concordantly, they can offer input on improving design or strength of materials of the existing technology—shear angles, steam, distillation. We want to make the impression that the tech they have is quite close to ours as far as it will go, which is true, and that only our space travel is more sophisticated."

"That's brilliant."

"Well, I do try." McDonald grinned cheerfully.

"I want Stephens along. She's about the best at grasping the relationship of the technology to society, and she's studied it enough in that context to hold a conversation without having to resort to notes. They have to believe we regularly use the same tech. But caution here. She's incomparable, but talks too much, and her opinions are not diplomatic."

"I'll send someone with her to keep her in line. Zihn, maybe."

"Good. He's very astute and a nice guy. How's he doing, by the way? Got enough to keep him busy?"

"He's an astronomer, but has enough training to help a lot of others, and a variety of interests. He's very enthusiastic about studying their technical development."

"Good. I don't want people getting bored or feeling left out."

"No chance of that."

"Please work with Irina—Lieutenant Shraybman. And here she comes. Hello, Lieutenant. I need a tour rotation set up. We have to keep our people going to see their society, in order to gather more information. We also can't be too reserved. They could decide we don't care, or are being dismissive. The presentation has to be of near-equals with different nuances, not of invading master race."

"Sure, that makes sense. So I should manage this?" Shraybman asked.

"Yes, but . . . I want that rotation to be scientists with closed mouths. Some of them tend to jabber, especially once you get them started on their area of expertise. I want a reliable military escort for each one, also—an officer, an intelligence troop, or security or one of the Special Warfare people."

"You're using the hell out of them, you know."

"Yeah, but I need to." He grimaced.

"Don't worry," she reassured him, "they love it. Do you know how rare it is for them to get used as more than shock troops or kept in 'reserve' to do nothing?"

"I hadn't thought about that. I was an intel analyst. What about your people?"

"What about them? Documentation specialists, public affairs, we get neglected, too, and left to make crappy soundbites and pretty pictures. We're hard on this." She grinned.

"Good." At least he wouldn't have trouble at that end, and he could use them more, then. Great to know.

"We can use cameras now, too. That's a relief."

"Yeah, I'm wondering about that."

"Yes?" she prompted.

"Every time we see a new Ishkul trick, we trot out the equivalent, only better. They know we have all the tech they do and then some. I see hints of resentment. Even Vlashn gets snippy when it happens. We're impressed with how far they've come. We can't say so without sounding patronizing. They can't help but feel we are anyway."

She furrowed slightly and said, "That's a PR problem, sir. Let me think about it and I'll see what I can do. Worst case, we borrow some of their stuff in some case or other, and thank them."

"That's disingenuous."

"That's public relations." She grinned.

"I'm also wondering about espionage. Is our recon technology good enough to sneak bugs into their society?"

"We probably can. We'd have to have Special Projects devise an exterior shell that could pass as a local insect. But if it gets found . . . what's the outcome?"

"I'd apologize and admit we were doing it. They know we can see them from orbit, so what's the problem?"

"They may not see it that way."

"True. But I can claim we do, and play the embarrassed and stupid card."

"I guess it depends on how much you need that info."

"That much. Please arrange it. Check with me on each step."

"Will do."

With his commander forward deployed, Connor had charge of the security detachment for the embassy, effective customs control, and the euphemistically called human-acquired information resources, or espionage. He had troops out all the time spying on the UN, and on the press, the industrials, all the incoming interest groups and any passing Ishkul researchers who could be recorded for information. Now he had to go back to school, with four Freehold Mobile Assault troops from the *Healy*, and two UN Marines.

He didn't mind learning new combat tactics. That's what he was all about. Learning them from the Ishkul was fascinating. Teaching them as much as possible about a skill he had to admit humans had largely forgotten, while not revealing anything that would suggest the far greater capabilities humans had, was a task.

The Ishkul training area wasn't dissimilar from how he'd arrange a training field. Open space marked off for practice, dummies of wood and straw and padded weapons for sparring. The primary gave a yellowish tinge and he could feel the local dust and pollen despite his nano treatments. He coughed and cleared his throat periodically.

The translator barked, "Parry, counter, high attack." He tried to do all three correctly in the right order.

"Not correct," the Ishkul, Fightmaster Misk, as near as he could translate it, said. "This way," he demonstrated a vicious parry, "then here," what was probably the counter. Connor knew of them in theory, but wasn't very good. "Then of course up here for the high attack, just as you'd attack any beast-mounted troop." If Misk would slow down, Connor might manage to duplicate that twist, arc and spiraling thrust. Assuming, of course, his knees bent that way.

Of course. Anyone could do it. Assuming they regularly fought cavalry and trained for it.

"I'll try again."

"Query: Would it be better to show me how humans do such, and I will compare to our joint angles?"

Busted.

"Our warrior ethos requires I finish learning the task to the best of my ability before I move to the next step," he said. The other humans snapped to attention in response. He refrained from grinning. Good catch.

"Very good," Misk said, with a flourish that was probably a salute. "We shall."

Hopefully by the time he'd learned it, Connor would be able to fake the "human equivalent."

Otherwise, it was going to be a very tough tour.

Sergeant Thomas walked in, or more accurately, stumbled into Mark's office.

"Sir, the lieutenant tells me you have medicinal booze handy."

She looked rather groggy.

"Yes . . . if you can tell me why." He didn't want to pry, but he needed to know the cause. He kept a concerned eye on her as he reached into a cabinet and brought out the three bottles he kept on hand.

"Ow . . . things I didn't need to see. The biologists wanted my documentary skills."

"A dissection or such?" he asked as he passed over a bottle of whisky.

"No . . . I could handle that. No, sir. Reproduction. Ishkul sex. Then the humans did a demo in return. But the Ishkul . . . those legs. Oh, I don't want to think about it. It's going to be bad enough having to edit the video and encode it. And those weren't the two most attractive humans either. Not that they were very imaginative. Then I realized I could do better . . . and that made it worse."

She knocked down a double shot and winced, eyes tight, probably from the liquor.

"Not what you signed up for, eh?"

"No, sir, it's *exactly* what I signed up for. Stuff no one else can do, in rough conditions. It still gets to me at times, though."

"I imagine. I do appreciate the work you do."

"Don't get me wrong, it was fascinating," she said. "It just put me in mind of spiders, those long limbs . . . I hate spiders. I don't like pseudarachs, either."

"They . . . we've been keeping you busy, haven't we?"

"Oh, yes, sir. Shooting vid, editing, analysis. I'd love to have a couple more people just to keep the volume up."

"Can we get them?"

"Not likely. Typically we're a two—to three-person shop. Yancy didn't make it back from leave in time to be aboard, and since Lieutenant Shraybman is trained and can supplement, our complement was down. I found three people who can fill in, and a lot of the scientists have decent skills for basic documentation. The gear's the limitation, and I'm the only one the captain can spare for groundside. They're still doing a lot of study from orbit."

"Yes, how's that going?"

"How much do you know about what we do?" she asked.

"A little about the technicalities, less about operations and organization." Something else he needed to learn.

"Well, it's a big planet," she said. "We don't know where to start. Since there's a ground element here, they've been radiating out from here as orbital observation allows. They deployed some remotes, but it's hard to tell much from a distance. We look for fields or other signs of development, zoom in and look for habitation, zoom in and look for details. Some of it can be automated, but since a lot of what we'd use as keys—certain elements, large energy outputs—doesn't exist here, it takes a lot more brain time."

"That makes sense. Should I gather they've found nothing obvious yet?"

"You'd be told if they had, and so would I. I'd likely be asked to help crosscheck some stuff, which I'm fine with. Also, the technology the natives have is far down our study list. We're trained for military recon, not anthropological. We've been getting some consults, but it's still going to take months to get good images of the entire habitable zone."

"So they could be hiding several million people and a few more pocket civilizations and we wouldn't know?" This was interesting and a little disturbing.

"Exactly, sir."

"Sergeant, that's very useful information. Thanks."

"No problem, sir," she smiled. "Ask any time."

He didn't comment as she left that she'd forgotten about her earlier distress.

It seemed to Mark that his function here was to sit at a desk and relay bad news to people, and be ready to take the blame for anything that went wrong. So far, he'd seen very little of anything save his office and the courtyard outside. This wasn't the way it worked on vid. He should be visiting palaces, making overflights, examining the society in detail and pronouncing policy.

The reality was that his training was in politics and business, and those could not take place until the other scientists had done their job. Aggravating, but each had his part.

He needed to follow up on that possibility of other nearby cultures, though. Could he ask Vlashn? Or would it be better done discreetly?

Nurin Russ knocked politely and stepped in. His expression was tired, and indicated he was worse off, since he got regular floggings from above as well as below. On the other hand, he might possibly find someone to pass the blame onto. Mark had no such outlet.

"Nurin, what can I do for you?"

"I need to talk. Unofficially official, if you gather what I mean."

"I think so," he agreed. "We're never not official, but I'm not going to hold it against you if you need advice or backup."

"Yes, some of each would be good."

"So talk," he said. He reached back to the cooler behind him, filled with ice, not mechanically cooled, and brought up two bulbs of beer.

Russ sat uncomfortably and blurted, "Look, Mark, none of this is personal."

"Meaning you want to put me on the spot." Mark grinned. It was a posed grin, but he wanted to hear this out. He handed over a beer.

"Thank you. No, meaning I'm told to. I got stupid orders." Russ popped the top and took a swig.

Mark said, "It's my experience that orders from outside the event are usually misinformed."

"Yeah. I'm supposed to promote your nation's 'militarism' and history, its independence from the rest of human society as a detriment, and generally paint you as rogues, with us as the good guys." He sighed.

Shrug. "Well, you could do that. It's one-sided, but reasonably true in that context. I gather you're reluctant to?"

"Yes, because it is one-sided. The Ishkul might just decide that since we did attack first—historical fact—that we were the bad guys, and your independence a good thing. They also might decide to deal with the more aggressive or militant or capitalistic power, based on their carnivore genetics, or so the scientists tell me. If that happens, I'll have to try to duck the blame, and you get the advantage. You understand that I'm supposed to gain the advantage here."

"I understand that. Now, let me be frank about your leadership. They seem to think this is a win/lose competition. I don't see why it can't be a mutual event."

Russ grinned, but it looked sickly and defensive. "That's because you don't have the cultural indoctrination to see independence as a bad thing, and the desire to prove its failure by any means necessary—plus existing outrage at the War."

"I can see that, intellectually." He didn't want to point out that failure to get the message that the Freehold really didn't care what the UN did, as long as it was left alone itself, could be construed as a statement that the lesson of the War had not taken, and needed repeated. Not that the Freehold wanted or planned that. Massive bureaucracies were remarkably slow to change, though.

"So," Mark led, "do you have any alternatives?"

"I do," Russ nodded, looking wry. "I said I'd let you lead, wait for you to fail, and pick up the pieces."

"I see." He let that sit for a moment, not wanting to jump to conclusions. "That comes with a large assumption attached."

"Yes. At the same time, I don't want to use their idea of trying to scapegoat you. But if you pull this off, things go bad for me."

"For not doing it their way, which is the dumb way. I see. I suppose you've decided that doing it their way to cover your ass is a nonstarter?"

"It has too many open variables," Russ agreed.

"That's a reasonable analysis," Mark said. "So why are you telling me you want me to fail?"

"Because I do want this to be a mutual thing. Or rather, it's best if it is. That way they can't publicly goat me."

"They still might professionally, though."

"I'll take that risk. This is more important than one man's career."

Mark considered offering support from the Freehold if that should happen. He decided to just hint at it.

"We have resources we can use, and would help with legal support if that happened. That's not a bribe, that's a consideration."

"Yeah, I see the difference. I appreciate it."

"No problem. While I'm supposed to help my nation's interests and corporations, I see long-term advantage to a mutual deal, too. So if I can do that, I will. Nor do I have any problems along those lines. If Egan and Margov and your own people, who haven't landed yet—"

"I suggested they not, to keep the arguments simpler."

"—Thank you. If they get upset, they can complain, but I doubt they'll get anywhere under the circumstances. And as long as I get them something, they'll shut up and take it."

"Yes, you do have that advantage." Russ still looked put on. "I guess we proceed as we are, then. We have been sharing info?"

"You've seen at least as much as I have," Mark shrugged. "You can issue orders to your interests. I have to make suggestions and back them up with stalls, delays, evasions and the occasional gunboat."

"I suppose I should be happy I have a venue I understand, since I'd be lost in yours," Russ said with a raised eyebrow.

"Likewise." Mark grinned. This time it was real. "Stay and finish your beer. I could use the reprieve, and 'affairs of state' is the only bulletproof excuse."

"I have a few minutes. Sure." Russ tilted his bulb in toast and drank.

"So, is this in leadup to the conference? How do you want to approach it?"

"We can both give our side of things about the other. I propose Stephens and one of your historians come up with the least biased timeline possible, and try to pitch it as a misunderstanding."

"I agree," Mark said. "Only . . . six plus billion dead on both sides is a hell of a 'misunderstanding.' Want to just mention that cities were destroyed, without tacking numbers on? The idea of twenty times their global population being wiped out in a misunderstanding would not likely help things."

"Yes, we'll both need to vet the summary. We don't have long, either."

"Right, that's tomorrow. I'd have asked for more time, but we don't have it."

"Especially when we have our troops out corralling someone or several someones."

"Yeah, I need to follow up on that, too. Look, Nurin, I have nothing against you, nor does the Freehold in this matter. I keep saying that. It's true."

"I believe you. I wish I could get it clear higher up."

"Well, do what you can. I'm not withholding anything from you."

CHAPTER 12

On the trip back from the exchange conference, Mark sat collecting his thoughts.

The round table had been grueling. Parts of human history that were critical to development were painful. Discussing mammoth hunters was one thing. Discussing ritual human cannibalism wasn't too painful. Hitler, though, and Pol Pot, and Jaksa in Indonesia and their lesser aspirants . . .

The good news was Somle and Vlashn knew it was frank. Mark's perception might be incorrect, but revealing the existence of brutality and scientifically devised torture in human history was being blunt and honest. On the other hand, the Ishkul had nothing similar, or not that they admitted to, he reminded himself. Some of their comments, though, were on the pragmatic side of fascist.

"Query," Somle had asked. "If these groups were perceived as a threat, why not directly issue an order to those ruled to exterminate them at once, cleanly and dispassionately?"

"That would have led to civil war and societal destruction."

"Your telling indicates that was the resultant fate, with external interference and suppression of all aspects of such societies, including those you perceive as good. The cost benefit of a direct action would have been cheaper, less burdensome and much faster."

There was a hint in that answer that the Ishkul were not nearly as peaceful and mild as suggested. A strong one. Other answers had indicated likewise. He wondered just how efficient they were with those bows and spears, and what their tactics and strategy were. Was it possible those cities the scientists thought were abandoned as resources shifted were echoes of some conflict?

He brought up a file and scanned some of the camera images.

"That road bothers me," Stephens said. She was looking at the terrain below their flight.

He looked up, jarred from his concentration. "Why so?"

"It's too straight and even for a nonelement using culture."

He looked out the port behind him, craned his neck and could see it.

"The Romans built very straight roads and aqueducts. Their tech was inferior, and not industrialized in any way. There were large irrigation systems in Meso-America that I recall. This doesn't seem too far removed from that. The larger population density means more labor available, too." He examined it as he spoke. It looked normal enough, and older in style. It was nothing like the impact-detonation carved cuts on Grainne, or the bored and fused ones on Earth. It seemed to be a dug and layered roadbed with graded gravel atop.

"I know. I'm just looking around and it feels wrong," Stephens said. Her unease was obvious. "A lot of excavation was done here. I'd expect the road to go over the terrain, not through a cut. It's efficient, but it's advanced by several decades over their best tech level so far."

"You feel that's significant," Mark said. He was paying attention.

"Yes, Citizen. I can look at an artifact and tell you within fifty years when it was made, if I have a good background on the culture, even without specifics on things like paints, glazes and mineral finds. This road screams twentieth century. I'm not seeing why it's so advanced. There's no reason for it to be, even with labor, even allowing for overburden to be used as fill elsewhere. They don't carry that much traffic. One doesn't typically install a restaurant type kitchen in a house, for example. So I'm bothered by the cutting and removal of that much material." She clearly was adamant about her belief.

"Keep me informed. It's a reasonable concern." Mark still wasn't convinced, but if a scientist was, he would take it under advisement. "Would it make it easier to move vehicles?"

"Definitely, and certainly the low-level steam they have. However, it's a lot of labor for a few vehicles. Unless they're planning far ahead. . . ."

"Entirely possible, given the background so far."

Stephens grimaced. "Yes, that's also disturbing. I know the slower pace has enabled them to develop socially to a much higher level than their physical skills would suggest. It just feels wrong from this end."

"It's all information. I wonder if we're getting too swamped in forest to see trees. We have entire theses already, but little understanding."

"It will come. These things have a way of bursting open all of a sudden."

Mark said, "I think one of the problems I'm facing is that I can't possibly learn all I need to in the time allotted. Asking certain questions will indicate a certain direction on our part, so I can't. I can only acquire what we happen to observe, and make educated guesses."

"I'm sure we'll get a handle on it, sir. In the meantime, it's a great learning experience."

"Yes, it is." He reflected, though, that great learning experiences in politics often had far more severe repercussions than in history or linguistics.

Why does every negotiation get tougher and more involved? Mark thought to himself. By all logic, it should get easier. But this was a ball of snakes.

With the information available, he'd made the decision to call in the corporate sharks for a face to face. They arrived politely and promptly, of course, with the possibility of acquiring something. He knew they weren't going to like the news, though.

Margov took it seriously. She arrived wearing a basic pair of field pants, neatly pressed, and a shirt and sun hat. No flash, no glitz. Maybe he was giving her too much credit, though. It was possible Shraybman's presentation had taken the wind out of her sails. He wondered how long that would last. The look she gave Shraybman as she entered was cool but definitely not friendly.

"Mr. Egan, Ms Margov, we've put together a presentation so you can see what we've discovered so far. In front of you is a standard nondisclosure agreement. We will proceed as soon as you sign it."

Taya signed at once. Egan paused and read through the entire page, then paused some more. He looked up at Mark, realized he wasn't going to get anywhere, and finally scrawled along it. Shraybman grabbed both sheets, scanned them into file at once, and dimmed the lights slightly.

Both sat stunned as the video tour unfolded. They couldn't record anything, but they were going to remember every detail they could. Sergeant Thomas had edited all the available footage from diplomats and scientists and distilled the high points down. The probable peak of Ishkul technology was laid out, and impressive as hell.

"That's one small part of the productive capability of this city," Mark concluded as the presentation ended. "We must keep this quiet. You see the technology they have. It's taken them millennia to develop it, a little longer than it's taken us. The important part is that they developed culturally and philosophically with equal time and attention. They have a stable, rational, largely peaceful culture that needs to be protected."

Taya Margov said, "I will if he will, but I suspect—"

"Hah," Egan said. "That makes it even bigger. There are beyond billions here, possibly beyond trillions. We don't even need to train them up, just make the pitch. I'm more than willing to wait, as long as it's conceded that HMG has first rights."

Mark knew it was pointless, but offered, "You realize that a drastic improvement in their tech base means hundreds of thousands of laborers unemployed all at once from technological obsolescence?"

Egan shrugged. "Something will develop with the influx of money and materials. Buggy whip makers got displaced. So did computer programmers."

Margov saved Mark when she said, "Certainly you'd have a claim to a percentage of everything, though I am not conceding the claim until it has been heard in Citizens' Court, only that you would have basis for a claim, which I would certainly dispute on behalf of my company. However, the fact that a number of interests are now in system, and have seen potential you did not on your initial scan would be evidence toward negating large sections of that claim. Thusly, other outfits would be able to negotiate their own deals for other resources, and at most pay a royalty to HMG, especially as HMG would need to outcontract most of such development, it not fitting your charter of intrasystem space-based raw materials. Collate in the necessary diplomatic exchanges of information to create a good bargaining position, and your claim is not nearly as grandiose as you would like us to believe you think it is."

Holy crap, if anyone was going to negotiate with the Ishkul, it was she, he decided. He also made a note to keep an even stricter eye on her, not that he could without assigning people to follow her to the bathroom and sleep with her, considering the surveillance he already had in place. He suspected she knew several times as much as she was admitting, in a variety of fields.

Watch the bitch, he thought again.

He noted, "It's likely a war will result from such displacement. Especially as they don't have much in the way of military technology. One side would have the overwhelming edge."

"So we sell to all sides. Keeps it equal and limited. Low intensity conflict was common for most of human history."

Wow. Mark was . . . stunned. The callous attitude of, "So they're killing each other? Sell ammo!" was jackal-like.

Biting down and keeping calm, he said, "Yes, but we evolved with it. They apparently have not."

"That's . . . true." Egan actually admitting there was a stumbling block? "I'll consider that, but it's an issue to be resolved, not a bar."

Still, it was something.

Mark pointed at the screens in front of them.

"Before you are the fields we are discussing with them. Tactics of existing weapons are on there. Weapons are not. Medical techniques for surgery and therapy that can be done by hand are. Cellular, chemical, nano and advanced biotech are not. Technology for steam and transport are. If you have any leads in any of those fields that we do not, you are welcome to put a package together, and you, I and Vlashn will sit down with his experts and negotiate an exchange."

"That's strictly information, and little of it anything HMG—" Egan cut off, bit his lip and clenched up tight as soon as he realized the admission. Hah. Got him.

Egan paused, and tried again. "I presume the existing cultural exchange will not be paused while I bring in an expert from out system?"

"You may assume so," Mark agreed. "We came prepared. If you didn't, you'll have to play catch up."

Margov said, "I do have some limited resources in system. I will be happy to offer their services free to the Freehold, and the UN, without any expectation of favoritism or other return. I will admit our goal is to create a favorable impression with the Ishkul for further development." Her smile was acid sweet.

"Accepted, on those terms, subject to review through this office," Mark said. Yes, Taya was quick on the rebound and never missed a chance to get a foot in.

"I'll call my ship and see what resources are available," Egan said, controlled enough not to sound as if he'd just been stomped.

"Do that. We'll gradually move into actual technological development, and you'll both have claims you can push in court. I will be willing to testify as to your input and assistance."

"Thank you." Egan rose carefully, gauging reactions, and decided they were at a stopping point. He shook hands, offered formalities and left. As he cleared the door he broke into a run.

Margov rose easily. "Mark, Citizen, you negotiate well, but I fear you've softened a little working for the Council. Time was, you wouldn't concede the sky was blue."

"I really am trying to open things up. The less time I have to keep warships here, the less time there is for things to blow up.

"One other thing, Taya," he said. She cocked an eyebrow.

He'd been about to mention the landings. Maybe not. Keep that card for now. He improvised. "While I will testify as to events, I won't come out in favor of anyone. That will be for a Council vote, seeing as it is extra-system in scope."

"Of course," she said. "Realistically, any agreement that includes us is positive. Obviously I will ask for the biggest slice possible. But pie is pie. And so is schadenfreude." He could see fangs when she grinned.

He grinned back. Same old Taya.

"Good day," he said.

After she left, he turned to Shraybman.

"Obviously I don't have to warn you to watch her. She'll make a pass at anyone she thinks will give her a slice. She's not cheap, but her cut of billions is enough to make her warm up to anyone."

"She already made a very subtle and charming pass at me, sir." Shraybman grinned.

"Oh?"

"If it were social, I'd do her in a second. Considering that her purpose in fucking me would be simply to fuck me, and us, in several ways, I pretended not to see it. If she's still interested after the fact, I'll think about it."

Mark considered. "I actually have no idea what her type is, or even if she has a type, other than someone with assets she can assign to DSR."

"Pity, if so. I'd like to hope there's an actual soul under there somewhere."

"So would I, but I'm not betting on it. Watch yourself."

Shraybman laughed. "I'm all duty. *If* I meet her in port, then I'll size her up. She is quite the eyecatcher, though."

"Indeed. They also must not hear about the civilization to the north, assuming our photos are correct. I don't even discuss it here if I can avoid it." The photos probably were correct, but assumptions were just assumptions.

"Is that why you haven't mentioned it to Vlashn?" she asked.

"Partly," he agreed. "I also don't want to complicate those negotiations. We'll work with the people who contacted us first, then smooth out relations with other, less sophisticated groups."

"Yeah, we have enough factions on our side without splintering theirs, too."

"That's my thinking," he said tiredly. "And on that, I need to consult with Lieutenant Phelan again, if you can send her in?"

"Will do," she said. "Don't strain yourself, sir."

"Well, not more than I have already," he said with a forced grin.

Taya Margov sat in her prefab hooch, busily building a list of assets. Several lists, in fact. One list was people she might exploit, either with money, ego stroking, or something more blatantly whorish. She never lied to herself about her morals. Her goal was to get what she wanted, through the simplest route possible, without disgusting herself more than the return would dictate. Sex with Egan would disgust her unless it yielded at least 70 percent of her base goals. People with less pull she might offer a bit to in exchange for information to go around him. It was an irony of the market that the less someone had, the more that tidbit might be worth. One scrap of information had a base price. A thousand scraps came at a steep discount, especially as all information aged fast.

As sweat permeated her clothes, she wished for better climate control, but most systems used metal for heat exchange. The polyceramic system she had available was enough to cool her comm and gear, make it bearable for sleeping and clean the air, at a modest price. Trading for it in system had cost a few credits, and had also made a ship's stores petty officer grateful, and a bit beholden. It wasn't major leverage, but she might need more assets later.

Her company had very good scanners in system, for their purposes. She knew to within close order the mass of exploitable metal in the local halo, the usable gases, and had an extensive writeup on Ishkul technological levels and probable development. She didn't have her own anthropologists along, but a certain UN grad student had been amazed at the "assistant attache's" interest and lay knowledge of the subject—knowledge she'd acquired from a ten div marathon read of ten college-level texts—and happy to elaborate on his findings. Nothing classified, of course, but classification could take time, and someone untrained in intelligence operations let a lot of information slip through the cracks. So far, it had cost her some time, some interest that was only half feigned—she did like the subject and he was nice enough—and a few segs swapping innuendos and gropes. She always escalated slowly if she could. Once you nuked someone, you had nothing bigger to play. She'd gone too far with Russ's assistant, and had gained little intel. The man was a lackey for his government, his associates lackeys for him. Mark wouldn't fall for it at all, and Shraybman, Thomas, Adair and others had only been interested in social get-togethers after the fact. She wouldn't even think about one of the "Blazers" who were almost certainly Black Ops. It would be fun, no doubt, but yield nothing. Dead end on human intelligence otherwise. McDonald, Stephens, Zihn, others, all professional, didn't even notice her, and knew she was off limits.

She decoded a message that came in from the *Milton*. The mercs inland reported favorably. The locals there were indeed interested in better ceramic blades, power ground and with unseen molecular treatments. Their price for allowing mining of their territory, and any future territory, was a permanent supply of such blades. The local chief was savvy enough to demand regular resupply for any member of the tribe or its tributaries, maintenance of the deal to the surviving group if they were subjugated, and a periodic review of available technology. That worked out to about two percent, in Margov's estimation. A reasonable return for mineral rights. She had no illusions of persuading every group on the planet to accede. She just needed enough that HMG's claim was diluted. That would tie things up in court. The longer they were tied up, the better her position, and the more likely HMG would cut them in, just to end the case. Best case, that would lead to a solid claim for DSR that would let them take a sizeable percentage. Shutting them out completely was not likely, though if Egan pissed off the wrong people, it was vaguely possible.

There was no further word from her recon bugs aboard the *Healy* and *Margin*. She assumed they'd been found. The military might have used them for counterintel, but in this case no one would bother. The bugs would just be smashed, irradiated, zapped with electricity and either used as reaction mass or just flushed out an airlock. No matter. No report was no report. That made her anthropology geek that much more interesting. Fortunately he was clean and attractive, though enough billions made that irrelevant, too.

Recon was a long, usually boring and uncomfortable process.

The ten Operatives worked in five pairs, each taking a div at the observation post overlooking the distant village. Once done, they took a slow, careful march around the area, each one on a slightly different track, seeking evidence. Then they rested.

Chinran awoke stiff. She'd managed to keep herself still while asleep; a couple of troops had already learned that stretching out caused contact burns with the local sap. However, the position wasn't the most comfortable, made more awkward by a desire not to tear up the ground and leave evidence. She had her groundmat, and a carefully cleared little coffinlike tunnel under the brush. It was barely noticeable, quite cozy, just breezy enough to not be stifling, uneven and full of bugs.

She made an audio check for safety, opened her eyes, shifted her net and shimmied out into the clearing.

She cleaned up, including wiping off dust with a chemically treated cloth, to prevent skin damage. It helped, but they were all getting red and irritated, much like a sunburn. Keeping sleeves down and salve on the skin helped, but the dust and pollen still snuck in. She grabbed a shot each of the nano and oxygen to be safe, blew gunk out of her nose quietly, and edged over to the OP. She left her spear, bow and quiver, but took her shorter blade and a knife, all ceramic composite made to look like stone.

The two she relieved said nothing, just handed over notes written in careful block letters, timed, dated, giving all details, in a code that wasn't easily deduced but she could read handily. She nodded and they drew back, to head out on patrol. Moose wiggled up next to her, the tiny woman taking up little space. Operative Meuser knew what she was about, and set to making her initial notes for the shift, confirming ranges, sectors, landmarks and weather. Very methodical. Her face, as always, bore an expression of concentration. Everything was a problem to be solved to Moose.

Chelsea left her to it and carefully punched for an intel and weather update from *Healy*.

The village seemed to contain about a hundred inhabitants, and resembled medieval European villages quite a bit, even to thatched cottages. It had commons with grazing animals, a couple of streets, specialist workers and a small stream as a water source, which also powered a mill of some sort via an overshot wheel. Fields terraced down the stream slope with irrigation pipes, growing a mix of grains, ground fruits and probable pulses.

The stream was more than a trickle, but not big enough for river traffic. Two cart trails headed in different directions. The shore was about ten kilometers away, and there were larger towns there, per satellite recon. Chelsea wondered why the traders hadn't chosen those, who'd certainly have more resources to offer. Presumably, this remote site was a test case, and they'd spread out from here. Or so they might hope. She was here to stop that.

Nothing happened for half the shift. They chewed rations, a piece here, a bit there. They sweated and itched quietly, only occasionally twitching to an intolerable irritation. Except when eating, they kept filter masks over their mouths and noses against pollen, dust and detritus.

It was a pity, she thought, that the local growth was so toxic. It was quite pretty, ranging from green to red. That probably meant it was an efficient UV absorber, if she recalled correctly. Higher frequencies went in, lower ones reflected. Smaller or dimmer stars would create darker growth, as plants attempted to absorb as much radiation as possible. The flowers were quite bright and rather wildly shaped. Goddess knew there were plenty of bugs, with eight or ten legs, mostly crawlers but some airborne ones, too. Few local animals presented themselves, but the humans probably smelled rather bad. No larger predators, a few scurrying types that looked like four-legged kiwis.

About midday, Moose said softly, "We have a violator."

Chelsea twitched and shifted.

"I see him," she agreed, looking through her own binox. Human. Male. "Let's assume he has friends. We also need to find out who he works for."

"As soon as he turns around. I'm recording already. Audio should be up in a few seconds, but I can do better live if I see his lips."

"Sandy, Anjin, make a second perimeter sweep through the growth. Squirt me updates. Think you can do it in two divs?"

"Yes, ma'am," Anjin agreed. He was small but stealthy and light on his feet.

Moose said, "My concern is who they hired. Almost certainly FMF vets, but from where? Any of ours?"

"Almost impossible," Chelsea said. She recalled a rogue once. She'd been toe-to-toe with him as her father took him down. Operatives were generally about as loyal as could be, as were most Blazers. There were lots of very good Scouts, infantry, Assault and other vets who'd be amenable, though, for enough money. Nor was there any regulation or contract against it, for anyone, as long as anything nondisclosable wasn't disclosed.

That just increased the incentive to resolve it nonviolently. Besides intel and such, professional courtesy mattered. She'd prefer not to kill one of her own.

Anjin circled back before night.

"They're definitely a lower tech level than near the landing," he said. "Selectively bred plants and crops, some draft animals. No sign of gas, steam or other power. Earth sixteenth century, maybe. Mostly peasant farmers."

"And our friend?" Chelsea asked.

"Yeah, he's talking to them. I don't see any signs of those elements. I do see them paying rapt attention as he shows them how to use a pedal-powered grindstone. I'm not sure they traded that locally, though they may have."

"Either way," she said, "they're teaching tech to the locals and it hasn't been cleared through Ballenger. Violation. The problem is, unless I see the banned elements, I can't actually do anything."

Moose asked, "The UN can. Do we dare go there?"

"That's a fascinating question," Chelsea replied. Could she?

If she called the UN and suggested it, they could pick up the salesmen, who'd scream and get ransomed straight back to Ballenger. They'd head right back here, with diplomatic protection against another apprehension. However, in the meantime, she could see that whatever facility they had was destroyed and so unusable as to make a new start necessary. In the meantime, since the locals knew who humans were, a small detachment of scientists could be brought in, with the inevitable politicians. She wouldn't be the one making contact or stirring up trouble. She'd still be the officer on the spot, and as long as the UN agreed to that up front, it wasn't a problem. Ballenger would back her up. That line wouldn't be crossed, since everyone had the same goals here. The only injured party would be whichever of the corps had these reps on site.

"I like it," she said. "I'll be sure to credit you with it."

"In case it fails?" Moose grinned.

"Of course. I'll place the call."

Lieutenant Jetter was far more patient than his Marines. On the other hand, as warriors, reconnoiterers and athletes, they understood the need for planning.

The good news, as he reported back, was that the trade so far only included better lithic tools. Whichever group was sponsoring this incursion seemed to be figuring to bring the Ishkul up slowly, or to trade for advantage. There didn't seem to be an intent to offer them the universe. He suspected it was one of the political groups looking to make friends and build a presence that the natives would request in any negotiations. Sneaky. Also very well thought out. He had a précis on the groups involved, and this didn't sound like most of them. That was for intel to deduce, though. He simply reported his observations. No craft apparent, no landing sites on any scans. The humans on site were in excellent physical condition, likely hired military types. He saw a lot of stone and ceramic axes, improved handles with a curve suited to the native physiology to increase moment. So whichever group it was had actual scientists working for it.

"All in all, I would describe it as a very professional operation," he said over encrypted link to Ambassador Russ. "There are twelve humans, six of them on rotating security shifts, six doing the negotiations. The humans are armed with bows and spears, but my sensors indicated some heavy small arms in one hut, including an M Twenty-Three squad weapon and some flame projectors. So they're ready for trouble."

Russ replied, "That raises the question of did whichever group that hired them approve of that? It could be a discreet way to order them pulled, if some peacenik group is behind it, and can be identified. Tell them their mercs were prepared for actual violence and have them ordered back for violating the vision of universal peace."

"That was my thought, sir. Let them run out a lot of line, then yank. We don't want them weaseling out and trying again, only better."

"As long as the visible trade goods are moderate improvements over the present, with no blatant increase in capability, nor any substantial military advantage, you are to continue to observe and not interfere."

"Understood, sir," he agreed. "You're placing a lot of faith in my observational and interpretive skills, sir."

"Should I not?"

"Sir, I believe I can handle the mission. I am just reminding you I'm a Marine, not a scientist. Perhaps one could be made available?"

"You raise an excellent idea, Lieutenant. We should do so. I don't know that we can, but I'll explore the possibility."

"Thank you, sir. I will report again on the same local ephemeris tomorrow."

"Well done, Marine. Relay the congrats to your platoon and continue."

"Roger that, sir. Jet out."

So they'd wait and watch. That wasn't a problem. They were good at that.

CHAPTER 13

Mark did not want to reveal the presence of the other incursions to Vlashn. However, he didn't see that he had a choice. If Vlashn found out from some other source, that would be worse. The only logical, honorable course was to fess up early and let him know the details.

Still, he paused for several deep breaths before he entered the courtyard where Vlashn was due to arrive. He'd rather be fashionably late, but that would be out of character.

So he sat, enjoying the local sunlight and fresh air, with its irritating tickle. He'd need to remedicate shortly. While he waited, he enjoyed a thick, crusty chunk of bread with a generous dollop of apricot preserves. Chef Finley from the *Healy* had been offered the position of chef on the planet and quietly but cheerfully accepted. Mark was glad. The man was discreet, observant and a phenomenal cook, even deprived of metal pans. His breads were a high point of the cuisine.

Vlashn and his usual escort arrived, and Mark's usual bodyguard escorted them in. All the human recording was now automated. Vlashn brought parrot things, but Mark hardly noticed them anymore.

"Good morning, Mark."

"Good morning, Vlashn. I have information for you today." He stood and swapped greetings.

"I am interested in anything you will offer."

"I hope so. First, I must update you on human events." He took another breath.

"I hope you have not had another war."

Mark laughed nervously. "Was that meant as a joke?"

"Fractionally yes." Vlashn glugged. "I deduce it is better than even odds that two human groups somewhere are fighting, based on the summary of your racial history you provided." Vlashn didn't sound bothered, but how could he, through a translator? Mark decided to address that first.

"That is correct, Vlashn. However, no dispute affects the relations between Freehold and UN or between humans and Ishkul at this time."

"Very well. I wish for that to remain the case."

"I have no doubt it will. There is a different dispute that you need to know about, that both UN and Freehold are in agreement on."

"In human colloquialism you are 'stalling for time.' "

"Sorry. There are other human landings on your planet," he said in a rush.

Vlashn replied at once. "I understand. You seek multiple groups to observe and negotiate with."

"If we thought it wise and had more ships present we would do so. These are groups from the Freehold and from the UN who have landed on their own initiative, in remote areas, to commence trade with your less advanced societies."

"Query: To what purpose is this?"

"Their goal is to transfer technology, without regard for implications, and at a price most favorable to them. I don't have a problem with the latter per se, except that it will affect long-term relations between our peoples."

"Query: What do you plan in regard to these landings?"

"I have dispatched a special class of warrior who specialize in observation and information gathering to watch them. No other action will be taken yet. If need be, the warriors will relay the concerns of myself and Ambassador Russ. If that is insufficient and the situation degrades they will use minimum force to interrupt the humans and they will be brought here."

"It is moderately troublesome, Citizen Ballenger," Vlashn said, "that your people are arriving all 'over the planet, both largely traders and very much warriors. You tell me you are their second-level leader and speak for them, but you are unable to exercise control I would expect of such authority. There is a logical disconnect here. Power proceeds in a line with control or influence. If you cannot influence your people to the level claimed, I must presume your status is not as great as you would have me believe. I am decrementing my confidence."

Blast. The man—alien—was right. Or at least he was from his own point of view, which was all that mattered here.

"Influence is more accurate than power, Vlashn," he said. "I am consulted when others have problems. If they do not see a problem, I ca . . . my ability to interfere is limited. Much as I can't interfere with your function, those I protect,"—yes, that was a good word, fatherly—"have their own roles and hierarchies."

"Query: If I ask for your interference on my behalf, will that increase your ability to influence?"

That was one hell of a question. And if Egan still thought these people were savages, he was heading for a collision that was going to be painful.

"I can speak for any Freeholder who asks," Mark said. "They must be Resident in our territory and pay a fee per year to make it official."

"Query: Does this apply to humans with exclusion?" Vlashn asked.

"I don't know that it has to," Mark said. Tricky bastard. Did he want to let the Ishkul go there? Maybe . . . "The law says that the person must be a Resident of the Freehold. Clearly, you are a person."

"If I become a Resident of your Freehold and pay this fee, you could speak on my behalf." It wasn't a question.

"I could do so," Mark agreed. That was a huge step. On the other hand, it would mean a *formal* agreement with the Ishkul ahead of the UN. He grinned. That was fucking beautiful. But there was one problem. "You would have to visit the Freehold, take our oath, and pay the Residency fee," he said. "That can be done, but it will take several weeks to arrange travel, among other issues."

Vlashn paused only briefly. "Queries: Is it a complete requirement to be on your planet for this to take place? Is there somewhere closer? You have mentioned territories in space. Would your ship meet the requirement?"

"No, ships do not count as territory. They have a separate status. Any territory we control, the Halo, Jump Points, embas—"

Embassies.

Damn. "Please bear with me for a moment," he said.

"Of course," Vlashn said, with a human nod.

Mark called for Shraybman. She burst through the door and he said, "Irina, I need anyone you can vouch for who has a chunk of land in Capital District."

"Yes, sir," Shraybman said, looking confused but not arguing. "Lieutenant Phelan does, I believe."

"Perfect. Get Cochrane, too, please."

Shraybman grabbed a radio. She called through and made the request. Phelan arrived moments later. Cochrane was right behind.

"What do you need, sir?" Phelan asked, panting and eager.

"How much land do you own?"

"Me or my family, sir? My share is about a thousand hectares. Prime bottomland along the Amassippi. Not much use for anything."

"It will be perfect. Would you be willing to trade one hectare of your land for one hectare of . . . the local land?" He realized he had no idea what name the Ishkul gave to their planet.

"Oh . . . of course," she said, and stifled hysterics. Yeah, it was obvious. Why hadn't they done this at first? Too damned timid, that was the problem. They'd know better next time. And so, of course, would the UN.

"Will you also buy an additional small plot for cash?"

"I can. I'll be the first human landholder. I like this."

"Ideally I'd have a nonattached civilian do this. Better change quick. Get out of uniform. Irina," he said, "Please have the captain issue leave orders for Phelan, effective as of her last shift, running for say, two days."

"I will do that, sir," she agreed. She sounded very confused now.

"Lieutenant Cochrane, print me out the Oath of Competency in Ishkul, as best as you can manage. Or an audio translation."

"Vlashn, this is how it is done," he said. "If you wish, you may swap land with Lieutenant Phelan. This means you own a section of land on Grainne. As a nonresident, you can't own land, but she's donating it as official territory for you to hold an embassy. In exchange, you are paying her in the equivalent land here, which she is selling to the Freehold for our embassy. That means that this section surrounding the ship in a one hundred meter square is Freehold territory for our diplomatic use. We are willing to relocate later and adjust the terms accordingly."

"I understand to a substantial degree," he said.

"You should also sell another hectare to Phelan for one thousand Freehold credits, our currency. She will write you a draft."

"I understand the statement but not the motive beyond a low level."

"You must have cash, or liquid assets, to pay your residency fee."

"I believe with great certainty I understand the entirety of your plan, and the ramifications of it." Before the translation box strangled out the complicated logic, he was glugging the wet throaty sound he used as a laugh.

In a few segs, the first land trade was made, the land sale transacted, the draft signed back to the Freehold Council, Vlashn sworn in as a Resident in the now official Freehold embassy, and had officially requested Mark's assistance in enforcing his needs.

"Can he speak for the entire planet?" Phelan asked. "That seems presumptuous and challengable."

"We'll work on it," Mark said. "For right now, we have official standing each way. The corps and the UN don't, nor will any newly arriving groups. They have to basically swap hostages and treaties for diplomatic status. We just bypassed weeks of admin."

"Power of attorney."

"The very thing," Mark agreed. "Vlashn, if you have an executed agreement, either signed or witnessed, that others are entrusting their property or decisions to you, then you have legal standing to ask for assistance. At that point, I can issue a great level of orders to all Freeholders that they must comply with."

"I comprehend in large part the sociology. Your culture tends to clans, if that is the word, and you exercise power generally within the clan, rather than holding a great amount of property and regulation directly to your person."

"That is an excellent summary," he agreed.

"Those I represent consent to a high level of my control over their location, and I or my staff may claim property for use, subject to a future decision for like compensation. Individuals may refuse generally freely and depart or withdraw as the situation suggests. Does that meet generally your 'power of attorney'?"

"Close enough for government work."

"I deduce a likelihood of that being a jest indicating a high level of confirmation. I greatly enjoy the nuances of your language, even after a translation."

"And I find yours to be refreshingly precise and easy to understand. How may I help you, Resident Vlashn?"

"I would like to limit access in this district to that approved by myself or my Equal Somle. I actively seek interviews with applicants and request an office adjoining your embassy be tasked with scheduling those. I presume without intent of offense that more money will be needed to execute this."

"Done and done. Lieutenant Phelan, please write up orders to that effect on behalf of myself, plenipotentiary and speaker for this mission, et cetera, pursuant to a request by a Resident. Round them up, bring them back, glue the notice to their foreheads if need be, and use force if that's not enough."

Turning, he continued, "Yes, Vlashn, it will cost money, however, once the initial word is put out, any violations devolve to the violator. In other words, you only have to pay to have the message delivered. If they dispute it, they'll wind up paying for my decision, and for your time and trouble."

"Your system strikes me as simultaneously effectively fair and highly mean. I presume you have spent as much time in developing it as we in ours."

"It's stable," Mark agreed. "All human interactions can get complicated and emotional. One party always feels wronged. Our system grew from desire and necessity and manages to get the job done. Eventually we hope for something better."

"Query: Would technical and qualitative analysis of your leadership techniques by Ishkul researchers be of help?"

"It actually might," Mark said. Oh, hell yes. "We'd certainly find an outside viewpoint useful and informative. We can likely work that into a trade of some kind. For this one, I'd like to thank you on behalf of all humans. That is certainly one of the things we can exchange."

"I am quite gratified to have secured the first item of trade where Ishkul have a reasonable expectation of exceeding human capabilities, in addition to an agreement of exchange in embassies."

Dammit. Time for more diplomacy. "Vlashn, there are a number of things you do better than we do. Part of the problem is trying not to reveal certain other knowledges in the exchange."

"So you have said before. I am quite patient. Those I speak for are not always patient to that degree. Your scientists and ours talk in equal measure when discussing scholarship and analysis. It is not as apparent to those Ishkul farther from this location that we share that equality. They demand with increasing insistence for a commencement of technology trade."

"I know. So do my own people." Vlashn seemed to be hinting at political unrest.

"I have made arrangements," Mark said—actually he hadn't yet, but he would—"for Ishkul scientists to attend a conference with human scientists, at one of our universities, to study all the skills we share in common and exchange information. I'd like to focus not on that we necessarily do these things better, but that we do them differently. That of itself is very interesting to our historians and developmental scientists."

"Query: Humans will share their technological development at this conference?"

"Absolutely." Way to pass the buck, Mark, he thought. Still, it was a concrete offer. Even if implementation was going to be a bitch, it wasn't going to be his bitch, and it was possible. Let the experts juggle it. He couldn't do much of that, though. "I see no reason we can't take a small number back with us, since you can breathe our air, while some of our researchers remain here."

He would have to secure them, though. Vlashn might be a very stand up guy, but Somle had suggested casual elimination of opposition, nor did Vlashn see a logical problem with forcing information when he could, *and* he was incredibly astute.

"That is excellent progress," Vlashn said as he rose. "I will depart to discuss that with those who advise me."

"Of course. I will do the same. We have our first proper exchange." He extended hands to shake. Vlashn took them in his own scaly skin, shook and left.

Exhaling deeply, Mark turned and headed inside.

In the science section, he sought Dr. Stephens.

"I have a proposal from the Ishkul for an exchange." He outlined quickly, not that there was much beyond bones yet. "I don't mind if it's at a UN, Freehold or GA institution. Just make sure everyone is prepped accordingly. How would we arrange that?"

"It should be either Freehold or UN, such as Caledonia," she said. "Somewhere with the technical means to handle it, but remote enough they can build a site away from any interference or large cities. That keeps certain elements out of the discussion. The problem is, discussing the history of steam without mentioning those elements . . . we'd have to duplicate a lot of development, fast . . . and I'm worried that the only alternative we have to go from is the Ishkul model."

"You don't think it's workable?" he asked.

She shook her head. "Sir, I doubt very much it is. It's a good stall for time. I presume you're hoping it will be a nonissue by the time we leave?"

"I am. I also anticipate that, just as we're a bit remote here, the Ishkul will need to be remote from human interference from the bazillions of people who want to meet them, until they feel up to it." He recalled the list of freaks Shraybman said she was holding back. Then he wondered if a big part of the reason for the canned tours humans were getting was the same deal. Keep the aliens away from the nuts who wanted to have sex with them, ask them for money, to fix their appliances, offer magical religious insight, accept the One True Faith, etc. He chuckled.

"Sir?" Stephens asked, looking quizzical.

"Nothing, I just gained a new measure of empathy for Vlashn. Thanks for the input, Doctor. Please let me know what I can do to facilitate it. Can I leave that concept with you to summarize? Do you have time?"

"I can summarize it fairly quickly because there isn't much yet," she said. "However, I don't really want my name on it at this point. It's not within my field of expertise, and it's too undefined at the present. I also see a likelihood of it either going wrong or morphing dramatically before conclusion."

"I understand. Would you like to keep the option of being credited if it does work?"

"That really doesn't sound fair, sir, if someone else does the work. I'll offer some ideas and that's all I really need credit for. If it works."

Yes, she really thought this was a nonstarter. Ah, well.

"Understood. I'll note it was at my suggestion, too. The buck stops here."

"That's appreciated, sir." She looked relieved.

"Good day, then," he said, and headed back for the diplomatic section.

He sought his UN counterpart, and found him finishing a plate of fruit and cheese. Russ wasn't a vegetarian, but also wasn't comfortable with killed meat rather than vat grown. Most of the food brought down from *Healy* was grown, but some of the choicer cuts—those Finley preferred to use—came from real animals.

"Ambassador Russ, I'd like your assistance, if you can."

Russ finished swallowing and looked up.

"Really. As little as we've done except read reports recently, I was beginning to wonder if the UN was still welcome, or if it might trigger another war."

Ouch. "Sorry. It's been a mad scramble. However, you will find this interesting, and, I hope, enlightening."

"Then enlighten me."

"We've opened embassies with the Ishkul. Vlashn has applied for, and received, Residency status in the Freehold." Russ sat up and looked interested and more than a bit offended. "He has asked for assistance in controlling off-planet interests. In order to slow HMG and that Egan asshole down, I'd like to request UN forces apprehend his agents and return them here. By the time they sort that crap out in the courts, I hope to have a resolution for us."

"I see. What does the UN gain from this?" Russ was a bit less prickly, but clearly thought there was some catch.

"I will encourage and assist in the creation of your own embassy, to be autonomous as soon as we complete this initial meeting. Obviously, I hope and expect we will continue to swap knowledge and proceed in a measured fashion."

"You're a very strange capitalist elitist, Mr. Ballenger," Russ said. "The deal is acceptable."

"Of course, I will have to officially protest your actions on behalf of our Residents, and threaten to follow up diplomatically later."

"The usual stern note of protest?" Russ said with a smile.

"I see we understand each other," he grinned back. "I'll give you a whitelist. Nail anyone else, detain them, deliver them to the *Healy* after we protest, secure their landing craft as contraband for 'later negotiation.' When you return it intact and undamaged, I can shrug shoulders and say they suffered no harm."

"I have your assurance the UN will not be found liable for economic damage to them?"

"Most of the groups have no economic interest. Those who do, I hope to give them what they want, eventually, and tell them to shut up about it. If they push a claim, I'll argue against it for reasons of practicality. If they win, I'll see that we grant some status or other in compensation. You have my word. I can't speak for the Council, but we need a practical resolution and you know we're good for that."

"Agreed. I would like that in some form of written communication for backup."

"Can't," Mark said with a firm shake. "I cannot indicate I'm prejudging a case, nor would I do so. It's barely possible they'll have some case with merit. What I'm saying is, as it currently stands, they're outside our law and I don't intend to find on their behalf. What I can offer is that since we now have diplomatic relations with the Ishkul, they must pursue any such resolution through Vlashn. I can't guess how he'll decide, though."

"That's fair enough, I guess," Russ said. "It still carries a risk for me and my people, and I have no idea what Vlashn might decide."

"Neither do they," Mark smiled. "Until someone knows better, it's a great threat."

"Yes, but . . . do you think some of these third parties living in close contact with the natives might have a better idea how such a decision will fall?"

Oh, shit. That idea had escaped him completely.

"So I guess we better bring them in ASAP," he said with a weak smile.

"I'll make some calls. I also have a visit scheduled," Russ said, grabbing his plate and heading for his office. Mark decided he should be in his, too.

He spent the day wading through routine approvals of scientific supplies that McDonald had signed off on, and some upgraded tools he reluctantly agreed would help, but he added a caution to please keep them out of sight of Ishkul. Someone brought food through. He couldn't recall who, though. It was a productive day, and he even dictated a press release with his name on it, rather than one of those "for" him by Shraybman.

He leaned back and stretched and heard sound in the corridor.

Bootsteps preceded a knock accompanied by one of the guards, half dragging Louise Thomas, who staggered and tripped. Mark came out of his seat to help, but she'd already been placed in a seat. The guard stood and spoke.

"Sir. You have a report." He left at once, but stood to as he closed the door. Nor was that door soundproof. He was offering professional courtesy, and would not "hear" anything.

Thomas's eyes were glazed again. This time, she'd clearly tranked herself. Mark looked her over and decided to leave her for now.

"Are you all right?"

"Forget any notions of gentleness. These people are as brutal as humans," she blurted.

"Oh?" he prompted. He was concerned. She looked rough.

"Execution. I watched an execution. Believe me, you *do not* want that video getting to the press. I'm prepared to deny under oath it exists for now." She swallowed hard and shook her head.

Wow. The nice aliens had capital punishment. Apparently, beyond a simple injection or shooting. "Can you tell me?"

She replied in terse bursts. "Vivisection. The condemned admitted his guilt, hoped his death could serve a useful purpose. They peeled him down for spare parts without anesthetic, while school children drew anatomical diagrams. Oh, Lady." She shook her head and gestured for a drink.

"Messy?" he asked, handing over a full bottle from his desk. He wasn't sure how it would react with tranquilizer. He wasn't going to ask, and she didn't seem to care. She chugged a slug, grimaced and swallowed.

"No. Neat. Surgically, professionally, dispassionately neat. And he uttered very little. It was . . . barbaric is the exact term. Primitive honor culture stuff. Like seppuku only more so."

"It does sound a bit like that. I'll have to watch it."

"Take this, sir," she said, handing back the bottle. "You'll need it. Oh . . . damn." She leaned forward, head in hands, and shivered. If it affected a combat photographer and photo recon tech like that . . .

Someone knocked at the door. It was Russ, looking similarly stunned.

"I think one thing both our societies agree on," he said, groping for a chair, "is that capital punishment is wrong." He was lightheaded.

"For different reasons, yes," Mark agreed. "I just heard."

"I understand the crime," Russ said. "I can't condone the punishment."

"What was the crime?" Mark asked. He was glad he'd missed this. He could be more clinical and professional from a distance.

"The translator had trouble. It translated as 'causing societal trauma.' As I understand, Vlashn and Somle have very large discretionary directorial powers."

"Yes, they can order people to relocate, change direction of industry, education. Great power with great responsibility, which is why they and we are moving slowly. It will help . . . but you've got something, please go ahead."

Russ nodded. "This individual led a group that falsified a number of reports on minerals, arability, et cetera, that indicated a certain area was more exploitable than it actually is. Orders had already been issued to build a new town, uproot people, start damming a river, when it was discovered. They do have an adversarial justice system. It operates very fast, though. It was proven to Somle's satisfaction that the individual had knowingly created this problem. He spoke up and accepted all responsibility at that point, and exonerated his underlings who acted on his orders and simply provided data that he massaged. They were then released. You've seen what happened to him?"

"I've only heard. It does sound swift, punitive and very dissuasive."

"It's utter evil. They don't believe in rehabilitation for things like that."

Thomas said, "Hell, I'm scared straight from here. I will refuse to answer an Ishkul. I will *never* lie."

Mark could comprehend their rationale. "Well, I can see that. Intellectual dishonesty at that level is potentially disastrous. They value science and intellect highly. Of course, our position is that a dispute is between parties, and the State has no right to decide life or death. We don't even imprison people often."

"No, you just allow them to shoot each other down in duels."

"That would be between parties, and none of the State's concern as long as all parties consent," Mark said. "We're getting off course. We're both bothered by their system, but is that system going to affect us?"

"It . . . shouldn't . . . though I wonder how our capitalist friends will respond, if it turns out that they'd be liable." Russ almost grinned, even through drugs, then shook his head again.

"Better," Mark said, "is not to ask the Ishkul, and present it as an assumption to our developers."

"Isn't that intellectually dishonest?"

"I'm not going to state that it applies to them. I'm just not going to state that it doesn't. After all, I don't know. It's reasonable and polite to abide by the local laws when one is a guest, and that's what embassies are for—to smooth over such problems. Obviously, if I had to smooth over such a problem, it would be of great cost to the Freehold . . . a cost that the Government would have to recoup from the party in question." He grinned.

"If you don't mind, sir," Thomas said, "I am not going to edit that footage. Show it to them raw. You'll hear me retching twice. I managed not to actually throw up and disturb our hosts. I expect recognition for that."

That last sounded like a joke, except there was absolutely no hint of humor in her voice.

CHAPTER 14

Chinran had her orders. "Apprehend and detain." The UN would send a boat to collect them. An actual water-based boat. Chelsea didn't ask. She trusted things would work out adequately, even if not exactly as planned. She focused on directing her team to bring in the interlopers.

There were six of them, one fireteam. She assumed they had military training and were Freeholders. She had the edge in surprise and numbers, almost certainly in training, but the others had advantage of local position and possible allies. She waited patiently. Nothing would be gained by rushing in, and the Citizen had specified "discreet."

Shortly, movement started in the growth near the hut, quiet but not tactical. Natives arrived, and called from a distance. Five of the humans came out, waved and walked toward them. Some gesturing and talking took place, then they left, carrying assault packs. That gave them a day's worth of supplies, maybe two if they stretched it. One human remained.

At a sign, her team advanced behind and ahead of her, slipping closer a bit at a time, keeping tree trunks and tangled growth between themselves and the targets. Once hidden again, she peeked low, verified it was still clear, and shifted a bit closer.

The remaining human came out to look at a miniature weather station that might harbor other intel gathering devices. She gauged the distance and concealment, made a sign, and rose to a light, fast run. Her target was male, twenty-fiveish, clearly experienced but occupied, and unarmed except for a headset radio.

Chelsea had learned this from an early age, and had years of professional experience. She flitted through the trees like a wraith, slipped up to the man by timing the shadows, and was almost on him before he noticed anything. His attention triggered on something, and he started looking about for the disturbance. She was the disturbance, and she tackled him before he was cognizant of her, rolling into the coarse grass and alighting over him. She relieved him of his radio with one hand and twisted him to his knees with the other, using his right arm as the fulcrum. He was in decent shape, average sized, but that was not even close to enough.

"Explain quickly and quietly or I will kill you," she hissed in a sibilant whisper.

"I am on contract as security," he said at once.

She noticed the omission of details. "More," she ordered.

"It's too much to tell at once. Ask questions."

She gave him credit for coming up with a creative evasion.

"You're smuggling. Who for?" she said to hasten things, with another jerk of his arm. He grunted sharply.

"Yeah, I'm a smuggler. But that's not what I'm doing here."

"You're showing modern weapons, gear and metal, idiot." The crushed plants under him were probably leaking through his pants to his legs. Good. A little redness and irritation, and no one could cry foul about it.

"They've seen them. There's no real danger. They know we have better tech."

She decided not to argue the point now. She wanted intel. "What the hell are you all doing right now?"

"Helping them against the baboonalogues."

"What?"

"The local ape analog is armed with rocks and sticks, and fights in troops. Not well organized, but aggressive and moblike."

"Another sentient species? Oh, shit, don't go there." If that was true, this was a nightmare.

"No," he replied, "not sentient. Semi at best."

"Explain. Quick. I'm not going to say that again." She jerked his shoulder until he grunted again. She needed intel, she needed it now. He was a source that could disappear. As he was not on any human world nor allied with any national government, he was quite expendable. She'd save that threat for later, though.

"Simple enough," he said after a gasp. "The ape things are growing in numbers and are aggressive. The locals are expanding and cutting into their territory. They attack in mobs with simple weapons. They're capable of dismantling a house and getting inside. They can't start fires, but they're not afraid to spread them, or they may do so by accident. Not even half as smart as a leopard."

"Thanks," she said. And thanks for admitting you're a vet, she thought. He'd mentioned leopards. It was unlikely a civilian would do so. "Come with me." She pulled on a joint and he came along, his alternative being to have it dislocated. She wasn't in the mood, nor did she have time to be nice. She frog-marched him back to their hide and shoved him to a squat in the clearing.

"What evidence do you have?" she asked.

"Video, stills, reports. They raid every couple of days and are getting bolder. It's a growing problem."

"So, to make nice to the natives, you plan to help them wipe out a hostile tribe, then offer better weapons and gear?"

He looked around, decided his life span depended on answers, and that he wasn't being paid enough to take that risk.

"I don't have many details, but the boss said we were only going to trade finished goods, not base technology. It's not as if they can refine the ores here."

"They can't. Those in the capital probably can."

He bit down on an answer.

"Talk or be made to," she said with a leering grin.

"I think our employers figured the technology will be transferred by the time word gets from this remote area, and that they'll have a solid trade advantage. They're going for subtle."

" 'Subtle' you say. I think I need to talk to . . . who was it you said hired you?"

"Not a clue."

"Of course you'd say that anyway."

"And of course I was paid cash by some guy I've never met who didn't say."

"I believe you. I also believe you're going to find a way to get us more intel, or you'll just be left here, alone. How long can you survive like that?"

"Not very long," he admitted, and sweat burst from him. He was a low-level merc, not used to playing with the big boys. He obviously wasn't one of those involved in issues like the conflict over moissanite mining rights in the Hinterlands. They were hardcase killers.

She'd need documentation of all this. However, if it was the case, it made it ridiculously easy to take care of this problem. She would put the attacking beasts down and steal his credibility. He could hardly complain to the government. At that point, a recognized diplomat could take over and start with a good score.

"Right. We'll do this then," she said, and whistled. The squad phased in from nowhere.

"You'll help?" he asked.

"No, I'll lead. You will do as I say or I'll hogtie you out of here."

"We're running things here," he argued, sounding firm. "The locals trust us and we have a base of operations."

"Military. My field. Want to bet? I've been in your base. I can have it gone without trace in a div." That was a moderate exaggeration, but he seemed to believe her. Just in case, though . . .

"Ow." He responded so well to those nerve points. "Fine."

"I knew you'd come around." She grinned. "Now let's call your people and get started."

"I can't speak for them," he said.

"You mean I'll have to persuade each one?" She reached toward him again and he flinched.

She laughed, on purpose.

The other smugglers were quite easy to catch as they came back. The Ops team had the advantage of holding their camp, after all. Ranid, the one she'd nabbed already, was gagged, bound and guarded by Anjin. He didn't seem disposed to trouble, but she was taking no chances. Moose and Sandy were behind the five humans, following them in. That left five others. Two on each flank and Sackett with her. She nodded to him. They rose together.

At that signal, the team closed in. Moose and Sandy had the rearmost down. Each flanking pair took one, she and Sackett hit the two foremost, hard, tackling them straight into the brush, rolling them and cuffing them before they could do more than raise arms and yelp. Sandy looked a bit tousled, Moose had some red marks from impact, but on the whole it was a very smooth takedown.

The five of them were propped up against trees, facing away from each other but close enough to be aware of each other. They made tentative attempts to glance at each other or make tapping codes. A couple of swift, vicious punches put a stop to that.

"Captain Jelling, representing a joint UN-Freehold mission. Do not talk, do not argue, do not struggle. Save any discussions for the diplomatic staff. You are my prisoners. You will answer my questions quickly, honestly and completely. I am in no mood to play games. There will be only one side of this story told. My side. Is that clear enough?" She didn't want to make an actual threat for legal reasons, but needed them to understand the ramifications and kowtow fast.

"I'm assuming your mission against the animals," she said. "After that, you will graciously make your goodbyes, to maintain relations with the natives. Then you will be leaving. We will take over the diplomacy. At that point, you have a choice. Identify yourselves and be remanded to the appropriate government for them to deal with, or remain reticent and we'll keep you confined until such time as you are IDed. If you're not Freeholders, you revert by default to the UN. Think carefully before you say anything."

The five said nothing. She thought that wise. All were over twenty Grainne years, thirty Earth. All were male, and in reasonably good physical condition. She wouldn't make assumptions about what that meant, but it was relevant.

"So, I need an answer from one of you. What did you plan to do to the local animal? The baboonalogue?"

There was a period of shifting and glancing, then one said, "They're a threat to the Srevnk."

"I assume that's the local tribe. Yes, I had deduced that much. And?"

"The plan was to attack them, hurt them, drive them off."

"How much do they resemble baboons, socially?"

"They're ground based, with arboreal habits for observation. They fight in mobs, with sticks and stones. They're carnivorous, and willing to eat Srevnk if they kill or cripple them."

"So you planned to kill this troop to show your intentions, and possibly your capabilities, thus to woo the . . . Srevnk into favorable relations."

He didn't reply to that.

"Then that's what we'll do. You can surrender your weapons and I'll put in a good word, or not and I'll ensure it's used against you. It's my word versus yours."

"Our employer might have something to say about that," the same one, presumably the leader, said.

"Oh? And who might that employer be?" She had a bet with herself.

"I prefer not to say."

"My bet is you don't actually know. Do you really think they'll say anything to screw their deal when they can just abandon you?"

"I . . . " he started, then ran out of commentary. He obviously didn't have anything to offer.

Win. She giggled on purpose and said, "You should take better care to have some kind of dirt on your employer. If you do this again. If you live to do this again."

She left them sitting in the tepid, humid air, being bitten by bugs and rashing up from sap to ponder their position.

Mark came out of his office the next morning, looking to take a break. Here he was surrounded by fresh air and daylight, even if the air was a little hazardous, and he was stuck behind a desk. He saw Shraybman down the corridor. She caught up to him as he entered the courtyard.

"You're going to love this, sir," she said.

"I suspect from your tone I'm not." He took a seat on one of the human chairs. Quite nice, slanted well back with legs at a comfortable angle to sprawl.

"Vlashn has set up relations with Earth." She adjusted one to face him and sat down leaning forward. She showed a lot of cleavage, but he suspected she couldn't help it and it wasn't intentional.

"He what?" Mark didn't want to have heard that. Just the thing to ruin a nice, sunny day with a gentle breeze.

"He signed a treaty agreement with the UN, and a mutual defense pact." She nodded with an askew smile.

"Russ is laughing at me."

He'd suggested the idea, of course, but he'd anticipated being involved. The "mutual defense pact" part bothered him. He'd kept the military out of it. On the one hand, that was bonus pull for the UN. On the other hand, it might come across as militaristic.

On the other other hand, the Ishkul seemed to be both practical and unafraid of using force. They might prefer to deal with the more militaristic group.

"Document everything," he said seriously.

"So we can do it right next time?"

"And to keep us out of disgrace or indenture this time."

"Don't underestimate Vlashn," she said.

"I've been trying not to," Mark said. "Assume they will sign other treaties with everyone they can. I need to talk to Vlashn again, very soon. I'm not sure how I'll phrase it."

"I suppose the good news is that it means the governments have more authority to control the situation. Though I'm not happy with that kind of precedent," she said.

"You're not happy? Try being me." He sighed. "Here I am trying to violate everything our system stands for. I could wind up being in history's dirtpile for starting the growth of government excess, like Lenin or Roosevelt."

"I have faith in you, sir. We'll all help. We'll find the leash and yank it and make these jackasses heel."

"That is such an odd mix of metaphors," he said.

"Or we could just shoot the mule and see if the rest learn."

"Tempting. But no."

"Yeah. How are our troops doing on that, anyway?"

"I'm told Captain Jelling has it well under control. For some reason I don't find that reassuring."

"Oh? Is that based on knowing how her unit likes to operate, or her real unofficial background?" To his expression she added, "I had a brief that included her at one point. I won't say anything."

"Yeah, please don't. Nor around her. She seems to take it personally, and I guess I can't blame her. Her father accomplished his mission, did save our society, and as far as her unit seems to figure, it was well within the rules. That's why it doesn't reassure me."

"They also follow orders very well."

"Yeah, which makes me wonder what orders I'm actually giving. Not reassuring."

"Shit, sir, you need to get drunk and unwind."

He nodded. "Yeah. A day aboard ship making use of the rec facilities would do me a lot of good. Problem is, stuff is coming up so fast I have to be here to piss on fires."

"You'll manage," she reiterated. "Let me know what you need."

"Thanks. I do appreciate it."

She turned and left him to worry and think in the corrosive fresh air.

When the call came from Captain Chinran, he decided he needed a drink.

Captain Chinran sat in a leafy blind and stared at the creatures, studying them. She looked at the zoomed image, looked at the enhanced analysis, considered their anatomy and structure.

Finally, she asked, "For record, can we consider those sentient?" She really didn't want to step wrong on this.

"Semi-sentient," Moose said. She wasn't an evolutionary biologist, but she was the squad's veterinarian, and knew quite a bit. "They use tools, but they don't make tools. As our host says, about like baboons on Earth, but more organized and better able to communicate. I suspect we'll find about a hundred distinct referents in their vocabulary."

"How does that compare to animals?" she asked.

"Dogs and cats have about twenty," Moose said. "Chimps can sometimes be trained to use a couple of hundred, as can dolphins and leopards."

She nodded. Fair enough, if that was the assessment. Bright animals, but just animals, and violent, xenophobic and *ugly*. It was unlikely anyone was going to start a campaign to save these things, even if they heard about it. Ballenger had eventually approved her suggested action, provided it helped keep the natives happy and transferred contact from the mercs to diplomats and scientists.

Still, she was going to look for every out. Subtle, he'd told her. Yes, she did know how to be subtle.

"Do you think they can get the idea without being killed?"

"I suspect not," Moose said. "Pain is a motivator, but their determination seems high. They're not bright enough to deduce that Ishkul . . . Srevnk make the food they steal, only that they have it. That's worth fighting for. In essence, they're hunting the Srevnk for the food they have, using small unit tactics of a crude but effective nature."

"So we have to hurt them badly . . . and if we're wrong and they're sentient, I'm the brutal warmongering bitch everyone on Earth expects me to be."

"No one here knows who you are, ma'am, and few people know who your father was."

"These things slip out. They always do."

"Not through me, ma'am."

No, not through Moose. Nor Sandy. The others didn't know, or if they'd found out, never mentioned it.

Chelsea pondered the situation again. "The idiots used explosives, but that means we can, too. Low order stuff only. Arrows and traps. Looks like all that low tech improv we did in school, that some people bitched we'd never need to know, is going to come in handy."

Moose said, "So we're looking to enfilade them, blow them up, shoot them up and set them on fire."

"I'm a big fan of subtlety," she said. "I get it from my father."

"You'll be the slip, ma'am, with comments like that."

"You're correct. I'll stop."

First, she needed to keep control of the captives, while ensuring she had them available for further questioning. Simple enough; they'd be lashed to trees and she'd take the one useful informant with her.

Second, weapons. Rather than explosives, the two rifles the mercs had would work well. Accurate distance kills should be more unnerving than apparently natural random blasts. They had knives and spears. The beasts were about hominid size, and gravity was low. They could be tremendously strong, though the limb length suggested not, and she had no doubt human intelligence and Special Warfare training would give them the edge.

"So, Ranid," she asked, "where do I find this troop of monkeythings? I assume they aren't far from here."

He seemed to have accepted that his best bet of getting out of this was to cooperate. He said, "Out on the plain, about three kilometers. The Srevnk say they've been moving closer."

Sandy said, "Yeah, I did see a bunch of them. Ugly fuckers."

"How often do they come in?"

"Every three days or so. Today's day four. We were . . . " He paused. "Well, we were getting ready to help the Srevnk."

"By wiping out an animal tribe. I don't suppose you considered scaring them off?"

"We did," he said with a disgusted glare. "Flares, bird bombs and such didn't work. One got burnt and they got angry and tore the framework we used apart after it cooled. We shot one, and they went on a rampage, destroying crops, tearing down a cottage, almost killing the occupants. So now we're sworn to eliminate the problem."

"That was just brilliant," she said. "I take it you stopped to think, and forgot to start again."

He didn't reply. There was a lot she could say, but what would it help?

"Okay, so we get to clean up your mess. Pay attention, then."

She grabbed him by his bound wrists and he grunted as he came to his feet. She lashed him back to a tree near his friends and went to work. She had to have this ready before the troop returned, which could be any moment, apparently.

She stationed a second watch, this one on the open terrain, which meant six people on guard—village, prisoners, hostiles—and three making preparations as she managed. By nightfall, they were ready. They also hadn't slept in an entire cycle. They napped in snatches as best they could, and she offered metabolic drugs all around. It was time to earn their pay.

Mark was surprised to hear that Somle was approaching. She'd visited twice since they'd built the embassy, that he could recall. Still, as he understood it, she and Vlashn were equals. Though she'd sentenced someone to death, and had been the one to ask why humans didn't just kill troublemakers. Vlashn had not. It might not be significant, but it also might be. He let that wander through his brain as he went to meet her.

Someone announced her entrance, and he hurried to the inner plaza. The weather was a bit cool, cloudy and breezy, with occasional splatters of rain.

"Greeting, Mark. Apologies for needing much assistance of your time."

He avoided a sigh. She meant she had a problem she couldn't handle, probably involving humans. He had two guesses as to which groups might be involved.

"By all means. That is why I'm here." He gestured to the couch, and watched the tableau of guards and recorders take their usual positions.

"Father Dunn is being opposed in debate by Shaman Lo Thing and Reverend Felts."

"Oh, my. That must be . . . interesting." He'd invited them. It was his fault if something was wrong.

"It is most interesting and highly educational as to your species and motivations."

"I wish we could record it." Yes, "interesting" was probably a very good word for it.

"Our parrot recorders have taken it down, and we can also transcribe it if you wish, though the latter will be a translation and moderately lack nuance."

"No, that's fine, though I'm curious as to your thoughts."

"Father Dunn is highly interesting. He is very logical and reasonable and patient, while persisting in faith in what he admits is an unprovable series of unlikely events. Reverend Felts clearly opposes everything Father Dunn stands for, and all of your current sociological standards and mores. I can actually state the absolute. He is, as firmly as Father Dunn is, convinced of the same series of events, but interprets them in a violent, aggressive and illogical manner, attributing widely separated events to wrath by the God entity in response to other events and activities.

"The secondarily interesting one to me is Shaman Lo Thing. His mockery and arguments are clearly intended to underscore a disbelief in either system. Yet Father Dunn is frequently able to respond with a logical and insightful answer that is open-ended, metaphorical or allegorical. Reverend Felts finds this very upsetting and his physiological markers almost always graphically spike at such times. Father Dunn and Shaman Lo Thing will talk rationally and with the appearance of friendship. Reverend Felts will not."

"Felts doesn't surprise me. He comes from a long line of hatred and idiocy. Lo Thing is what we used to call a 'jester.' They use mockery and derision to defuse anger and make points that are memorable."

"He is certainly memorable. His Sacrifice of the Virgin Kitten was highly amusing even without understanding the finer details of the translation of the service. He intoned two words I did not comprehend even out of context. 'ACK!' was one, emphasized in that fashion, as nearly as I can reproduce the sound, and 'Ramen,' which I understand is a ground grain meal bound with protein and stretched as a thread. 'Beer volcano' was translatable but I don't grasp it, nor 'stripper factory.' "

"I truly have no idea. I'm sure it's hysterical in context, though."

"As do I. There is another issue, with the other human landings."

Ah, here it came. The meat of the visit, and she might be the enforcer . . .

"Yes?"

"You are aware of them."

"I am."

"Query: What is their purpose?"

What should he say here? He couldn't pretend not to know of them. That would make him look incompetent. So would admitting he'd been blindsided. He'd discussed this with Vlashn. Why was it being rehashed? On the other hand, that proved he was not some omniscient monster. On the other hand, what stories had gotten back to the Ishkul? Did they have some form of eavesdropping, either infiltrators or the parrot creatures? Some paid shill? Their own intelligence network around the planet? Was there anything he could say that wouldn't make a mess of this?

"Somle," he said, "I apologize in return, for needing to ask for clarification. 'Purpose' can cover several intents and meanings."

"It seems highly likely you are being evasive. Humans have landed in three different locations. Query: What is the reason or reasons for this?"

"Somle, please recall that I speak for one planet, and as a buffer and go between for others. Ambassador Russ speaks for one planet, by proxy for several others, and by interim agreement for most of the rest. Neither he nor I have been able to contact all human groups and discuss with them. As I told Vlashn up front, I am aware of the landings. I do not yet know who they specifically are. I can assure you they don't have sophisticated weapons, and don't intend violence."

"It is bothersome to a moderate degree that you continually insist on a nonviolent intent for so many groups, when your admitted history indicates violence is the norm."

"We have changed from those times, Somle. Even when we do fight, it is from failure to resolve issues, not from desire."

"You are reticent to a high degree, extremely so on several subjects. Other subjects are not discussed at all. A majority of Ishkul, including Clan, Tribal and Citylode leaders find this mentionably alarming. You are partly aware of the nature of our meritocracy. Vlashn and I are expected to provide answers."

"Things will be troublesome if the answers are not satisfactory to the others?"

"If we cannot provide information about a situation, it indicates a failure of leadership. This would lead to the possibility of a change in leadership."

"Obviously, I must give you more information quickly." But could he?

"That would aid in resolution of the situation, depending on the information and its nature and reception."

"I will have to discuss this with Ambassador Russ, as well as our staff. I will get with you shortly, if that is acceptable."

"It is. I shall wait in the courtyard."

"It might not be that short a wait."

"I will wait," she reiterated, obviously comprehending. She rose and left.

Great, that was another stressor. It might be cultural for them. It was overbearing for humans. He'd have to hurry, obviously.

Wait . . . three different locations. Did that mean three locations, including this one, or three locations different from this one? The adjective was important. Why specify *different* locations? By definition they were not the same. This seemed to indicate there was another landing site the Ishkul were aware of, that he so far was not.

He couldn't ask.

He didn't dare risk human infiltrators or intel devices in the local society.

He'd better have intel get cracking.

CHAPTER 15

From a hasty hide under an explosion of shrubbery with two others, Chelsea watched the pack of animals dither and wander toward the outer fields of the village.

Moose was tracking the creatures via a tiny drone that could be mistaken for a large insect. That info built into a map and assessment that she relayed by comm to the team, with occasional quiet comments to Chelsea.

Ranid was smart enough to say nothing. His status was half prisoner, half advisor and all hostage. She didn't think the other violators would care if he died, but Ranid was likely to provide all the intel needed in order to prolong his life span.

The creatures loping across the grassland were *vaguely* reminiscent of baboons. They did live in trees, in troops, and had brachiator limbs with semi-opposable thumbs. They carried sticks, some for poking, some for clubbing. They had arm pouches of loose skin in which they carried rocks. The intent was obviously aggressive, as was the fact there were about a hundred of them.

The face structure, though, made a baboon look pretty. Their gaping mouths, coarse, orange dental bones, and drool running from fleshy protrusions, combined with the high nostrils and wide, downward-canted eyes made them look as if they'd already been well-clubbed, at least in the face. The loose skin and matted fluff didn't help. Their gait was ... bizarre. Even compared to the Ishkul. They pranced, like ponies crossed with bantam roosters.

Still, that would mean less bad PR. Talk about faces only their mothers could love. . . .

They were definitely bright, though. They moved in a single unit but with good order and noise discipline. There was almost a leapfrog component to the move, but it was more that of the brave leading the way in bursts, growing insecure, and waiting for the tail to catch up. Still, give them a few thousand years of incentive, and they just might rate "sentient" on some scale the scientists used.

"Do they seem aware of us?" Moose asked in a nonsibilant, breathy whisper almost in her ear.

Chelsea bent over and replied, "Not yet," in the same voice. The esses were voiced almost to lisps to keep the noise minimal.

"They're warm."

She raised a finger to confirm and acknowledge. Yes, the creatures were very hot blooded. They were easy enough to track. She wondered what the visual range of animals here was, generally. Presumably, their visual range ran lower than humans, not to violet, and likely into the near infrared, but that was an unproven assumption based on other planets. It was probably the case, but variations happened.

She raised her hand, signaled, and rose carefully. She knew the squad scattered behind her was doing the same, but she heard nothing. Good. She picked her way through the brush, looking several steps ahead to let her keep a good pace.

Woodswalking looked ridiculous out of context, and even more so here, with the need to avoid brushing toxic plants: Stepping high, moving on the balls of the feet, arms in and held high. It was already a caricature of itself, and amusing to watch, assuming anyone was around to watch it and survived the team approaching in that manner.

The forest petered out quickly, to scrub, brush and grass. Out on what they'd taken to calling the saveldt, they squatted and scurried, low enough for the grass to conceal them from the baboonalogues' rear guards. They moved in fits and starts. She closed the distance steadily, to within ten meters of the rearmost, and decided to push on. It was good practice, they had the element of surprise, and it should be even more effective on animals.

She oozed down into the growth as the hind one turned for a scan. He wrinkled his nostrils, cast his eyes back and forth, obviously aware of something, then turned and resumed moving. He was no more than four meters ahead of her.

As he turned, she slunk sideways into the path he'd left in the grass, let gravity draw her down and forward, then pushed off. She slipped an arm around the matted, greasy feather-fur, under the nonexistent chin and raised his head. With the other, she shoved a knife in the side, under the ear and pithed the brain. She stuck again, then sliced forward in a rolling cut that severed lots of blood vessels and the windpipe. He made no more sound than a gurgle.

He thrashed, though.

He also stank, she noted, as the others turned and screeched. It wasn't exactly a screech, more an ululation with a nasal overtone from their odd sinuses. Either way, in seconds the creatures were counterattacking.

They fought as a marginally disciplined mob, but the fuckers were strong. Her hat stiffened against a blow but it still stung. She responded with a spear thrust that probably didn't pierce anything critical, being near the shoulder, but should have been painful and crippling.

Luckily, the numerical difference didn't matter for long. Chelsea had one fireteam stationed to the right, shooting into the mass, shortly enfilading it as it became an offensive line.

The line broke up and started to retreat, and the humans pursued, clubbing, stabbing, beating the howling animals.

However, the creatures were definitely semi-sentient. They regrouped and pressed the attack again.

This was getting bad.

She signaled, the humans drew back and formed up, with a defensive line in front and archers in back. She wasn't keen on escalating to this point, but Ranid's advice seemed valid. The creatures were a serious threat, would be even to a well-armed Freehold range station in the Hinterlands.

"Flame," she ordered firmly, and five molotovs flew forward to hit the creatures and the ground around them.

Cord-slung flares arced high overhead, providing illumination and drifting shadows as their tails spread into parachutes. Ghostly shadows, lights and yellow and blue flame billowed, adding to the confusion.

The creatures saw the humans clearly now, and drew back. The goggles, shifting camouflage and weapons had to be intimidating. They still had numbers, though, and pressed again, while several of their mob screamed and thrashed, flames turning feather into stinking smoke. They seemed familiar with flame weapons.

Chelsea gutted one laterally and thrust into his buddy. The mob drew back in rings, fearful and respecting the fighting ability of these new, strange animals.

Then they were retreating, and several crashes from a hidden sniper using a rifle confiscated from the smugglers dropped their numbers. Less than half left as running wounded. Chelsea ran up and speared one of the thrashing, burning ones through his neck. There was no need for them to suffer.

"Casualties," Moose said.

"Right. How bad?"

"Mostly scratches, two bad bites," she said and pointed to where they were being treated. Ranid was one. Sandy was another. "And you." She gestured at Chelsea's arm.

"Ah. Yeah," she said as she glanced at the laceration. Now it hurt, and it was going to fester and react to the local chemistry. That was going to sting, and probably leave a mark. "Did we get enough?" she asked, trying to distract herself as Moose douched the wound with peroxide and wrapped a dressing.

"We got tens of them. The mob was perhaps a hundred. We got well over half."

She shook her head. "Not enough. We need to get near enough all of them. We can't leave enough to regroup."

"We're going to take casualties hunting them."

"We have to," she insisted. "Let's move."

She pulled the elastic dressing tight around her wound; it settled in place, nanos seeping in to start repair. Then she realized the dust and smoke, and particles of grass were in her eyes, burning, itching, despite the goggles.

"Eyes, rinse," she said at once, reached up and snatched off her goggles. Moose poured two large splashes of saline into them; she grunted and let it drain. "Now let's move," she said, redonning the night vision. She rose and took the lead.

"Keep shooting?" someone asked in her ears via radio.

"Yes, envelop from the south and keep moving. Try to drive them back this way."

A sharp report slapped her, then the world exploded.

She ducked down, hugged the ground, shut her face, opened her mouth, and rode it out. Bright orange flashes came in a kaleidoscopic whirl, and a cacophonous thunder, like a fireworks finale or a time on target artillery barrage.

Only there was no artillery here.

The thunder subdued and echoed away, leaving a hiss of dust, a drumming of falling debris, animal cries of pain . . . and Moose's voice in a pained whisper.

First, though, was security. Chelsea rose enough to get a good scan, wishing she had more than a spear to protect her. Someone had called in heavies, probably orbital.

Sandy was already on Moose, slapping drugs to her and apparently putting a tourniquet on her leg. Chelsea swore, made a visor scan, and saw two other casualties, and one missing light. Not red, *missing*. Buckley was . . . gone. If that was an orbital kinetic strike, even a few grams would have blown him to vapor.

Oh, shit.

A wave of adrenaline-driven rush, nausea, shock and anger washed over her. Someone had violated the rules, hell, had nuked the rules.

And she'd made a promise to Ballenger to be diplomatic.

With casualties being treated, and no action available but to wait and ensure things were under control again, she let her anger out in the only way she could think of: pounding the ground with a fist and a booted foot. She grunted in exertion, then got a lungful of the crud she was stirring up. The resultant spasm of coughing made her decide to stop.

There would be a reckoning. It might be a while, but someone was going to pay dearly for that insanity.

"Sandy, stay with Moose. Find a hole. Civilians will remain, too. Troops, with me. Let's finish this."

She knew anger was driving her, and she knew she had to keep it under control. She'd save it.

Mark had Somle invited in from the courtyard. It was chillier now, and it wasn't just the weather. He and Russ went as a pair, with Russ making it clear it was a favor. Mark couldn't blame him. As far as they knew, both infiltrations were Freehold based. The UN outfit was still in orbit.

"Hello, Somle. I'm sorry you had to wait."

"I chose to. It is part of my (untranslated. Duty? Choice? Task?)."

"That is an interesting word with no exact human match yet," he said. "But I understand you. Here's what we have, much of which is what I told Vlashn: Two human groups have landed, one in this archipelago," he indicated on a map, "and one south of here in the continent. Both are attempting to set up trades with less sophisticated locals."

"Understood. Query: That will be more problematic for them than trade with us, correct?"

Russ said, "Yes, but is offset by being distant and unregulated. We speculate they plan to use that as a bargaining chip with us to force a deal more favorable to them. It also may be intended to drive a wedge between Freehold and the UN."

"Statement, query: This would appear to be antagonistic to both and an act of aggression and defiance. What measure of response do you plan?"

The two human diplomats looked at each other. Mark flushed and felt a tingle.

Here we go, he thought. Gloves off.

"We have observed. We have determined that your assessment is correct. At this point, they are being recalled and ordered to report here, by our warriors. If they refuse, they will be engaged and probably killed. This is in line with our policy of noninterference, and with Vlashn's request as a Resident that I stop the incursion. It also matches with the mutual defense pact you have with the UN."

"Approval. Query: Per said agreements, what rights do I and my Equal Vlashn have in regard to these persons?"

With a nod and a gesture, Mark let Russ go first.

Russ said, "With our agreement, you have the right to be kept informed, to offer input and suggestions, to meet with and interrogate the respondents in our official inquiry, and to file charges for damages."

"Understood," she said, then turned to Mark. She said nothing, but blinked and maintained eye contact.

"Per our rules, you have the same rights. If you are not happy with the resolution, you may demand duel with the defendants."

"I confirm: Per the translation machine, the word 'duel' appears to imply direct confrontation."

"That is correct. You may challenge them to a contest or fight. They would get to choose the conditions. Such conditions would have to be modified to meet the local environment. They would likely argue against this, but I would hold them to it."

And hope I don't choke and wind up in duel myself. Ah, well.

"This appears to be the preferred option for myself and Equal Vlashn. Presumption that the stated resolutions apply to personnel from your respective groups."

"That is correct," Russ said. He looked both relieved that he wouldn't be held to violence, and disgusted that Mark was. Or was he disgusted that Somle seemed to relish the idea?

"Query: Do you have the means to determine which group individuals belong to in this context?"

That was a very good question. Curse these aliens and their intellect.

"We will find out and deal accordingly, and you will be involved in the resolution," Mark said.

"That is the majority of information and resolution to this issue that I sought. Expression of general satisfaction. Thank you, Citizen and Ambassador. I will now leave you to proceed and await updates to the situation."

With a movement Mark knew he could never match, she took her leave, turned and walked away.

"At least there isn't a third landing," Mark said. "She only mentioned the two plus this one." He walked back toward his office.

"We only mentioned them," Russ said. "She might be the type to take that to mean the other one is not on the table, and she's free to do as she wishes."

"I think that means we need to up the intel and share better. Do we want to invite DSR and HMG's ships to help with scans? If they're both looking for the other, they might be inspired to end any activities they have."

"I like it," Russ said. "If you're asking my approval, you have it. Should I ask ESO to help, too?"

"Good. But it occurs to me . . . the group my troops have found claim not to know who their employers are. That seems to be a likely MO for the others, too. I'm sure they'll help us find any anomalies. It also means they get free access to as much exploratory scanning as they can do, and they can even turn in their own people, if they decide they don't need them anymore."

Russ was silent for a moment.

"You know," he said, "I was about to make a nasty comment about capitalist whores. But I think our own corporation might do the exact same thing under the circumstances, and they have a charter from the General Assembly."

"You call your troops. I'll keep up with mine. We've got to shake this down fast."

"I agree."

Lieutenant Jetter got the call in early morning, well after sunrise but before the dew lifted.

"We're supposed to round them up and bring them in," he told his troops. "We're authorized to use force."

"That is both cool," Acting Platoon Sergeant Ruark said, "and disturbing. Who did what to who to get that approved?"

"I'm not sure. Still, we're the right people for it," he grinned. "Okay, gather round." He waited while the Marines shimmied and crawled in closer, still being discreet and all but invisible. Damn, it was good to lead professionals.

He drew in the dirt and said to his people, "We're going to approach. I want a narrow pincer there and there, so we can cross fire without endangering each other. I'll want a couple of guys here to prevent anyone fleeing that way. Make noise as needed, attack and kill if you have to. These clowns have managed to piss off the UN, the Freehold and the Ishkul."

"That took some talent," someone commented.

"Yeah, I have to wonder what they did. But we're the ones taking out the trash."

Ruark said, "I recommend six and five plus you for the pincer and four for the block, sir."

"Sounds good. You'll take the six."

"I'd like to take the block, sir," Okubo said.

"Good woman," he agreed. "Can we all be in position in three hours?"

"I hope so," Ruark said. "If you plan for that, sir, we'll figure to do it. I'd suggest having some slack if we need it."

"We can have slack. It does have to be quick, though."

"So let's move, Marines," Ruark said. He stuffed a few items into a patrol pack and picked troops out by eye.

Shortly, three abbreviated squads wormed their way through the scrub and along woodlines.

Their quarry seemed rather shy and insecure. They had two well-camouflaged tents and a lean-to of local brush, but they were a solid kilometer from the native village downstream. They were also well back and out of sight of the river. Jetter understood the one in the tropics was closer to a farming village. This group definitely didn't want to be noticed.

"We'll give them a shout first," he decided. "If they'll come in quietly, it's better all around. We don't want the locals to decide to get involved."

"How loud a shout, sir?" Ruark asked through his ears.

"A quiet one. Smoke puff or something else they can relate to."

"Roger."

Once in place, Jetter had one of the troops move laterally to be directly upwind, about a hundred meters from the position. On his signal, the Marine popped a green smoke, let a generous billow chug into the air, then kicked it into a hole and dumped a spadeful of dirt on top to damp it. The cloud lazily drifted over the camp and began to dissipate.

Someone either smelled the ammonia or saw the green tendrils. He came out with a rifle, looking suspiciously around. He tried to locate the source of the smoke and made a rough guess that was close.

Jetter said just above conversation level, "Now would be a good time to talk."

The opposition didn't seem to grasp the realities. A cloud of grass and debris kicked up with a crack.

"You did not just shoot at me, pigfucker!" Jetter said in loud exclamation. He'd never seen real combat, and hadn't expected to from civilian humans on an alien planet.

Still, if that's where this was going, he'd have at it. Although he had bow and spear, and they had rifles. Utter violation of the rules. He'd have to make them pay for that.

"Advance by section, first section forward!" he ordered. "For God's sake use cover. There's no suppressing fire. Second section, shoot anything you can. Cover! Second section, forward!" He rose and moved, got a scrubby tree between him and the shooters, sprinted and dove, getting a faceful of dirt.

Then he remembered the ground was toxic. He shrugged inwardly. He could decontaminate afterwards. For now, he needed to close.

The nine opposition boiled out of their tents and spread out for envelopment.

"Teams break down by pairs, flank and kill. Stop team, come on in, you have the enemy's rear. Use your judgment, Marines." He rolled away from the tree, sprung from all fours and covered down behind a grassy hummock. Someone was good; dirt erupted over his head. He flinched, flattened out, took a glance and decided the dirt was solid enough for now.

From his forward left, shouts indicated one threat was neutralized.

That meant eight more in good cover. There were going to be casualties.

"Go, Marines!" he said at once for encouragement. "Another on the right. Take him!"

He moved again, just in time. As he rolled through the spiky grass, a wave of heat rolled over him. Someone had broken out the flame projector.

"Got the squad weapon," someone reported. Kate Okubo.

"Well done. Hang onto it."

"Got one," Osis reported.

"They're surrendering."

"Smart," Jetter replied. "Roll them up."

Thankfully, there were minimal casualties. One of the civilians had a serious gash, already being sutured. Two Marines had injuries, one a minor bit of frag and one a serious bruise from impact. Everyone had skin irritation from the dirt and growth.

He stood in front of the gathered captives for psychological effect. He also had the numbers and had just defeated them with "inferior" weapons. He wanted to debrief them hard and fast.

"You've been recalled by both UN and Freehold, so it really doesn't matter who you are, who you're working for or what you want to say. You don't have any bargaining chips. I'm also authorized lethal force, and no one will ever know if I decide to leave a body behind. So your best bet is to come along quietly. We're going to hike out a good distance and get picked up by air. Then we're going to the main mission embassy. After that you're not my problem. Anything to say?"

He didn't expect anything, and there wasn't. Still, they seemed rather calm. It made him suspicious.

He turned and muttered into his mic, "Ruark, I want a thorough search of the camp. Get a scan from orbit and see if any . . . element is buried. We've got to make sure it's sanitized."

"Will do, sir. That's going to take a few."

"We're not in a tearing hurry and want to do this right."

"Of course. I've got three troops on it now."

Excessive force was authorized, and Chelsea planned to use it.

For now, she was using it on the aggressive beasts. Soon, though, she'd use it on whoever had ordered an orbital strike on her people. It had been a very precise one, too. That narrowed down the technology, and the intel gophers promised her they'd get an answer. Once she knew . . . someone was going to regret being alive.

For the pseudo-simian animals back in their tree-dotted grass, this much force wasn't necessary, but she was the commander and had broad powers, so she gave the order.

"Boost up and take them." Then she triggered her own Combat NeuroStimulant.

Her implant was even more sophisticated than her father's, and she felt the controlled ripple start. Extra oxygen, hormones and sugars flowed into her blood-stream. The dosage would increase for about ten sec-onds, which was easier on the metabolism and allowed better control than the sudden shock of Boost the troops had during the war.

It was also a thrill to the pleasure receptors.

Add in anger, frustration and vengeance, and it was better than sex.

She rose to a high-step sprint which increased in speed as the drug hit, then increased again. She covered the hundred meters cross country in under seven seconds, while the creatures turned in confusion, wondering what the apparition was, then deciding that even bipedal, and alone, it was a threat.

She wasn't alone for long, either. The others were just a moment behind as she tore through the mob, slashing underhanded. She wanted tendons under the knees. The first two she caught collapsed from the wounds, and the others didn't seem to be sure what to do. One in front opened his mouth and she raised the spear, jabbing it straight through his face with a wet crunching sound. With a twist, jerk and roll of her wrists she drew and reversed it, then gutted another behind her.

Vaguely, she knew these animals weren't responsible for the attack, but they were in the way, and there was nothing wrong with enjoying her work. She'd need her composure later.

She turned to go for more, but they were all down, except a bare handful, perhaps five, running into the growth. A few moaned or shrieked but someone finished those off. Seeing that, she whirled and heaved her spear in a long, flat arc. It chunked into the shoulder of one last beast, that howled and ululated and thrashed in agony until someone walked over and speared it again, mercifully ending its shrieks and whimpers.

As the thudding in her brain and heart slowed to something close to normal, and her burning gasps softened, she idly wondered how widespread this particular species was. Had she just eliminated a burgeoning sentience?

Not her problem. Soldiers fought. In this case, they fought to protect a group that wasn't even of interest to them, except that some other group of humans had made it so.

Now she'd find out what that group was up to.

Lieutenant Jetter led his unit on a forced march. The open prairie was harder to navigate than the tropical grassland his counterpart was on. Had he known, he'd likely still have taken the mission. He got a lot less acidic chemistry. Here it was irritating rather than injurious.

But it was irritating. The saw edges of the grass chafed the skin and then it itched, like cat scratches or nettles.

Flying pollen and the chalky coating of plants got in the eyes and swelled them to weeping redness, even with goggles on. Everyone was constantly coughing and clearing their throats.

Behind them, the camp was tattered fabric and a scorched pile of ash of everything plastic or technical. A few items like transponders were distributed among his Marines, and as many extra rations as they could carry. They'd need them.

The captives didn't resist, bound and surrounded by a larger number of professional troops. They clearly weren't eager to leave, though. There could be several reasons for that, including fear of repercussions or pending criminal charges. Caution suited Jetter's plans, so he just made note of it for now.

A hypersonic crack indicated a bullet.

Without thinking, Jetter went prone and pulled his ruck strap disconnects. So did his Marines. Okubo managed to hide her slender form in a depression mere centimeters deep. Good girl. He wished he could do that.

Then he remembered that no one had rifles here. These idiots had given, or allowed, the natives access to modern materials and weapons.

"This is definitely going in my report," Jetter said to himself.

At least two of the interlopers were running away, back the way they'd come. He saw two others fighting with Corporal Garry. That wasn't well thought out. Garry was a huge, muscular Forward for the team. Not the first choice one should pick to fight. Two other Marines waded in to seize them, while the rest kept the remaining captives at spearpoint.

Everyone flinched at a second shot.

"Okubo, Tahere, find that rifleman."

The two slithered off without a word.

"Marines, try *not* to kill whichever native has the rifle. We must be hands off. We also must get that weapon, at all costs." Dammit, he hated giving conflicting orders, but what else could he do? This was just a giant ball of suck.

Ruark scurried around, very flexible for his age, and ensured the captives were restrained. It looked as if he was cuffing their ankles. Smart. They could be left here and recovered later as needed, and under the circumstances, if they got eaten, Jetter would just shrug.

The rifle fire picked up, rapidly. Shit. One of the humans had reached it . . . but who?

Then it stopped, then picked up again.

"On our way back," Okubo said in his ears.

"Report," Jetter insisted.

"One of them asked for the rifle from a native. He commenced fire. Tahere and I flanked him. When he turned to Tahere, I sort of stabbed him in the kidney, and Tahere sort of gutted him. The natives ran off and we let them go."

"That's better than I hoped for. Well done."

"Shoot, sir, we're Marines," she said cheerfully. "I'm not sure who these clowns were, but they were hired cheap."

"Or in a hurry. Let's not assume they're all bad quality, though."

"Roger."

Jetter turned to the bound captives.

"Nice try. Didn't work and you lost one. We're not going to look for the survivor. He's on his own. Since we either have your gear or destroyed it, he's on very limited hours. I'll leave him this," he said, and dropped a flare. He dug in his ruck and pulled out a signal panel, kicked it open to bright orange and looped it over the flare handle. "If he finds it and uses it, we'll send a bird for him. There will be no more trouble. I've already risked my people more than I care to, and I'm the only one who gets to make a report. Fuck with us again, we kill you. All of you. We leave the bodies here, and no one has any idea what happened. Nor is anyone going to waste the money to look for you."

The defiant stares were tinged with hatred, but that was all buried under a dose of fear.

CHAPTER 16

N urin Russ wasn't a big fan of sea travel. He always got seasick. Some medication or other was helping, but he felt odd from it, and still a bit dizzy and nauseated. Warm, moist air didn't help. He'd prefer it cool. Still, the archipelago natives were far less sophisticated technically, and he'd agreed not to bring the first aircraft or spacecraft they saw. This was a secondary first contact, with the Ishkul holding to the same rules of not contaminating native development. It was an ironic effect.

They had approached within thirty kilometers by air, then done a hot cast into the water aboard a large Freehold assault boat. That had taken them cautiously within ten kilometers, and here they were in an Ishkul boat, downteched to use only wood and fiber. He was thankful for the flotation vest of some corklike material, though he didn't imagine it would help much if they actually sank this far away. He'd confirmed the orders himself that human tech was not to be shown this close to the islands. If they went down, they'd likely drown or get eaten, poisoned, or sunstroked before anyone could respond.

He wondered what the Ishkul escort had made of the lander. Russ had never seen inside a Freehold military vessel. It had a certain elegance to it, in that it was a very sturdy, simple, reliable design. One would never mistake it for anything but a technical military craft. The crew had been perfectly polite and unforced; it had been he who was agitated and terse.

The shore lay ahead. He could now see the breakers rolling gently over it. Relatively gently. He was still a little queasy and grateful for the approaching landing. He wasn't going to consider how the return trip might be, under the circumstances.

"People on shore," his bodyguard said. The four crew/escorts were Ishkul warriors. He and one Freehold guard were the human contingent for this mission. There was one other human, to escort back the prisoners on shore.

Shortly they were sailing/rowing ashore, the sail furled to a quarter its full size, then they were thumping in the breakers and hissing up the sand, the crew out and heaving on ropes. An actual plank was put in place for Russ. On the one hand, he appreciated it. On the other, it came across as effete.

The people on shore were the Freehold military team and their prisoners. Or he assumed so, since they were human. He strode up, the sand hissing and squelching under his boots. The field gear he wore was borrowed but fit well and was of excellent quality.

He enjoyed the fact he was actually getting some time away from a desk. Even before this, he'd actually done more exploring than Ballenger. That was actually a probable advantage when it came to serious negotiations. He didn't have a good feel for the Ishkul, but he certainly could read them better than his opposite number, who was just now figuring out that Somle was the enforcement arm. He'd share such info as was needed, and exploit the rest.

One figure was in front of the others. Female and in field uniform and gear.

"Ambassador Russ, I'm Senior Sergeant Meuser. Captain Jelling is at our camp, maintaining reconnaissance. You'll need gloves, hood and respirator in the woods. This tropical stuff is even more toxic than at the landing site."

Meuser looked like hell. She was bruised, stained, swollen, covered in cuts and scrapes and had her right lower leg splinted and obviously operated on. She was probably quite attractive underneath, but he couldn't tell from her appearance now. She'd been here a week and looked like that. Not encouraging.

"I'm ready to travel," he said. He was glad it was only a few kilometers. Not being an athlete or soldier, he'd normally have expected vehicular transport. That not being possible, he'd have used an exoskeleton to increase strength and endurance. That being partly metal, and therefore not possible, he anticipated a grueling walk even in the lighter gravity.

"Yes, sir. Sanderson will lead you. I'll travel back with the prisoners. Good luck."

She limped rather quickly toward the boat, and two others prodded the captives along.

The troops herded the prisoners aboard, forcing them to wade through the surf with no plank. The boat probably would have grounded with their additional mass, but Russ didn't think that was the only reason. They needn't worry, he thought. They were very much wanted alive.

While he made constant political use of the "fact" that a UN discovery would have immediately led to a quarantine, he wasn't so sure. It was impossible to secure a system against phase drive. ESO's presence was proof of that. It was possible, even likely, that a UN mission would have neglected to maintain the intensity of patrols that would be needed, and just as likely that the Freehold corporations would invest in the best stealthing technology available to get in clandestinely. Given the bureaucratic tendency to disregard anything outside one's narrow scope, and to evade responsibility or even ignore threats, the same situation or worse was likely to have occurred. That didn't mean he wouldn't use it to hammer Ballenger, of course. A tool was a tool, no matter its source. Just like these captives, who were a source of information on the exploitation attempts.

The crew tossed several large packs onto the sand, then rowed the boat away, using cupped sweeps that were more complex than human oars, and bent over their pivots. The boats seemed quite efficient, but were obviously very labor intensive to build.

Sanderson nodded, handed him what he assumed was a night vision visor, gestured and started walking, slowly but with a presumption of being obeyed. Russ donned the visor, found the knob to adjust the brightness, and followed, pulling on gloves he found in a pocket, along with a face scarf. Sanderson grabbed one of the packs, and each of the others—there were four of them—did, too.

They shifted at once into the trees, following what he assumed was a "game path." It was faintly worn, but easier to maneuver in than the growth proper. They had to squat and crawl once or twice, but he'd expected that and had padded knees. Still, it was strenuous. He sweated, strained and found the local chemistry was that toxic. His exposed skin itched, which he first thought was psychosomatic, then it burned.

"How far are we going?" he asked Sanderson in a low voice.

The man replied likewise, "About eight kilometers. We managed to move our OP closer to the village, and we've made initial contact only. They're very eager to resume their trade."

"Trade?" He hadn't realized any had actually taken place.

"Yes, sir. The infiltrators furnished them with a few steel knives and sharpening stones. The natives appreciate the resilience but are unhappy with the need to constantly sharpen. They do a lot of cutting. A substantial future deal was offered, along with promises of other artifacts. To our advantage, we wiped out the tribe of animals that's been destroying their crops and killing them, so the trade deficit is in our favor."

"I had only inklings of this," he said.

"Sorry, sir. I expect a lot of it happened since you left the capital. Things are moving very quickly."

"Right," he said, then concentrated on walking.

It made sense, though. He, an ambassador, was along on this remote contact to ensure things got straightened out. It wasn't that someone else couldn't do it; it was that he would take a lot of hits if it wasn't handled properly. Under the circumstances, hands on was the best way to protect himself.

Eight kilometers wasn't very far. Unlike a lot of Earth dwellers, he did keep in shape. Still, the trail they took was irregular, narrow, twisting and had steep inclines to scrabble here and there, rocks and protruding roots. It wasn't like an exercise track or even a road course. The island was sizeable, about that of Ireland, but the elevation rose rapidly here. He tired quickly, and felt his skin itch and burn as sweat mixed with airborne matter in the tropical warmth.

They stopped to rest.

"How far so far?" he asked, trying not to pant. The Blazers barely looked winded. He scratched at irritated skin and it got worse. Probably crud under his nails.

Sanderson said, "Two klicks so far. We'll stop every couple. Want some salve for that rash?"

"Please."

"Here you go, sir," the man said as he tossed a tube.

Russ squirted out a handful and slathered it on his exposed arms and neck. It did help, a lot. It seemed to be some kind of wax base with a mild alkali. It tingled, but the irritation stopped almost at once.

"Good stuff," he said.

"Yeah, that supply load that came with you has more, and food of course."

"Do you get supply drops, I assume?"

"Yes," the man nodded. "Way away from where we're stationed. This is actually easier."

"I hadn't thought about it. My food is prepared from the stuff on site."

"Sure, but even that is replenished every day or so. Ready to move again? Drink some water. That tube on your harness."

"Right, thanks." He hadn't realized how thirsty he was, and drank deeply. He stood as Sanderson did, and resumed walking. At least his boots fit well. No trouble so far.

As they hiked, he rethought the situation here. That Captain Jelling was very capable. Here she was, equipped with strictly local tech, and had apparently engaged a significant fight. Nor had his own intelligence section seen the infiltration when her team arrived. They were furiously and intently scanning every minute of every record since she'd disappeared to find out how the Freehold had done it. If that didn't work, he was considering the possibility she was twins. He didn't think there'd been any attempt to show off, either. She was the woman for the job; she came and did it. One moment at the embassy, within twenty-four hours on the ground half a hemisphere away.

These were the same type of troops that had destroyed chunks of his planet; only now they were not his enemy and were functional allies.

That would take getting used to. Still, there was no reason the two nations couldn't get along, but six billion corpses less than a generation ago would take some effort. To be fair, the UN had been the aggressor, no matter the official line, and had used WMD first, on Freehold civilians. That was going to take some effort, too. Large parts of Earth were still rebuilding. It gave him something to ponder while sweating and huffing and slogging away.

After that, he was going to have to try to explain to a local tribe that they really couldn't get any more of the marvelous magic knives just yet, but if they started negotiations all over again . . .

Mark got the word that the first load of infiltrators, from in-continent, was about to land. The others were en route from the tropics and would arrive local evening.

He had some ideas on how to deal with them, but meantime he planned to shake up the two reps. They were a constant irritation to him. It was time for some response.

First, he was going to call Egan. He was easier to get riled up, whereas Taya wouldn't twitch if she was caught strangling a puppy. He asked Shraybman to make the call, or rather, send a runner to the area Egan had set up in.

Egan entered the office and said, "Citizen, how can I help you?" He wore his negotiation smile.

He was either very good, or he really was clueless. His glance betrayed nothing.

Mark projected six images onscreen. "You can help me with these men, who say they work for you." If a jab didn't work, follow it with a hook.

"Who are they? I have no idea what this is regarding." He did look completely confused.

"A team down in the archipelago, making nice to natives, giving away *element* knives, fighting a war against a local species of pseudo-sentient, offering deals, demonstrating explosives, carrying firearms."

Egan's expression was odd, but definitely negative. "Citizen, I swear to you they are not part of my operation. You have my word, and I'll duel on it if need be."

He sounded sincerely pissed.

"There isn't any way for me to check that."

"Have your crypto experts check our manifests." He flipped open a phone. "This is Egan. The military needs to access our manifest. I authorize this. Code two one one two eight one two."

"I'll check," Mark said. "Though I don't know enough to know if we can prove anything. The effort is appreciated."

Egan was twitching now. "You want to know where to look? Try that liquid helium bitch. I'll put five hundred credits, man to man, she's got skewers in someone."

It was possible, even likely, that Margov had done exactly that, Mark reflected. It fit her personality, capability and ruthlessness. How could he check that? Though her current negotiations made it unlikely, which he couldn't discuss with Egan.

"You also know nothing of the military attacks against the UN and Freehold forces? Dropping the bar on the troops we sent to intercept them. One casualty, one wounded."

Egan blanched and grabbed a chair for support. He wasn't faking. He had no idea.

"Sir. At this point, I'm caught between wanting to help, and believing I need to hand this over to our legal division."

"Either way, you need to start talking."

Egan sat down heavily.

"Sir, I want control of this system. I've made no bones of that. Inhabited or not, we're the first human contact, we should get to write the deals. You want honesty? I don't mind oversight. If there are to be limits, that apply to everyone, bring them on. As long as we get first pick of every deal, and a reasonable percentage of the rest, we'll be happy. It's an entire system. We don't have many."

Mark said, "You have three. All red dwarf, all marginal. Systems like this are few and far between, and most have some kind of native life and have been colonized. You'll need to move way out to improve on that, and you're an ore mining company, not an economic conglomerate poised for colonization. Admit it. Outside of the materials business, outside of the Freehold, HMG is a small player."

"In private, sure, I'll admit that," he nodded. "We won't get bigger without working at it. That doesn't include fucking over the government we operate under, nor attacking the troops we'd need to bail us out if it got ugly here."

"Thank you for your honesty. I request you allow my intel people to view your operation so far."

Egan hesitated. "I'm not comfortable opening up our records to that level, even though I won't admit to anything actionable."

Mark leaned forward. "Mr. Egan, any charges against you will come from the military, whom you seem to have attacked. Clearing that up saves you some trouble. Vlashn or local groups might make claims. Those claims could seriously undermine your claim to rights in this system. Clearing that up will definitely save you some trouble.

"You want to get that 'liquid helium bitch,' as you call her?" He jabbed with his finger. "Open up to me. Prove your bona fides. That leaves her playing catch up, and presumptive bad guy. Win for you. If she opens up, it ends her scheming. Win for you. If we find it's some third party, you both get a claim against them, and shut them out from the word go. Win for you. You want this to proceed? Stop fighting the people who want to help you, and try for some real compromise. You can't have the whole system. You could certainly have chunks of it."

Egan nodded. "I have a lot of decision-making authority, but that goes beyond it. If you'll assist me in getting a message through, fast, I'll endorse that idea."

"This is where I admit we always have a boat standing by to drop a message through, if we have to. Good thing the UN has opened up the Jump Point. Now I have to negotiate using it with Ambassador Russ. See how this works? We all put in, we all get something out."

"I'm honest about this, sir," Egan said. "But please keep an eye on Margov."

"She and I go way back. I trust her less than you," he said.

"I'll cooperate. Anything I show the government is granted privacy, though, and any hypothetical plans we have are strictly that."

"We both know how this is played. You plan for every possibility, legal or not, and fight it from there. I won't hold you accountable for theories, only for overt actions."

"I will discuss that with my advisors and get back with you."

"Do so."

Egan left, and Phelan came in moments later.

"Information from *Healy*, sir," she said. "I have it on your system."

"Show me," he said, turning to the wall screen and motioning her over.

"We have a very small spike here." She pointed at a pair of flat charts showing a point so it was IDed in three axes. "It's a phase drive entrance, but very discreet and quite far out. Someone was willing to waste fuel and spend money to be discreet. Now, both HMG and DSR brought ships in openly. They also know the risks of pissing us off. This was someone else who wanted to tie them both up and didn't really care about repercussions in the short term. They also didn't figure to get caught, or the likely results. So they're not Freehold. None of our businesses are likely to be that stupid or shortsighted. Here's where they launched a minisat, and these are the orbital parameters. It's what launched the Thor attack against Captain Jelling, and undoubtedly was tracking everyone."

"Makes sense. Who?"

"We're guessing UN based, just not of Earth. The direction makes it very unlikely to be Earth or Caledonia, so we've narrowed it down to two probable suspects."

"And not one of our two?"

"Obviously, we can't prove a negative, sir, but Captain Betang said he'd give long odds against it. It not only doesn't make sense, it would mean at least a double phase jump, and no one is tracking one going out from the Freehold or into any appropriate system."

"In other words, they originated somewhere quiet in UN space." It just kept getting thicker, didn't it?

"Almost certainly, sir. They may have had intel from elsewhere, but the responsible party and the ship came from one of the UN's systems out that way. Ours are clean."

"I'm glad. I'm also not letting them off the hook until they cough up, bend over, and offer major concessions."

"Oh, of course not, sir. It's also still possible they contracted it, too."

"Yeah, but that would be sloppy and a security risk. They didn't. Someone just wants them down and out. Even if we don't find out now, we wait to see who makes the next bid and look at them."

"In other words, whoever it was has likely cut themselves out being overeager. Well, I'm glad our own people didn't decide attacking us was a good idea, and that no one officially involved with the UN did. It brings the tension down."

"Yes, sir. Intel is looking at traces and scanning back through records to see when the satellite showed up. It wasn't a dedicated weapons sat. It had a defense package that was reconfigured, probably by a local signal. That's why it wasn't very powerful, and it means whoever it was does have a presence here."

"Dammit." He thought furiously. "Send a summary to Russ. As soon as he gets back, I want him to check out ESO again. In the meantime, if we can tag their ship, do so. I want to make them face off. Especially as there could be murder charges."

"Yes, sir."

Phelan left, looking just as serious as before. Her humor the first day, and when he'd had her help buy land for the embassy, seemed to be her off duty and relaxed mood. On duty, she was a severe perfectionist.

Still, there was nothing more to be done about that issue until he had more intel. Meantime, he needed to talk to Margov again. She was the tougher nut and if anyone had dirt on Egan, she did. If she thought it would help her case, she'd slice his hamstrings and throw him to the rippers.

Mark decided on a direct approach. He let her come in and sit down, and kept his demeanor nonchalant.

"So, Associate Margov, I have some of your clandestine agents here. Interestingly, they were found far out of the agreed area, with HMG ID," he lied. "I wonder if you can enlighten me about that?"

"That's certainly an interesting allegation," she said smoothly. No dissemblance. She was an amazing actress.

"Very. Especially since HMG agreed to open up their manifests. Intel confirms they didn't doctor anything."

"You don't think they're that good?"

"You know as well as I do they're not, but my intel gophers are." He let his grin get colder. "I wish I'd had these kind of resources back when I was playing. It's neat."

"Obviously, I wouldn't admit to it if it were true, and deny it if it wasn't. I'm not sure what you hope to gain here." She still smiled, but it looked posed. Barely, but he could see it.

"We'll see if they talk, since I do have the authority to hold their accounts, and them. I imagine that given time they'll want to share."

She shook her head and smiled. "I'm not worried by that possibility."

"I can see you bribing over this, Taya. I can't see you killing."

"Do please let me know what you find out. If any allegations with substance are forthcoming, I'll certainly address them. By which I mean, 'Refer them to legal counsel.'"

He'd known he would get nothing from her. He'd have to find some leverage.

"Very well. You won't mind what I do, then."

"No, not at all."

She didn't seem quite as casual when she left, though. Connor came in after her.

"Sir, the prisoners are arriving," he said.

"Good. I want them all together."

"Sir, normally—"

Mark cut in, "I'm aware of sequestering POWs and criminals. I want this bunch together." He didn't mean to be blunt but he was in a hurry.

"Understood, sir. We'll bring them right in. Any pre-treatment?"

"Let them use the toilet. A patch of ground should do, with guards standing by. Look for anyone particularly bothered. That might help narrow down where they're from. I also want to make them as uncomfortable as possible psychologically. I'll make them wait, too. They're on my schedule. The guards are welcome to snicker quietly, but no touching or comments."

"Got it, sir. They're pathetic and beneath our contempt."

"Exactly."

Mark gave them more than an Earth hour to sit and sweat, literally, outside. They were sequestered out of sight, but without shade, given a bottle of warm water each but no food. They had a low concrete slab to sit on. After taking care of some other business, he wandered out, casually dressed, alone.

"Gentlemen," he said, "and I use that term very loosely. You've had a hell of a vacation. I assume you either don't know each other, or aren't going to admit to knowing each other."

He was unsurprised that they looked around at each other and said nothing. The way they studied, though, between the groups, indicated they had been unaware of each other, though a couple might recognize each other. They didn't nod, but there were indicators in their body language. All of them seemed to be sizing each other up.

"I'll also assume you aren't going to admit to attacks on both UN and Freehold military personnel, either of which could be considered an act of war, terrorism or just plain criminal stupidity."

There was some uneasy shifting. A couple of them looked less confident, more hesitant.

"Unfortunately, since I don't know who is a Freehold Resident, I have no reason nor authority to hear a case on your behalf. Likewise, Mr. Russ can't do anything for any UN residents, until they identify themselves. This puts all of you in a very gray area with no law. Outlaw, in the old meaning, if you will. You'll be staying here for the time being. Eventually, we'll have to do something with you, or offer you to Leader Vlashn for disposition under whatever rules the Ishkul have for disturbing the peace, crimes of violence, etc."

"That . . . " one of them said, then stopped.

"Yes?" Mark prompted.

"The Ishkul are a nation, not the species. They only control part of this continent."

"Shut up," another quietly said, from across the ground.

"It's nothing that will ID anyone. It might save some trouble," the one said, looking vaguely defensive. "Not that I'm offering to sell out," he continued, facing Mark, "but you don't know as much as you think you do, Mr. Citizen."

"I think I know very little, or I'd have this resolved by now," Mark said, shattering the man's attempt at a play. "I'm offering no deal, but if you have useful information, it won't hurt to share, and might work to your advantage. The Ishkul are who we're dealing with; that's who you'll be remanded to if not us. They apparently find medical research and criminal justice compatible."

They'd apparently heard that. Some of them looked a bit queasy.

The man said, "I think that's all I'm going to say for now."

"Fair enough. All of you might want to consider that your employers could renege on any deal at this point, and leave you hanging. Unless you have a contract against them you'd like to enforce, you have no claim, are no loss to them and utterly deniable."

The shifting and mumbling happened again. Whomever they worked for, they weren't convinced of their employer's support.

"Just consider the ramifications of being attempted murderers in the Freehold, or of our military personnel. Also consider Earth's probable response. And the Ishkul. There's little in your favor. Lock them up somewhere, Warrant," he concluded.

Connor had an assigned MP or uniformed soldier for each of them, and escorted them off to the rear of the compound. He'd wanted to stash them in a cell aboard *Healy*. Mark insisted on keeping them here where they were available for more questioning.

After they were well gone, Shraybman asked, "Sir? I don't think we can have any actual repercussions if we can't prove their involvement."

"Of course not," he agreed. "I'm betting at least one of the Unos doesn't know that, and at least one of the Freeholders, too. And I have one intelfiltrator, to coin another phrase, in the group. We snuck him in with the others, in pairs. If they don't talk, they don't ID him. If they talk, we get intel. Either way, he gets to observe and deduce."

"Sneaky. I like it."

"We'll also start working the deniability angle. If they can't monitor their accounts to even know if they're being paid, they should start having doubts very quickly. Whoever sent them made a series of mistakes I intend to exploit."

Taya swore in a string of physical obscenities and impossibilities that went on for a long time. Her team had been placed to make friends and influence people. They weren't supposed to have real weapons along. It made her wonder if that was sabotage by someone from HMG, or from the lately arrived ESO.

Considering the attack on the Freehold team in the archipelago, which she had not been behind, she definitely suspected a third party. There were rules to industrial espionage. Murder and terrorism were off limits, for the risk of payback if nothing else. Someone had screwed her over badly, and HMG too, not that she cared about that, other than she might take the heat.

The team she'd contracted, indirectly, had definite orders. Make friends, sign deals, make them reasonable, undermine HMG. No transfer of metals, nothing that a reasonable, uneducated, vid-watching yokel would see a problem with.

Now she had to figure out which group or groups would risk pissing off both the UN Marines and the Freehold Forces. Whoever that was had bigger balls than brains.

Not only didn't it fit HMG, it was sloppy. She had her own complaints about them, but that was not one of them.

In fact, it was almost blatant enough to be obvious, as if someone was trying to get them both busted, at least long enough to swing a deal. That meant it was one of no more than four competitors, including ESO, though that wasn't really their thing. Or had some government done it? That was borderline conspiracy theory, but some of her hires were ex military. What if one or more of them wasn't ex, or was on payroll? Shit.

No, the UN wouldn't risk war with Grainne by attacking Freehold troops, and neither would have allowed modern weapons. Silly idea. It was a competitor.

Was that important, though? It didn't matter who. They were doing it, and they had to be stopped. Some large leverage was needed, or concrete proof of who it was. They'd deny any accusation, as she was doing so.

Then something occurred to her that made her stop still. It couldn't be that obvious. Surely someone else would have done so . . . but she hadn't . . . and what if . . .

The grin that curled her mouth would have terrified anyone unlucky enough to be in bed with her. It was sexual with overtones of almost cannibalistic eagerness.

She would contact that nice Lieutenant Shraybman at once, and the ambassador's assistant, and invoke Freehold and UN privacy rights.

Then and only then would she admit to the first score of the game.

CHAPTER 17

Within the day, the prisoners decided Mark was right. Unfortunately, they didn't know much.

Still, Phelan interrogated them one at a time, with Connor playing bad guy. Mark let him slap them around as long as no permanent marks were made. Thomas caught everything on video, with a file to kill and a file to save. She also went through every file and highlighted anything that looked like dissemblance or deception.

"Here's a summary," Phelan said as she threw an image on the big screen in Mark's office.

"You managed to track bank accounts," he observed.

"Yes. It took an entire day to get information relayed, and two jumps so a ship could transmit, since there isn't regular traffic. So when this is over, someone owes the cost of two gate jumps."

"Ouch." That wasn't going to be cheap.

"Anyway, they were paid by three different cover companies." She indicated transaction records on a chart.

"Three."

"Yes. Two members of each team were hired by one payee. The rest of each team is a different payee. All of them are dead ends, of course. One account holder is 'Knullen Voide.'"

"Interesting. So someone did infiltrate."

"Someone with a *lot* of resources in our system."

"You think so?"

"Obvious. They set this up on less than twenty divs notice, between open business one day and midnight the next. Someone had an ear to the ground, as it were, and money ready to spend." She pointed out two more items. Very complete, detailed and professional. He believed her that they were dead ends. If there was any kind of lead, this woman would have dug it up and chased it.

"Competition, you think?"

With a shrug, she said, "It wouldn't surprise me at all if it was ESO. They do have a ship here, but graciously agreed not to land."

"Yeah, but they were also ordered to by Russ, and they do complain about it."

"Sure. But two other companies snuck teams down. Why haven't they?"

"True," he agreed. Yes, it could be. Still . . .

He continued, "Follow that, but also follow up on it possibly being either another competitor, or one of these anticorporate nutjobs, or anyone else with an ax to grind. Even the UN. They'd love to slime us with both events, and try to manipulate it for advantage."

"I will, sir," she agreed. "I've got three people in my section, and nothing else pressing, duty wise. I'll need an open encrypted channel to the *Healy*, and I may have to make a couple of trips."

"Supply shuttle comes down every four days. If you need it more often, it's approved. Have someone keep track of it. When the lawsuits come about, the military is going to dun the guilty party for all expenses. Troopdays, fuel, even the bookkeeping. Don't be stingy with the estimates, either."

"Will do, sir." She grinned. "And now I have real work to do at last."

"Go get 'em."

He was just wondering what to do next when there was a discreet knock, and Margov stepped in cautiously.

"Yes?" he asked simply.

"Sir, I am here to help you."

"Taya, you can't possibly expect me to believe that."

"I don't, but in this case, it's true. I stand to profit, but the deal will be of significant help in your negotiations. May I discuss it?"

He sighed. "I have a little time. What do you have?"

"A trade proposal with the Ishkul, for credit on account. We'll be interacting to their benefit and I freely welcome your oversight."

That was an interesting offer. What the hell had she come up with? There had to be a catch. There always was a catch with Taya. When it came time to pay, she generally came out ten points ahead of the deal, even if you did get what you wanted.

"I'm hostile, but listening," he said.

It took her fifty seconds to outline her proposal. Then she stopped, and smiled. It was coy and sweet.

"Taya, you are a genius, and a sadistic, sociopathic bitch. I'll relay an invitation to Vlashn."

She smiled triumphantly.

"You say the sweetest things, Mark."

"See if you still think so after we spend all day on this. You came up with it, you're going to outline it and head it up."

"May I have a connection to your net? Restricted access, obviously."

"I'll set it up." Yes, and he'd keep an eye on that himself.

Nurin Russ read the summary of Phelan's report with interest. He had to admit, the Freehold people were good at what they did, and they did seem to be keeping him in the loop.

There wasn't much he could offer, though, and certainly not from this hut in the tropics. He did encode a signal authorizing the UN forces and intel to cooperate to the extent of finding out who the third party in the equation was.

ESO, though, was generally scrupulous about not committing violence, so there might be some *fourth* party at work here. He'd relayed that to his assistant and to Ballenger.

He tabled that. He had to meet with the Srevnk again, and their tribal Chief, whatever his name was. It was utterly unpronounceable, so Russ had programmed the translator to call him "Joe" for convenience.

He could see Joe coming up the slope from the village, with a couple of elders with him. Unlike the urbanite Ishkul, the Srevnk did have a religion of sorts. It wasn't close to anything human, and as far as they were concerned, their gods didn't reward or punish anyone. They created things on whims and sent them to see how people interacted and responded. Joe was very pleased the gods had sent humans, and very aggravated that the deal had changed partway through. To that end, he visited every day, wondering if perhaps the deal had changed again. He wasn't pushy, just stubborn.

"Good day, Ambassador Russ," he called as he approached. That was cultural for them. Your host should have plenty of notice if your intentions were good.

"Good day it is, Joe," Russ replied. It was. Sunny and warm, the dust down quite a bit, and slightly breezy. That and meds and a good coating of salve and he felt okay.

"We are still enjoying the new knives." Joe's language translated more colloquially than Ishkul. It still left huge gaps in style, comprehension and vocabulary, though.

"I'm glad to hear it. Unfortunately, it still isn't time to resume that trade and I'm not sure when it will be. My own leaders haven't given any new information. However, we have other knives you will enjoy."

"That is good," Joe said conversationally, now that he was face to face.

Today he wore blue pants and a vivid tunic with a collar that worked as a short cloak. Their garb was simple and practical, sleeves and legs loose enough to roll up for labor. His face was even rougher and scalier than the Ishkul. His hands bore scars.

Russ said, "And I can still offer advice on farming. We have studied your fertilizing methods and devised some improvements."

"Those are welcome. Are these also paid for, as with other offers?"

"Yes, Joe. You have offered a fair price and we are still trying to make up the difference."

"But not with knives, though."

"Not with those knives. The new ones are better."
He gestured and Sandy, as the NCO liked to be called,
brought one over.

The polyceramic matrix was harder than steel, and
about as resilient. Just to be safe, he let Sandy demonstrate by splitting a section of tree limb, shaving off a
thick curl of bark, and notching it.

Joe looked impressed. "I see. These are said to be
better than the other knives?" He accepted delivery of
the knife, a large, leaf-bladed oval with a lovely grain
that really did look like polished stone. He examined it
and hefted it.

"A lot better. The agent who was here misunderstood
the value of your offer, and didn't return as much as he
should have. I apologize for that. I will exchange the new
knives two for one of the old ones."

"The old ones work well, too." He was busy examining
the new one while he spoke.

How to respond? Russ improvised. "Yes, but they are
personal property of our ship pilot. He was angry that
they were mistaken for the trade goods."

"I understand. I will see they are returned promptly,
and two for one is more than fair."

"I am sorry, Joe. The human who initially greeted you
made a mistake in offering those, as I've said. We will
offer other technology sometime soon. It won't be at
once, though. Also, I will have to leave tonight, and the
warriors will in a few days. I know we will return, but
my leaders have not said when."

It was handy, he reflected, to be a subordinate answer-
ing to others, who always said no.

"We will look futureward to your return, and the
knives."

"I will do what I can, Joe. Our people desire trade, and your land resources are quite rich. Be sure you get a good price for them. Always refuse the first offer."

"If you advise that for your people, I will do so. I am sad to hear the offer we got was not fair."

"It was badly advised. I or another ambassador will try to make sure you get treated well. Now I'm afraid we must prepare to go."

"A safe trip across the sea to you, Ambassador."

"Thank you, Joe. I hope your crops are productive and bountiful."

Good. One more fire put out. The polyceramic blades would break with use, but they'd last a lot longer than native stone. Afterwards, they'd look just like waste rock, except for resisting all efforts to knap them with native tools. These natives had no contact yet with the Ishkul, nor did the Ishkul see any need to deal with cultures so far from their own and so far behind. So the pieces would wind up in the ground somewhere, well-camouflaged, and hopefully before anyone recovered one, other issues would have passed them by.

Captain Jelling came around from behind the tent.

"I heard, sir," she said. "That seemed to go well."

"Indeed. I'm glad we could resolve it."

Every time he saw her, he was reminded of how harsh this planet was. She was a stunningly gorgeous woman, despite her military haircut and Olympic physique. Yet the chemistry, exertion and mental wear made her look like a very average person who'd just been hit by a truck. He wondered how he looked at this point.

She said, "I'm going to send three troops with you tonight. The remaining six of us should be out of here within the Earth week. We have our final drop of supplies tonight."

"More salve and field rations?" he asked with a slight grimace.

"Yeah, it's a nasty place, sir. But that's what we specialize in. Anything you don't want to take we'll salvage or destroy, but I wouldn't plan on getting it back."

"That's fine, Captain. The less I carry the better. Use what you can. I assume that's a hint to pack?"

"Yes, sir," she smiled. "It's never too early to get ready, and dusk is in about five hours."

"I'll be glad to see it. Travel safely when you do."

Mark watched the trio of experts work. Lieutenant Phelan tracked movement on a screen, Sergeant Thomas squinted and zoomed in on photos and made marks, and some other technical expert, down from *Healy* and in petty officer uniform, did something.

"That's probably one there," Thomas said.

"I concur," the tech agreed with a nod.

"Is that?"

"Mark it anyway," Phelan said.

Mark watched silently until he was noticed.

Thomas looked back, nodded and said, "We're going over the in-continent site. There were a few element artifacts left behind, and possibly some transmitters. We're trying inductance fields. If we do find any, they may yield intel as to their source."

"Very good. Don't let me interrupt," he said.

Bad, and good. Artifacts left behind, but the infiltrator's sloppiness could kick up new evidence.

Phelan said, "Not at all, sir. Be advised, though, that even if we find a traceable component, it will take time to determine its original disposition from surplus sale or manufacturer, and that may not yield information on later transfers."

"In other words it probably won't find anything."

"I'm sure it will find something. It just may take several months."

"Well, meantime the bill is building."

He decided he'd keep the information on possible traces away from Captain Chinran. She had a score to settle, and he didn't want her settling it here. He was sure she'd eventually find out and do so, just so long as she was discreet.

Later that day, Lieutenant Shraybman came in.

"Sir, Lieutenant Phelan gave me a brief for you. They have possible leads on the secondary infiltrators."

"That's interesting," he said. "I understood that was going to take several months."

"To determine some things, yes. However, it seems our self-appointed Ishkul activists are a bit on the eager side, and naïve of technicalities. That latter's not really surprising for a bunch of luddites."

"Skip the pleasantries, please, Irina," he said, but smiled. She was enjoying this.

"FreeTech bought one of the transmitters outright, surplus from us, the day the news leaked."

"So eager to play they didn't even stop to think."

"Sir, I doubt they're really that smart. They just bought it and thought they were being sneaky."

"Any group that shares technology has to have some grasp of it."

"Not them," she almost snapped, and bit down after she said it. For whatever reason, she really didn't like FreeTech. Personal?

He said, "Oh, I doubt the leadership actually bothers. Their sources have to, though. The joke here is they didn't think they needed an expert on mere transmitters."

"I'd be surprised if they could read the manual, sir."

Yes, she definitely had an ax to grind.

"So how did they get in system, then?"

"ESO," she said. "That was the only nonmilitary vessel that came in afterwards."

"Would they have time to get the transmitter to a ship in Earth space and get it aboard in the time available?"

"I'll have that checked, sir. But unless there's a ship we don't know about, it has to be. Neither our ships nor the UN's entered this system in that timeframe. ESO is it. The signal hopping frigates on commo duty are the only ones coming in and out, and they don't get in system."

"But ESO must then have stealth capability to get to the other company vessels."

"No, sir. They docked and had exchanges. I doubt they had stowaways, but they either had existing infiltrators or paid someone new. They threw a fairly complex but unsophisticated package together in a hurry, and completely discounted the blatancy of it."

"That's pretty typical for that type of thinking."

"Yes, sir," she agreed, smiling. Negative comments about them made her happy.

"Well, that doesn't prove anything, but if the military wants to swear out a complaint, I'll have Russ look it over. He's on his way back now. He'll deny us jurisdiction, of course, but we'll threaten to let the Ishkul decide it. Of course, we can't because of the information that would leak out. Still, we can tie them in knots while we clean this up."

"Got it, sir. Let me know if you need any help."

By evening, they had confirmation of many of the facts. FreeTech had one paid shill in HMG and two infiltrators—one each in ESO and DSR. The ESO man provided instructions and tools to the others.

However, the HMG shill decided his best bet was to talk. He was out of a job after this, and likely to be sued, but word of the stack of charges had unnerved him. He told all, except for motivations and which parts were personally his, not that of the group. He admitted the presence of other infiltrators, and that he'd been warned of the orbital attack.

The complication, of course, was that HMG and DSR were tentatively off the hook for the actual attacks. Whether or not ESO was involved was still unknown. Still . . .

Russ arrived, and Mark greeted him.

"Damn, man, you look like hell."

"Yeah, thanks," Russ replied.

He did look rough. His skin was not only inflamed but puffy here and there, likely from insect bites. He looked very tired, with sunken eyes, and the backs of his hands were blistered. He'd showered, but that only emphasized the damage under the former dirt.

"Harsh environment, I take it," Mark said.

"Yes, like here but more tropical, active and humid. It means actual contact is going to be from sites like this, more than likely. I came right over because I heard you had updates on the infiltrations."

"Yes, I do. It's becoming a lot clearer." He gave Russ a summary and displayed some logic charts he'd created on who was doing what.

Russ said, "As far as ESO, it's enough for me to order them to remain in place near the gate and go nowhere. As far as UN persons go, I control this system."

"Must be nice," Mark said. "Do so, then. I have enough evidence and statements to stick FreeTech to the wall until it's heard in court. That tramp freighter everyone came in is going to be rather full and cramped. I have valid reason to suspect anyone who argues with me and stuff them aboard."

"Better, from a point of view of keeping control."

"Yes, so far."

"So far, at least," Russ said, "the business interests have been smart enough not to flash any element here. How long will that last?"

"A while, I hope," Mark said. "They want to get good graces first, then offer stuff slowly. Making a massive pitch at once means a one-time sale, and what do the locals have? First, they have to find out who's nominally in charge, try to create concordance on the idea of mineral rights, and swap those rights for finished goods. Slower development actually works in their favor. And they have flashed element as finished goods, which they failed to keep adequately secured. No serious leakage happened that we're aware of, but it's still a bad precedent. Add in that without their presence in those unauthorized, and in fact, prohibited or 'strongly advised against' landings, our FreeTech scum wouldn't have had a means to do what they did, and I'm going to nail them as accessories."

"They certainly don't act like slower development is of interest. You're also correct on the modern materials, which are bad for several reasons." Russ looked frustrated and bothered, hand gripping his jaw.

"No, they want to move slowly, they just all want a monopoly and that in writing now, so they can be the only ones to move slowly."

"Do you think they'll abide by our judgment now?" Russ asked.

"Yes, as long as we maintain a presence and have legal claims to hold over them. No longer."

"ESO is going to find a lot of its government contracts being audited," Russ said.

"Just to annoy them, eh?"

"Oh, no. The contracts are quite detailed and involved. It's virtually impossible for a company to comply. As long as they deliver per contract, though, no one looks too hard at the nitpicky details. In cases like this, however, as much dirt as possible is dug up, thrown around, used to embarrass their public image, tarnish the ranking people and cost them money in accommodation, defense and compliance, along with frequent punitive fines and interest."

"You play the same game," Mark observed, "with slightly different rules."

"Yes," Russ agreed, smiling. "It's just that I know these rules and don't know yours."

"I am going to shut off communication between Margov and Egan and their ships. From now on, all their commo can go through the military, which I will furnish graciously free of charge so they can't complain."

"They must still have some kind of code."

"Yes, but I have cryptologists and scientists. They'll be cautious. I'll also have all written communication paraphrased."

"You've done this before," Russ observed. "I was told you were brand new and untested."

"I was just such a corporate negotiator on the other end of the deals, and before that I was an analyst in the military, doing a bit of what Phelan does only on specific technical developments. I have the ball and they are now going to play by my rules. Care for a drink?" he concluded, reaching for a bottle.

Russ laughed. "Delighted."

A knock on the door was followed by the appearance of Shraybman, who said, "Sir, sorry to interrupt. Vlashn just arrived to see you."

"Well, show him in, I guess. We'll meet him in the conference room."

"Of course."

The two men rose with their drinks.

"That's almost suspicious timing," Russ said.

"It could be luck." Mark shrugged. "We'll see."

They stepped into the meeting area. Vlashn was still standing, his assistants discreetly in the corner.

"Greetings, Vlashn," Mark said.

"And likewise," added Russ.

"Greetings, Mark and Nurin. My unscheduled visit is to discuss new events."

"Of course."

"My information is that you have removed and sequestered the unauthorized visitors."

"We are just completing that process now, Vlashn. Ambassador Russ went personally to deal with one such." At mention of his name, Russ nodded.

"Thank you for your attention, Ambassador Russ," Vlashn replied. "Thanks to all those you collectively represent and/or lead for their efforts. I remain convinced of your good intentions and confidently believe your ability to accomplish your stated goals."

"You're welcome, Vlashn. Is the exchange with Associate Margov helpful to the situation?"

"It is helpful in that we have agreed on Ishkul and other Drazl products and resources she believes she can profit from with other humans. It is moderately problematic that such exchange is only tentative and exchange cannot take place. Also, no human benefit to Ishkul exists save a tentative study opportunity."

"Yes, that's one of the last hurdles to be resolved. Once I convince them to an accord, exchange of knowledges you don't yet possess can begin, which will then be moderated through your office."

Vlashn leaned upright on his couch. "It is blatantly clear that these interests wish to discuss business with us. Obviously, this is connected to transfer of technology. The problem I and other leaders face is balancing a desire for knowledge with a moderated rate of transfer to avoid socioeconomic disruptions. The rather ironic feeling of this event is that while I am extremely better suited to make this judgment than you, I am part of the receiving society and therefore must remain ignorant of the relevant technology. I would prefer not to trust your judgment, without prejudice or intent of insult, due to your far lesser familiarity with our society. I am forced to do so because of your familiarity with your society, the technically superior. Conversely, there is a different and lesser risk of harm from transfer of cultural theory, in either direction." Vlashn stopped talking long before the translator finished. Their language was not only precise, but efficient.

Russ replied, "That's exactly the problem, Vlashn. We hope it will be resolved very shortly. We're working to that end."

"Query: What can Ishkul do to assist and expedite this process?"

"We need as much technical information on your society as we can get. We need to know the philosophical history and current practices. Our scientists are working on that now. Once that is done, there will be complicated, but I hope brief, discussions, first between the

Freehold and the United Nations, then between that
alliance and the nongovernmental interests to resolve
points they present as concerns for people. After that, a
binding policy will be created for our corporate interests.
I strongly recommend you retain a human legal advisor
for those negotiations."

"I will take that under strong advisement." Vlashn
glugged a laugh. "I have been party and/or witness to a
representative plurality of these meetings. Three of these
groups claim to represent the interests of my species. As
I only represent those of this district of the continent,
such claims are inaccurate though with a strong probability of intention to be beneficial to us, yet considerably
amusing to me."

"Yes, they are the nongovernmental groups we will
have to deal with."

"Your complicated alliances and treaties, between philosophies, business, warriors, statesmen, · geographic
locations and financial groups are strongly reminiscent
of our (untranslated) era, approximately (one thousand
Earth years) ago. I am surprised."

Mark said, "Yes, Vlashn, we believe your development
has been slower and more mature. We're open about
that fact. We can learn from you, too."

"You are learning. We still await the beneficence of
your technological gifts."

"I recognize the sarcasm you imitate, Vlashn. You do
it very well. I also understand your concern. I will authorize our scientists to offer further improvements to your
steam engines and mechanical transmissions."

- "That is appreciated. I remind you that you have not
answered the question that was implied in my comment
on your near-tribal interactions. Also, you were hesitant

to discuss the war with Earth and do not discuss technical details of how so many were killed. The complete avoidance of this subject is of high interest to me."

Sigh. "Yes, Vlashn, we and Earth had a knock down war. They killed a lot of our people. We killed a lot of theirs. We have resolved things and are here together."

"I am led to believe you were highly more successful in your infliction of casualties and degradation of infrastructure."

The two humans looked at each other for a moment. Russ gestured and Mark replied.

"The latter is debatable. They had a lot more infrastructure to start with. The former I concede is true."

"Impressive. The energy release needed to destroy a city, or power a ship through the interstellar spaces is multiple I will not guess at this moment orders of magnitude greater than we have attained. I understand your caution in dissemination. Concurrently, I am highly interested in seeing my people develop further in that direction to bring a balance, and better development of our planet."

"That is how things are done. We hope you'll believe that we also desire to see you achieve parity, so as to negate these complicated exchanges and ensure your people will retain their self."

"I believe we have a near unity understanding of the political summary each of the other. I am unable to convince related and nearby second order leaders of your collective generic earnestness. This is directly and indirectly causing upset and political friction I must deal with."

"Vlashn, humans have a tradition of using alcohol to celebrate and bond. In many cultures, there is a male ritual of doing so with one who could be considered a friend, an ally or a worthy opponent. I would like to offer you a human beverage."

"I will accept in all three male ritual meanings and in the generic." Vlashn . . . didn't laugh. A friendly chuckle?

They seemed to like strong flavors. Mark grabbed the bottle of Silver Birch he'd brought and poured a shot. He grabbed the local bottle and poured a triple, not knowing how much Ishkul drank and wanting to be sure the amount was sufficiently non-dainty.

Russ was letting him take the heat, the bastard. Though to be fair, he'd taken the authority, so it was his problem to deal with. Bastard. He poured another glass for Russ and handed it over.

Raising his own, he said, "A toast, to enemies past, now allies in exploration, discovery and peace."

"To openness and development, so that many cultures can become strong from sharing their virtues." Russ offered. Ick. How syrupy.

"To sharing our mutual understanding and bond with those subordinate to ourselves, in sufficient time to prevent their uprising in revolt."

Mark tried not to choke.

"Vlashn, no matter what happens, you and I are friends. You are welcome to visit my house whenever you can get to Grainne."

After the diplomacy came the practical dealings. Mark met with his staff, military and technical, and posed the situation and question to them.

"So what can we send?" he asked when done.

Dr. Zihn spoke up. "Actually, sir, I think I can be of help here. They have telescopes. Also water clocks and excellent plotting pantographs. Send me, a ceramic engineer and an optician, and we can see about improving their refractive scopes. It's positive for them and I don't see any negatives for us."

There was silence for several moments, but it was thoughtful.

"I like it," Mark said. "Land?"

McDonald fingered his beard, then replied, "I tentatively approve. I can't see any negatives either."

"Dr. Stephens?"

"It seems very good, sir. Positive, peaceful and helps their long-term scientific position. I'd do it."

"If anyone finds any problems before end of business today, let me know. Otherwise, I'll offer it to Vlashn first thing in the morning."

Stephens said, "Also, sir, I can state with confidence that the culture to the north is another nation. I would assume word of our presence has reached them. They will respond at some point."

"Can you guess how?" he asked. It was inevitable, really. It was also very inconvenient.

"Not without seeing the culture up close. However, there are no obvious signs of conflict along the border, nor major military activity. We can hope for peaceful contact."

"I hope they're not more capitalists," he said with a wry smile.

CHAPTER 18

Vlashn and Somle continued to alternate their presence, for longer periods of time. The temporary camp used to signal the humans on first arrival had been abandoned, and was now reopened on a smaller scale, occupied by scientists and warriors. The Ishkul researchers constantly pestered the humans and were gaining knowledge bit by bit, both from what was said, and what was refused.

Russ visited the site and reported to Mark when he returned.

"They have limited field plumbing. They've arranged a windmill-powered well, have their own logistics train, and—are you familiar with semaphore?"

"The concept, yes," Mark agreed. "Swinging arms to send signals."

"Yes, that's it. They use that for communication. It's fast enough, considering. So they have quick communication with the capital and daily arrivals and departures of supply wagons."

"I am constantly amazed at their development," Mark said. "They have proper surgery, too, with anesthetic, antiseptic, antibiotics, reconstruction and physical therapy."

"All that and more," Russ agreed. "I wish it had been a scientific expedition that found them."

"Heck, even if it had, the same bunch would show up."

"Surely," Russ agreed. "But it more likely would be one of our expeditions than yours, so we'd be able to slam the door on them."

"Maybe. It hasn't worked so well this time, with all the power plays."

Vlashn appeared again the next day from the landing camp. Rather than one of the three scientists who regularly escorted him, he had a completely different assistant, who carried both parrot recorders and a writing kit. This Ishkul assistant took a couch, prepped his—at least, Mark thought he was male—writing kit and waited patiently.

Vlashn sprawled on the couch and looked over with those intense, alien eyes.

"Father Dunn is a highly fascinating man, and his ideas are of unprecedented interest."

"He's spoken to you of his faith?" Obviously he had; but it was a leading question. Mark still felt a bit foolish, after absorbing some of the direct and logical communication of the Ishkul. He saw the scribe was busy making notes.

"Yes, he has spoken of his philosophy, of the Savior and God. I'm quite intrigued."

"How so?"

"A large number of humans subscribe to this metaphysical construct. They vary from token acceptance to deep conviction of this unprovable resurrection and salvation, and it guides their life and business, and there are residual components in the philosophies of most humans we have met so far."

"Yes, that's true. One of our antecedent cultures was entirely Christian."

"I observe you don't consciously subscribe to it anymore."

"Well, some—" Mark pulled up short. The statement had been precise. "No, I don't. There was a reconstruct of an earlier religion a few hundred years ago that was colored by the base culture of the time, which was Christian in basis even if the devout adherents were few. That's the primary philosophy of the Freehold, but it was colored by further influxes of Christianity, some of Islam and lots of skepticism. It's taken for granted but most regard it as a philosophy, as you say, rather than a faith. I am not religious."

"Query: So a faith is more than a philosophy?"

"That's more a question Father Dunn could answer, but I believe a faith requires a belief in something unprovable. The need to trust in the unknown creates a courage to accept things a . . . more rational person would not. I dislike phrasing it as 'rational,' but people with strong faith in their philosophies will do things that look insane from the outside."

"Having discussed this at length with Father Dunn, I can now hear the inflections it makes into your English.

It is a marginally precise but highly subjectively gorgeously colorful language. It seems to my study you can express an almost infinite array of emotion and feeling, but you use specific sub-dialects for precise technical matters."

"That's a good summary."

"Query: How long have you had your sciences?"

"I believe the actual principles of the scientific method date back about eight hundred Earth years."

"This 'Christianity' dates back several times longer."

"Yes, about three times as long, with earlier religions it may be drawn from. Certainly some of the early parts of the Bible are."

"Father Dunn and I discussed the Mesopotamians, Zoroastrians, Greeks, Romans and others."

"It sounds like he's covering it very well." So far, this was a much more palatable subject. Vlashn should be encouraged to do more of this and less worrying about technical matters. It seemed unlikely to happen, though.

"Yes. I deduce from his reaction my analysis disturbed him to a level humans might consider insulting."

"That's possible. Matters of faith are very intimate." Oh, dear. What had the alien said?

"It was partially about faith and partially about English human culture."

"Okay, tell me."

"I said that by still allowing faith to interfere with science and society to a low but measurable level, rather than drawing a definitive boundary between the two, you were still of a high order of savagery."

Mark raised his eyebrows. Wow.

" 'Savagery' is not the Ishkul word. I worked with the machine at an intense level, but was unable to find a word that would fit better."

"No, I think you and the machine are correct. Humans have many motivations, a large number of them not based on rational analysis. That is why we specifically brought the experts we did, and there are still some frictions."

"You have managed to develop a more robust technology and star travel despite that. Our scientists believe you have developed high-energy chemical bonds in your ceramics, and have ready access to long molecule chains you can form into this." He slapped the plastic of the chair. "What isn't clear is how your initial step from the planet to space proceeded. We know resources in space are easier to access."

"I wish I could discuss that, Vlashn," Mark said. Damn. Did they have the periodic table of elements? Did they know there was a vast hole of elements they had no access to? Could they access metals enough for ceramic matrices? There were light metals in many of their ceramic molecules, of course, but no sign they could refine them to purity. Most took high energy or electricity, neither of which the Ishkul could achieve. "We have had experiences where cultures were damaged by exposure to new technology, plants, philosophies."

"Query: Why did you allow Father Dunn in with his faith?"

Shit.

"As I have implied, Vlashn, we have never before encountered a nonhuman, sentient, tool-using species. Some animals use rocks or sticks, or move things around. We have experience, earlier in our history, of encountering other races. Without exception, one culture was subverted to the other, or destroyed by its influx and numbers. Humans currently number near fifty billion, to your one hundred million. As your planet has less sophisticated groups, so do ours. But those groups are easily able to travel here and can create problems for everyone else."

"This attitude sounds highly protectionist and derogatory of our cultural identity."

"I'm afraid it does sound that way," Mark agreed. "I can only say that we would feel a racial shame and guilt if we were to inadvertently damage your society. Our caution is because we want you to maintain it."

"Query: What is in it for you?"

That question had to have come from Taya. Had to.

"Vlashn, we don't know that anything is in it for us. This is costing a sizeable but absorbable amount of funds. The survey ship that found you was seeking an uninhabited system to acquire minerals from. Since you are here, that was not possible. But it is not the only system that was not viable at once for commerce. You have developed very differently from us, and that is of scientific interest. Our traders hope you will become a market and supplier for them."

"I continue to sense a level of condescension."

Blushing, he said, "Yes, Vlashn, you do. It's a racial and cultural issue for humans. Be glad you didn't meet our ancestors of a thousand years ago, who would have landed in the millions bent on killing you and forcing you to accept some religion. I don't say they would have been successful. But you clearly see the event would be disastrous."

"As I learn more snippets and bits about your cultural past, I become both impressed and fearful. It seems your race should have spent more time on social development before constructing spaceships."

"I can't argue with that, Vlashn. Yet here we are."

"Indeed. We must deal with the situations we have, not those we would like there to be, were a choice available."

After a pause, Vlashn asked, "Query: What minerals?"

"Vlashn? I didn't understand that." *And does he believe me when I lie? Or stall?*

"Query: What minerals do your traders seek, that are so different in space than on a planet?"

Mark prickled again. Shit. "That's not a subject I'm familiar with," he replied.

"You mean you don't intend to answer."

"Vlashn, I hope that soon we have enough knowledge of culture, language and your sciences that we can answer those questions. We do get closer every day, and our exchanges are hastening the moment. In the meantime, there are many humans, of many cultures, who I readily admit are not as sophisticated as yours. Whether or not they would cause damage to your culture, they would embarrass ours and cause further tension."

"I will remain patient," Vlashn said. "I understand only a little of the many human motivations, but I generally trust your subjective belief in your own field."

"Thank you. It is my intent to ensure my people get what they want, without causing damage to your culture, and without offending our neighbors in the UN."

Mark wasn't sure if that defused things or not.

He needed resolution, quickly.

"Query: The United Nations are larger and more powerful than you?"

"That depends on your definition of power. During the war eighteen of our years ago, we were able to fight them to a standstill. Both our planet and Earth suffered badly."

"Ambassador Russ spoke of entire cities suffering extremely severe damage."

"Yes. The power sources we use for interstellar travel, several types, can be released in million parts of a second and do a great deal of damage, as I think you deduced. We try to avoid it, and have managed to become friends again, as I have said."

"You present that you don't believe that would happen here."

"I don't. Nothing here would cause such to happen. You must be familiar with displacing other cultures, though."

"I am. Such is part of Ishkul history. I am making these circumlocutions to lead to a point."

"I can sense so, Vlashn. I am prepared for your point."

"Our neighboring culture north and inland is not as well-placed, in terms of resource availability and exploitability. They are more numerous, and as technically sophisticated. They are moderately aware, first through clandestine information acquisition, what I believe you would accurately call 'spying,' and recently through the obvious to us necessity of public discourse, of your presence, and our summary of your abilities."

"Thank you for the information, Vlashn." Oh, shit. Exactly one of their potential fears. "We will need to consider them in all activities, though for now I prefer to negotiate only with your group."

"We both see the logical necessities. I request you make an official expedition in a moderately short timeframe."

"I'll try, Vlashn. Part of the problem is that should I do so, I would also have to send warriors, in order to maintain order among my people. This expedition was hurriedly put together and is not as large or equipped as we'd like."

"I inferred such. I repeat my urging."

"I'll see what I can do. Thank you again."

This was not how first contact happened in vid.

"The (untranslatable, sounds like Homna, proper noun) are more aggressive in our view, a developmental necessity of having less access to resources. Attempts to share such have been marginally successful. They claim to perceive you as offering advantage to us which would increase perceived inequality of development."

Mark realized he needed to do something about that.

"Can you bring one of their envoys here, with our gracious greetings?"

"I will arrange so. I must advise it will have the appearance of great fanfare."

"You want to make them feel honored. I understand."

"I was sure in advance that you would. That raises the issue of how much of your diplomacy is for our benefit rather than your own."

"I am trying to minimize it, Vlashn. We would be far more elaborate with Earth."

"I accept your statement as truthful and appreciate the ramifications."

"Thank you."

"You are welcome."

After Vlashn and his scribe departed, Mark let out a deeply held breath. He retreated to his office for privacy to think.

He had just reached his office when Warrant Connor's voice came through the speaker. *Anything* broadcast or wired indicated an emergency.

"Sir, you need to take a look out the window right now. Northeast. Airborne."

Mark rose, jogged across the building and took a glance toward the city.

What in the . . . ?

A skywriter. Someone had a drone or a small aircraft and was skywriting, in Ishkul.

He didn't know anything beyond theory about the written language but he knew that had to be stopped now. He really couldn't use violence, but he might not have much choice.

"Warrant, that has to be stopped. Suggestions?"

"Shoot them down . . . Harass them away . . . Wait. Disrupt the smoke as they do it."

"Do the latter, now, but the trace would still be readable. Disrupt them, too. Avoid shooting. We're still peaceful."

"Got it. Hold, sir." He changed channels, then shortly returned and said, "Emergency launch from *Aracaju*. Superstratospheric fighter. I'm on my way in."

"Understood—break—Lieutenant Shraybman, get Mr. Russ now."

"He's on his way over, sir."

Russ arrived right then, fumbling with a headset, escorted by a Marine.

Mark said, "I was going to say to meet me in the courtyard. Let's go." He headed out at a jog.

"I heard," Russ said as he moved alongside. "*Aracaju* says the fighter will take damage from this reentry, and has no fuel to recover. They're not made for space launches. Survival mode only."

"We'll bill whoever it is, once we force them off. How long? I see two words now. Lieutenant, get L T Cochrane. I need to know what is being said."

Shraybman said, "Cochrane's on air with me. She says it's 'You collectively are a patient of an action' "

"Right. They're trying to disseminate information." Hell, that was obvious, but it was provable. It also had to stop right the hell now. He felt helpless. He'd given all the orders he could, and it might not be enough. Further orders would be silly, like "hurry" or "do it now." Everyone involved knew that.

Connor arrived at a sprint, with an extensive comm system in hand. He dropped it, grabbed controls—it was a military brute force model and had manual controls, not a sensor field—and resumed his work.

There was the fighter, dropping in, and the shock wave shattered the words. It also tumbled the craft, which looked to be either kit built or an ungainly little drone.

"How the hell did that aircraft get here?" Mark meant the drone, not the fighter. He realized the imprecision of English now. Why was his brain focusing on that at this moment?

"Not sure," Shraybman said. "It had to be one or more of the packages of construction material that came down for either corp, or a space launch."

"They wouldn't be that stupid, that blatant, or that wordy. This is showy but amateurish."

"So they've been infiltrated, too."

"We knew that." He sighed. At least the crude fixed-wing was veering off.

"The fighter will have to force land here. Not enough fuel for a return."

"Can he land without a runway?"

"No, that's why I said, 'force.' "

"Sigh. Get combat rescue ready to pull the crew. Get a DGO down to recover and sterilize the area. Have combat air control find him somewhere with few or no natives. Or can they do a water crash?"

"This is going to cost millions and make a scene," Russ said.

"Can't be helped."

Connor interjected, "Water is worse for recovery from our POV, but might take longer for Ishkul to do anything with. Their dive depth is limited."

"Deep ocean?"

"Continental shelf, shallow, south of here."

"Do it. Pass the word." He looked at Russ for any disagreement. It was their ship he proposed to splash, after all.

Russ shrugged. "I don't know what else to do," he said. "I'll comment if I need to." He turned to his microphone and said, "I concur with the Freehold decision. Proceed."

Connor tapped and spoke, turned and nodded. "Done."

"And I want that intrusive crew. Here."

"Sir, I will have to proceed to location, with the captain deployed."

"Go. Take what you need."

Connor was already gone.

By the end of the day, that disaster was mostly cleaned up.

Captain Jelling was back, but deferred to her exec. Connor had a summary for everyone. Shraybman, Cochrane and Phelan were present.

The more I try to make this a diplomatic mission, the more it becomes a military action, Mark thought.

"First," Connor said, "it was a remotely piloted drone. Control signal came from the *Milton*."

"Margov's ship," Mark said. "I strongly doubt she was behind this. It's clumsy."

"I concur," Connor said. "However, I have used this as an excuse to board and search."

"Of course. How did that go?"

Connor looked at Phelan, who said, "There was a transceiver, hidden in one of the crew cabins. DSR handed said crewman over at once, with no hesitation, and provided his record. I can't tell you much about it yet, but it's fake, beginning to end. Pretty enough to get someone hired, and as long as they're adequate at their task, in this case, housekeeping management, no one would question them. It took very little time to find gaping contradictions. They subbed for a 'sick' crewmember just about the time we left Freehold space. I've tagged said crewmember, and *Milton*'s commander has willingly offered to help, to the point of furnishing contact info so we could have him held back home."

Mark chuckled. "I'm sure they did. At this point, I'm starting to wonder if they did set it up to deliberately look clumsy. Taya would cover her ass, but after that, every inquiry would be met by cannibalistic lawyers. Still, their cooperation makes it hard to nail them. What's next? Captain Jelling?"

"Sir, I just got back," she said. She looked like hell, too. Those tropics must be fierce. "So I'm deferring to Warrant Connor. I'm an observer at present."

Connor looked from her to Mark and said, "Good news as our operation goes. The fighter landed on eight hundred plus meters of water. We pulled the pilot, recovered all the pluggable controls and recorders, delivered them all to UN authority, cracked the hull and sank it. If need be, we can drop a localized incendiary to slag it into the sea floor."

Mark suspected the removable controls had all been photographed, scanned, checked ten ways including inductance and neutrino scans before return. Or likely not neutrino scans. That took more resources than were down here. Or did it?

"Thanks on that," Russ agreed. "We have all the records from the fighter. Also a bill." He smiled and handed over a stick.

"I'll ensure someone pays it," Mark agreed. "Lieutenant?" he asked, looking at Cochrane.

"Nothing more was written after you got my translation. For what it's worth, it was in very crude Ishkul text. Without photos or an immediate sketch, they may have trouble with it. I deduced the intent from context and clunky translations through our gear, which is probably the way it was assembled."

"We'll have to find out what Vlashn has to say, if he does."

"And make sure he doesn't know about the crash site," Shraybman added. "Hopefully, it was out of sight of any Ishkul."

"That should be simple enough," Mark replied. "They have telescopes, but what range? Then there's curvature of the planet."

"There's also lots of sailing ship traffic to other continents."

"Ah. Crap." That hadn't occurred to him. It should have.

"Other . . . I guess the race is 'Drazl' . . . nations are aware of us, of course. The inland tribes, the large nation north, several overseas undoubtedly, as well as that archipelago. The word's hitting them as fast as it hits human space."

"That's a lot to deal with. I guess I . . . we, because Ambassador Russ needs this too, need ongoing updates on all this. Keep me informed, at once if it's urgent, twice a day if it can wait."

They rose and left. Russ hung back, let the military depart, then turned back.

He sighed. "I have a problem at my end."

"Go ahead," Mark prompted.

"My government has asked me to deemphasize and discourage the missionaries. Unofficially, they said they'd like Father Dunn gone first."

"That's an odd position."

"Not really." Russ sighed again. "How familiar are you with this subject?"

"Religion or the politics around it? I've read some of the history, and I know summaries of most major faith groups."

"Christianity is not well regarded on Earth, by the majority Muslims, as far as faiths go, or by the atheists."

"Same on Grainne, but it's not an issue."

"It is for us. Catholics, specifically, are held in disdain for their conservatism and their strict rules."

"I thought the purpose of a faith was strict rules, to challenge the spirit for development. And I've never heard of Catholics having problems before."

"You're probably familiar with Reformed Catholics, specifically, Second Reformation. Byzantine Catholics and Orthodox don't have major problems, except by association. Roman Catholics, though, are something of a pariah, the way conservative Jews are in many cultures."

"That can't be officially endorsed or even allowed, though."

"Officially? No. There are enough millions of people in the UN government that official policy is very vague.

Some of the Church's positions are regarded as 'hate crimes' even though they're hundreds of years old and not enforced."

"Do you want me to cover for you?" Mark asked. That was simple enough, as long as it wouldn't create waves. Russ seemed embarrassed by this, so he felt obligated to extend the favor without strings.

"I'm afraid you'll have to. I'm told all religious groups are denied status as either government or Non-Governmental Organization. Some of the specific charities funded by various groups are allowed. So far, no Catholic institution has made that list. Partly that's due to the way they manage their groups, and I won't state that it's a conveniently written policy." He wasn't denying it, either.

"That's fine. I'll host them through our embassy. I will have to vet them again, except for Father Dunn. I can offer him asylum through our people, and a Catholic Diocese on Grainne."

"Thank you." Russ seemed embarrassed to the point of agitation, and ashamed.

When Vlashn arrived, he immediately mentioned the skywriter.

"Mark, the factions you have mentioned in minor detail to me are apparently attempting a diversion around you and Ambassador Russ."

"Yes, they are."

"I retain my confidence in your ethics and position. Supportively, I offer an undefined level of assistance without expectation of favor, should it be helpful to the situation."

"I appreciate it. We did manage to get things under control and I thank you for the offer. Vlashn, I must speak very frankly without intent of insult."

"We know each other well enough, Mark. Please do so."

"Obviously, with billions of humans, we have a great many different motivations. You've met several groups with a variety of motivations already."

"We have. Egan is blatantly obvious in his multiple motivated desires for large commercial gain. Mr. Russ seeks detailed information and agreements for control of all facets of interchange. I deduce you are highly agitated at the multiple and conflicting interests, and exceedingly nervous about negative side effects."

"That's exactly true, Vlashn. I'd like to speak on that."

"Please do."

"Obviously, we have technology you don't. We can fly in space, faster than light. Our ability to observe and transfer information exceeds yours. There are other skills we have. One of our concerns is the effect such knowledge has on development. Conversely, while we are less concerned by the reverse effect, it also exists. You have knowledges we never developed, that should be cautiously exchanged. It is important that both cultures gain maximum return from their knowledge, while causing minimal trouble. This requires strong leadership. My own culture prohibits that level of leadership over the individual. The UN allows it. Both our approaches lead to problems of different types."

"We face the same problem with the ocean and southern primitives. Some have traded finished goods to these groups, causing reduction in their organic production levels and increasing their dependence upon trade through point or limited sources."

"That's exactly the problem we face here. My culture's predecessors previously encountered primitives on our own planet with a similar but lesser technology to yours. This happened several times, coincidentally on islands, and to the south, but elsewhere as well. In all cases, the indigenous culture fractured into local wars for dominance of the trade routes. It also led to that dependence on the trade, displacing the existing culture, as you have observed."

"Much of that depends on social development. I judge there to be a good likelihood our social development is high enough to avoid this, possibly higher than your own. This decreases such risk."

"It probably does. I hope you understand I'm not willing to take the risk without further study."

"Queries: What do you suggest, Mark? Should we not engage in commerce?" It was hard to tell if Vlashn was agitated.

"We certainly should. It should be in a slow, methodical manner. Our scientists will take some years to learn the intricacies of your technology. Yours will take years, possibly decades for the reverse. However, in both cases, the knowledge has developed over millennia. In our case, we had dramatic shifts periodically, much like you had when you developed your present language. These shifts affected entire continents of sto . . . primitive cultures. Your culture develops steadily and with guidance. Our multiple cultures develop in leaps and directional changes. Also, we have several planets. I believe any transfer from your culture will be soaked up by ours into the existing zeitgeist. Did that word translate?" He waited for Vlashn's assent and continued, "Good. Inversely, I believe any transfer from ours will cause dramatic upheavals to yours." Damn, he was actually starting to grasp their communication, in whatever limited fashion a human could. He then realized that thought was phrased almost the same way. He almost laughed.

"I grasp the risk completely but do not understand your implied proposal."

"We need to continue the scientific missions. Your scientists should learn our science. You should have a solid, reliable group of scientists, politicians and commercial developers who can keep secrets. Each development should be released and allowed to propagate before the next is released. This might take decades. In the meantime, we should have an agreement so we can prevent intruders from interfering. I find your society, culture and technology to be fascinating, beautiful and admirable. I don't want to see it suffer."

"I agree. However, those I represent are becoming impatient and demanding a transfer from your people to ours. If they are not quelled, there will be disagreement over my position. The situation is somewhat less than critical, but more than urgent." He seemed to indicate such disagreement would involve some degree of violence or at least subversion.

"Then we must give them something."

"I hoped for that outcome. Ambassador Russ has offered a moderated cultural and technical package."

Yeah, turn it into yet one more digital copy of every other UN planet, or every corporate owned megaplex. Just lovely.

"I will definitely offer something by this time tomorrow."

And the gloves were off. Vlashn could now play each group against the others for his own benefit.

After Vlashn left, Mark felt a ripple of shock.

The Ishkul leader had not mentioned Margov. She had certainly been consulting, though.

Egan was going to find she'd taken him for everything, before this was done.

CHAPTER 19

The Ishkul semaphore was busy that day and part of the next. Mark asked about a translation, but got nothing.

"Sorry," Cochrane said. "The language is tough enough even with AI assistance. This is a representation of the language, distilled as a shorthand and encoded as well. We certainly can break it, but we can't do it in time to matter."

He'd just have to wait and see. In the meantime, he had information on his desk. Zihn's party reported that the Ishkul were eagerly digesting all the advice they could get on quartz glass, coated optics and various prismatic lenses. The telescopes they had were good. The human ones were better.

Wait until we show you reflecting and radio telescopes, Mark thought. Soon.

Somle sent messengers with updates. The messages were written in stiff but clear English with odd word choices. That was disturbing on its own.

Mark warned everyone when he realized that. "Assume they can understand us, even with the translator off."

"That shouldn't really be a problem," Cochrane said. "We tend not to talk in their presence."

"We don't know that someone hasn't provided them a radio," Phelan said.

"Oh. Yes."

Mark said, "McDonald tells me it's just possible for them to build their own using chemical means. I didn't understand it, but that's how it is. Of course, they wouldn't know our encryption algorithms, but let's be extra paranoid."

Somle sent word that she'd visit in the afternoon. True to her word, it was right at 1300 local when she came in view. She had no entourage.

"That's different," Shraybman murmured.

"Yes. Let me see her alone," Mark insisted as he went to greet her, dragging a translator node.

His bodyguard for the day protested but didn't hinder him. Mark strode quickly and met her a good hundred meters outside the berm. There was a well-worn path by now, the growth beaten to the ground and brown. On either side, a strip of a few meters was trimmed, the tall stalks of ground cover flat and drying after being scythed or similarly cut.

"Welcome, Somle," he said. "I presume this meeting is intended to be discreet."

"It is," she agreed. "Spoken words can be overheard and written words are available to copy even if not understood."

"Go ahead, then," he said. He shivered slightly. It was a cool day, and the wind drove the point home. Somle wore a cloak with sleeves and a hood. His shirt was quilted, but not enough for lengthy spells outside.

"The Homna are our neighbors to the north. They are not as technically sophisticated as Ishkul, in any field, but are closing the gap quickly."

"Understood. You recall I mentioned the technology gap between West and East that we endured. This seems to be similar."

"From your telling, I believe the two are similar in many regards. They have a different political structure, based on popular opinion."

"We call that 'democracy.'"

"This is not the same as that. They elect a leader who has very broad power without consult. It is similar to the early monarchic systems."

"I will keep that firmly in mind, Somle."

"Thank you, Mark. You should expect that their leader or representative will seek status and precedence."

"I'll remember. How do you recommend I respond?"

"You should try for great status. However, if the Homna become upset it may lead to a military action. They are and will be prepared for it."

"I understand. Can you speak on my behalf or as an intermediary?"

"You would lose immediate status for such, as well as imply that he was not worthy to talk with you directly. He speaks Ishkul in a poor yet comprehensible fashion."

"I understand. When should we expect him?"

"He should arrive in our capital in two days. Vlashn will bring him the next day, as he will not treat with a (gender? Status? Undefined). We can create a delay of less than a day if it will prove useful."

"Thanks, but no need. I'll meet with him, as will Ambassador Russ."

"Your promptness is and will be appreciated by all parties."

"You're welcome, Somle."

"The envoy will push for status, then will demand as much tribute in the form of knowledge as he believes he can acquire. He will start with a larger set of demands and be prepared to discard the more extravagant. He will offer exchanges. The greater his perception of his initial exchange, the more he will demand in return."

"I am very familiar with that method, Somle. I appreciate the warning. I believe strongly I can handle it."

Indeed. If this neighbor wanted technical advances, they'd make heavy offers. That had to be delayed, possibly indefinitely, unless he wanted to play favorites and give the Ishkul the upper hand . . . though their own culture was not the kindest, gentlest of sorts. He didn't find it impossible to imagine they'd eliminate a potential threat, given a large enough technical edge.

Of course, the Ishkul had not asked for such. Had, in fact, only urged he provide something, and had been very eager to discuss peaceful and scientific technologies. On the other hand, all technologies eventually were used in a military context. They might be betting on their ability to reverse engineer something.

Hell, he couldn't second guess himself like this. He had to come up with answers.

He didn't want to order everyone off planet, but he might not have a choice.

"I will await your messengers and we will meet with your neighbor. Do you advise meeting here or in your capital?"

"Here is to be preferred, and your query is taken as a favored gift. Query: Should I explain why?"

"I can think of several reasons, Somle. Unless something is relevant, no need." Suggesting their capital showed trust in them. That was probably it.

"Very well, then, let us conclude. Expect visitation by myself or Vlashn tomorrow, with regular messenger correspondence. Query: Is the correspondence comprehensible?"

"It is. Thank you. Good day, Somle."

"Good day, Mark."

It was two days later, midmorning, that Shraybman and Connor came into Mark's office.

Shraybman said, "Sir, I think you can expect that envoy any time, even if you haven't heard from Vlashn or Somle."

"Why, what's happening?" he asked.

"Traffic on the main north-south highway. There's a convoy that's definitely some kind of expedition, with honor guards."

"That's useful. Thanks."

Sure enough, that afternoon an Ishkul messenger delivered a letter from Somle, that Mark should expect the representative and her Equal Vlashn the next morning. He confirmed the appointment and then called everyone he could.

"I'll try to be back," Shraybman said. "I have to go topside and talk to the press. I've been putting it off for ten days."

"I'll manage," Mark insisted. She was certainly a great help, but he had faith in the other officers, too. And the enlisted.

Mark made sure Russ had also gotten the message, and invited him to a joint meeting. It was largely politeness; they both knew it would be a joint meeting so they could back each other up. Much of the tension from the beginning had dissolved. Mark was unlikely to be friends with the Earthman. They had little in common. He could work with him, though. That was what mattered.

Sergeant Thomas got busy setting up additional cameras. She promised she could record the meeting from four axes and obliquely from above, with focused audio. Connor's section, Mark's de facto bodyguard, had a connection to an observation post not five seconds away if they kicked out a wall. Connor would be on hand personally, as would Lieutenant Jetter. Russ admitted that his remaining assistant was actually a bodyguard with no real administrative duties. Mark wondered why he'd bothered, though the UN was big on oversight and support. They also had the budget to have assistants whether needed or for show. The Freehold did not.

Mark pulled Captain Chinran aside. She looked better than when she first returned from the tropics, but was still a bit beat looking.

"I need you to make absolutely sure neither Margov, nor Egan, nor any of their understudies get anywhere near."

"Can do, sir," she agreed.

"Don't leave any marks. I want to be able to laugh at them if they make any accusations."

"Of course."

"I suspect Margov won't be a problem. She's got some initial negotiations started. That's absolutely secret, of course."

"Sir, I can do it. Just worry about the Homna."

"Thanks. I appreciate it. You and your team have been great so far."

Wardrobe. Mark had to worry about wardrobe again. He and Russ and the Ishkul had dropped that after two days and he'd gone to casual slacks and pullovers. This called for more style. He chose a full length coat tailored to bulk him out. The natives were tall and sinuous. He wanted to look forceful.

Next morning he made a final check of the indoor patio of the courtyard. Chairs, couches for the natives, a couple of tables, assorted snacks for both species, all looked in order. Russ arrived and nodded.

"Round two," he said.

"Yes, with their mean neighbor. I'm a little concerned."

"What I was considering is that the Ishkul managed to keep their own traders, reporters, pretty much everyone except select scientists away, with us within walking distance of the city. Walking distance for natives, I mean."

"Right," Mark said. "We look pretty crappy not being able to keep people from landing."

"I believe I have the advantage there," Russ said with a sly smile.

"As far as they know, yes. I haven't mentioned your company's infiltrators yet."

"I appreciate it. I haven't tried playing the card yet," Russ said.

Rather than play along, Mark let it drop.

"I gather we're about ready?" he asked.

"I feel ready."

Connor leaned in and said, "Sirs, they're on their way. Walking from the camp now."

They both replied, "Thanks."

Mark took a seat and waited. Russ paced slowly, examining minute details of the structure. Six Freehold segs, ten Earth minutes, passed agonizingly slowly and silently. Connor stayed just outside, within view of his observers. The low tech approach really hadn't been that hard to adapt to, Mark thought.

"Here they are," Connor said softly, and stepped aside.

Both ambassadors rose, and Mark could see Vlashn escorting what had to be the envoy, with a bodyguard of twelve. Those spears looked rather sharp. Still, letting them retain their weapons was a friendly gesture, a gesture of power and Connor assured him it wasn't an issue.

The Homna with Vlashn resolved as he came closer. He was slightly shorter, still a good two meters tall, and his outfit screamed tin-pot dictator with an undertone of native shaman. He wore what almost looked like bandoleros over a golden silklike robe with iridescent green trim, sleeve bands, a kiltlike garment with badges and spangles of lacquered leather and wood, and a garish dagger in a beaded sheath.

They entered the courtyard and slowed to a casual walk rather than a hike. They entered the patio; Vlashn stepped forward between the parties and said, "Citizen Mark Ballenger, Ambassador Nurin Russ, Elected Exalted Tilfoma," he then stepped back.

Tilfoma had obviously been coached. He stepped forward and offered a hand to each.

"It's satisfying to meet our outworld visitors. I greet you," he said. His Ishkul was quite simple. It was clearly not his first language.

Russ said, "We greet you, Tilfoma, on behalf of humanity, and the United Nations of Earth, the Freehold of Grainne and as interim speakers for the Galactic Alliance."

"Please relay a hospitable welcome to your traders and let them know they are welcome."

"We will, with thanks," Russ said, fielding that one. "The more trade and exchange between cultures, the more we shall all benefit."

"This is also our thinking. I am aware you have traders with you. I desire intercourse."

Russ twitched in a way Mark knew meant he needed backup.

"We do have traders," Mark offered. "We are having some difficulty finding an equitable trade. Our cultures differ considerably." He was also amused at the intercourse comment. If anyone needed to be screwed over . . .

"I await their presence."

Tilfoma's demeanor came across even the species barrier. Arrogant and willing to back it up.

Mark gulped.

"Of course. I'll arrange it."

Russ gave him a "what the fuck do we do" look. This character was crass, pushy, clearly wasn't leaving if he wasn't happy, and had a small army on hand.

Mark took a deep breath, and called, "Lieutenant Shraybman."

Sergeant Thomas came in at once. "The lieutenant is not down from the *Healy* yet, sir. How may I assist?"

Adrenaline burst through him, but he calmly said, "Please have Mr. Zihn and Ms Stephens brought in at once. Our guest wishes to discuss their trade offers." He held eye contact.

"The traders, yes, sir, I'll get them at once. Mr. Zihn and Ms Stephens specifically, and not their subordinates, sir?" she asked with a slightly cocked eyebrow.

"Elected Exalted Tilfoma wishes to speak to the trade leaders directly."

"At once, sir," she agreed with a nod, and a completely neutral expression.

Oh, shit, she was good. The trembling tension he'd been fighting drained away. He figured Shraybman would have caught the play, but Shraybman had been dealing with him for weeks.

He'd never paid much attention to combat documentation personnel. He decided he should make a study, and recommend additional uses for them.

Zihn and Stephens arrived shortly, slightly out of breath and dressed in suits. Well done. Tilfoma might not recognize human styles, but then again, he might.

Stephens swept up, offered a hand Earth fashion, and said, "Exalted Tilfoma, it's a pleasure to meet yet another of our gracious hosts. I look forward to commerce between our peoples."

Zihn was less wordy. "Greetings to you, sir. I hope we can reach an acceptable deal."

Tilfoma stood. "Excellent. There are many abilities you have we do not. I am interested in airborne travel, steam power and photographic imagery initially. Query: What can I offer in exchange?"

Mark had no idea how this would play out. He'd called them on a whim, since they were smart, used to dealing with officials and known to him. He was winging it. So were they.

Dr. Stephens stepped right up and went for broke.

"That's been the nature of the delay dealing with the Ishkul," she said, taking a seat and stretching her feet out. She looked so comfortable and so unimpressed. "Truthfully, while there is much social knowledge to be gained from your peoples, there is little in the way of tangibles we need, given our access to space. I'm sure Vlashn has been reluctant to discuss this, but we came to an impasse over our initial offer of technical knowledge and tools in exchange for land."

Tilfoma paused for a moment, apparently digesting the content. "Query: How much territory?" he asked. He rose up fractionally higher, trying to look more imposing. Zihn took that moment to sit down too.

Stephens said, "A hundred million square kilometers was our initial price."

Mark almost choked. Holy crap, the lady didn't start small. That was twenty percent of the planet's surface, more or less.

"Impossible to agree to. No nation or tribe controls that much area."

"Of course not. Obviously, it is up to you to come to an agreement between yourselves to make a viable counter. Shoreline and arable land rate higher, of course."

Zihn cut in, "If you found some of your neighbors to be resistant to the idea, limited technology could be made available to persuade them, with an additional percentage for the risk, of course." He steepled his hands in front of him and leaned comfortably back in his chair.

That made Mark blanch. It was the type of offer this warlord just might accept. Though it seemed Thomas had briefed them on his attitude and they were prepared to throw it right back at him.

"The offer is impractical. As traders you know this. I assume interference from your leaders."

"Not at all," Stephens said. "We offer an advance of several hundred years of technical knowledge and skills. We expect commensurate resources we can use for our own holdings. I'm not about to provide large amounts of valuable knowledge out of the graciousness of my heart. I have investors to answer to."

"I deduce you are evading," Tilfoma said directly. "I will take a token of your technology with me, as deposit for future exchanges. You may consider it a demonstrative exchange item," he stated.

Hey, mister, got any free samples? Mark thought. Only it wasn't phrased quite like a request.

Zihn said, "When it is clear you are ready to make a worthwhile offer, we will be happy to grant a sample. As it stands, there's little here we need, and uninhabited systems we can take with no argument." The dapper man looked annoyed, bored, and did condescending very well. He stood.

"Conversely, a sample will convince other tribes of the value, and ease the way. This is obvious and reasonable."

"No," Stephens said. She shook her head and gave a slight frown. She seemed utterly unimpressed, almost disinterested. She rose, too.

"I am prepared to strongly support my reasonable requests," Tilfoma said, with a caress of his dagger.

"It is not quite that easy," Mark said. He raised a finger to the guard watching on monitor, who had also picked up on the attitude and flashed an inquiry on the glass, unseen by Tilfoma.

Tilfoma seemed agitated as he said, "The time for evasion is over. Your ships fly through space. You have other technical achievements we don't. Furnish one."

"I am not offended by your demands," Mark said, "but I will not comply."

"Is that phrased as refusal?"

"It is," he said. "You seem to value the direct statement. I will give you such. I will decide when it is appropriate to transfer technology, with my own counsel. I absolutely will consider your people in this, but I will not respond to demands."

"Nor will I," Russ replied. "My people are not threatened."

Tilfoma had little to say. He stood for several segs. Neither he nor the others moved.

The tableau stretched out. None of the humans broke role. Vlashn seemed prepared to wait forever, as did Tilfoma. The silence moved in and enveloped them, and not even the spectators did more than breathe. Everyone waited for the cusp to resolve to . . . something.

Finally, Tilfoma spoke.

"I will pursue this further at another time," he said. He left with no formalities, simply turned and strode out with his guard rushing to catch up.

Facing the "traders," Mark said, "Thank you both, and Sergeant Thomas."

"That egotistical little prick has a stick up his arse," Stephens said with obvious distaste. "I wouldn't negotiate with him even with fair value."

Russ said, "Steam power, flight and photography are great dual use technologies. We wouldn't be giving him weapons directly, but it's pretty clear they'd wind up being used for intel and logistics. Apparently, he either doesn't know or doesn't care that we can figure that out."

Mark turned to Vlashn. "You are sure no military threat exists?" he asked.

"I am not sure. I suspect strongly it will not come to that. His entourage is in Ishkul territory unharmed and without causing undue harm, other than normally expected from a large movement. Our relations are as peaceful as your own."

Mark wasn't sure if that was a naïve statement, or if Vlashn had figured out the uneasy détente that existed.

"If you need to follow him, Vlashn, please do. We can talk at our leisure."

"Thank you. I will do so. Good day to all of you." Vlashn left at a less hurried pace.

With all the . . . Drazl gone, Mark looked around.

"Well, that was interesting. What's our followup? And thank you, Doctors. That was well played." He walked toward his office and indicated for everyone to follow.

"It was the first delaying tactic that came to mind, sir," Stephens said.

"It worked beautifully."

"I'm a bit worried about followup," Jelling said.

"Oh? Captain?"

"His entourage has a distinct military look. Warrant Connor has been conducting reconnaissance."

"Please elaborate," Mark said, facing Connor. He wasn't sure if the reconnaissance had been on foot or by remote. He wasn't going to ask at the moment.

"He brought a large entourage. It has a lot of vehicles. There's an ongoing supply train to it."

"That's not that surprising. We started with two hundred, mostly military, then withdrew most, and have daily supplies."

"His could number in the thousands. Easily."

Russ said, "Yet Vlashn doesn't seem worried."

"Or," Jelling put in, "Vlashn doesn't want to get in the way. Or, Vlashn figures to see us tested by his annoying neighbor, or for us to put down his annoying neighbor, or hopes his neighbor will put us down, resolving the political problem and keeping blood off his hands, though that sounds more like Somle."

"Well, show us what you have and we'll go from there." He entered his office and pointed at his system.

Connor nodded. "It's all satellite at present. I haven't risked sending anyone in on foot, mostly because of the time involved." He stepped over and brought up a screen.

There were lots of possibilities.

Dr. Stephens asked, "How long have you been observing this area?"

"Where they are now? Since yesterday specifically," Connor said. "We have routine low-res photos since we landed."

"How does traffic compare? That road looks fairly well traveled."

"It is a major trade route," Connor admitted. "The traffic doesn't seem right, though."

"Can you be more specific?" she asked.

Mark let them wrangle.

Connor said, "My concern is this convoy, and I use that term specifically, has a military feel to it."

"Okay, go ahead," said Stephens.

Others gathered around. McDonald had arrived, Zihn was still present, along with several military personnel and technical staff.

Connor pointed at details and explained, "They're in good order and spacing, they stopped in an organized fashion with a perimeter at night. It's not a lot, but it just feels that way."

"Oh, don't be paranoid," Stephens said. "That's standard for any caravan that might get attacked by bandits, predators, any number of threats. There are hundreds of vehicles along these roads every day from all indications."

"I agree that would be true for Earth," Mark said. "Though I'm not seeing anything to indicate bandits or predators are in the area."

Stephens looked a bit put upon. That was likely as much as she'd show in public.

She said, "It's practical behavior, carried forward from when they did. We don't really know how long they've had their current security and borders."

It was true. The Ishkul were as reticent as the humans on various issues.

Mark said, "That, and if it were military I gather Vlashn would have something to say about it. They wouldn't just roll in. He did mention their safe passage."

"It's possible," Sergeant Thomas said, "that they've got a mutual force agreement. Or perhaps Vlashn isn't aware of what they brought. As the doctor says, hundreds of wagons come through a day. It wouldn't take much camouflage, though it would take a lot of planning. From here, though," she indicated the screen, "one wagon looks much like another."

Still, Thomas had arrived after Jelling's statement, and her thoughts were similar. Was that military training speaking, photo intel thinking, or common sense?

Zihn said, "He also may be aware of it and unable or unwilling to do anything under the circumstances."

"Assuming it is military, what can it do, and how do you find out?" McDonald asked. "We might as well cover all bases."

Connor said, "Well, first I'd scan for weapons, either dense ceramic or dense element, and look for patterns. Obviously, that is precluded."

"Obviously."

"As to threat, I can't say. We've consistently underestimated them."

Mark asked, "What weapons from the early twentieth century might we face?"

"I can't imagine aircraft. Artillery would of course be impossible."

Stephens offered, "World War One was basically nineteenth-century trench warfare supplemented by occasional use of radios, photography and more modern artillery, plus machine guns. Aerial bombs were rather late."

"They can't have machine guns, they can't have aircraft or artillery. They can't have radios without element. . . ."

McDonald offered, "Actually, it's just possible to use chemical matrices to generate and receive radio frequencies, as I said, but they'd be bulky tanks of liquid and not portable."

"I want to hear about that," Connor said. "But let's finish with the other stuff first. I can foresee portable, highly efficient siege engines, and obviously massed archery formations."

"Any threat to us?"

"I would say at least some."

"If those are cargo wagons," Stephens said, "they could carry sheaves of arrows. A thousand human bowmen can fire up to fifteen thousand arrows a minute. Proper logistics would let that sustain itself for a while."

Jelling said, "Our armor will stop even high power arrows, but most people are wearing torso armor at best, not limbs or head. The building will stop them, but a two hundred kilo boulder in a high trajectory can smash almost anything, certainly anything we have down here."

"So the threat is credible in its potential," McDonald said.

Connor said, "Sir, all military threats are based on potential. If someone can hurt you, you—"

Mark cut in, "—plan for the assumption that at some point they will. I did threat analysis."

He nodded. "Yes, sir. As Dr. Stephens says, it's paranoid. That's my job, however."

Mark said, "So we need to treat this as a potential threat. Everyone needs to wear their torso armor. I know most don't bother. We need tourniquets for immediate action, and good surgical kits. I assume everyone knows enough biology or first aid to understand that arrow wounds are painful, debilitating and potentially lethal even in extremities?"

Everyone nodded.

"I have no idea how to defend against incoming boulders. I'm hesitant to ask Vlashn. He knows we can see from orbit, so if this is hostile and he's involved, I give away the advantage by admitting I know it's a possible threat—"

Connor said, "Though it might make him reconsider."

Jelling leaned over and said, "Yes. It's also possible he doesn't know about it. It's also possible the Homna are arranging a trade convoy, as Dr. Stephens suggests, and I don't want to offend by suggesting a threat. That also makes us look like suspicious types who think of things as threats."

"We actually know very little about their history of warfare," Stephens said. "I believe I mentioned that early on, but I've been constrained from finding out." She sounded snippy and miffed. "We also don't know that the Homna, assuming it's they who would be attacking, don't have a valid claim, for their culture."

"You were right, of course, Doctor," Mark said. "We also couldn't go there. 'Tell us how we can best defeat you' is not something that can ever be discussed."

"Is it possible Vlashn doesn't know about this operation and would we be doing the right thing to ask?" Connor asked.

"That's the other issue." Yeah, on the other other hand . . . "We still look suspicious and snoopy. They know we can scan like that, but doing so while they can't, and without foreknowledge, comes across as deceitful. Also, will we be interfering with their development? If this is a war between two nations, which side is correct? We don't want another Mtali or Balkans or Cameroon."

He continued, "I'll find some diplomatic ways to probe without actually asking. Russ has more experience, and he'll need to share this with his people, too."

"That increases the threat of intelligence compromise," Connor said. "Sorry, sir."

"You're correct, no offense," Russ said. "I would appreciate our Marines being brought in on this."

"Of course," Mark said. He turned. "Somedays, Warrant, you wake up in a world where you just can't get what you want," he said with a frown.

"That's typical for my line of work, sir. So far, though, that's been every day for everyone here."

"I'm sure Ambassador Russ will be discreet. We can't keep the lid on this forever, though."

Jelling said, "One of the other problems . . . I've researched their 'democracy.' The UN of course loves the theory of a pure democracy, while shunning it in practice for obvious reasons."

"Careful of the politics, please; tread carefully," Mark cautioned.

She looked only slightly chagrined, and continued with her point. "Sorry, sir. The Homna are a pure democracy, but a militaristic one. Whoever gets the most votes is in charge and suppresses the minority. It's stable, because the scapegoats get wiped out one at a time."

"That's . . . you know, we're going to learn a lot about the social systems of this species, and I'm not sure we're going to like much of what we learn." The Ishkul were very sophisticated, very civilized, and still rather brutal. Their neighbors were positively fascistic.

Shraybman returned that afternoon, while Mark and Russ were still discussing how to proceed. Mark invited her into his office.

"Please keep Ambassador Russ updated, too." He indicated his opposite.

"Can do, sir," she agreed and took a chair. She nodded to Russ, then spoke to both. "Sir. FreeTech of course denies being involved in any of the incidents so far, but I understand there is sufficient evidence to suggest so."

"Yes, they're shut out, permanently," Mark said.

"Understood. Captain Betang has Mob troops aboard that vessel, and they've got it locked down. Only one airlock is in use; we control it."

"I hate to bring it up," Russ said, "but have you considered that some of these . . . people might be willing to fake an accident and use an abandon ship order to take emergency craft down?"

"Actually, sir, we have. Everything's locked out. They can't even escape unless our people release controls."

Mark cringed at the liability there, and he hadn't considered someone might try a stunt like that. He agreed it was possible, though. Nor could he think of a better solution.

"Good," Russ said. "I take it we're not allowing them down to be part of any negotiations at all?"

"Not given their likely involvement in the incursions, no," Mark said. "They have no economic interest, and they can't play the morals card now. However, we pretty much do have to let HMG in, and I'd much prefer to have DSR as a counter."

"What about ExtraSolar?" Russ asked.

"That's a good question. How do you feel about them?"

"How I feel isn't relevant," Russ said. He looked thoughtful. "If there are Freehold interests in the negotiations, I really do have to insist that some UN group be involved. I'm very unhappy with it being ESO, seeing as their actions were at least as unsavory as the others, but I don't think there's time to get any other group here."

"I concur, and a counter to them complicates things for us. Of course, it also complicates things for them, which is not entirely a bad thing."

"Right."

Shraybman asked, "What about press, sir? They're not happy with the updates, and even all the video frameage Thomas and her crew put together doesn't appease them. They want back on the ground, or in the case of the newer arrivals, on the ground at last, and to get down to their business."

"Lieutenant, do you think any of them can be trusted not to reveal element technology, not to ask questions the Ishkul can't back calculate into intel and not try to milk what they call 'controversy' out of this?"

"There are one or two I'd personally trust, sir. I won't officially sign off, though."

"Exactly."

Russ asked, "Is it possible to have them escorted and just shut off the translator if there's an issue? Not that I like them, but if we can make them back off . . ."

"The Ishkul can record the English with their parrots and play it back later."

"Ah, point."

"Also, the more information leaks out, the more people will try to come here."

Shraybman said, "Sir, do you think Vlashn can be trusted with more information? I understand he's aware of the existence at least different 'minerals,' as he calls them."

"He might even have the periodic table," Mark said. "We can't ask; he'll have to offer. But even then, if the twenty-first century developing nations hadn't known about plutonium, and suddenly had, it wouldn't have made them less likely to have nuclear programs. It would have been easier if the Ishkul were primitive agriculturalists, around our Bronze Age, or even as late as the Middle Ages. They had that technology when the Romans were just building their first roads, though."

Russ stood up. "I think it might be worth consulting with the scientists again on that. Ask them how much we can release. As you pointed out, knowing the material exists and knowing its capabilities are not quite the same. It takes that extra step. How long did it take to get from uranium to the newest artificial element?"

"Number Two-Twenty-Three is still speculative, I think, but you're right. The early researchers never found the mythical stable massive atoms they wanted. Nor did they have any real idea what to do. So yeah, let's ask the brains again. No mention of the rules on press and other parties at this point." He rose to his feet, too.

"Of course," Russ agreed.

CHAPTER 20

The scientists had a new toy to play with. They had detailed photos of the Homna city.

When the diplomats entered the lab area, Stephens was busy with a laser and a zoom control, and was running her mouth too fast for most people to keep up. They all looked confused as they gamely made notes as they could.

"—and this type of structure is probably a compacted substrate of several previous levels of development. Rather than relocate along the river as space, resources and industrial capability demand, this seems to be a long-term, ongoing staged development. You'll recall the Schliemann and Evans excavations in Troy. It wouldn't surprise me to find fifteen to twenty distinct strata, given the timeframe and development involved. Then over here, we see what appears to have been a canal at one point. Given the latitude and geography, I can easily imagine this was at one time a glacial riverbed. The silt would be easy to remove for construction, and would have led to localized building to make use of the material, as this urban crowding seems to indicate. The canal would be both cause and effect of the longitudinal development, which we see repeated here, but not on the river. The shallow banks hinder proper use of barges. Now—"

Mark watched silently for a while. He'd studied some of this, could pick out some other details as military intel, some of it was logical, but this scientist was basically writing the history of the entire city from a photograph, and he'd bet her timeline wasn't far off whatever they eventually concluded.

She turned, half winked and kept talking, with a querying glance as to if she should stop. He gave a nod, and she paused, after another paragraph of dictation.

"—My point being that this culture will expect things to be stable and consistent, but more than that, they'll be less flexible to change. The Ishkul change constantly. The Homna do not. That also explains in part why their technical base isn't as developed. Granted, this river is not as large or powerful, but it could be exploited more than it currently is. Sorry, let me stop for now. Good afternoon, sirs."

"Doctor, I will never question your instincts on this subject again," Mark said. Behind Stephens, lots of people could be seen sighing as they tried to wrap up their own conclusions from her lecture.

Russ said, "I'm amazed. I wish I could lurk here all day and pick up what you all have to say."

"I can easily provide a daily summary," she said.

"Thanks, but even that would be too much for us."

Mark said, "This is a general inquiry session. With the Homna stepping up, we have to provide some kind of developmental information, or else we have to leave. Leaving is only a temporary solution, weeks at most. We can't seal an entire system against phase drive. So that's not an option. We've offered them a little information on surgery, as I understand it, and on ceramics and glass. How much better can their steam engines get?"

"Without element?" McDonald said. "Not very. They've reached the technical limits of the materials they have. We did help their optics a bit, or rather, Dr. Zihn and Dr. Volk did. We can't do much more without a lengthy study. They really have developed their technologies as well as we've developed ours. Even the new group, the Homna, have less energy to work with, but that's their only limitation. They have distillation, limited steam power, the works."

"So what can we give them? There are some existing deals," he hinted without naming Margov or offering any details, "that are building up credit on their account, but we need something to offer them in exchange."

Stephens said, "Without damaging their own development, creating a rift of obsolescence or a war with their neighbors once the information gets out, which it will?"

"Exactly. We have a couple of days to come up with something to start with, even if it takes longer to get rolling." He heard groans and curses.

"I suppose we should start brainstorming," McDonald said with a resigned smile. Mark had never seen him bent out of shape over anything. He was utterly calm.

A loud bang shook the air and ground, and a pressure wave slapped in through the swinging door.

"What the—" someone shouted. McDonald lost his calm and got down behind a bench fast.

"Explosion," Connor said. He sounded professionally laconic, almost bored.

There was another. This one was closer and the over-pressure was painful.

"Local manufacture," Connor continued. "High veloc-ity, medium pressure."

"Impossible!" Russ shouted. "They don't have a mod-ern weapons culture."

"We are taking fire," Mark said, amazed at how rea-sonable he sounded. Incoming fire, find hard cover. But there was no hard cover. They were in a crate in the middle of a broad plain.

"That was it!" Stephens shouted. "The road cuts. Drilled slopes, indicating boreholes for explosives. That's why the roads are so advanced. They have explosives!"

What a great time to find that out, Mark thought, as another blast sent gravel snapping, whining and rattling through the air and against the walls.

"Apparently they have delivery systems, too," he said. *I still sound calm.* "Now we understand why they have advanced body armor."

"May we return fire, sir?" Connor *still* sounded unper-turbed.

"Return fire. Rockets and launcher grenades only, no rifles. Try to disable first. We don't want to escalate when we're outnumbered that much." *Damn, I sound calm, too*, he thought.

"Yes, sir!" Connor grinned, looking reassured. He spoke into his mic.

Mark had tried to balance diplomacy, force, minimal response and revelation of technology, and was glad he had troops educated enough to understand and agree. Now to see if the natives got the hint.

It was less than ten seconds later, after two more incoming eruptions with dirt and smoke blowing around, before a series of thumps and a HISSHH! indicated outgoing fire. There was only one more incoming blast, sounding rather half-hearted.

"Scared off, sir," Connor said. "Minimal casualties inflicted. We have several superficials among civilian staff. Military unharmed, fully effective. Twelve grenades and one Thunderbolt missile expended."

"Don't pursue."

"I understand, sir. I don't have to like it."

"Neither do I." At least they'd managed to use apparently comparable force. The Ishkul, or Homna, didn't need to know how much better human explosives were, or about guidance systems. They could probably calculate the former, though, and deduce the latter from intel.

Mark strongly considered sedatives. He was now in charge of the first armed conflict between sentient species. He had to bring it to a rapid conclusion. Just like a marriage, first rule is to apologize.

"Is there any way to get hold of Vlashn?"

Russ said, "Only if we send a ship. They went back to the city."

"If we must . . . no, wait. Would that be seen as hostile?"

"It . . . could."

"Should I assume this is not his group attacking?"

"It wouldn't make sense for them to. They could get in among us easily enough. They know we have advanced tech. I suspect this is an outside group, almost certainly the Homna."

"I thought they had less access to industry, given that they don't have large streams to power equipment."

Stephens said, "Either we were wrong, or they traded, or they've been building up a long time and never had a need to use the stuff. The technology is not beyond them. I'd only question the amount."

"Warrant Connor, can you minimize any further casualties?"

"At their end? Yes. I can use sonic stunners if they work, or widely dispersed simple concussion weapons. As for us, concussion can kill, but shock stabilizers and good nano treatment for hemorrhage boost survivability. Body armor will stop most critical fragments. I recommend having helmets handy, in case of further attack. I'll see about reinforcing the walls, too."

"It's very important that we appear defensive and reluctant." Mark needed to stress that a lot.

"Yes, sir. I've got it." His nod was serious and attentive.

"I recommend we cut and run," Russ said.

"What? You're not serious."

"That's the book policy for this situation."

"What book? You have a manual for dealing with sophisticated aliens?" Mark wondered where this was going.

"It's what we should do." He looked uncomfortable.

"If we pull out, everyone with an ox to gore will be in here at once. The place will be a shambles. Wars will break out. Millions die, the Ishkul hate us, and worst case, they come after us. That may be unlikely, but second worst is they never trust us and we lose everything we've worked for."

Russ sounded very bothered. "I realize all that. Still . . ."

"Forget the stupid book.".

"There are . . . reasons I can't do that." He was flushing red now.

Mark was getting tired of chills running down his neck. "You have orders. That means with the Jump Point open there's a comm tunnel."

Russ said nothing.

"You do. Can you please express to whoever is in charge that access to that communication will make it easier for me to assist you and them?"

"I'll mention it." Russ really looked uncomfortable.

"I will not be cutting and running. You're welcome to stay. In fact, under the circumstances, I believe for anyone to leave would endanger my people. Should any mishaps result because of it, I will consider it a breach of our treaty, and demand serious reparations. I'm not above seizing UN assets in system."

"Obviously I must protest your aggressive stance," Russ said. He was smiling, though. "I will remain in the interim, under protest, and will file an appropriate complaint through my government to yours."

"Is anyone keeping track of all these swapped protests?" Mark asked.

"I hope so, or not. One or the other."

"We'll talk later. Or you can come over to our side. I'm going to get a tactical report and share it."

"That's appreciated. I'll stay here. Not by choice."

Mark suspected the UN security detail would gibber if a diplomat went out in the middle of a potential battlefield. Fair enough.

"I'll send the info."

Connor stepped back in with Thomas and two others. "Perimeter secure. I've got an update."

"How bad is it?"

"Bad. And now that the gloves are off, I'm sorry we didn't see it sooner," Connor said, sounding embarrassed.

"What do we have?"

Thomas brought satellite images up and Connor pointed and spoke.

"This is in Ishkul territory. This is in Homna territory. Excavations here and here. Large scale chemical operations here, including acids. Massive guano and manure processes here. Nitrates. Explosives."

"Eh, could have also been fertilizer," Russ offered.

"Ceramics factory here, almost conjoined. You don't use ceramic nozzles for fertilizer."

Mark said, "True, but that's fairly esoteric and you couldn't have known about the nozzles. Was there any reason to look in that detail?"

"You pointed out the body armor, sir. As soon as we knew the body armor could stop modern weapons, above ceramic blades, we should have figured something was up. Nothing they develop is by coincidence. It's all carefully planned and very scientific."

McDonald said, "I'm wondering what other technology or weapons they may have. We know they have fertilizer, explosive and fuel chemistry, medical chemistry, steam power, hydraulic power, and sophisticated selective breeding. They've been open about showing us things we see from orbit, and they have telescopes so they can at least guess at the resolving power we have. If we don't mention it, they don't bring it up unless they need to, and they're very reticent about discussing certain subjects. Anything technical that might be used for military or intelligence purposes. They were reluctant to show us armor, weapons or cameras so far, at least."

Russ said, "It's not as if they think they might have better than we do, but they seem to want us to underestimate them."

"I can't blame them for that," Connor said. "It's one of their few advantages."

"Certainly. So tell me about range and capabilities."

"We're assuming no electronic guidance. These are ballistic rockets only. They have a decent degree of precision, and we're assuming T and E, Traverse and Elevation, controls for the launchers, possibly including bubble levels or plumb lines. We're assuming respectable maps and elevation charts. That envoy may have had a pace counter or something even more sophisticated —they could parallax to get distance. They may be able to account for wind, barometric pressure, and temperature effects on launch, in fact, I'd assume so. Every team of ours has a combat weather specialist who's trained to use improvised sensors in an emergency. Theirs are bound to be more sophisticated than that. We assume spotters for terminal guidance; we know they have lenses. Range appears to be about five thousand meters. I would not rule out longer ranges. They also seem to have a mortar version for indirect fire over barricades. Fragmentation appears to be vitreous ceramic. Sharp and nasty, but not much range. Explosive filler is on the close order of one point five, similar to nitroglycerine. Old TNT is a one on that scale. RDX is one point six six. Some of the modern hyperexplosives are close to three. It's a linear scale."

Mark said, "Impressive. Now we understand the body armor." It would stop some pistol rounds, he'd been told. Now they knew.

"Yes, frag protection. The same rationale we use. Protect the torso and skull."

"We always thought aliens would be drastically different, but really, similar environments require similar solutions."

"Their bows, if you recall, are a different configuration, but as efficient—up to eighty-seven percent. Draw weight is close to fifty kilos, even given the low gravity. Their long limbs give them a lot of leverage."

"World War One equivalent, from a threat perspective?"

Stephens said, "I'd say quite close, yes. No aircraft and no radio. Otherwise, quite similar. If you recall—"

"Thanks, Doctor, hold on please. That was a very ugly war." Her input would be useful but distracting.

Connor said, "I don't think there's ever been a war that wasn't, sir. But I understand your statement."

"Are the Ishkul going to get dragged in?"

"I have no idea, sir. I know you want to avoid that at all costs."

"Almost all costs. If Vlashn knew they were bringing in this much stuff, then he allowed it to happen to test us. I can't really blame him for that, but I am not happy, either."

"That's a very good observation, sir. I'll see if we can recon some information on that."

"*Very* discreet, Warrant. And I don't want to know about it."

"I didn't say anything, sir."

"Dr. McDonald, I'm going to leave you and the scientists to brainstorm on trade. I need to talk to Ambassador Russ, the troops and our ship and see what we can do to avert further violence."

"Of course. Good luck, Mark."

"And get everyone familiarized on body armor and have it ready. I'll see about getting more and helmets.

Warrant, I need to see about further defensive earth-works."

"Already on it, sir. I'll have every available troop digging and piling."

"Between photos I'm available," Thomas said.

"So am I," Shraybman insisted.

Mark added, "Take any volunteers you can get. We're all in this together."

Russ said, "I'm sure our Marines will be happy to help, and I'll work with the scientists if they can spare lab personnel. I know how to use a shovel, too."

"I can, also," Mark said.

"You can also get back there and work on tactics. You have military training, I don't," Russ said. "Keep the brains where they belong."

"You're right." Mark sighed. His lot was to be stuck in an office.

Mark awoke to an explosion. Dust flew, the air shook, and people shouted. He rolled out of bed, grabbed his helmet and pulled his body armor with him. He pondered shifting to a bunker, or behind the ballistic panel in the corner, but he wasn't sure what was happening, or if further incoming would occur. Better to stay where he was. He was safe so far.

A bit later, he started awake. He'd actually dozed off on the floor. Still, no further activity, and no one had come to get him or check on him. It must have been minor. He doffed the armor and crawled back into bed.

The next morning he dressed very casually, just pulling on slacks, walking shoes and a shirt, and skipped bathing for intel. He found Connor in his command area, with a radio headset visible and his comm online.

"There was an attack last night," he said.

"There were three."

"Three?"

"We intercepted two. I think we managed to express our displeasure without causing permanent harm."

That was interesting. Good, but interesting.

"Any captives?"

"I deemed that would be taken as hostile. We just told them to clear off, after disarming them. Humiliation possibly creates additional ill will, but I had to give them some kind of sting."

"That's fine. Any word from Vlashn?"

"None. Orbital recon shows a local force moving into place to interdict the incursion. I assume the Ishkul are moving to protect us. We've become a resource the natives are willing to fight over."

"We have a war starting. It's our fault."

"That's probably how history will record it, yes, sir."

"Get me those smugglers, again."

"Yes, sir. I wondered at keeping them here, but it seems to make sense now."

"That's largely luck and instinct, but I learned to trust them both as intel and as a dealer."

"Sir, if it's stupid and it works, it's not stupid."

A couple of segs later, the twelve smugglers were standing in the bay, surrounded by Operatives holding spears and knives.

Mark didn't bother with introductions.

"As you are aware, we've been attacked, we've retaliated, two groups of locals are moving into place for a battle. I don't suppose you've ever seen a battle with spears and arrows."

Dr. Stephens said, "We can expect severed limbs, mutilation, disease, slow, painful death. The Ishkul may blame us. Certainly some other indigines will. The press will. At present, all that attention will be heaped on you."

"We've got drones up to document it. Ultimately, whoever takes the blame could be facing a massive suit for damages by Vlashn and the Ishkul, by the UN, the Freehold, the scientific expedition, HMG and or DSR, various NGOs. Someone will be owned, or called to duel. This assumes the Ishkul or other local groups don't make a claim to try the accused here under their laws."

He had no idea if the latter was possible, or what punishment might be meted out. On the other hand, neither did they.

"Now would be a good time to make a statement," he suggested.

"We're probably paid by DSR, but I can't prove it and you can't," Ranid said at once. "As we said, everything was done on the sly, with cash." He looked nervous, but open. He had nothing to hide now.

"I have military and scientific experts. They will work with you and find out who. I suggest you cooperate completely."

"Yeah, we will," he said, with a glance at his compatriots, who nodded vigorously. "I want it on record that we acted in good faith to our contract and offered no violence."

"The more you give us, the better your chances. I'm not granting or promising anything. Talk first, then we negotiate." He sent them back to their cell with a dismissive gesture.

Thomas came in, sweaty and dusty from digging.

"Sir, Vlashn is on his way. He has a squad-sized element of Ishkul troops."

"That doesn't seem threatening, just cautious. Can I ask you to greet him and show him in? You have a duress word, I assume?"

"I can, I do, and yes, sir," she said, turned and started jogging.

Hopefully he wasn't sending her to be a tripwire. Logically, she should be fine, but there was that element of the unknown.

Connor's troops came back and took defensive positions. Whichever engineer had designed this facility had incorporated a lot of handy pillars, turns and cuts that served as fighting positions.

Thomas led Vlashn in without any sign of trouble, no gestures, no duress word.

Vlashn spoke without his usual greeting.

"Citizen Ballenger, I offer an element of our warriors to assist in your defense."

Mark closed his eyes to rub them, then reopened them.

"It was brave and considerate of you to come, Vlashn, but I can't accept. Our law on this is that we have to resolve it alone. We can't drag you into it, even willingly. We have to limit all repercussions. I feel rude sending you away, after you've shown such loyalty and support, but I must."

"The offer is not entirely for human benefit, Mark. I know that you have far greater military capability than you have shown. I intend to deescalate the threat to save many lives of our neighbor nation. Should that be effectively unobtainable, I urge you to use potent weaponry at once, to overawe them and minimize the need for further hostilities."

"Both are very valid. Both are impossible at this time."

The warriors stirred and twitched. Insulted? Quite likely.

"You lack detailed knowledge of our tactics. There is insufficient time for you to learn. We noted how hard it was for your warriors to learn basic counters to cavalry. I deduce you have many more vehicles and little use for animal-mounted transport. Consider our reluctance to share such information. You wish to minimize your response. This is the appropriate alternative."

"I agree, but I can't do it. With the greatest respect I must ask that you leave. We must handle this, to prevent escalation among your people. We would be held at fault by our rules if that happened."

"I wish to talk when this is over. I place a strong likelihood on your survival."

"Thanks. I appreciate it."

"You should be aware that we knew of the Homna military force and decided against informing you at the time."

"We were aware of them all along from orbit, and assumed your inaction indicated fear rather than hostility. Was this incorrect?"

"We and they agreed not to fight in order to avoid violence between us, to maintain our strength against you, if it was needed, and to maintain our peaceful image. They promised, and have maintained, minimal interference with Ishkul. You are their target. If I order the battle joined I will place our nation at risk. I am prepared to do this from both hospitality as host and because of the threat that force will offer to us should you either depart or be defeated. I have also considered possible repercussions from your own nations. I consider it a very low probability that you would burn our citylode, but I know you have the capability and must consider the risk. I intend no insult, only accurate exchange."

"I understand, Vlashn. I'm not offended. I wish I could accept. I assume you are reluctant to offer intel directly to us?"

"I would, but Somle and I would be considered damaging to our society to share such. I deem it more prudent to remain alive and offer continuity of counsel."

"As do I. I'd offer you exile status if it came to that, but I fear that would damage our relations."

"I concur. Mark, events are at cusp. I wish you good deductions and reason. As you request, I shall leave you to resolve it. I look forward with moderate expectation of a resolution we can both accept. I believe the English term is, 'good luck and give the bastards hell' or similar."

"It is. I shall see you soon, Vlashn." Where had he learned that? Did someone provide him a history? It sounded like something from the European wars of the twentieth century. Stephens would know exactly.

Vlashn turned and left, with his entourage, who twitched again. Yes, they were agitated and a bit insulted.

Well, that was that. Defeat the Homna and maintain status quo. Lose and die, and incidentally destabilize a planet with societies on the verge of star travel. What crappy options.

CHAPTER 21

"**S**ir, I have an update, sensitive."

"Captain Ch . . . Jelling," he greeted. "How can I help you?"

She stepped in and stood to at his desk. She had recovered from the close encounter with the native environment and once again looked far too decorative to be what she was, until she moved and he saw the muscles flex.

She said, "Apparently, our freelance delegations tried to sneak in again. They now have angry sentients on one side, and angry semi-sentients on the other."

"Poor them. What's the bad news?"

"Someone has to rescue them. They're apparently deniable. Neither group is accepting the blame. They're willing to let a few agents die rather than admit the screwup."

"They want us to do it, without violating the rules they've already violated, at our expense." He leaned back and considered that.

"The captives promised indentures."

"Of course. How deniable are they? Can we get concrete evidence on one group or both? Not that the Freehold officially cares, but others may have cases to bring, and I sure would like to know who gets the first bite."

"We can probably get something, since otherwise we own them. They'd rather we owned their bosses."

"See if the UN can send a boat."

"Yes, sir. As a favor, on contract, or . . . ?"

"Hell, I don't know. Ask Russ, I'm sure he'll say yes. He and I are about done fighting at this point. It's us against the rest of you. No offense." He was almost giddy. What a relief it was to actually have control of the situation at last.

"None taken, sir. That's a healthy position for this." She grinned and took a seat at his gesture.

He buzzed Lieutenant Shraybman. "Irina, I need Margov and Egan so I can mock them."

"With pleasure, sir," she replied.

Margov arrived first, escorted by one of the troops. She obviously hadn't had time to dress up and was wearing field clothes. She didn't look intimidated, but she didn't look entirely in control, either. She said nothing, but assumed she could sit and did so. Mark said nothing. He made eye contact in passing only and went back to his screens, which didn't show much of anything useful, but the pretense was a good cover.

Egan arrived before the silence got too uncomfortable. He looked unsure if he should bluster or plead. He looked at the military officer and decided to stay mute.

"The two of you don't get it," Mark started. "You can't keep sneaking people behind my back. You will wind up paying a hefty price."

"Uh . . . sir . . . " Egan stuttered. Mark raised an eyebrow and locked gazes with him. "I don't have anyone here, per your orders. If they say they're mine, they're lying."

"That's possible. And you, Taya?"

"Sir, you know I have been most cooperative, and apologized for our earlier transgression. It's not us. I'd prefer to be left out of this."

"Oh, I am quite prepared to leave you alone," Mark said. "The UN is controlling the Jump Point. I now have a stealth recon craft looking for phase drives precipitating into the system." He didn't, but how would they know? "I've given orders to destroy any craft that doesn't clear with us. Two local nations have requested that contact only be through our embassy to theirs. Given the background of violence, any other landing will be considered hostile. I'm on solid legal ground here. So whomever you have on the planet is stuck here and will stay here, until they get our attention to recover them, or you go ahead and tell us where they are.

"Now, I know the kind of cutthroat bitch Margov is." He nodded at her. She didn't smile, but she didn't protest. "I assume you're comparably skilled and sociopathic, Egan. However, I'll be very interested to see if abandoning people to die fits into your corporate model. The potential lawsuits and public embarrassment from that should add up to a lot of lost assets. I'm sure you'll still make a profit, but it will be tainted, and you're not going to impress our hosts in that fashion. Once it becomes an open market, because you can't dictate to them who they deal with—and if you're thinking Vlashn or any of his peers are stupid enough to grant any kind of exclusive, you're the sucker in this game—you get shut out.

"So how about doing the smart and honorable thing and play with the rest of us? Tell the captain where your shills are."

Jelling said, "Better yet, I'll tell them where their people are, and they can nod agreement. If I miss any, they can keep silent and let them die, or improve my intelligence gathering." She brought a map up on screen. "Six here, yours." She pointed at Margov. "Eight here, yours," another point at Egan, "and they had *element* blades and wire. Six here, unknown, with firearms."

"We didn't provide firearms!"

"Nor did we!"

"Of course not, ExtraSolar Ores did, or so we're told. It's just a party over there, isn't it?" Jelling grinned. "I am prepared to believe you don't know about it. ESO denies having anyone there, incidentally. So I'm guessing they suborned your personnel, and they're trying to use you for cover. We could just abandon them to teach them professional courtesy."

"Tempting, but we can't," Mark said. It occurred to him that a standard military sized team was another item to help track them with. Not quite tricky enough. He wasn't going to mention it.

"Sir, you can embarrass all three groups. Think of it as an extra level of control."

"Extortion?" Egan hinted, clearly annoyed.

"Politics and business," Jelling smiled back. She looked mean, and clearly still wanted vengeance on whoever had killed her troop.

Mark said, "If you're willing to claim them, I'll slap you with a fine for each. You can appeal if you wish. I'll investigate the weapons further and you'll avoid those charges, which Vlashn is indirectly pressing—'introduction of unapproved technology in violation of agreement with the Freehold and UN missions on behalf of their governments.' It's his rule, not ours, and he has legal standing. You won't win. If you're not liable, and we suspect ESO is, they take the rap from us and from the UN. You look better. In the future, you might hire a better class of mercenary and pay them enough they don't sell out."

The two glanced at each other. It was a fair enough deal, and Mark hoped they'd take it. They weren't going to get nailed for the weapons, and the fine was not going to exceed a few million, which was not much of an addition to the development costs in question anyway. It wouldn't hurt them.

"Agreed," Egan said. Mark was surprised he was first.

"Yes," Margov said, sitting back thoughtfully.

"Thank you," Mark said. "Give me the details and I'll assess a fine. If you really want to delay it for Council and lawyers, you can, but things aren't getting better."

"No, I accept your judgment from bench," Egan said.

Yeah, I bet you do, Mark thought. *This way it's quiet and discreet. You can still push for a deal.*

"Then you better give me names so I know who is who. You're losing points for competence here. I believe you got blindsided. It doesn't mean I trust you or you're off the hook."

"I'll send names in a few," Margov said and left at a slow walk. Egan said nothing, but beat her to the door and held it, then ran past her.

When consulted, Russ said, "ESO does not have any official representatives in system. Research only."

"Interesting. How do you plan to proceed?"

"I'll seize everything you don't want, and I'll lock assets based on suspicion, pending investigation. They have to argue back home. Similar to what you're doing, but I don't need to play legal games, I can just do it."

Practical. At the same time, that much discretionary authority raised hackles.

Mark said, "On the one hand, I'm glad I don't have that authority."

Russ smiled. "I'll be the other hand."

"That works."

Sergeant Thomas didn't get to do much digging. A ream of new photos came through the comm link, with more backed up the pipe behind it. She and Connor wound up in Mark's office analyzing them.

"It's clear now that huge convoy of the last few days was in fact a military supply line. Not a big one by our standards, though," she said.

"Please elaborate," Mark said.

"These are their launch sites. I see scorch marks here and here from launches."

"Got it," he said. They were small on this resolution, but clear enough now that he knew what to look for.

"I'm guessing that these lines are supplies of fuel. It looks like they can load variously sized charges as well as adjusting trajectory. If so, they can fire a time on target salvo."

Mark whistled. "That's pretty damned sophisticated. I'm going to assume they have incendiaries as well as HE, and that they have longer than a five-kilometer range."

"That would be a cautious idea, sir," she said. "I'll keep going over this."

Connor asked, "How do you feel about Vlashn-Somle after this, sir?"

Mark shrugged. "He came clean. I really have no cause to blame him. Politics is like that. Aliens land, neighbor wants to test them, are you going to try to get between them initially? He did ante up once he realized the score." Though Mark wondered if Vlashn anticipated Mark's refusal and had expendable troops ready in case he accepted. Or he may have hoped for humans to rid him of a dangerous neighbor. They'd refuse if asked, but if presented with a threat, and once attacked . . .

However it went, Vlashn was still non-hostile and worth negotiating with. He was no more a schemer than anyone else in this mess.

Mark spoke to Connor. "Do you think you can handle this? And how big is 'not huge'?" He looked back at Thomas.

Connor said, "I'm confident. We have decent ballistic protection. Their accuracy isn't pinpoint. They'd have to get a direct hit, and I doubt they can pack anything large enough to do serious damage. It might be about as annoying as guerilla mortar fire, just like last night."

"How long can they continue that?"

"Sergeant Thomas?" Connor asked.

"It's not a simple answer," she said. "They can continue the logistics train indefinitely, unless we or the Ishkul interdict it."

"Can they bring in anything larger, if they have it?"

"Possibly. They'd have to assemble here, which would require an area with tools. We'd see that. They could have some kind of steam-powered war wagons like that Italian engineer came up with."

"Leonardo da Vinci," Connor offered. "Some of those actually existed later, I believe, and I know horse-drawn war engines did."

"Keep an eye on them then," Mark said.

"Will do." Connor touched the tiny transceiver on his ear. "Sir, a messenger from the Homna just delivered a message. It's in Ishkul."

"Get Cochrane."

The message and the linguist arrived within seconds of each other.

Upon being handed the note, Cochrane said, "Oh, hell, sir, I can't translate this in any kind of time. Sorry, sir, you know what I mean."

"If we assume it's some kind of ultimatum, does that help?"

"Not really. The language is positional and structural, sort of half alphabetical and half pictorial, with tone indicators. I'd need days. You need an Ishkul."

Thomas said, "Vlashn's people have abandoned the landing camp. They're in the city."

"I don't think it matters," Mark said. To their looks he said, "Oh, do please work on a translation. It's useful to you and me. I have no intention of giving them anything, though, and I need to keep working out a deal."

"Yes, sir," Cochrane said. "I'll take it and start in, with photos for record of course."

"We should send a message to Vlashn as well. Warrant Connor, you're prepared?"

"If they attack again, I have counterfire, recon in force and infiltration options ready, organized between myself, the captain and the Marine lieutenant. I might suggest bringing a few Mobile Assault troops down from orbit tomorrow."

"How many? A squad?"

"That should be enough. We don't have the tail for a large battle, and we're limited on tech. I'll likely have them working defense while we do offense."

"Do it."

When Mark got back to his office, he found Father Dunn waiting. The Jesuit wore very worn field clothes. He still looked serene, even more than McDonald did.

"Good day, Father. I'm surprised to see you." Mark offered hands.

"It was deemed unsafe to remain in the city. I'm here for the time being. I'll stay out of the way, but if anyone needs someone to talk to or guidance, of any faith, I am available. I also have credentials in emergency medicine. I will pray there is no further violence, but I offer my services."

Mark had to smile. "Sir, you are a refreshing breeze. I realize you have an agenda, but it's so mild compared to the rest, and I'm sure we're all grateful for the help. Check with the military and see if they can give you a kit or task. And thanks . . . I will take all the prayers and moral support we can get."

"Then I shall check with the officers and retire to pray," he said. "May the Lord bless you and your mission with continued success." He made the sign of the cross, turned and left.

Just at the end of twilight, the next Homna attack commenced.

Whooshes followed by loud bangs announced the landing of a fresh salvo of rocket shells. Some debris rattled on the roof and walls of the embassy. A flurry of pressure waves rattled windows and whuffed through the air, pushing doors and curtains with ghostly hands. The lights went out. Deliberate, to make them harder to spot.

Mark cursed, rose quickly from his desk, grabbed his armor and squatted down to don it, then sat in the sandbag barricade against his inside wall. He wondered how many volleys it would be this time.

A second sequence landed, in timed bursts with punctuating rapidfire salvos.

This time, the incoming fire went on and on. Ten, fifteen series of shots, with steady harassment in between.

Connor leaned his head in the door.

"Sir, you need to take cover now, and put on that filter you brought. Now." He was still dead calm under his own mask, voice elevated slightly to compensate. He clearly meant it as an order, though, and Mark decided it was valid. He grabbed his respirator, donned and cleared it and snugged his helmet down.

Connor was all the way in, now. He wore helmet, armor and a small combat pack. He said, "Glad you're in cover. If you feel any gas, close your eyes. We don't know if they have blister agents or not."

Gas. The Ishkul and Homna had chemical weapons, to go with their rocket artillery.

At least now he knew what the evasion at their end had been.

What if the aliens find out we're violent? Both sides were playing PR games. Vlashn had hinted at such when he'd said they were as peaceful as humans. Not very.

It had to stop. Soon. The locals were going to start a civil war over this that could be planet-wide.

He stopped thinking as another volley of rockets exploded. *Yeah, think you're pretty smart, don't you? I could order counterbattery to go with the satellite intel and have you vaporized in seconds. Or drop the bar on you from orbit. But if I do that, I blow the whole operation.*

As the blasts echoed away, he tried to resume thinking. Where was he? Oh, yes. Part of him wanted to dump a coil of copper wire, a thousand metal spears and a hundred rifles. Let the natives realize what they were facing. That would lead to them being a protected, effectively a slave species, though. The UN was pushing for that. The typical government elitism that people aren't smart enough to handle their own affairs. He also wasn't going to award a monopoly to any group.

They needed to concentrate on what could come out of the system, but what could come in in exchange? Technology, except the locals didn't need any, except that which they couldn't have.

Dammit.

He did see some vapor. It could be smoke, dust or steam, but it was acrid and close. He closed his eyes. He hadn't thought to need a gas mask. He hadn't thought to meet rockets.

Another incoming volley got replied to with outgoing fire. The troops aimed by parallax and laser ranging. The natives probably had the former. They'd been consistently quite accurate, more so than common rebels on human planets. Some of the shells slammed, others thumped. More gas.

Was it actually possible the locals would defeat them? The irony was staggering. Here were the two highest tech militaries in human space, and no one had thought to bring a gas mask. It wasn't as if the threat was serious.

It had been centuries since anyone used chemical weapons militarily. Terrorists sometimes did, and a few despots had used them for genocide against civilians. Militarily they weren't viable.

It seemed they were here. Connor came back after the next volley.

"I've got filters blowing in here, sir. We should be safe. Keep the mask on. We're responding through the windows. If we lose too many more, the filters will be useless. No overpressure."

"How's the fight going?" His voice was tinny through the mask. He wanted to know and he wanted not to worry.

"I think we have them convinced we're a serious threat, despite our numbers. We can't risk the gas yet, though. At least some of it is blister agent, and considering the chemistry here, it's hideous stuff. I've got a man who is going to need a skin graft on his arm."

"Ouch. How'd that happen?"

"We had to test it somehow."

Mark had no idea how to respond to that. He knew his Operatives were hardcore pain and adrenaline addicts, but that seemed to push the envelope.

Another blast shattered a window. Air slapped and swirled around him, dark and dirty with debris.

"Close your eyes! Get down and back!"

"Complying," he said, crawling fast. One finger was stinging. Had he caught a piece of shrapnel? "What range are they firing?"

"Estimate around four thousand meters."

"That's pretty impressive."

"Yeah, I imagine their heavier stuff can go a few klicks farther. You were discussing if they had rockets and spaceflight? I don't think they're far off at all."

"Definitely. It just gets worse all the time."

"We're almost certainly going to have casualties. The captain led two teams, one of ours, one graciously volunteered squad of UN Marines, to infiltrate and take out some of those batteries. They're going through gas, toxic terrain and into a large mass of troops. We've got to stop this, though, and with minimal retribution, as you demanded."

"I wish I didn't have to."

"Hell, sir, it's a challenge, but it makes sense. We'll do it." He sounded cheerful.

A moment later Connor was talking into the air. Implant transceiver, obviously.

"Understood, Lance. Return ASAP. Out. Sir, we got three of the vehicles. You may hear them any moment." He stopped talking.

In fact, Mark could hear a crackling string of reports, very reminiscent of the big holiday fireworks. That should hopefully give them pause.

The moment stretched. No further missiles came in.

"It seems to have worked."

"For now."

He cautiously rose and looked himself over. Yes, his finger had a minor cut, clearly from some kind of frag. One of the windows was out. He doubted the plastic pane had shattered, so there must have been a second blast that threw shrapnel.

How ironic. He'd never seen combat in the Forces. Now he was a civilian and a diplomat and had a bona fide, if minor, wound.

He left his battle gear on. He hadn't been given an all clear, and didn't want to be a guinea pig. He did need to at least make notes, though, and check with everyone he could as to status and intel.

He reached his desk just as the next wave hit.

This was neither a ballistic shell nor a roaring rocket. It was a shrieking scream and a much bigger *bang!*

As the walls and floor shook, Mark dove prone. The armor was tight and pinched his armpits until he shimmied to work it down.

What in the fuck was that? he wondered, heart drumming, sweat bursting, head aching. His ears rang. That had been some significant firepower. Another window was out now.

Seconds later, another one shrieked and banged in. It was a rocket of some kind, he decided, and much bigger. Probably longer range, too. The nearby battery having been corrupted if not destroyed by the military, the Homna had diverted the attack to a second unit, one with near strategic munitions.

He crawled cringing across the floor into the little sandbagged cubby and considered pulling some over on top of himself. He wondered if earplugs were a good idea against noise, or if a close burst would create more overpressure and rupture his eardrums. He settled for cupping his hands. It was awkward under his helmet, but he managed.

Shriek, boom. Shrieeek, boom.

What the hell were they firing? Not that knowing would change anything, but it might help him grasp it intellectually and feel better.

"Sir?" Connor called. Mark heard him fumbling around near the desk.

"Here," he called.

Connor ran over in a crouch and squatted.

"Good, keep the mask on, sir. This seems to be mostly HE, but we don't know when or if more gas will come in. Or incendiaries for that matter. Two fires already."

Shriek, boom. The walls shook again.

"What are they shooting?" he shouted over the echoes.

"You can't tell? Pulse jets. Buzz bombs. Low enough pressure they can do it with their materials. They only last a few seconds before failing, but about seventy percent last long enough to be in trajectory. I'm guessing ten-kilometers range. What level of response do you want, sir?"

"Can you accurately counter those launchers with something non-met . . . element?"

"In theory, very easily. As it stands now, we didn't anticipate this and the only explosives we have that are clean are a few grenades."

Another blast, not as near. He still cringed.

"Not enough range?"

"Thirty-two hundred meter max. There's no reason for squad level weapons to do more, and we were leery even of that. Sorry, sir."

"Not your fault," he replied. "I should have had a backup plan."

"The Homna are not real bright, sir. They know we have better tech. What if we used it?"

"They seem willing to take that risk to gain intel, or threaten, or to hopefully have us attack the Ishkul instead."

Another blast sent crashing sounds through the building. It must have hit within the walls not far away.

Connor shouted, "*Aracaju* has equipped some debris with guidance systems and is offering fire support. Rocks, basically."

"Yes, show them we can cause meteorites. Pinpoint only. Don't do it if they can't." Things didn't fall out of the sky very often on this planet. It might have an effect.

After a mumbled exchange, Connor said, "Yes, sir. They report four hundred, nineteen seconds to impact. They say they have the launchers. Five kilo rocks with guidance and ablation shields."

"Let's hope in the meantime, then."

"Yes. I recommend getting outside, sir. You can see a bit better, wind will disperse chemicals and we do have some overhead cover. Also, this building is a target."

Mark was already up and moving. If his combat expert suggested it, he was going to do it, unless it flew in the face of diplomacy. Probably then, too, actually. He was scared and he was pissed.

Connor led him through a haze-filled hall and out the rear. The officer was still receiving intel and said, "Update for you, sir. Chemical fillers are choking or blister agents. No sign of nerve agents yet, nor is it probable that nerve agents for natives will work on Terran life. I would not assume it wouldn't, though. Cyanide-based blood agents are entirely possible, though they'd have to figure that out from our blood type. Of course, from the biology exchange, they might have. Irritants are very easy. Any plant sap would work. It depends on how advanced the enemy espionage and chemistry are, but they seem on par with the Ishkul.

"The good news is we have night vision. They can see near-IR, which helps them a little, but we can see a lot better in much lower light. They have definite advantage of numbers and years of specializing with their weapons. We have superior communications and can evacuate if need be."

"Yeah, I'd really rather not, though. Once we do, it's all wasted. Are you sure we have the upper hand?" He could discuss it like this, without having to think too much. Part of him was sure the Homna, and Ishkul, had nothing that could do more than annoy them, apart from killing anyone they got lucky and actually hit. The odds of that were remote. At the same time, every overhead scream, every bang of high explosive, made him sure he was going to be that one. Outside felt more exposed, though Mark realized he'd evacuated a target and now only faced misses or lucky shots.

Connor replied to the question Mark had forgotten asking only a second before. "Of course. I'll also put our people against theirs." His mask was separate from his goggles, and hanging around his neck now. Mark left his mask in place.

He asked, "What are you basing that on?"

"Balls."

"Fair enough." Even if it wasn't true, there was a fifty percent chance, improved by the attitude.

Outside was a bit clearer, though smoke and dust were quite present. There weren't any billowing fires, but smoky, oily embers and low blue flames showed here and there.

"Ah, shit," Connor said.

"What?"

"Can't you . . . oh, sorry. IR spectrum, sir, and I'm remoted through my visor to outside. I can see it, but I can't do anything about it with what we have on hand."

"About what?" Mark insisted.

"Balloons. A squadron of about eight."

"They're going to use them as bombers?" Mark peered to the west. There was no light pollution this far from the city, and with multispectrum sensors, there was no reason for the humans to have illumination up.

"That would be my guess. Let's find some heavier cover. Luckily, they can't carry much payload, even in this gravity."

They hunched and sprinted back toward the rear of the embassy, and Mark was glad for the reinforced lower walls and integral bunkers. It was standard construction for military engineers. They hadn't asked, they'd just done. Good on them.

No sooner had they zigzagged in the cofferdammed opening than a brilliant brightness came up, like a blood-red sunrise, followed by a wave of searing heat, moist then dry then beyond.

"Napalm, of course," Connor said. "No . . . stuff to improve it, but basic naphtha and some kind of oil thickener are all they need."

"And gas," Mark said, feeling his face burn and grabbing for an alcohol wipe to blot the skin around his mask and neck.

"I think that's just residue and the normal chemistry, but . . . ohhhh, shit."

"What now?"

"Air assault troops, rappelling down." A series of pops presaged a brighter orange glow. "And illumination rounds."

"How big a balloon does that take?" It didn't sound possible to carry more than a couple per balloon. He edged around the shelter's opening to look.

"The balloons appear to be hopping and bounding from upwind. They have enough lift to clear the wood line, descend, then lift again. There are at least twenty balloons now."

Mark snugged his mask tighter into place, looked out and up, and was impressed, right before he realized he should be terrified. Tens of natives fast roped down, not the same way humans would, but with equal effect. They had bows, spears and, apparently, grenades. The shifting shadows from the orange parachute illumination was creepy.

"Twentieth-century military tech, too."

"Yes, I see," Connor said, sounding pissed, but in a general fashion, not at Mark for stating the obvious. He raised his bow, snapped off an arrow, and spoke into his mic. "Jack, to your left. Robin, to your point eight. We've got them in a three-way cross fire." He shot three more arrows as fast as he could, then ducked.

"Sir," he said, "if it comes down to it, use this." He rummaged in his ruck and produced a Merrill 11mm pistol. "Yeah, I know about the rules. You stay alive to enforce them and sort it out afterwards."

Mark almost refused to take it, except that he was afraid Connor would actually use it if he didn't take it. Not that the mechanism was much beyond the natives, it was just the half kilo of metal and the advanced composites it was made of that were an issue. He grabbed it, stuffed it down into a pocket, and said, "I've had reasonable training with sword and bow, too."

"Sir, no offense, but this is an all or nothing event. They've trained all their lives. 'Reasonable' means you wind up dead. Stay out and let us fight."

"Understood." He hated it, though. He was a veteran, did know how to fight, and craved to do something other than cower with his head down.

Arrows clattered off the reinforced panels of the building, and an explosion tugged at the air.

"Arrow launched grenade. Impressive." Yes, he was that calm. Panic just wasn't going to help.

Connor slipped sideways, balanced on the balls of his feet, rose up and drew back the bow in one motion, the string twanged and he skipped back behind cover.

"I got him."

"Good."

"But there are a lot of them."

A massive explosion rocked the ground, slapped the air and shook the walls. A sandbag to his right popped open and oozed a trickle of dirt. Then he realized that sandbag was bare centimeters off the ground. He found he had to pick himself up off the ground, rolling to his knees and rising to a squat.

"Yeah, they're still aerial bombing us," Connor said. "Sir, we need to take the balloons out. They're semi-anchored and maintaining station. They're going to keep doing this."

"What do you suggest?"

"Flyby."

Mark thought quickly, though he was still dizzy and having trouble. Was there any reason not to? The locals knew the ship existed, knew it flew, no additional contamination there. It would be effective. It would probably not kill many, and it would certainly save humans.

"Do it."

"Already did. Thanks for confirming, sir."

Mark really wasn't sure if he wanted to make an issue of the presumptiveness or be glad of it.

There couldn't be more than a few tens of Homna, but they had home planet advantage, weapon familiarity, and it seemed likely only the elite would be tasked for such an expensive and complicated attack.

It seemed forever before Mark heard an engine howl. The courier.

"They've noticed that," Connor said. "And here we go."

The engine howl rose sharply, cracked in what sounded transonic, but was probably just exhaust roar, then dopplered away. "That hurt them!" Connor shouted. "Yeah!"

Mark stuck his head out and took a peek. Indeed, the balloons had been jostled and several were sinking, two burst. Though he was struck again by the local sophistication and reason.

One of the huge balloons, a troop carrier, came down *fast*. The eight warriors on the ropes raced it down, getting as close as possible to the ground, then swarmed back *up*, to slow their impact from as low an altitude as possible. The ones nearest the ground simply dropped and rolled. The swarmers did so as a trained unit. Clearly, this was a planned tactic for just such an event.

"These fuckers have a lot of experience fighting," he commented.

"Yes, I'm seeing that," Connor said. "We're hurting them, but they brought enough numbers. Are you sure about that technology bar, sir?"

"No, but it stands."

"Yeah. Ah, well." Connor shrugged. He was a first class soldier, of course. He didn't have to like his orders. He'd follow them as best he could and gripe later.

A roar overhead indicated the courier returning. A hot, pungent wind blew through, clearing some of the smoke, haze and grit. It was easier to breathe, even with the added presence of fluorine fumes and ozone. The local crap had built up slowly, but between natural toxins, war gas, smoke, nitrates and petroleum distillates, and dust, the billowing air was sooty and gray-green. The incoming air was near clear.

"I'm glad we have the Marine contingent," Connor said. "That adds a number of professional troops."

"How do you rate them? Better than average?"

"Consider that I regard 'average' troops as a three, civilians as zero to one. Marines are about a four to five, maybe a six. Our hosts might reach a five, but have lots of numbers."

"You're a ten?"

"If I fight fair, yes, sir."

"As soon as we can not fight fair, I'll let you know."

"Much appreciated, sir. Let me know soon. They're getting numerous."

Mark sneaked again, was shocked at the numbers he saw, and said nothing to Connor's shove that took him out of sight again. There were possibly a hundred troops on the ground now, the balloons providing arrow and aerial bombing support. He saw one equipped with a fast-firing ballista, shooting spears, probably with armor-piercing heads. Another had what looked like an over-sized slingshot. Half-kilo grenades projected from it, steadily and with decent accuracy.

The human forces held up well. They had better armor, were good enough with the weapons, and weren't psychologically overwhelmed, once the first shock was over. This was all archaic stuff, if creative, even genius in its development.

Still, those formations of spear and arrow were close enough to pike and musket, or pike and archery, to be a credible threat. Others arrived in several inconsistent streams, mounted as cavalry, drawn in carts, on foot and from the balloons. A couple of shapes dropped from the rearmost balloons in the formation—hang gliders. They were likely recon or penetration troops to disrupt the humans.

"Gliders, I see them," Connor said, apparently having given up on keeping Mark out of view. "They don't have night vision, radio or the power of explosive we have, so we will win, but you want to do this as peacefully as possible, right, sir?"

"I do. I'm not above some psych warfare, though. Can we do a nice bright, powerful airburst to make them pay attention? Let these assholes realize their numbers aren't enough."

Connor grinned broadly, a rictus under his goggles. "Can do. Thank you, Citizen. Stand by." He spoke into his mic, "Irish Two. Air mission. Support. Air burst for psychological effect. Target, balloon formation. Grid—" He rattled off numbers. "Collateral military damage acceptable."

Mark felt a ripple of shock. Did Connor intend that as an excuse to kill more than he had to? Or was it a legitimate advisory? While he pondered, Connor said, "All: standby for flash. Splash."

He squinted and ducked his head. The burst that followed was brilliant right through his eyelids, a sparkling firework charge in his protected vision.

BANG! The report slapped at the air, an overpressure spike that was a definite attention getter.

Cautiously, Mark opened his eyes and looked. That had been effective. The locals seemed rather quiet and reluctant, and several more balloons were out of the fight, either descending from leaks or outright burst and falling. Alien officers shouted, though, and they continued their attack.

"Leapfrog retreat to embassy grounds, take positions at perimeter, then in building on order or if needed," Connor ordered into the air. He turned and said, "Sir, we're getting close to that magic point where we accept our loss nobly, or kick some teeth."

"Once you've retreated here the gloves are off as far as explosives and air support," Mark said.

"Understood. I'll prepare for a perimeter mine drop, and a supersonic flyby."

"Do it."

Another flight of something went overhead, low and fast, with a resonant scream.

"More pulse jets?" He stared up, and saw the shapes unfolding. Paratroops. Dropped from rockets? That was insanely brave. "That . . . is disturbing."

"I'm more disturbed by the incoming ground troops."

True. There were more of them. Plus others on the ground, plus those who'd vacated the balloons.

"I need a bow and spear," Mark said. "At least to defend myself. Your talents are wasted as a bodyguard."

"Agreed, sir. Follow me."

Connor dropped to the ground and started low crawling. Mark followed, curious but trusting. The ground chemistry would cause irritation. Arrows and explosives would cause death.

The ground changed from gravel to grass interspersed with bare dirt that hadn't been overfilled back to gravel. Connor rose and darted whenever some structure, debris or terrain allowed. The few low hummocks, a couple of bushes and a crate of something provided cover on one side, concealment on the other. A figure trotted across in front of them, birdlike legs pumping.

Instantly, Connor whipped his spear around and took a leg at the ankle. The Homna glugged and keened and dropped. Connor brought his spear up, over down and into some critical organ. With a twitch and a kick, the alien stopped.

"Take my spear and bow," he said, dropping the spear, unlooping his bow and quiver. Mark grabbed them without asking. Connor snatched the Homna's blade, which resembled an Aztec thing . . . Macahuitl? Ceramic edges on a long baton with a bone point added. There was a belt of grenades and a pseudo crossbow. It looked magazine fed. Had some Earth culture done that? It seemed familiar. Connor grabbed that, too. The Homna armor was a long jerkin with plates, leg wrappings of sinewy leather and a helmet of scales over hide. Connor had speared him right underneath and up into the belly.

He stopped studying as Connor said, "Follow me, move!" and rose to a sprint.

Mark flexed his arms, pushed off and followed. He ignored the bangs of grenades. He had body armor and there was nothing more he could do. He shifted his helmet as it flopped.

At least, he tried to ignore the grenades. Just behind him, about where he'd been lying, something landed and slammed his spine with the concussion. He cringed, clenched all over and ran faster.

He stumbled on something, felt Connor pushpulldrag him upright and shove him into a much sturdier bunker. He could feel movement but saw nothing other than a bare glimmer. Night vision, right. All the military had multispectrum visors on. This was their command post, and it was as bombproof as it got around here. It was also rather comfortable. In between little action, they'd spent their time paneling, painting, building furniture and making it homey.

He took a seat and breathed deeply through the mask. There was a bare tickle of irritation, but even some nonlethal human chemicals did that. He wasn't going to worry if no one else here did.

He pulled his feet out of the narrow walkway. Five soldiers in here had comms set up and were plotting, directing, managing. Mark smiled. It had been a long time since he did battle management. He wondered which one had his job.

Connor said, "Sorry to have you running around so much, sir. It's a bit disorganized."

"No, this is perfect for now. Can you tell me how the scientists and Ambassador Russ are?"

"The Marines have them bunkered on their side of the compound. Pretty much everyone is out of the main building at this point. It's an obvious target. We're monitoring and prepared to slag it completely if we think it is compromised."

"Ouch," Mark said. That would mean a lot of research and information lost, anything that hadn't been uploaded to orbit yet. Still, modern conductors and semiconductors could not be allowed to fall into native hands.

"Dammit!" Connor said.

"Warrant?"

"McDonald, Stephens and Zihn. They stuck around to upload as much information as possible and secure physical copies. They're still in the embassy lab."

"I can easily see Land doing that, and Stephens is stubborn."

"Yeah, well now we have to get them. That end is embattled and there are no spare troops in the line."

"I'll come with you."

"Sir, I—"

"I'm Chief of Mission, it's my responsibility." He also was damned well going to be useful.

"I disagree but will comply, sir," Connor said.

Yeah, the sole diplomat really shouldn't do this. Mark Ballenger, however, was a veteran and in charge and needed to.

Connor had four troops from somewhere. They just showed up around him. Mark adjusted the quiver he'd been given. It was very nice work, with belt and shoulder strap. The arrows were right at his fingertips over his right shoulder. The bow . . . he tried a couple of practice pulls. Stiff . . . very stiff. It had to be close to fifty kilos, but he could draw it if he had to. He checked the short spear and decided it would work like an escrima stick or walking cane. He'd trained with both at one point. Okay.

Connor said, "We're going through the end door, straight down the corridor and into the lab. We grab them and don't take any argument. We retreat in good order. The outer perimeter will fall back. We slag the comms and gear. We regroup at the rear bunker. Sir, are my gloves off yet?"

Mark had already reached a decision. "As long as we recover any element from the bodies, do what you have to."

"Thanks. May I have my pistol back, sir?" He held out a hand.

Mark dug into his pocket and pulled it out. He handed it over butt first. It seemed there was another pistol, too. Not one for everyone, but one of the troops pulled one out. Hopefully enough. If there were two here, there were probably others elsewhere. Mark knew he should object afterwards, but as long as they weren't compromised he would keep reticent.

"Where's Ru—" he started to ask and was cut off with Connor's, "GO!"

Nothing to do but stay with the current fireteam. He ran along, clutching at an arrow and worrying it onto the bow while running. He clutched that in position and made sure he could reach the knife/spear if he needed to. Connor had said Russ was secure, yes?

It was hard to suck enough air through the mask while running, so he doffed his helmet, yanked off the mask and looped it over his quiver. He pondered losing the helmet, but another explosion reminded him of the very real risk of frag. He dumped it back on his head and snugged the straps.

He choked for a moment on the acidic, dusty, smoky, haze-ridden air, then found that breathing through his mouth made his throat burn, but reduced the coughing.

It took seconds to get to the embassy building, then they were sprinting down the hall. There was debris on the floor from the overhead dome, and there were apparently a couple of breaches up there, but it was largely intact. The materials and shape made it quite resistant to shockwaves.

He had one soldier behind, two in front, Connor in the lead. Connor rose and twisted, sidekicked the lab door right off its hinges and landed like a gymnast.

Three scientists turned in shock, clutching at benches. They recognized the intrusion was by humans and not Homna.

Mark saw the beginnings of argument on Stephens's face already, and beat Connor to the draw.

"I am Chief of Mission. You will get your asses out of here *right now*. If it's in your hand, bring it. If it's not, leave it. *Now*," he repeated.

It worked, though the presence of guns, bows, knives and the door lying on the floor might have had something to do with it, too. The three grabbed several items each, swept the table's contents into valises, started to reach for items on the floor and thought better of it. They started running as best they could. None of them were in bad shape, but all were older and not very athletic.

Connor took lead again, one of the troops behind and to his left. The scientists filled in. Another soldier picked up behind them. The last gestured to Mark to run ahead, then brought up the rear.

Outside, it was chaotic again. The Homna troops had managed to cause some disruption and were scattered throughout the camp. One of them turned just in time to get stomped and stabbed by Connor.

The Blazer or Operative with him, it had to be one of the two, suddenly burst ahead as fast as any Olympic sprinter. *Combat NeuroStimulant*, Mark thought. The man had a short spear and a pistol and he cleared a swath. A Homna appeared with a bow, and went down with a bullet through his face. On the way down, the soldier sliced his throat with the spear.

A squad-sized element of natives had positions in low spots, a crater and behind a gear pile. Mark saw one of them drawing a bow. He ducked aside and dropped while fumbling an arrow into nock. He had little experience with bows, but the idea was to keep outgoing fire, while avoiding incoming. The Homna arrow flew right overhead as he shot back. His accuracy wasn't great, but he was within a meter. The Homna flinched and paused his own shot. That was enough time for someone else's arrow to take him in the thigh. He convulsed and dropped to the ground, but still tried to get an arrow off when someone ran up much closer and shot an arrow into him from a couple of meters.

Mark was on his own, now. Connor and his assistant were clearing the way, and the other two were chivvying

the scientists toward safety. They must have decided he
knew what he was about and could take care of himself.
It felt good. It was also rather scary.

Mark heard a sibilant, growing scream, knew its
source, and dove for the ground, plugging his ears and
opening his mouth. Incoming.

A wave of heat slapped him, tumbled him. Another
pressure wave crossed it in a roiling roar, under which
he could just hear shrieks and gurgles of fear and pain.
He heard punctuated bursts of rocket fire, and there was
no more incoming.

He saw someone rushing toward him and shouted,
"What was that last?"

"It felt like conventional artillery. I suppose they could
have bound tubes. It worked for the old Chinese. Possibly rockets in a high trajectory. I think we have them
now, though."

He didn't recognize the speaker at first. It was the
Marine officer, sheened in sweat and dirt and nursing a
bloody elbow. It appeared to be skinned, not stabbed.
He'd probably run into something.

Crackling gunfire and the definite sound of human-
designed explosives increased in frequency.

Then faint white streaks to the north resolved to thun-
derous, ground-shaking echoes.

Four hundred and nineteen seconds. That's all it had
been since he'd authorized orbital bombardment.

The incoming tapered off, as did the gunfire.

The faux meteorite impact did nothing to stop the
troops on the ground, though they seemed minded to
retreat.

"Let them go," Connor ordered. "They have an
escape route."

They seemed willing enough to take it.

CHAPTER 22

By morning, things were pretty well back under control. Most of the Homna had retreated in good order, taking their wounded. Some of the worst wounded lay under a tent. Humans bandaged them and gave them water, and a message had been sent to the Ishkul capital via lander. Mark hoped they could be kept alive until professionals of their own species arrived, but that was up to Vlashn. He really couldn't force such.

The dome had two gaping holes and the engineers had them half fixed. A munitions team was out safing and occasionally biping—Blowing In Place—the Homna UXOs. Several of the smaller outbuildings would have to be rebuilt, if a human presence stayed. Some gear had been lost, about equal amounts attack and self-destruct. Nothing appeared to have been captured. All but two rounds of ammo were accounted for, and both troops were quite sure they hadn't been left in wounded aliens. If the natives did find a few small pieces of tungsten, they were unlikely to be able to do much with them, and that shouldn't happen any time soon. Mark made a note to have another search of the area done.

Casualties: several wounded, two dead. They'd lost one Marine and one junior lab technician.

The Homna seemed to have tried to limit damage. Connor and Chinran were sure they could have used bigger charges. It seemed their plan was to take the human site intact and ransom it. They were not stupid, and he made a note to remind Connor of that. *Don't underestimate your opponent. He always believes his approach is valid.*

A roar unhindered by the missing windows in Mark's office announced the courier craft returning. He stood and took a look. Ah, good. Those Ishkul would be medics. Vlashn was along, too, with an actual squad of body-guards this time, carrying real weapons. Mark wasn't worried and thought that a wise idea. He walked out to meet his friend and counterpart.

"Vlashn, welcome and thank you for your assistance," he said.

Vlashn slowed his walk and said, "You are welcome. Citizen Ballenger, I need your assistance."

Vlashn was being formal. That wasn't helpful.

"I'll do what I can."

"I request Freehold assistance in settling the dispute along my nation's northern border. I am not opposed to the use of military force."

Mark had predicted that.

"It's complicated, Vlashn. First is the rule about not interfering, though in this case, our presence has exacerbated and perhaps caused the problem, so that's arguable. Then, this is not the Freehold. I can't deploy troops for combat operations without a sponsoring body, which you offer, and a vote by the Citizens' Council."

"Query: There is no way you can assist? This is a vital issue to our discussions."

"There's one way, and I won't do it."

"Query: Please explain."

"I could do it easily if your lands or your planet were Freehold territory. If you signed over authority to my government. I will refuse to allow that."

"I would never consider such. I am reassured moderately well by your refusal to do so."

"You're a Resident with out-system territory. I can control my people at your request and offer diplomacy and hearings. I can't get involved with an outside party."

"I strongly desire a resolution, Mark. Your culture offers much with great confidence. For your information, Ambassador Russ offered membership in the United Nations, or a sponsorship for the Galactic Alliance. I refused. I comprehend the wellness of his intentions. My trust is extended more toward you for your lack of such an offer."

Jackpot.

"I am obviously pleased to hear that. I want to help find a solution." Damn, this was tricky, almost intimate. Mark's nerves prickled. This was the cusp, but he was greatly limited in options.

Finally, he replied, "I will have to consult with my warrior class."

"Axiomatic necessity. Presumption: A low majority of your warriors conclusively appear to be technical specialists, with combat a secondary skillset."

"Most of them do have a technical skill. I assure you they can all fight, very well."

Vlashn said, "Thus far, your warriors' ability is comparable with the mean level I expect from our own class. Their handling of weapons appears median, within one standard deviation. I am reassured that in this pursuit you do not excel, as in so many others."

Wait until you see them with modern weapons, you poor bastard. Or our Operatives one on ten to yours.

Outwardly, Mark replied, "I'm glad you're reassured that our intentions, all of us, are peaceful. There are disputes as to approach, and we are a chaotic, anarchic species, but desire to cause injury is outside our norm."

He continued, "Please wait. I will consult and see what options we have. Can you assist in repatriating the Homna warriors after they are treated?"

"There are negotiations for that. I will act as your agent."

"Thank you. Stand by, please."

Mark turned and strode inside. He needed advice fast.

Mark gathered both Connor and the Marine lieutenant, plus Shraybman in his office. He had a channel open to Captain Betang if he needed it. Chinran/Jelling was available on scrambled transmission.

He summarized the situation. "So, the Homna, having failed to pin us down, are now exploiting the open path into Ishkul territory."

Shraybman said, "It comes across that Vlashn was stuck with a no win scenario—fight them or allow them in. Now they're in. Now he has to take care of it fast or his own people will disown him."

"Yeah, I think that's the case." Heck of a society they had. Screw up and get dismembered. He knew he didn't have enough background to determine how valid it was, but it still seemed excessive.

Connor asked, "Since we are the cause, can we take the responsibility for stopping them?"

"Not with any technological means. We could negotiate."

"I have an idea, then," Connor said. "Captain Chi . . . Jelling is positioned behind the attackers."

"I don't want casualties, and certainly not in any fashion the locals would regard as objectionable."

"I was going to suggest she move between them and negotiate. Perhaps argue them into a contest, or to attack her instead of each other. That should take some time to sort out."

"That's ballsy."

"That's what we do."

He thought it over for a second only. "It's worth the diversion at least. Do it."

"We still have conflict in the central continent."

"Yeah, and riled up natives and animals in the archipelago. We've got to rein this all in fast," Lieutenant Jetter said.

Shraybman said, "I have some useful information, sir."

"Do tell."

"We have some recent news sheets from the Ishkul, with translations they say are from the Homna. They're well aware that we have space travel and flight. Publicly admitted, and our presence. It, the alleged Homna story, concedes we have superior technology, but is amused at our unwillingness to use it. It's politically taken as weakness, as near as I can tell."

"Hand it to intel, and let me see, too. I did traffic analysis, but I can gain something from it."

"Yes, sir."

"Let's tentatively have Captain Jelling move between them. I also want a show of force over the Homna capital. Provoke them, don't initiate."

A light flashed and Mark let the message through. It was Stephens.

"Sir, you should come and see this field surgery, and bring Sergeant Thomas. It's very interesting."

He was sure it was. Could he pull away? Sure, a few segs wouldn't hurt.

"We'll be there in a moment."

He called Thomas, who replied, "I'll meet you there. What kind of gear?"

"I'm not sure."

"I'll bring enough," she said and disconnected. That was a bit terse for someone of her rank. Was she getting familiar? Or just brusque when in a hurry?

"I'll be back in a few. Do please relay the message to the captain, Warrant," he said. He headed outside.

Things were quite a bit neater in the compound; the engineers and the lab assistants had cleared a lot of ground and removed a lot of debris. He saw a substantial pile of Homna artifacts, with a handful of technicians sorting and collating them for study. Excellent. Firsthand intel of their weapons was good. He stepped around a small crater dug up by some blast or other.

Sergeant Thomas hurried up to him, toting two cases and a backpack.

"Can you get photos of that pile when you're done here?" he asked.

"What do you think I was doing? Sorry, sir," she added. "I've been very busy since last night and I forget my manners."

"That's fine. Did you do any fighting?"

"Yes." She left it at that so he did, too.

Under the tent, supplemental dividers now partitioned it. The engineers had been and still were busy. Stephens gestured from one divider, clearly agitated and wanting them to hurry. Mark jogged over.

She said quietly, "Come see how they operate," and waved.

In seconds, Thomas had a camera out of a case and on a tripod, and was dialing it in. Mark slipped through the fabric behind Stephens and stayed close to the divider.

There were a handful of humans, military and civilian, watching the proceedings. Father Dunn stood back out of the way, reciting scripture or prayer. It didn't matter what faith or even species, Mark thought. The priest would do what he thought would help.

A Homna warrior with a rather damaged leg lay on a table, anesthetized. Mark assumed it was by gas from the mask over his face.

The surgery in progress was quick, efficient, and impressive. With wooden tools, glass scalpels, bone and horn needles and pins, pseudo-silk sutures and distilled alcohol and anesthetic, it was quite modern. Two Ishkul operated, one assisted. It was frustrating, maddening to see the heights of their technology limited by their environment. They were far more socially refined and scientifically minded than most human cultures. He had no doubt that if he were injured, they'd try their best to reconstruct his bones.

He snuck back out. Thomas stayed to shoot more video. Stephens followed him.

As they left the tent, she said, "I'm told that their return presents some difficulties. The Homna culture isn't one that handles failure well."

"That's unfortunate." Poor bastards.

"Yes, but that also means if we manage to cow them, they should stay submissive. Or at least the way I read the signals. Of course, I'm following human bases here and have no idea how accurate it will be, but I can draw a lot of roots for Ishkul behavior."

"Have Lieutenant Shraybman arrange a meeting with you and Vlashn or Somle to inquire."

"Thank you, sir. I was going to suggest that."

"I need to follow up on some things. Please let me know what you find out," he said.

Back in his office, he had messages on screen, on paper on his desk, and people waiting.

Russ was one of those, and said, "Through the Ishkul, the Homna have agreed to meet our champion."

"Good . . . and bad. Connor, I know her background, but are you sure Captain Jelling can take one of them? I'd hate to lose her, on top of the political issues."

"Sir, I understand she could take out a grown man before she hit puberty. Absolutely vicious fighter, rated master and has created new forms, and outrageously strong. In this gravity, no contest. She'll tie him in knots. I'm stronger, but her analyses are faster, and as commander, she kind of had to volunteer first. We lead from the front."

"Have you met her father?" he asked, offering the hint.

"I have, and I've seen some of his contract work. He does rescue ops only now. Generally without weapons,

of course. I've seen her and him spar. I tried a couple of
rounds myself. You've seen her physique. She's a combat
leopard in human form."

"What did it cost you?"

"A broken knee, three ribs and a dislocated shoulder."

" . . . I . . . was assuming a cash bet."

"Oh, hell, it was just for points. And she was pulling
her blows. Took me a week in regen. She doesn't know
how to fight fair."

"I'm glad we came to terms with Earth. It could have
been a lot worse on both sides."

"Indeed."

Mark saw the interested look on Russ's face and
decided he better change subjects.

"Still, with that in mind, I'm going to perpetuate
that philosophy."

"Sir?"

"Assuming she wins, though it doesn't matter either
way, I want combat aircraft over the field after the bout
ends, and I want a flyby of the Homna capital. A slow
one."

"Yes, sir. They may have air defense that is of moderate threat."

"I'm hoping so."

"Yes, sir." Connor grinned broadly.

Mark didn't want to waste any time, nor did anyone
else. The next morning, a courier took him, Russ, Stephens and Thomas to the Homna bivouac area. Stephens
confirmed her opinions on the way.

"I still could be wrong, of course, but based on their
envoy's presentation and their response to our refusal,
as well as their attitudes about failure and their political

system, I confidently believe if we beat them in single combat, we have the upper hand for a long time."

"Good," Mark replied. He was thinking that if it went wrong, he'd lose a first class officer, then likely have to retreat to avoid more fighting. He was tense and nervous even though he wasn't the champion.

Chinran had asked for backup and they'd flown up the night before. Mark trusted her implicitly and hadn't asked why she needed them. Still, a lot of preparations had taken place for this single combat. Thomas had one of the lab techs assisting her, with more recording gear. Vlashn was to meet them, with his own entourage. This was almost as big as the initial landing, and might be more important.

They landed in a broad meadow, a field really. There were obvious signs of the battle here, too. The human bombs were more powerful, had left deeper craters and blown down trees. Damaged gear looked to have been burned in place or cannibalized for parts. The Homna knew they'd met a worthy opponent.

Once the loadmaster gave clearance and dropped the tail, they debarked. Mark and Russ came out first, and a Marine guard snapped to attention. It made sense. They were ranking plenipotentiaries, they needed to appear that way to this honor culture. They walked down the ramp into the sun.

Vlashn awaited them with his own honor guard. As the day before, they carried real weapons and wore real armor. No more pretense, and no one trusted the Homna.

"Greetings, Mark and Nurin."

"Hello, Vlashn."

"Good to see you, Vlashn."

"I offer to explain the proceedings to follow."

"Yes, please."

"The Homna and humans are drawn up across from each other. The cleared area in the middle," he pointed at an area that looked mowed, "is where the contest will be fought. Both entourages will enter. I advised your female third level element leader on weapons and protocol."

"Thanks. When do we . . . they start?"

"As soon as we signal we are ready."

"We might as well get it done with. Go ahead," Mark said.

Vlashn turned to one of his soldiers, who made a gesture, dropped his weapons and ran toward the other side, arms out. Once he was spotted, one of the Homna did the same. The two met, appeared to speak briefly, then turned back to their own lines.

Mark looked around. Thomas was recording, as was her borrowed lab assistant, and one of the Blazers was using something to do some kind of recording and observation that was probably tactical, but blended in. The Ishkul had a couple of their odd cameras and some artists.

One of the good things about this, Connor had said, was that the Homna weren't moving around and were organized enough to make counting and analyzing them easy.

The Homna champion arrived to much fanfare, carried on a portable dais and with both weapon and shield bearers to hand him his accoutrements. Everything was bright colors, polished stone and hide. The warrior in question was taller even than average for this species, and looked very solidly built. He strode out into the open field, stood in an aggressive pose with his weapons and awaited a challenger.

The human and Ishkul crowd moved aside as that challenger came forward. Her entourage led the way. As it did, Mark and Russ had to move. He had to shift around to get a good glimpse of her through the mass of people.

Captain Jelling was very brave, with a flair for showmanship.

She was also absolutely bugfuck insane.

First, she was dressed in a grass skirt, face and bare breasts painted in complicated patterns that were neither Celtic nor Amerind nor Pacific but a combination of all three that must have taken all night to do. Second, she was carrying only a short spear and a hide shield. Third, she was leading an entourage of Blazers and UN Marines, all dressed likewise. They marched in a perfect step that would make any crusty sergeant major weep with envy. Nor did they look silly. They looked flat out *mean*.

It was pretty clear to all that she intended to be the champion, and that the expression on her face was not a smile.

No word was said, or needed. The humans moved aside to let the unit through. It moved in utter silence, even the grass trodden underfoot not daring to intrude. The warriors stepped forward, marched in a calculated series of angles and finished in a triangle with the captain at the apex, snapped to attention, then parade rest, and placed their spears in a perfect matching angle. All their spears were two meters. Hers was a meter. Something from history niggled at Mark. Something about that . . .

The Homna waited only a few moments, to be sure the humans were in place. Then they started chanting.

They sang in unison, formal and rehearsed. Moments later, they were gesturing with spears. They waved, swayed and sang. It was powerful, evocative and loud. Mark was impressed. He wasn't awed or fearful, though he knew that was part of the intent.

Then the humans responded. Chinran walked around and through the formation while shouting loudly.

"Ringa pakia!" she called, which was followed by a slapping of hands on thighs, as the warriors bounced and spread into a low horse-riding stance.

"Uma tiraha! Turi whatia! Hope whai ake! Waewae takahia kia kino!" The thigh slaps gave way to a perfectly timed foot stomping that quickly became palpable, vibrating through the soil.

Her voice rose a level as her arms waved, leading a call and response. Mark had no idea what any of it meant, but the emotion and power was clear.

Jelling shouted, too loud and too deep to be feminine, *"Ka mate, ka mate!"*

The troops bellowed to shake the ground again, *"Ka ora, ka ora!"*

Jelling: *"Ka mate, ka mate!"*

Team: *"Ka ora, ka ora!"*

It was all accompanied by hand waving, stomping, pointing and movements reminiscent of wrestling or kung fu. Also, it was even louder than the natives' challenge and there were only about twenty humans. The ground palpably shook.

The roar that followed was painful, as the platoon gesticulated threateningly with spears and bellowed into the sky, vocal rhythms matching the beat of hands, feet and spears.

"Kairakau o te whetū
kia whaka whenua au i ahau!
Hī aue, hī!
Ko Aotearoa e ngunguru nei!
Au, au, aue hā!
Ko kairakau o te whetū ao e ngunguru nei!
Au, au, aue hā!
I āhahā! Ka tū te ihiihi, ka tū te wanawana!
Ki runga ki te rangi e tū iho nei, tū iho nei, hī!
Matakīrea!
Kairakau, aue hī!
Āpiti!
Kairakau, aue hī, hā!"

It was obviously some war song, and had tonal similarities to Indonesian. Mark caught "warrior," "life" and "death." Maori? The skirts seemed to suggest it. The dance definitely looked like a haka.

They made a final jump that took them a good two meters in the air, athletic bodies fighting low gravity and winning for just a moment.

As they landed, Jelling sprinted forward, spear and shield clutched midsection and held in close to her body.

Her native opponent apparently realized he was behind the count and sprinted out to meet her. He expected her to stop, but she ran past, still at a sprint. As she passed she dropped her speartip and slashed low across his right leg. She leapt, spun, turned the momentum around and came back. He was halfway around by then, and her tip caught the back of his left leg before he whipped back the other way, his shield crashing into her haft.

She let the impact swing it, and brought it up and over while punching with her own shield to block his incoming thrust. Her shield wasn't exactly hide, but the locals would never know the difference, nor that her spear was a cast dendritic ceramic, tooled to look as if knapped and ground. She turned the motion into an overhand thrust just past his face. For a moment, she was standing on his legs and torso.

He bent upright and she nimbly bounced back. He thrust, and she twisted aside, batting his spear and slicing across his arm. He drew his back and across, both of them taking slash wounds from the exchange. Still, it was three to one and she'd gotten in two near misses, the advantage of the lead, and had virtually climbed atop him, which had to be disheartening.

Of course, this was not a human, Mark reminded himself, and couldn't be assumed to react as a human would. He seemed quite focused, though his actions did seem to be a bit defensive. Though without seeing more of his style, and without being an expert at hand to hand combat, it was impossible to say.

The two met again in a press, shields and hafts jammed into a tangle, butts drawing out, tips thrusting past. Jelling took a wound near her knee, and returned the favor. The inside of the exposed Ishkul knee was hard to reach, being set back behind the torso, but was a soft and inviting target. To that end, the locals didn't seem to have developed much in the way of draw cuts.

She spun sideways and made a forehand/backhand combo that had her foe backing up fast. She was all attack. Even when blocking, she was still stabbing or kicking. The different geometry of the two species dictated different tactics, but she was certainly holding her own and getting a little better than he.

At that moment, he got through and nicked her across the shoulder, but she dropped and thrust and sank her blade a good three centimeters into his torso. He gurgled and screamed as she bounced back into guard.

"Will you yield? Or appoint another champion?" she yelled into the distant translator, which echoed her words back.

The foreign army shifted about and started jabbering. Their leader raised his hands for attention.

"You would shame him as a slave?" he asked. "Or do you require his execution?"

"I prefer to fight to the death," the champion said through the speaker clearly and flatly, though he was in obvious pain. The contrast was odd, disturbing.

Chinran sighed. The ritual called for an honorable death. She knew what was expected, she obviously didn't like it.

"Let us fight," she said and dropped back into guard.

The alien moved painfully but with skill, guarding his torso and keeping his blade in close. That was standard for humans, but seemed to indicate defensiveness for the Homna. Perhaps her use of that stance had caused some trouble in determining her threat level for him.

She leapt, stabbed and jumped back, drawing her spear out of his abdomen, grating over his belly ribs. With a suppressed growl of pain he worked himself upright on his spear haft, tossed away his shield to get a two-handed grip, and advanced.

In a moment, she flung her own shield at him, took her spear in both hands and swung it like a great sword. He raised his to block, and her ultramodern edge shattered the base of his blade and sheared through the wood. She drew back into low guard and shot the tip out in thrust. He staggered back and she followed through with a butt slash, a smash that he tumbled away from, and a blade slash that took him across the throat and down the thorax. She leaned into it again and drove the point into where his liver should be. He gurgled softly in contrast to his thrashing limbs, and died.

The applause wasn't a shock, but still unexpected. The opposing army cheered loudly, extolling her skill and the bravery of their now dead comrade.

All around Mark, the human warriors tensed. Connor had a link open to a gunship high overhead, and was ready to, and had assured Mark he could, blast a cordon sanitaire within meters of the human position. Mark was caught between needing to watch that and needing to see the outcome of the event.

Somle strode forward, alone. Mark couldn't catch the conference and conversation between Somle and her counterpart from the Homna. It seemed civil enough, though. They gestured and moved, speaking at length. Finally, they bowed and touched fingers.

The army dissolved back into formation, ready to march away. They started forming their wagons into convoy. It would obviously take days to get moved, but it seemed the problem was resolved.

Captain Chinran came over, limping slightly from minor wounds and strains. She'd already brought her breathing back to normal. Mark suspected that was partly training, partly pride and partly psy op. The only thing worse than an unbeatable opponent was an unbeatable and *unflappable* opponent.

He extended his hands. "Well done, Captain."

"Sir," she said and shook them. She still seemed a little out of breath.

"That was a haka you opened with, yes?"

"Yes, sir. The Rugby team uses it for opening their games. I changed the words slightly, though the Homna wouldn't care either way. I wanted the rhythm and the noise."

"It was impressively loud. What did you change it to? Wasn't the original about outsmarting an opponent?"

"I think so, yes. This one was . . . well, let me recite it.

"Slap the hands against the thighs! Puff out the chest! Bend the knees! Let the hip follow! Stamp the feet as hard as you can! It is death, it is death. It is life, it is life. It is death, it is death. It is life, it is life. Warriors of the planets . . . that's the closest translation I could get to 'Marine' or 'Mobile Assault' . . . let me become one with the land. This is our land that rumbles. It's my time! It's my moment! This defines us as Marines. It's my time! It's my moment! Our dominance, our supremacy will triumph and be placed on high. Spearhead! Warriors! Attack! Warriors!"

He grinned. "You just had to create something special for the occasion, didn't you?"

"How could I not? It was a moral imperative." Her grin that was not a grin was half friendly and half taunting.

"I agree. Well done again, and thanks. All of you have performed beyond all expectation so far. I know you'll continue and I hope we're done soon." He winced and sighed.

"Good luck to you, sir, and I'm impressed in return. If you'll excuse me, I think my medic is about to sedate me if I don't drag myself over for treatment."

"Here." He offered an arm.

"Thanks, but no." She smiled and started walking, with barely any sign of a limp. Right. She'd not admit to any injury while still visible to the Homna. Her people were indestructible in every way, and don't you primitives forget it.

Mark motioned to Connor, who came closer. He'd stayed back to allow the perception of privacy, though Mark was sure he'd heard every word, and equally sure he'd never talk.

"It's Plan A," Mark told him.

"Of course." Connor switched something in his hand and spoke into the air. "Plan A."

"Plan A." Zig Hensley brought the gunship in low and slow, as ordered. He was a bit nervous and felt threatened, but confident enough. Hopefully, he'd get to show these savages what real weapons were.

The Homna capital was reminiscent of Greece or Rome. It was actually quite a bit more aesthetic and inspiring than Ishkuhama. They lacked the huge river for the massive industry, but managed with manpower, apparently slaves, and the terrain they had. It didn't seem to have slowed their weapons industry down, either.

Slow. He drifted in below stall speed, using vectored thrust for lift, generating a tremendous amount of wind noise. Below, the Homna came out of buildings, stared, ran back in, huddled, pointed. The distant news of aliens was now a blatant presence in their skies.

"Stand by on door guns." Though really, if it came to that, they were probably done for. Still, it made the crew happy and gave them something to clutch. That was useful by itself.

"One ready, Two ready," his copilot said. Dutch sounded firm and confident, and that was good.

A launch warning buzzed loudly and flashed. He grinned. A primitive solid rocket was no real threat. He slipped sideways and let it rush harmlessly past. It would have to come down somewhere . . . but that was the Homnas' problem.

A second launch followed, this time a volley. He let the automated defense suite take them, staccato bursts shredding the tubes into confetti that flash burned, the propellant residue sparkling. He dropped lower to taunt them.

Third shot.

"Sergeant Lemke, will you be so kind as to surgically remove that threat down to the ground?"

"Yes, sir!" Lemke called back through the net, punctuating with a burst of cannon fire. The dense ceramic bullets were almost as effective as metal.

Really, it was little more than a heavy machine gun, but more than enough for ceramic and wood, even that used for armor against the local armament. The burst shattered the roof and housing of the launch facility, and native troops started running. Lemke gave them a few seconds to get clear, then proceeded to fire raking shots along the perimeter and across the magazine. Explosions and flames engulfed the collapsing debris, and in moments the building was useless rubble. Hensley fired one explosive missile, which slapped the air in a horrendous report that was sure to make the locals notice. It scattered the rubble over a broad area, to leave lots of souvenirs. Then he lifted the craft slowly and with dignity and accelerated back to the south.

He deliberately detoured near two other installations, but neither took the opportunity to shoot at him.

Message delivered to the Homna. The visitors were only friendly up to a point, and nothing from the ground could touch them.

Mark received a followup report the next morning, and relaxed a little more. The Homna were retreating in good order and another emissary had asked Vlashn-Somle to negotiate for them. No native war. At least, not while the humans were present, and not this visit. Chinran's use of the Maori Haka reminded him of something called the Musket Wars, and he did recall the Japanese acquisition of firearms. While those might not be his problem at present, they still had to be guarded against.

His musing ended when Marguerite Stephens came in.

"Sorry to interrupt, sir," she said, "but I have an idea that may help with cultural stability."

"No trouble, do please tell me," he replied. Heck, more good news would be welcome.

"It occurs to me that we can provide political support to Vlashn and Somle just by publicly stating that we wish to continue our negotiations with them directly. No threat need be implied. It's simply a statement from a powerful party that we like the existing arrangement and changing it would be awkward. I expect the Ishkul would find it logical not to do anything that might anger us, and pull back from any discussions of replacing them."

That was good.

"No need to anger the powerful aliens, eh? Just keep negotiating, with no loss of face locally, and the public never needs to know. I like it. I just need to find a way to present it to Vlashn. Actually, I can just tell it to him like that, as a de facto statement."

"That's how I'd do it, sir," she agreed. "There's no need for them to understand our machinations at this point. Tell those bloody Homna to make their requests through the Ishkul, too, or piss us off further."

It wasn't as simple as that. He now had to juggle the presentation of that superior force with good faith negotiations and maintain the safety standards. Still, he liked Vlashn and Somle, and if he could keep them alive despite their culture's insane demands for perfection, he would.

Very soon now, the Ishkul were going to be released upon the universe. Citizen Mark Ballenger of the Freehold of Grainne was going to make history.

The problem with making history was that sooner or later one would screw up and become a villain to someone.

He couldn't think of a way to pass that off on Ambassador Russ, and he didn't really want to. Russ wasn't a bad guy.

CHAPTER 23

T he Ishkul great hall appealed to Mark. It was carved and polished stone with lovely grain, and all done with stone or ceramic tools and hand polishing. Amazing. Even with water-driven abrasives, the labor invested was incredible. It drove home again that any rapid changes in technology would lead to drastic societal upheavals. It all might be lost in a collapse, or a cultural shift. The outcome of both was likely to be what had happened to the Meso-American civilizations, or to the Koisan. Though the Warlordism of Japan was possible, too. None of the probable outcomes were good.

He nudged Egan and pointed at one lovely piece of quartzite, either agate or onyx or some similar veined stone. "I wonder how many days went into that?" It was a pillar, a good half meter in diameter and looked to be turned in sections.

"It is pretty," Egan agreed. He appeared distracted, but he did look for several seconds.

Mark glanced around. There was plenty of security, Sergeant Thomas and her crew had the only human recording gear—per a request he'd suggested Somle make—and Shraybman and McDonald stood by to field intrusions and handle inquiries. Good enough. He stayed back and let Russ handle this one. The UN could take any blame for actual technology transfers.

Russ had voiced that exact concern, but as he'd earlier complained about being shut out, he could hardly refuse the diplomatic opportunity. Win for Mark.

At least the Ishkul didn't go for elaborate ceremony. They were, in fact, rather terse by human standards. They always introduced everyone by name, title and position, almost like an abbreviated resume, complimentary but not exaggerated.

Vlashn, Somle, National Trade Manager Glimn, Most Senior Technology Developer Fusht—whom he suspected was female but couldn't clearly tell—he programmed the translator to keep the title in place—and Most Senior Sociologist Orgla on one side, with their unnamed assistants and a couple of guards, made up the official native contingent. Spectators lined the room in galleries all around. The guards looked quite relaxed, even with the crowd, so that was good. The broad stone floor looked like a single slab of polished agate, twenty meters across or more, and there was no central table or furniture. The humans sat on the other side, with side tables for equipment and writing, and a handful of Ishkul servants willing to run materials back and forth.

It was a little disconcerting a setup, but Mark had gotten used to it. He, McDonald, Zihn, Shraybman and

Egan and Margov sat across from the Ishkul, with Connor and another Operative as security. Chinran/Jelling was absent for discretion. Separated only slightly was the UN contingent: Russ, Stevens, ESO's recently arrived rep who looked to be strictly a lawyer, Russ's assistant and two Marines.

"We will now discuss a technology trade with our human guests," Vlashn said for the record. It was recorded by parrot beasts, shorthand-scribbling scribes, an Ishkul with a camera obscura and a couple of graphic artists.

Egan rose, and approached the spectator barrier. One of the Ishkul passed over a doccase, big enough to contain a large chart or graphic. That wasn't what bothered Mark, though. Why was he receiving it from a local? That was the question. He flushed and clenched his teeth. Around him, the entire human contingent stiffened and tried to restrain it.

Margov muttered, "You asshole," echoing Mark's thought. She locked eyes on Egan and seemed oblivious to everything else.

How the hell did that display get down here? Actually, it was quite obvious. The same way everything else had come down. Egan had just gone for subtlety for once.

Egan reached into a corner pocket and slid out what appeared to be a good, basic knife. No frills, just steel and a wrapped handle.

"Vlashn, Somle, a gift for you from my company." He extended it hilt first and Vlashn took it. He drew out another for Somle, and a chunk of what was probably ore-bearing rock.

"I can provide these, or the base material, in ready quantity."

It was too late to stop it, but Mark had reasonable faith in Vlashn to keep things under control, he hoped.

Vlashn took one of the blades, and the ore sample, and turned them in his hands. He ignored everyone else.

Egan was obviously aware of the inhaled hisses and silent but fiery stares behind him. He very carefully kept his eyes on Vlashn.

The Ishkul leader looked up, fixed Egan with a stare and spoke.

"I deduce this to be a mid-periodic table element with a lattice structure, refined in pure form. Our scientists predict it should have excellent tensile strength, be highly ductile, moderately elastic and much lower than average in abrasion resistance."

The resulting silence stretched out for seconds. Finally, Egan said, "Yes, that's exactly what it is. We call these elements metals. This is in a high-purity form with certain alloying elements."

"I assume this is the technology you've been hiding with less than adequate technique and extreme concern." He looked up toward Mark.

"Yes," Mark said simply. What else could he say?

Vlashn and Somle both glugged loudly, followed at once by their advisors. All the Ishkul started laughing. Their gestures indicated helpless amusement.

It went on for some time, while Mark and the company reps flushed crimson in embarrassment.

Finally, Vlashn sat up and faced Mark.

"Mark. Query: Is this the secret of your technology, the purpose for all this high amount of trouble?"

"Yes." He wanted to offer more, but decided not to.

"Interesting. I am of mixed feelings of amusement, insult and complimented. Query: Is there a need for an explanation from us?"

"No, I think we all grasp it from the laughter. You understand what metal is."

"Axiomatically we have refined certain ores in our laboratories. The materials thus far are exceptionally useful, but economically infeasible. Our estimation is that large quantities exist in space and deep underground, but are not reachable with our current technology. We of course assumed you had access to them. What confused our scientists was your lack of use of them. It was deemed inadvisable to raise the issue, though you should recall I hinted to you several times to do so."

"I do." Oh, he felt like an idiot.

"Our conservative faction raised the risk issue of offering a space-faring species access to these materials. I deemed this a minuscule risk, assuming that any such spacefarers would have developed a variety of materials. You showed none. My evaluation was that your ceramic knowledge was very high and detailed, but that you regarded them as secondary resources. Argument proceeded to your plastics, which are clearly more available than ours. This is where the argument reached before Mr. Egan's presentation."

There was much shuffling of feet. Really, Earth scientists imagined potentials for materials that didn't yet exist. Why wouldn't others?

Turning back to Egan, Vlashn said, "I am interested in conducting negotiations for access to more such material, and the tools to manipulate it."

"Excellent!" Egan said in triumph. "I'm glad to see you comprehend the advantages and technical boost that—"

Vlashn cut him off with a very human slashing gesture. "Stop compliments. Query: What is your offer?"

Egan was actually speechless. Mark tried desperately not to smirk as the master capitalist was called to the point by someone he felt was his genetic and social inferior.

"There are rocks in space, like planets but smaller," he began again.

"Planetoids," Vlashn provided the word. Clearly, he'd been talking at length with both sets of scientists. "You should recall Ishkul have telescopes."

"Yes," Egan agreed, becoming more nonplussed. "We use them for ores and materials."

Vlashn fixed him with an eye and said, "You ask a lot. Again. Query: What is your offer?"

"Ah, well, they aren't of much use to you," Egan said, obviously defensive. He'd been hoping for a trinket trade.

Vlashn said, "Currently such are not of significant use, but have obvious great potential. Other groups also can help us. If you want to trade for rich property, your offer must be of significantly similar value."

"The actual metal content is rather low. What—"

"You have plentiful power, unlimited solar influx. The useful ratio is low, we estimate on the close order of two percent of available planetoids, with their metal content on the order of eight percent. Clearly, you have a technology to exploit this based on your company name."

"Yes, that's what Halo Materials Group does. Since we have lead rights—"

"You have arguable lead rights for humans. I do not automatically grant inverse rights from this end, and reserve any and all unnegotiated rights. It is quite possible Deep Space Resources or another group will offer a more equitable trade."

"I would like to offer a counter to any such offers, of course." Egan almost cringed. His profit margin was dropping fast and his position was going from from "own a system" to "buy a few mineral rights." Mark was embarrassed and amused by the mix of events. They'd still underestimated the Ishkul, even after all this. He caught Connor's eyes with his own, and saw that he was rapidly upgrading their threat potential. Never mind the Japanese and Western firearms technology. This was going to be similar, but much more dramatic. Their lithic and ceramic technology weapons included rocket artillery and airborne troops. What would they devise with access to metals up through the artificial fissionables?

"We know a variety of metals," Vlashn said. "They are hard to refine, dull easily, corrode rapidly, and are quite heavy."

"Our alloys avoid some such problems."

"Obviously, we will purchase that information."

"Of course. I could easily include that technology in the exchange."

"I suspect that knowledge is relatively straightforward, a matter of content, temperature curves and solubility. There are others who can provide that, preferably at the same price your own students and technicians pay for the training."

Egan was wincing now. He'd thought to buy Manhattan Island. He was being handed his head.

Vlashn continued, "Query: What density of ore are the planetoids?"

"Your estimates were within close order," Egan admitted. Apparently, he'd realized honesty was his best policy now.

"To fifteen percent, HMG may add moderate and negotiated infrastructure development costs. Competing bids will be secured from ESO and DSR. The political concordance I speak for will mandate compliance to cost, and mandate a change in operator should estimates differ by ten percent or more. New operator to be required to conduct operations within budget, said budget to be administered by our contractor."

Sharp, Mark thought. He was requiring them to work on a shoestring. If someone underbid, they'd be given the entire mess, and required to operate on *that* shoestring, or be in breach of contract, at which point Vlashn could request new bids.

"The deal is mostly acceptable," Egan said. "You have our word to operate with fair expenses for building and development. The normal share in our industry is twenty percent, though."

"I have researched this and agree with your statement," Vlashn said, "and am offering fifteen percent. You have the right of first refusal, in your terminology."

"No, I accept," he said hastily. Fifteen percent of something was better than twenty percent of nothing.

"You must understand and agree that such rights are only for mining of nonplanet resources gravitationally bound to this system. All other rights are reserved for separate negotiations. HMG may retain no more than two contracts total at any time, and each contract will be in force for five Freehold years."

"Uh . . . that is acceptable to us."

"Our negotiations will be on behalf of all Drazl, unless another group entity or nation negotiates a more favorable contract, which will be binding on said group."

Mark remembered Vlashn's laugh and promise to "take it under advisement" regarding legal advice. It appeared the Stone Age savage was far above his human counterparts for diabolical scheming and shrewd manipulation.

Still, HMG was making out like bandits. They had the foot in the system, would be developing metals for the Drazl and could export their percentage straight from Halo to Halo via a Jump Point the UN had conveniently established for them, with standard usage rates. They were not going to suffer at all.

"There are also products and materials of interest on your planet's surface," Egan said.

"You speak of our artwork, philosophy, gems and minerals, bioengineered plants and other items noninclusive. I have secured a right of first refusal on those with Ms Margov. You are free to make offers on a case by case basis. Ms Margov, you may speak."

"Thank you, Leader Vlashn." Her smile was still dazzling, still cruel and with a hint of sadistic pleasure. Mark stifled a grin, because he knew what was coming. She rose and stepped forward. "Our opening bid is five years of free transit for a thousand Ishkul designees to any human function they can arrange attendance for, with accommodations and support. We will provide free marketing and wholesale of their products and technology, with an eighty-five percent return to them, at a guaranteed minimum volume."

"Guaranteed minimum?" Egan asked.

She named a figure. Mark cringed and clenched. Ouch. She probably could do it, too.

Margov continued. "As there was no restriction on *exporting* technology, I have already sent samples to ten major markets and secured opening bids and exclusive offers. Want to try, Egan?"

"I . . . will have to consult with my headquarters on that."

"Please do." Her smile was viperlike now.

Mark suspected she had all bases already covered. Still, that was for them to dispute. His concern was incoming only. Margov had taken a very shrewd position.

He looked around and saw Irina Shraybman grinning and exhaling. She looked more relaxed, too. What a fine officer she'd turned out to be, officially as public affairs. Her smile was friendly and had a saucy glint he hadn't seen in days. He hadn't let himself think of anything social since the mission started. That smile reminded him that he could, now.

He butted into the fray and said, "Leader Vlashn, obviously, these negotiations are well under your control. If it suits you, Ambassador Russ and I will take our leave and meet with you in three hours? And if you are agreeable, we will fly in and land here, as a show of our respect and trust."

Vlashn almost bowed. "I accept your suggestion and thank you for the respect. I will expect you and call on you."

Mark had not discussed departure with Russ, but he met him eye to eye and Russ nodded. The two departed at a brisk pace. He decided to leave the military and scientists to keep an eye on things. Ideally, he'd have remained himself, but he wanted the perception that the government was not involved. Pulling Russ out also set a precedent for the UN to follow, of letting business be separate from politics. That was largely a personal and culture-based—Freehold culture—decision, but he was damned well going to push the UN to keep as much out of it as possible.

As they exited the hall, Russ ran a hand through his hair. It was mussed, not stylish.

"Well done, Citizen."

" 'Well done'?" Mark asked. "It damned near started wars on two planets, and we almost destroyed our first sentient species."

"No, it went brilliantly. I observed and participated and was in charge of the UN mission, equal to you but de facto leader due to the size of our nations. It went brilliantly, due to your diligence and my advice. That is how I shall record it." He grinned, but there was a depth to his gaze. He was in shock.

"I wouldn't write it up quite that well," Mark said. "We got lucky in several regards."

"That's for the press to market. They'll try to criticize us anyway."

"True. The historians will work it out eventually. We won't be here by then. But you know what, Ambassador?"

"What?"

"I'm just glad it's over, without more pain than there was. Luck, skill, whatever combination it was, we did it." He was getting giddy. Weeks of stress evaporated. There were still issues to resolve, but his part was over. Whole legions of people could share responsibility and blame now. He had the credit, a place in the history books, and the accomplishment. And he hadn't gotten eaten by hostiles.

It was a false relief, he knew. He would have to write everything up, be debriefed, discuss the baboonalogues. Everyone else would defer to him and want advice on Ishkul philosophy and attitudes. If there were two sentient tool users in the universe, there were almost certainly more. He'd have to write entire books on this, and become a source for future such encounters, possibly even manage them. The rest of his life was set for him, and he had no choice.

But, he reflected, there wasn't anything he'd rather do more.

"Yes," Russ said simply.

"Oh, and there's one more thing Egan is going to hate," Mark said.

"What's that?"

"I'm going to make him pay for oversight, including transit and a station in system. I'm all in favor of capitalism. I just expect the capital to come from the capitalist. No free lunch." He grinned.

Russ looked thoughtful as they boarded their carriage. "I think I do see some advantages to pure capitalism. If you can keep it pure."

"That's been our fight for two hundred and fifty years, Ambassador. Not letting the cannibalistic sharks eat their own young or their keepers."

The driver nudged the beasts and they started moving. Russ glanced around, looked at Mark and made a mouth-opening gesture with his fingers.

"I believe we are secure," Mark replied, making his own check.

"Vlashn never lied to us, did he?" Russ asked. "Every factual statement was correct."

"As far as I know, yes. Why?"

"I recall him stating that Ishkul technology exceeded that of the Homna in every regard. The Homna have ballistic missiles, high explosive and poison gas."

Mark felt a chill. Yes, Vlashn had made that exact statement.

"I think the human race is going to learn a lot in the next few years."

"I agree. I just hope we don't learn it too fast."

"I hope we don't have to."

After all, if there were two sentient tool users in the universe, there were almost certainly more.

The following is an excerpt from:

DO UNTO OTHERS

MICHAEL Z. WILLIAMSON

Available from Baen Books
August 2010
hardcover

Chapter 1

Alex Marlow had just been tasked to guard the richest woman in the universe. He wondered why he wasn't twitchy.

Of course, his team hadn't been told that yet. Nor had he started the mission. Both of those would raise the stress level.

He and four of them were awaiting the sixth member, who was uncharacteristically late.

"Where the hell is Elke?" Aramis snapped in frustration.

"She's probably mining her apartment for practice, or defusing her comm, or having an intimate experience with her shotgun," Jason Vaughn offered. "Regardless, you're not going to make her appear faster." He smiled wryly.

Aramis was a bit more than half Jason's age, and it showed. He twitched, all youth and energy. Jason sat in a couch, comfortable and calm.

For calm, however, Jason had nothing on Bart Weil, the big German, who leaned against the wall and barely gave evidence of being alive. His eyes took in everything, though.

That left Horace "Shaman" Mbuto, the team's surgeon, as the odd one out. He was older even than Alex, ancient by the standards of executive protection, and making use of the time to inventory a surgical kit.

They seemed a bit motley, but in the executive protection business, they were the best, and had been a team for a year now. He couldn't imagine breaking them up. The mixed skill sets meshed perfectly, and the personality clashes were minor and only added flavor. They were Ripple Creek Security's star bodyguards, and paid accordingly.

Luckily, money was not a problem for their new principal.

His musing was interrupted when he saw familiar movement out in the turnaround.

"Here she comes," he said.

Eleonora Sykora, called Elke, hated running late. Admittedly she'd enjoyed the reason for it, but still.

They entered the Ripple Creek site on her password, and the gate flashed a warning that guest vehicles could go no further than the turnaround ahead.

She turned to Alaric and said, "If you want to kiss me goodbye, do it now. Last chance."

The car was on automatic. Alaric bent over and kissed her deeply, his hands roaming inside her jacket and all over her body. If he only knew how much trust she showed by letting him do that.

"Okay, stop now," she insisted, before he got too excited again.

"Why like this? What's wrong with kissing you good-bye when I drop you off?"

"Because they might think I'm a girl," she said with a smile. She measured the car's deceleration and reached for the handle.

He still looked puzzled when she jumped out. Without a word she grabbed her personal bag, closed the door and strode toward the building where she was to meet her former and again teammates.

She hoped the new job was worthwhile. Men could be fun, but explosives were so much better. Finding reasons to use them socially was the tough part.

Jason felt better when he saw Elke. He worried about her when she was late. They'd been friends a long time, and saved each others' butts more times than he could count. Probably everyone knew her persona was largely an act, but he knew the real Elke. She really was a performance artist who worked with explosives, but under that, she was very human. She just didn't let it peek out often.

She slipped in the door and closed it behind her. The window darkened with polarizing as Alex pushed the control, and she drew a heavy drape across. Jason activated the dampening gear on the table next to him, and a few other security measures happened. It wasn't as secure as some military areas, but it should be plenty for what they needed, he hoped. Alex seemed a bit twitchy, though he probably thought he looked dead calm.

Alex stayed sitting, but said, "I assume you all realize we have a mission."

Bart said, "I was hoping we would be told of a pay raise and free beer."

"You know better," Alex replied. "We have a medium duration project, on and off Earth, in civilian environments. That means limited weapons and explosives."

Elke said, "I will send you the usual protests on this theory."

Alex smiled back, "And I will file them in the usual way."

Banter aside, Jason understood the concern. High profile civilian missions could be worse than those in war zones. Everyone knew you were unarmed, and your response was basically to say, "Stop, or I'll call the police!" That, or throw yourself in front of incoming fire. It came down to tactics, evasion, diversion in lieu of any confrontation of any kind. That was always the goal, of course, but for putative peacetime missions it was a legal and real imperative.

Aramis said, "I notice we haven't been told who we're guarding."

Elke said, "I assume we haven't been told for a reason." She gave a hint of smile.

Alex smiled back. "You assume correctly. The OPSEC is necessary. However, you can be told now." He touched a command, which put the full screen up.

"This is our principal," he said, and gave them time to wrap their brains around it. The silence lasted about a minute.

Aramis said, "She's . . . "

Jason offered, "Stunning."

"Actress? Model?" Bart asked. "She's not one I recognize."

"Caron Elain Prescot," Alex said.

"The Prescot ExtraSolar Ores Group?" Elke asked.

"Yes. Daughter of the owner."

"He's worth how much?" Shaman asked.

Jason, now caught up, said, "There's no way to count. He's primary shareholder of the company, and they own an entire fucking star system full of readily exploitable minerals. More money than most governments can get to play with, and no need to worry about appeasing a populace. He treats his employees well, I understand."

"Yes," Alex said. "The employees are not likely to be a problem, other than the occasional awestruck miner who doesn't know who she is and wants a date."

"Do I recall," Shaman said, leaning back in his seat with a furrowed brow, "that several other major share-holders are unhappy with the state of affairs?"

"Former shareholders," Alex said. "It's been thirty years since Prescot Mining bought an option on mineral extraction rights for the system. The initial plan was ter-raforming. That proved infeasible, so the original title holders sold it off. However, Prescot was able to argue successfully that they retained rights based on capital outlay, not bundled with the rest. Several other nations and groups all bought in and out on rights to the system, in a decades-long financial poker game. Several times exploratory parties and habitats were started, and aban-doned. Eventually, they all defaulted or cancelled and abandoned."

"Which puts the system up for grabs again," Jason said. "Except that Prescot's claim was never abandoned."

"Right. They basically inherited the jump point and had mineral rights to the system. They landed a habitat and laid the balance of claim, and started shipping miner-als back, at a loss. Even some of the stockholders pulled out, and their consortium investors and backers dropped them."

"I remember watching that on the stock scroll," Jason said with a grin. He'd always respected accomplishment. "The volume increased as they plowed capital into development of new tech. Once they reached break even, they had this asymptotic growth curve for about a month, then it got taken off the charts completely because it buried everything else."

"From millions to billions?" Elke asked.

"From millions in a billion Mark operation to trillions, quadrillions, no one knows how much," Alex said. "The Prescot family holdings went from a significant minority to majority shareholders, they basically bought their family company back, and then acquired an entire system of assets."

"And it's our job to protect his daughter against jealous rivals," Bart said. "He can afford us, and they are hiring us because they think it's worth it."

Aramis said, "So a private citizen is spending enough money to buy a small house every week to have us watch his daughter? Why does that sound like we'll be earning it?"

"Yes," Alex agreed with a nod. "It's not just us. We get the daughter. Jace Cady's team gets facilities again—she's got the estate, basically. Our pilots are going to take over any ship with a family member on it, and unannounced. The boss will assign them from a pool at the last moment, so no one can make a concrete plan. This family earns in seconds what we earn in weeks."

"That doesn't sound like fun for them," Elke said.

"Yeah, imprisoned by your wealth," Aramis said, still staring at the screen. "She can't possibly have a social life."

"I think I would rather be back in a war zone," Bart said.

Shaman said, "Yes, there are definite issues we will have to deal with. This is going to be very rough."

"I can handle it," Aramis said confidently. "Despite the vomitously obscene wealth, I plan to be as cold and professional as possible. I won't comment on her at all."

Jason said, "Aramis, she's a high risk principal. You'll have to escort her up close, stay with her even in the shower, check her clothes when she dresses, check her skin for darts or poison patches."

Aramis paused and stared.

"Man, you're bullshitting me!"

"Well, yeah, but you started it."

Even Aramis howled with laughter at that.

Alex was glad to see it. A lot of the early personal clashes had dissipated over the last year serving together.

"Still," he said, "she is a beautiful young college woman, and that makes her a lot different from either a celebrity with fans or a politician with enemies. I don't know that any of us have handled a specific mission like this. Bart?"

Bart shook his head. "Celebrities, yes. Occasional executives personally. No one at this level, and not family members subject to kidnapping or death."

"So I want everyone to review their training, text, video and interactive. They're inadequate, but at least will help keep us in the right mindset."

Everyone nodded.

The Prescot industries were almost too large to manage. There was a Board of Directors, and various officers and departments, all of whom managed their share.

However, as CEO of the Group, Bryan Prescot had to track all of it to some degree. Details were almost impossible. It was just too large.

He did, however, make daily overviews, and occasionally zero in, on things that specifically interested him, or were of immediate concern.

The list was long, though. Tourism and casinos were easy; they were contracted out. The contractors paid up front, and a percentage of gross over minimum. His brother handled all that. Scientific research was officially a loss. The research agency ate up a lot of money to look at rocks, space, whatever it wanted. Those were charged against company profits. Of course, as always, the average was for the research to lead to new sources of revenue and improvements in operational efficiency. They were good PR as well.

Charities. The only real concern was giving away too much and causing destabilization. It was a serious worry. Prescot could easily make entire classes of people dependent, and Bryan did not want that.

Bio sciences produced the organics, hydroponics, vat grown meats, O2 producing bacteria, other bacteria that excreted assorted chemicals and enzymes, or cracked rocks. They were even trying to tailor one for that environment.

Materials science, physics, space transport, all interesting stuff.

His first love, though, was the mines. They were where the family started, and what they did. Digging rock, crushing it, extracting ore. The technology so far meant the human race would effectively never run out of resources, and made transmutation research a poor investment for the near future. Every mine on Earth, and even the asteroid mining concerns, were shutting down. They simply could not compete with a company that imported refined raw metal 500 million tons at a time, with the power to produce it supplied on site, effectively for free.

There he'd done what he felt was right, and hired as many of his former competitors as he could, and paid for their employees to be retrained. He was making large areas of Canada, Germany, Russia, China, Africa and South America into parks, but the people who'd depended on the former mines would have starved. They liked him well enough now, and their families were not suffering, which was the important part. The goddammed eco twits, however, still hated him despite the free parks he'd built. They'd never be happy.

They were on here, too, in Legal. Hundreds of petty, pointless lawsuits to stop his "corporate greed" and "facism" as they misspelt it, and "elitist concentration of power and wealth." They cost the company, at most, a few hundred thousand a month out of billions. They had to be watched, though, because a lucky strike with a commiserating judge could cost a lot more to fix.

Caron smiled to Ewan and Garrick as she left the elevator. They were fixtures here, had been guarding the family since before she was born. They were like uncles to her, as much as Uncle Uncle was. Ewan gripped the door handle and opened it for her. They still used manual doors here. Tradition.

"*Diolch*, Ewan," she said and smiled.

Her father was at his desk, and she held the smile until Ewan closed the door. It was traditional in look, but modern in its soundproofing. Once private she was less composed.

"*Tad*, I got the briefing on the Ripple Creek body-guards," she said.

"Good, I got mine, too," he said.

"I don't like it. It's going to affect my studies," she said. She breathed a dramatic sigh to emphasize it. Was it too much? If he caught it . . .

He swiveled in his chair. "Come here," he said, and opened his arms.

She did enjoy his closeness, and his empathy meant she'd given just enough.

"I love you, *Merch*," he said, gripping her tightly.

"I love you, *Tad*," she agreed. "That means you're not going to change, doesn't it?"

He leaned back. "Caron, we need them. I wouldn't spend the money if I didn't think we did. I'm almost sorry we've done so well, for the hatred we've gotten."

"Only almost?" she replied, feeling anger and jealousy. "Unload some of it. Let other companies buy in."

"Caron, you know that's impossible. The economic repercussions would be huge. We also can't exploit Govannon forever. We have to drag the resources out now, and keep control of the technology, which is where the real future is. Times change and so must we."

"Yes, I know we're not drift miners carting out coal anymore. I know we're beyond the Industrial Revolution and don't have children in the mines anymore. I'm being selfish by insisting on a normal personal life—"

"And melodramatic," he said.

Damn him.

He continued, "You've never had a normal personal life in a lot of ways, and I'm sorry. On the other hand, you've always had friends to play with, even if they're retainers rather than peers. I try never to treat our staff as anything less than friends and compatriots, and I know you do, too."

"They're not exactly poor, and they are part of the extended family, in a way," she said. "But I can't just go out and make friends."

"The irony is that if we were merely millionaires you could ignore the money and go out. With what happened since you took your tests, it's now impossible."

"I know, and I want to be a normal college girl. I'm half tempted to just drop it entirely and get tutors."

"I considered that," he said. "But I think the socialization is important, even as limited as it is. The environment isn't ideal, but you'll be more separated with tutors. You can't develop in a vacuum." He frowned and looked sad.

"Govannon is a vacuum, outside the dome," she said.

He grinned. "No, it's a toxic atmosphere at high pressure. Caron," he said more seriously, "I wish we didn't have to spend money on things like public affairs and security. I'd rather give more of it back to our workers and stockholders and keep some for ourselves. I don't like having to plan every outing around business and potential threats. But if we walk away, lots of people lose their jobs, lots of people relying on our stock for income and pension suffer, and we won't be any less hated by all those who didn't have the courage to hang on. We've had all these discussions before."

"I know, *Tad*, and I'm sorry. I'm just frustrated. I can't even . . . I can't even have a real boyfriend." She blushed. "Everyone is either trying for position, or knows they can't and are just a diversion, or doesn't get told who I am and then resents it, or . . . hell, you know all this." She tossed a dismissive wave.

He looked a bit uncomfortable. He knew she wasn't a virgin, and had had a sex life for some time, but he never liked mention of it. She wasn't comfortable discussing it either, but it did bother her, and she'd always been able to talk to him.

"If I could sneak you off somewhere for a year, I would. I am sorry." He reached for another hug.

She gripped him back this time.

"So am I," she said.

As she left, he sighed himself. She was a grown woman, and she was still his little girl. Now that little girl needed a security force.

Ewan and Garrick came in with Joe. Joe had gotten past the younger brother stage, eventually. They managed to interact as friends, after a fashion. Bryan lamented they were both too busy to actually socialize much.

That was as much his fault, of course. He checked the time. He had a vidconference in ten minutes and then a face to face with the County Council, just because it kept them thinking of him as a local businessman. He could skip it, but . . . and of course, his own security detail was arriving, too.

"We have to be quick," he said, "but what's the final take? Ewan?"

Ewan seemed slightly put upon, and well he might.

"They're trained for much more serious events than we are. Of course, I hope that's completely unnecessary. However, they have a reputation."

Joe wasn't as agitated as he'd been throughout the contracting process, but still wasn't comfortable.

He said, "There's the price, of course. I know we can afford it, but it's not cheap and I feel it's both unnecessary, and a copout. We're basically telling any threats we can be scared into that kind of expense. There's perception that being able to afford that kind of expense is immoral. Then, they do have a reputation for shooting things up and arrogantly disregarding any rules they don't like."

When he paused, Garrick cut in.

"They ignore rules that would hinder their ability to protect their principal. Yes, it sometimes looks bad in the press, but we know firsthand what the press is like. They are just about the best, and the only outfit that can offer the schedule and flexibility we need. I feel no moral failure in admitting I'm a Welsh hillman who's loyal to his lord, but cannot offer that level of expertise. I will, of course, manage oversight, but unless there are specifics, I'd prefer to just let them run things, and I'll be liaison to them."

Bryan pretty well knew all this, but he liked having everyone face to face. It made sure everyone took it seriously and understood it was personal, not just a business calculation.

Along which lines, he had to deal with the two next items on his schedule. He'd been glancing at his screen. A nervous habit.

"Well, we'll welcome them and work with them when they arrive. I'm sure they're neither as bad nor as good as stories have it. Drinks this evening if we have time."

"Can't make it," Joe said. "But have one for me."

"Of course."

They rose and left.